THE GREENSEED CONSPIRACY

PHILIP BENZ

VoxLuces

2016

THE GREENSEED CONSPIRACY
Philip Benz

Cover: Crockett Design & Philip Benz
Cover images: Sascha Burkhard©123rf.com, Kirill Cherezov©123rf.com
GreenSeedConspiracyTP2 85878 050116 Garamond Exp.0.2

Trade Paperback
ISBN-10: 0985813237
ISBN-13: 978-0-9858132-3-9
Library of Congress Control Number: 2016939089
VOXLUCES
WWW.VOXLUCES.COM
WWW.FACEBOOK.COM/GREENSEEDCONSPIRACY

AUTHOR'S NOTE

THE GREENSEED CONSPIRACY is an action-thriller. It's a work of fiction. It's partly about government failures and conspiracies, and these are easy to write about. It's also about crimes committed with the permission, if not always at the instigation, of governmental bodies—these require research and are more difficult to write about. In particular, I reference Avon Park, nuclear bomb test fallout over St. George (Utah), Holmesburg Prison, Sonoma State Hospital, Guatemala City, Tuskegee, Dr. Saenger's x-ray experiments, and the compulsory sterilizations of women conducted during the 20th century. These, unfortunately, are not fiction. Though readily available in the public record, they may make you wonder what information, in the government's files, is not.

I distinguish between our government and our country. Our country embodies a set of laws, rights, and principles that join our many diverse peoples together. Government, on the other hand, should only govern. With all of our problems and all of our failures, and even all of our unpleasant histories, I believe our country and even our government are still the best in the world. But those who serve the government do not necessarily serve our country and we must continuously examine the limits of what we want our government to do.

While writing THE GREENSEED CONSPIRACY, I drew much source material from current news. Technologies like CRISPR and three-parent mitochondrial DNA replacement are not science fiction and I hope these scientific capabilities will not surpass the wisdom with which they are deployed. A Glossary defining scientific and military terms and acronyms is provided at the end of this book.

My thanks go to all those who helped me with this story. I could not have written it without the support of family and friends, specifically including my wife, Rogene, and my parents, David and Inez. I also thank Bob Wiggins, who has generously shared with me his time and insightful critiques that helped make this novel better.

I hope THE GREENSEED CONSPIRACY will make you laugh and make you sad and offer something you didn't know before reading it.

Philip Benz
May, 2016

For those who served their country.

The GreenSeed Conspiracy

— HUMAN FERTILISATION AND EMBRYOLOGY ACT

In 1982, the United Kingdom's Department of Health & Social Security established the COMMITTEE OF INQUIRY INTO HUMAN FERTILISATION AND EMBRYOLOGY, in response to concerns about the increasing ease of manipulating human genetic material. Chaired by Dame Mary Warnock, DBE, FBA, FMedSci, the Committee examined the new technologies applied to human embryo development and published its findings in July, 1984. The resulting Human Fertilisation and Embryology Act of 1990 created laws criminalizing attempts to modify DNA in human embryos.

— EL PASO, TX

Summer sun blazed hot on railcars queued up on their tracks. Trains, as long as a mile, sat unmoving as others slowly rolled behind bellowing locomotives that snaked through the rail yard.

The heat didn't bother him. Not much. Helmand Province in July had been hotter. Except somebody said dry heat was easier to take.

They lied.

Duncan Stone, in grease-stained rail yard coveralls, crouched inside the cab of the MJ-9090 reachstacker, parked in the intermodal yard. The .338 Lapua Magnum rifle lay at his side, surrounded by empty protein bar wrappers. He had no idea how to operate the overgrown forklift that moved freight containers on and off railcars, other than rolling its windows down. Earlier he'd looked at the controls, thinking it might be fun to drive, maybe

1

something like a Camaro SS except it could also lift 40 tons 40 feet in the air. On a different day in a different life he might have had an interest in taking it for a spin—on this day, he only used its cramped cab for a shooting position. He took a sip of water and wished he'd brought a few more protein bars. He'd already told Manson he wanted real Tex-Mex after the mission and suggested steak fajitas.

Stone put his eye back to the spotting scope and focused on the semi-tractor lumbering out of the rail yard, which tugged a single standard intermodal container adorned with rust and multi-lingual graffiti. He watched it drive past shabby apartments and bare lots just outside the rail yard fence. Even at the distance of 200 meters he heard the aging transmission grind as it bumped over cracked asphalt roads. Stone watched it turn towards one of the nearby rundown warehouses. He correctly presumed cameras on at least one aerial drone circling overhead recorded what he watched.

The tractor turned into the warehouse parking lot, pausing and shuddering as the driver downshifted. It groaned again as the driver threw it in reverse and backed up the trailer to the loading dock.

Kids played soccer in the neighboring vacant lot covered by brown weeds, gravel and a rusty "keep out" sign. Portly mothers in loose dresses sat under the shade of the adjacent apartment building's covered parking area, sheltering from the late morning sun. The kids stopped their play as the tractor parked, and started walking towards it, waving. Several mothers heaved themselves to their feet and followed their offspring, scowling.

Two men stepped down out of the tractor, both walking like they owned the place. Stone watched the older man, Javier Salazar, grin while handing out $20 bills to the cheering kids. He could afford it. He was one of the men responsible for half the human trafficking in the Americas.

The other man, bigger by 30 pounds of muscle and sinew, stood next to him. Manuel Guerro, Salazar's lieutenant for over two decades, carried several scars that helped him earn his boss's trust several times over. His eyes constantly moving, he scanned the throng of kids and mothers. He knew the people here from many past visits to deliver their human cargos, and none had ever posed any kind of threat. Probably because of the cash Salazar handed out. Some of them, like that tall kid, Juan, who was good with the soccer ball—someday they might join the organization.

Five bodyguards carrying shoulder-slung Heckler & Koch MP-5 submachine guns emerged from the warehouse door. They didn't appear overly cautious, with good reason. They'd never needed to shoot anything since they'd started using this warehouse three years earlier.

Just because nobody had taken a shot at them here didn't mean it couldn't happen. Guerro called out in Spanish to the bodyguards. "Keep your eyes open, lazy bastards."

He walked out to the street and looked around. Nobody except these kids and their mothers. Funny how the mothers looked at you, like they were better than you, but they still took the cash.

Juan waved at him. "Hey, Señor Guerro."

Guerro waved back. Juan had good size. They could find him a place in the business. "You call me when you want to make some money, okay?"

Juan nodded and smiled as he walked away. Guerro walked around to the back of the tractor and chocked the trailer's tires. He lowered the landing gear and unhitched it from the tractor. After pulling the air lines and cables, he waved at Salazar, who stood near the warehouse entrance.

Salazar beckoned and two unarmed men from inside the warehouse came out and opened the doors to the container. Another stood by the warehouse door and watched as the other two started to herd the cargo out of the container. Guerro walked over to Salazar, and they watched the young girls, clothed in rags, as they stumbled into the warehouse. It would take a few hours for the drugs to wear off. Guerro still thought it a little odd how much some of these girls looked alike, like cousins or even sisters, from one shipment to the next. They must all be from the same town.

Mothers started walking back to the covered area, some goading their sons along. None would let their daughters outside when Salazar came around. The younger kids started back to playing soccer while the older boys hung around for a few more minutes, hoping for a glimpse of the girls.

Guerro felt his phone buzz and pulled it out to look at the display. He recognized the number.

Stone watched Guerro and Salazar. Two shots from the .338 would finish the job. He'd zeroed the rifle with a laser bore sight at dawn and at less than 300 meters, any body hit would do. Having used it at ranges of 1,000 meters in the Iraqi deserts, he knew from the size of the exit wounds that close enough was good enough. The 300-grain hollowpoint bullet moving at 2,700 feet per second would punch clean through anything that could bleed so he'd need to see only bad guys in back of his targets when he took the shots.

He turned away from the spotting scope and picked up the rifle. He pulled the covers off the scope and chambered a round. Stone glassed the warehouse area and saw too many people in the area who didn't need killing. Mothers and kids sauntered between the muzzle of the .338 and Salazar, or some kid would hang around in back of Guerro and gaze at the girls walking out of the container—until their mothers slapped them and told them to leave. He'd wait till he had a clear shot.

Stone put down the rifle when he heard the horn and engines of a mile-long train rumbling down the tracks. Its speed meant it wouldn't stop in the rail yard. It would keep rolling between the reachstacker and the rail yard fence just a few dozens of meters from the warehouse. Stone looked at the train, any hopes of gaining quick relief from the heat fading. He unloaded the rifle and looked through the spotting scope, watching railcars flash by, interspersed with brief glimpses of Guerro and Salazar standing at the warehouse entrance.

At 12 miles per hour it would take the train a little over five minutes to pass and by then who knew where his targets would be? He saw Salazar disappear into the warehouse and Guerro walk away, talking into his phone.

Stone covered the microphone on his headset against the din of the passing train. "Sierra Prime, this is Sierra One. I confirm targets. No shot. Going in."

He barely heard Manson's voice on the earpiece as he opened the door of the cab. "This is Sierra Prime actual. Roger that, Sierra One. Hold position for two. Sending backup, target site ETA five minutes."

Five minutes. Yeah, sure he'd hold position. His targets might be gone and that meant having his mission fail. There might be a first time for everything, but sure as hell not for that.

"I copy, Sierra Prime," said Stone. He liked Manson, but his by-the-book sometimes felt like a prostate exam. "Negative, negative on the hold. Going in. Advise backup to bring fajitas. Out."

He pulled off the headset and racked a round in each of his pistols, both SIG-Sauer P-226s. He screwed the silencer on the one he'd carry in the cross-draw holster under the coveralls. He'd use that first. After taking out the bodyguards, it wouldn't matter whether anybody heard gunfire. Stone checked the P-290 sub-compact pistol strapped in his ankle holster and zipped up the front of his coveralls. He slipped out of the cab, grabbed the chassis railing and swung down, hitting the ground at a run.

Zig-zagging between parked railcars and locomotives, Stone arrived at the track on which the mile-long train rolled. He ran parallel to one of the empty centerbeam flatcars, matched speed, then jumped onto its deck. Stepping quickly through an opening in the center partition frame, he took a running jump, landing hard on the ground. He rolled to take up the impact and ran to the rail yard fence.

Guerro put the phone back in his pocket and looked around once, then again. He knew the caller and had little reason to doubt the warning, but he saw nothing that represented a threat. Certainly nothing that five men with MP-5s couldn't handle. He walked to the street and listened. The late morning heat cooked up a faint odor of old tar into the parched, dusty air. He watched the kids kicking the soccer ball and the mothers watching them and scowling at him. He heard nothing except the train passing in the railyard, the thump of the ball being kicked, and the occasional shout from some kid who thought he would have scored a goal if only they had a goal. Guerro waved at Pedro, one of the bodyguards.

"Hey, Pedro. You see anything?"

Pedro shrugged. "*Nada, Jefe.*" He'd worked for Salazar's organization for almost five years, having been recruited from neighborhoods close by in Juarez. He hoped Guerro would let him off in the evening so he could go down to the clubs in the barrios. He liked the ladies and, for his good looks and nice suits, the ladies liked him. Someday maybe he could run girls for Salazar somewhere in the US.

Guerro walked back to the warehouse. He watched one of the men slam the doors of the now-empty container and walk back inside. He turned and took another look around. Kids playing soccer. Mothers watching them…and giving him the evil eye. Nothing unusual, at least considering they'd just imported two dozen girls to work for Salazar's pimps in the *Americano* cities.

Guerro paused for a moment, then loosened his pistol in its holster. Salazar would resent anything that interrupted his time with the girls—what he called quality control inspections.

It was probably nothing and Salazar would be grumpy for hours, but this was what Salazar paid him for. Guerro called into the warehouse.

"Hey, Señor Salazar. We have to go now."

Salazar walked to the doorway, his arm around a slender girl dressed in tight shorts and a t-shirt. Pretty, with long hair and dark big eyes. Add some lipstick and makeup, she might look like a girl on a magazine cover. They all did. Guerro looked her up and down and guessed her age at maybe 14. Maybe there's a younger sister for him later.

"What do you mean we have to go? I'm busy," said Salazar. He pulled the girl close to him and grinned. "This is Catalina."

"No, we have to go now," said Guerro. "I just got a call."

"Who called?"

"Our friend. He says there's shooters here."

Salazar stopped grinning and nodded. Their friend had never called with bad information. He went back inside, leaving the girl at the doorway.

Catalina leaned against the doorframe, not considering leaving, not thinking about staying, only gazing at boys her age kicking a soccer ball. She wondered how nice it would be to go walking with a boy, and maybe he might even buy her an ice-cold mango Jarritos to drink on a hot summer day like this. Just to walk around and maybe sit and talk and nothing else.

One of the kids missed a block and the soccer ball bounced out of the vacant lot onto the pavement, rolling into the pot-holed parking area. Juan sprinted and quickly cornered the ball, skillfully bouncing it against a curb and catching it. Before he turned to run back, he saw Catalina in the doorway and stopped and looked at her. Did she smile at him, a little? He smiled at the pretty girl, and ran his hand through his dark, wavy hair. He straightened up and bounced the soccer ball before going back to the game. Maybe he would chase the ball back here again.

"Hey, Juan, you better go back to your friends now," said Guerro. Juan wanted to look at the girls—except he probably wanted to do more than just look. Guerro walked over to Pedro. "Hey, go inside the warehouse and watch who comes in. We might have some people come around who want to shoot us up."

Pedro nodded and strolled inside, doubting they'd ever see any action around that old warehouse. At least it would be cooler inside. Guerro jumped up into the cab of the tractor and started the engine, then stepped down and walked back to the entrance of the warehouse, his eyes constantly moving. He leaned into the doorway and called, "Señor Salazar, let's go."

Stone ambled towards the bodyguard standing down the street from the warehouse. That he took no pains to conceal the MP-5 told Stone they knew this was their ground. He looked at the kids playing soccer and the mothers and the apartment building and only then looked for the other bodyguards. He memorized the locations of everybody, the trajectories of their movements and whether anybody stood behind his targets. He noted the bodyguard in front of him, and two others standing in the parking area. A fourth up the street, near the boys with the soccer ball. He would be a little tougher to shoot if he moved towards the kids. Guerro by the entrance, no sign of Salazar. Maybe 12 seconds to take out the bodyguards. Then Guerro. Then he'd have to find Salazar.

He'd seen Guerro start the semi-tractor, which meant that they'd be on their way in a matter of minutes. Which meant Salazar would come out in less than a matter of minutes.

As Stone drew near, the bodyguard grabbed his MP-5 and held up his hand.

"It's hot today," said Stone, in Spanish. Smiling, he raised his arm and waved and with his other hand pulled the front zipper of the coveralls down. "I want to find out—"

With barely a break in the movement of his arm, Stone drew

his silenced P-226, aimed and pulled the trigger three times. Two bloody spots appeared in the bodyguard's chest, two inches apart, just above the sternum. The third .40 caliber bullet hit him in his forehead and toppled him just as the brass from Stone's first shot hit the ground.

"—how loud this is," said Stone.

The jingle of the bouncing casings was slightly less noisy than the report from the sub-sonic 180-grain hollowpoint bullets, and was masked by the chugging of the tractor's aging diesel.

Without breaking stride he glided quickly into the parking area. Two bodyguards faced away from him, watching the kids play soccer. Stone's next two bullets shattered the second bodyguard's neck and pierced the back of his head, liquefying the brain stem. He died before he collapsed. By the time the third bodyguard noticed his partner lying face down in a puddle of blood, Stone approached to within five feet. Looking up from his dead partner, he turned just in time to see the muzzle of the silencer and likely never saw the fine mist of his blood expanding from the impact of the two hollowpoints punching into his face.

Stone heard the banter and shouts of the kids playing soccer abruptly stop. Everybody appeared frozen in place for at least 20 milliseconds, except for the last bodyguard. He spun around, following the direction of pointing fingers of mothers and their kids, suddenly aware that he was the last of a dying breed. Stone watched him grab his MP-5 and look around, taking another 80 milliseconds to identify Stone as the shooter. The distance, about 15 meters, was longer than Stone preferred when using pistols. He'd take his time.

Stone knelt and sighted, moving to keep his point of aim on the bodyguard's solar plexus as the man hurried to bring his MP-5 to bear. His first shot hit the man's arm, and the next three hit his chest. As the man stumbled he dropped the MP-5, screaming from a mouth spitting blood until Stone's last bullet jellied his brain.

Guerro had been looking into the warehouse when the sudden silence of the kids and the scream of his bodyguard alerted him that the caller had been correct. Pistol in hand, he looked around and spotted one...two...three...four men down. Guerro drew his pistol and searched for the shooters. He spotted Stone and his greasy coveralls and kept looking until he connected the pistol in

Stone's hand with the deaths of four of his well-armed men. Only one shooter?

As if moving with one mind, the kids and their mothers fled from the lot, screaming. Nearer the warehouse, Juan looked away from Catalina, wondering what the noise was about. Catalina kept looking at the now-empty lot, not caring about the dead bodyguards or anything else.

Stone had two rounds left. Not enough for two more targets. He turned to Guerro, aimed and shot twice. He heard the bullets bounce off the concrete wall of the warehouse, and dropped the P-226. He reached for its twin in his shoulder holster.

Guerro dropped to his knee when he saw Stone aiming at him.

"What's going on?" asked Salazar. He stepped out from the doorway, next to Guerro.

"Get back, what are you doing?" shouted Guerro. He stood and pushed Salazar to the ground, then fired twice in the general direction of where he'd seen Stone. Because Stone no longer occupied that space, the bullets missed and hit one of the fleeing mothers in her leg. She fell to the ground and screamed for help, which did not arrive since everybody saw too many bleeding bodies already lying on the ground.

Juan, confused, started running and bumped into Guerro, who pushed him away and fired again at Stone. He missed and adding injury to insult, Stone shifted his aim and quickly fired three times, one bullet hitting Guerro in his bicep and two grazing his cheek. Guerro grabbed his face and fell back. Stone quickly shifted his aim to Salazar, who by now regained his feet and grabbed Juan, one arm around his neck, holding him in front as a full-length human shield. His other hand held a big, nickel-plated Beretta, pointed by turns at the kid and then at Stone.

Stone aimed at Salazar, guessing the range at 20 meters, but now there was no time to take his time. He knew he only had a shot at half a face and at that range it could be a problem, especially for the hostage. Stone looked at Salazar, then at the hostage—the tall kid with the wavy hair, scared as hell, breathing hard, staring back at Stone.

The SIG-Sauer P-226 shoots notoriously accurately...for a semi-automatic .40 caliber pistol having a 4.4 inch barrel. Still aiming, Stone took two steps forward and one to the side to get a better angle on Salazar's face. He took in a half breath. Stone saw Salazar aiming at him but knew the shots would go wide. Salazar was scared. His hand was shaking and he'd jerk the trigger, sending the bullets high and to the right. Salazar fired…missed.

Stone took another quick step to the side, let out his breath—heard a gunshot—felt an impact thump his left shoulder, like getting hit with a sledge hammer. He stumbled as his peripheral vision saw the muzzle flash from Guerro's pistol. Not the first time he'd taken a bullet—it would have to hurt later. He recovered his footing as his heart rate accelerated and later turned into now. A scorching spark of pain replaced the numbness and Stone forced his breathing to slow. He re-acquired his target—a face on top of the front sight of his pistol—and fired a moment before he felt his left arm start shaking. Or maybe a moment after.

Guerro looked at Salazar, spattered with blood pumping from the man-made hole in Juan's face. Salazar let Juan drop to the ground, stunned by the shock wave of Stone's bullet, which showered him with blood and brain and bone from the boy who two seconds earlier had a heartbeat.

Stone watched the tall kid drop from Salazar's grasp and for a moment saw he had a clear center of mass shot at Salazar.

He didn't take it. More gunshots and his vision started to spin. He heard screaming and people running. He watched Guerro grab Salazar and shake him and shout "Get in the truck!" in Spanish. Guerro aimed at Stone and fired, then ran his boss to the tractor. He flung the passenger door open and shoved Salazar up into the cab.

Stone's ribs started to hurt and he had trouble breathing. He looked down and saw the bullet hole in the coverall and felt heat under where his vest took the bullet, probably a 9 millimeter hollowpoint, from the feel of it. He looked up and watched Guerro run in front of the tractor…shooting at him. A woman ran to the kid who had limitless blood pumping out of his face. She was the one screaming.

Stone found himself on his knees and staggered to his feet, looking at the semi-tractor. Tires skidded behind him. He guessed Manson and the backup team arrived a few seconds early.

— BENSON-PHILIPS FACTORY

Anybody watching the video feed from the drone's night vision camera would see lights shining brightly in the night. As it flew over the Benson-Philips factory, in the District of Columbia's southern corner, it only recorded a dark area, punctuated with the few unbroken lamps left in its parking lot. The drone's cameras lacked resolution sufficient to see the slowly rotating surveillance camera mounted on one of the light poles, though video feeds from it and the drone all wound up in the same places on federal agencies' data servers.

"For Sale" signs hung crookedly on rusting wire fences encircling the parking lot. Anybody could easily drive past the broken gate up to the factory building. They'd bump over broken pavement only to look at paint peeling off the walls and the large roll-up freight door. It might still open, though nobody had tried it in years. Bankrupt owners idled the factory after the economic collapse, when they realized the federal programs that promised so much delivered so little. They had only themselves to blame. They'd waited for the government to help, enticed by the trillions of dollars they later learned had been spent on nothing constructive. The main entrance, dark and rusting, waited for somebody to bring the factory back to life.

Inside, Stone, watched by an overhead camera scanning the factory floor, idly drove a six-ton forklift around in circles. Unshaven and dressed in a wrinkled security guard uniform, he drove slowly, chin in his hand, leaning on the dashboard and leaving tire tracks that were only slightly less dusty than the surrounding floor. Not thinking about its massive cousin whose cab he'd occupied over a year earlier, he'd taught himself how to drive it in near darkness, at least the part about turning it on and moving it in circles.

Bored, Stone finally parked the forklift in its proper place by the roll-up door and plugged in the charging cable. Someday it might be used again for something worthwhile. He stood for a few moments, under the 5-ton hoist of the bridge crane that spanned half the factory floor. Time to make his rounds, not that it really mattered. The bankruptcy trustees had put a night watchman on duty just to say they did so. Anybody stealing anything would need more than a week to get any of the machines out the door.

He brushed dust from his shirt and walked the corridors of the building, past the racks that still held rusting sheets of steel and pipe, and the rows of power hammers, saws, press brakes, and lathes. Nothing was small and equipment only got bigger towards the back of the factory. Stone wondered if they cut and formed steel parts for the Navy, or the oil drilling industry, or the heavy artillery industry. He walked through wide corridors bordered by 50-ton cornice presses, 200-ton stamping presses and a 500-ton punch press. Even with the power off, he paid attention when walking past, a little intimidated by the two-foot high opening between the press's ram and bed. Under 500 tons of pressure any body part caught under the 28-inch wide die would turn into a very thin layer of slime. He played the beam of his flashlight over the presses as he walked past, and then briefly, through the wide door leading into the back room that housed a machine shop, once used for repairs and maintenance on the heavy equipment. Grinding wheels and drill presses still occupied the area, along with benches and a lot of bare wall where cabinets might have once stood. The smaller hand tools had long since left, probably with the previous occupants.

Stone walked back to the roll-up door, passing the three large breaker boxes that passed enough electricity to power a small town when the factory had been running. He'd once switched on the master breakers, hoping for a little more light than what came from the remaining bulbs in the overhead fixtures. The din of the power hammers and presses took him by surprise, as almost every machine powered up and started cycling, as if their operators had agreed to leave everything running on the day they were all given their walking papers. He never flipped that switch again.

Stone finished his rounds and trudged off the main factory floor and entered a dark hall. He stepped into a room that contained little more than a sink, a rickety table and a frayed couch that might have been new two decades earlier. A bare bulb in the ceiling flickered on when he flipped the switch. A plastic clock perched on the sink, ticking loudly. It was the only sound Stone heard except for a slow cadence of water drops from the faucet hitting the sink, and his own breathing.

He opened a well-used grocery sack and pulled out a clean

cloth napkin. He laid it down, squaring it with the edge of the table, then pulled two pieces of white bread out of a half-empty bag and arranged them side by side on the napkin.

From the bag he pulled a sachet of sugar and foil bags of taco spice and bacon pieces. He'd had to sacrifice real bacon for the fake stuff starting a year earlier and maybe the taco spice wore a store brand, but there was one thing he wouldn't skimp on. He pulled out the spray can of cheese product, containing at least 51% real cheese.

It made the meal.

Stone placed the nozzle at the top right corner of the first bread slice. He sprayed a straight line of cheese product along the edge of the bread, then worked his way in concentric squares to the center. He opened the sachet of sugar and tapped it, sprinkling it remarkably evenly over the cheese product, then did the same with the taco spice and bacon pieces.

His hazel eyes regarded what he thought was almost a work of art. The wonderful thing was that the sugar and taco spice and fake bacon all stuck to the cheese product, even if you held the bread upside down. Everything in its place. He repeated his preparations on the second slice of bread.

Time to dine. Stone took his first bite, savoring the flavorsome interplay of cheesy goodness and sugar and bacon and spices. He took his time, dinner being the high point of each languorous day.

He carefully folded the bags of bacon pieces and taco spice closed and put them and the bread, in its white bag with colorful polka dots, into the grocery sack. He leaned back on the couch, and closed his eyes, satisfied for a few moments that at least one thing in his world turned out okay, even good. A brief smile.

"Can I cook or what."

Stone opened his eyes, vaguely aware of the clock ticking. Sleep came a little easier in the last few months as the dreams—nightmares—started to fade. That image of the mother holding the kid whose blood pumped out of his face happened less frequently. But every day he replayed that moment at least 10 times, wishing he could pull that bullet back into his pistol, but nobody ever taught him how to travel back in time.

Until that moment, Stone lived for the action. The hunt. The kill.

Life accelerated in those brief moments that had the maximum stakes possible—either bad guys got dead or he did. He never figured how the stakes got any higher until he shot that kid. He'd never had another mission bother him—but he'd got every one of those right and bad guys got dead. The one time he got it wrong, some kid who just wanted to play soccer and get laid died. It was the last time he worked a mission.

Stone once heard somebody say if you get thrown off a horse, get right back on, knowing you might get thrown off again. Otherwise fear rules your ass and you never ride again.

He just didn't know how to get back on the horse.

Stone leaned forward on the couch and rubbed his face, then stared at the floor in front of him.

Another day in paradise.

— SHENANDOAH COUNTY, VA

The prison van drove through heavy early morning mist, on its way to transfer its sole prisoner to the Big Sandy maximum security facility in Kentucky. The violence of his crimes made him too high a risk to keep in Alexandria. After only three days in the detention center he'd murdered a fellow inmate by crushing his windpipe and stabbing a pencil through an eyeball into his brain. The indictment that got him in jail in the first place was for murder, so the Sheriff's office was told, but only with a shotgun.

When the transfer order came in from the Federal Bureau of Prisons, the watch commanders at Truesdale Detention Center promptly arranged Cain's reassignment. They ordered use of leg shackles and handcuffs, the latter attached to a rail on the bench in the back of the van. Two guards watched him, in addition to the driver and the federal agent accompanying them in the front cab.

Cain sat silently in his bright orange prison jumper. He'd only stared at the floor for most of the drive, now occasionally stealing quick glances at the two guards. He'd already noted the van's driver didn't have video surveillance from the cab, which was separated from the back section by a metal wall too sturdy to punch through. One guard read his iPad, the other dozed, jerked awake, then dozed again. Despite Cain's size and obvious strength, the guards seemed not to care that they sat close to a seriously violent felon. The cuffs and shackles he wore had put them at ease. Cain slowly sat straight up, rolling his shoulders and stretching as much as his handcuffs allowed.

As he relaxed, he quietly released his seatbelt, then grabbed the edge of the bench with both hands, twisted his torso and spun a two-footed back kick into the face of the guard reading the iPad. The force of the kick fractured the bones in his face and knocked him immediately unconscious. Cain then bounced his feet off the floor and launched another kick into the dozing guard's throat. As the guard fell forward, choking, Cain balanced himself on his hands, put one foot on the man's chest and spun the other around to loop the chain of his foot shackle around the guard's throat. He then snapped his legs downward, breaking the vertebrae and severing the spinal cord. Cain pulled that guard's body closer to the bench, then turned and sat down. The keys to his cuffs and shackles were in the guard's belt pouch. Cain just needed to reach the pouch, open it and get the keys and unlock himself. He extended his arm as far as the handcuff chains would permit and found himself three inches short...the same when he tried with the other arm. He stopped moving and thought for a moment.

Bruised, scraped wrists and no keys meant Plan B. Cain slid himself on the bench towards the cab and pounded on the wall with his feet until he felt the van slow. He slid over next to the rear doors and waited for them to open.

— SHEPHERD PARKWAY, WASHINGTON, DC

Stone sat on the bus stop bench, waiting for the late summer sun to peek over the horizon, when he spotted them. Five days a week for the last seven months he'd sat on this bench after work and he hadn't seen them before. Bundled up against the slight chill of the pre-dawn hour, they must have walked quite a distance from wherever they came from. Not many apartments or houses nearby.

He stood to make room when she arrived with the young boy. She carried oversize shopping bags stuffed full of clothes and nodded thanks at him, not saying anything, English likely not her first language. She took good care of the kid, who looked maybe four or five years old. He looked well-fed and she inspected his jacket to make sure she'd zipped it up against the slight morning chill. Then she sat down, her arm around his shoulders. The boy leaned into his mother and yawned. He may have lacked for some things, but not kindness or love. Stone smiled.

He watched her enjoy fussing over her child, then turned away, briefly wondering what that would be like, to be a young kid and have a mother fuss over him.

— SHENANDOAH COUNTY, VA

A spark burned through branches of tall trees, heralding a sun that in minutes would rise into clear blue skies. The fog had cleared and Cain stood next to the van and watched the spark grow, averting his eyes when it brightened to blinding. He finished buttoning the uniform shirt that had the least blood on it, then tossed the prison jumper into the back, on top of the four bodies. He picked up the backpack the driver had kept in the cab and put the handcuffs, shackles and iPad inside. He buckled on the gun belt and checked the pistol the driver had tried to use after the other guard—some kind of federal agent—got too close. Most people didn't know that legs reached further than arms and almost always were more lethal when used properly, thus the success of his Plan B.

Cain pressed the rear doors shut, taking care not to slam them. He turned around to face the rising sun, eyes closed, and enjoyed the light touching his skin. After a few moments, he got into the van and turned the key.

— BENNING ROAD SE, WASHINGTON, DC

Stone stepped off the bus and wandered through the morning crowd on the sidewalk. The neighborhood had started turning around for the better, at least the part where he didn't live. Coffee houses, bakeries and bicycle stores established themselves alongside newly renovated homes, more than a few of which had once served the community as crack houses. He paused in front of a coffee shop advertising fair trade Peruvian "blond roast" beans. He didn't know what blond roast meant but he liked good coffee and reached into his pocket, wondering what he would find. With three days to payday he knew he wouldn't find anything in his wallet worth a cup of coffee. From his pocket, he fished out quarters and dimes and no dollar bills. He kept walking.

Stone plodded past a hairy man whose clothes had more wrinkles than his own and smelled much worse. The man slept on a street bench, a lit cigarette in the fingers of one hand and a well-used hand-scrawled cardboard sign cradled in his arm. It read: "Doing nothing. Need money and beer."

Stone started down the street to the ancient house where he rented a room when he felt somebody—two somebodies—following him. The last time that happened around here he'd put two punks in the hospital, both unable to walk or otherwise move their legs after attempting to rob him.

These weren't punks.

Stone spun around. "What."

He faced Edward Kimball, whose lean six-foot frame stood flagpole straight and wore that suit like it was a full dress uniform. His crewcut showed no more gray hair than the last time Stone had seen him, about a year earlier.

"No good morning, nice to see you, how you been?" asked Kimball, smiling. His accent came from somewhere between Arkansas and Georgia. He looked at Stone and shook his head. Unshaven. The wrinkled uniform. Didn't smell too bad but he probably gave himself that haircut without the use of a mirror. "Jeezus, don't you look like a bag of smashed asshole. Come on."

"I'm busy."

"Sure you are." said Kimball. He nudged the man beside him. "Martel, don't you want to say hi to Duncan?"

Martel Jaeger. Just another leg, but he could take bullets and beatings and still get the job done. The guy you want when you need strong backs, weak minds and no questions asked. Stone thought working with him was like working with Dracula. He sucked.

"Nice pressed shirt, Stone." Jaeger shot his cuffs, flashed his gold cufflinks, and grinned. He had decent fashion sense for a grunt four years out of Iraq. Stone had to admit, Jaeger looked pretty good in that suit, surprisingly not at all like King Kong wearing a necktie. Jaeger fingered Stone's uniform, then grabbed his arm and twisted it.

Stone twisted back, easily freeing his arm and putting the bigger man in a one-handed chokehold.

"I do my own ironing, Jaeger," said Stone.

"Stone, please do not damage my staff," said Kimball.

Stone released Jaeger and pushed him away.

"Thank you." Kimball turned and raised his hand.

The black Suburban parked a block away pulled away from the curb and drove up. Two men emerged.

Stone recognized Woltz and Barrett. Competent guys, seasoned, maybe two or three years out of running missions in Afghanistan. They knew how to work an op, shoot straight and follow orders. He nodded at them and they nodded back. Barrett smiled bashfully and waved with the hand that held a Taser.

Kimball nodded at the Suburban. "Just get in."

— MINERAL COUNTY, WV

Isolated by thick woods from everything, the dirty single-wide needed patching and paint. Carrying the backpack, still dressed in the guard's uniform, Cain walked up the dirt road, past tall weeds, old tires and weathered trunks of trees felled decades earlier to make room for the trailer. A battered pickup truck sat embedded in weeds off to the side, next to a row of propane tanks.

An old hound on a long chain trotted from around the back of the trailer and barked at him. He didn't recognize it…but he hadn't visited in years and dogs around this place tended not to last too long. Cain stepped onto the porch, past coils of copper tube, sacks of sugar and black plastic bags of empty moonshine jugs.

The front door swung open. Cain recognized the shotgun that appeared.

"Gotcherself some balls showin' yer face around here," said Jimmy Bob. Looking older than his 50 years, his remaining teeth brown from chewing tobacco, he wore only faded denim bib overalls and weathered leather boots. He cocked the second barrel and took one step out of the doorway, his eyes on Cain and his fingers on the triggers.

"Maybe I just got thirsty for some of your 'shine," said Cain. He smiled and rubbed a hand over his clean-shaven head. "Been a while."

"Clem ain't forgot you," said Jimmy Bob. "Neither've I."

— ALEXANDRIA, VA

She sat on the edge of the bed, on the side that hadn't been slept in, and looked at the photo with the black ribbon tied around it. Every morning for three years, before facing the world, she sat with dry eyes just to feel him look back at her.

Alex stood up and walked out of the bedroom, through the hallway decorated with photos and watercolors depicting cabin cruisers of a classic age long past. As she passed the open door of her son's bedroom she heard, as she did every morning, the crackle and boom of gunfire and explosions from the videogames. What did they call these? Multiplayer first person shooter games. Her education told her this might make excellent preparation for mass murderers. Her experience removed any doubt. She paused, worrying as mothers always would, but reflected that his grades were good, bordering on excellent.

At least he had the grades. She tapped on the door. "Milo, are you about ready?"

From out of the bedroom over gunfire, explosions and car engines revving, "Coffee's made."

"Thanks." Alex walked into the kitchen, and smelled the freshly made coffee, then saw the newspaper on the counter. She smiled. What mother had a teenage boy who made her coffee and brought in the morning paper?

Her gray eyes saw the photo and the headline as she unfolded the paper. "Suspect In Mall Killer Murder Escaped." Next to it was the photo of a man she knew. Elias Cain. Her smile evaporated. That must be the reason for her morning's first meeting. She brushed the bangs of her short dark hair back and thought, only for a moment, about calling to cancel.

Alex heard Milo close the door to his room and walk into the kitchen. She opened the refrigerator and pulled out the rye bread, cold cuts, imported cheeses and mustard. Milo loved her sandwiches, generously constructed for a growing teenage boy who had no body fat to spare. And whose unruly hair needed a haircut.

She spread Dijon mustard on a slice of bread, laid on Bibb lettuce and layers of smoked turkey. Alex asked, "What kind of cheese?"

"What do we got?"

Alex turned to look at her son. Her doctorate was not in English but she knew proper grammar and insisted her son use it—with his grades he had no excuses, other than pretending to mediocrity just to fit in. "What do we have?"

"Yeah—yes, Mom." Milo stepped next to her and watched his sandwich grow. He stood a head taller than his mother. "What do we have?"

"Cheddar, smoked Havarti—"

"Smoked Havarti, please."

Alex finished the sandwich and handed it, neatly wrapped, to Milo. Working in restaurants to put herself through school had lasting gustatory benefits for her son.

"Thanks, Mom." Milo opened the pantry and stuffed his backpack with a bag of organic truffle potato chips next to the sandwich.

"Do you want to work on the boat Saturday?" asked Alex. It had been two weeks since they'd visited the marina.

"Yeah, sure. Can we take her out?"

"We'll see if the engine starts."

Alex gave him a hug, then watched him walk out the door. All mothers worried about what the world might do to their children but she had better reasons than most.

Alex heard her phone ping. A text from her friend, Donna. "R U taking anybody 2 Karens wedding?"

She hadn't dated anybody in the years since Harry died and had no plans to do so. Between work, the boat and keeping Milo on his schoolwork and out of trouble, there wasn't time. She typed back: "Not unless I meet Prince Charming."

— WASHINGTON, DC

Stone, unhappy, sat sandwiched in the Suburban's back seat between Jaeger and Kimball. Through the window he watched people in suits marching on sidewalks and crosswalks, sometimes paying attention to stoplights as morning traffic inched past the Dirksen Senate Office Building, or Dirksen SOB for short.

"Got a new mission. It has your name on it," said Kimball.

"New mission." said Stone. He focused on suppressing any hint of interest and looked sideways at Kimball. "I want to work with you, why."

Kimball pulled out a pack of cigarettes after watching Stone focusing—too hard—on suppressing any hint of interest. He smiled. "Probably better than doing your night watchman gig. Some dirty, nasty, old factory nobody wants. Little guy doing a little job."

"Almost sounds like you care," said Stone. "I call how many times, nothing, now you show up and I'm all happy as a pig in shit?"

"Maybe happier. Just thought you'd want back in the game."

"Maybe I like what I'm doing. Maybe I'm busy planning my next vacation in Miami."

"Sure you are." Kimball laughed and tapped a cigarette on the armrest. Stone just didn't like being ignored for a year. He'd take a little convincing but Kimball would get what he wanted. He lit the cigarette.

"Get back on the team, play it right. No more little guy pissing around. But—" Kimball pulled on the cigarette. "Play it wrong, little guy's in jail for murder, parking ticket, whatever."

"I didn't do anything."

"So? Jeezus, you know how this works."

Stone looked out the window, at the Capitol building. "Yeah, I know. You're from the government and you're here to help. How lucky am I."

"Yeah, maybe your mother might care," said Kimball, to whom sarcasm came more naturally than breathing. He sensed Stone tense for a moment. "Forget it."

Kimball took another long pull on the cigarette and rolled down the window to exhale.

"Try and bullshit me, okay," said Kimball. "Just don't bullshit yourself."

A long black limousine inched along two blocks ahead of the Suburban, on Constitution Avenue, carrying its passenger to his third appointment of the morning. Chairing a dozen Senate committees kept his days busy and his short-cut hair gray. His driver thought he should have been in a good mood, perhaps even smiled at them, since a Federal Grand Jury failed to indict him—again—the day before.

Senator Walter Heidrick held his first drink of the day—he favored bourbon—while reading the morning's email and briefings on his iPad. He felt like sending an only-slightly-mocking email to the Attorney General for failing to indict him, but why chum the waters? Wiggins was probably already looking for another reason to send him to jail.

Heidrick usually read only a few words at the top of each email before deleting them. To a very few he'd respond, usually with a short note to contact one of his staff. Though he sat on their oversight committee, he dumped off onto a legislative assistant the official emails from the National Security Agency's Director and his Deputy. Only the underlings below them had proved useful to him, only because they thought he could help them advance their government careers. So he took note of the email that came from an unofficial but familiar account, which belonged to NSA Assistant Deputy Director Jepson. Heidrick read it in its entirety. Twice.

He tossed back the drink and poured another. There could be worse news. For example, a press release from Putin announcing he'd just annexed Finland. Heidrick carefully straightened his Hermès necktie, then pressed the intercom button on the console that connected him with his aide, who sat in the front seat.

"Kevin, I want to see Gidden. Now."

— MINERAL COUNTY, WV

Cain sat on the rickety wooden chair, long bereft of any varnish it might have once worn. He read the iPad, to see if any news about him made it to the internet. As he expected, there was no internet or 3G or even cell service where he sat.

He looked through the open door and watched Jimmy Bob, sitting hunched over the table. And what would Jimmy Bob do with the internet? Cain laughed. Jimmy Bob looked up, his swollen face and black eyes evidencing the thumping Cain gave him while relieving him of the shotgun. Jimmy Bob looked back down at the table, unable to put his face in his hands because of the handcuffs and shackles attaching him to the chair.

Cain, now dressed in faded jeans and a t-shirt, rolled up his left pants cuff, then peeled one end of a Band-Aid off his leg. He lifted a microSD datacard from under it and plugged it into the reader attached by cable to the iPad. The guard who had the iPad, conveniently, was very savvy in his selection of electronics and had the reader and a small carrying case filled with microSD datacards, each filled with various selections of pornography.

Cain believed his datacard contained something far more interesting and he only had to unlock it. He located two files and placed them on the iPad display's desktop: the first an audio file and the second an executable. He tapped the icon for the executable and a login window appeared on the display. He typed "gidden p15C" into the first box, "green$eed#@80" into the second box, and tapped the audio file icon when the third box appeared.

The voice, with its British accent, of Albert Gidden announced from the iPad speaker, "Login Gidden prime fifteen chelsea."

Dr. Gidden had been careless when he'd logged on to the GreenSeed system with Cain in the room, weeks earlier at their first meeting. He'd underestimated Cain from the beginning. The iPad display blanked and Cain waited. Presuming he remembered everything correctly, it would come back to life in a moment.

A chime sounded from the iPad speakers, then, in a female voice, "Gidden voiceprint confirmed indigo fifteen. Read-write file access enabled. Welcome back, Dr. Gidden."

— CENTER FOR HUMAN SCIENCES, ARLINGTON, VA

People who met him often thought he was the one who gave psychopaths a bad name. Pale, white-haired, with blue eyes that could go minutes without blinking, Albert Gidden sat behind his polished steel desk, dressed in his Savile Row suit. His sterile, modern-industrial office reeked of science. Through glass walls behind his desk, visitors could see lab coated, capped and gloved scientists peering into large microscopes of the ICellCo robotic workstations, designed to help them plumb individual human cells. They gazed at the micro-needles they controlled with nudges of their fingertips and at the aqueous blobs that, by turns, gently oozed from the needles or disappeared into them, all within the confines of a human ovum.

Gidden watched them for a few moments, as he did most mornings, remembering years earlier when his first big grant helped them move out of space that would never meet any clean room standard. With almost 3,000 square feet of ISO 2 clean room in Arlington, his labs now boasted some of the best intracellular micromanipulation equipment available, much of which he'd invented.

The intercom on his desk phone chimed and he heard his admin. "Dr. Gidden, Dr. Jones has arrived."

"Please send her in."

He turned around, heard a knock at his door and watched Alex march in. She tossed a newspaper on the desk, headline and photograph facing up. "Suspect in Mall Killer Murder Escaped," and Elias Cain's photo.

"I assume this is why I'm here," said Alex. "You could have just said so yesterday and saved us both the time and trouble."

"Good morning, Alexis," said Gidden.

"I told you months ago Cain wasn't reliable," said Alex. "Why didn't you—"

"Hardly unreliable. His temporary disappearance aside, he's performed remarkably well," said Gidden, quietly. His refined British Received Pronunciation accent softened the appearance he gave. "Mr. Cain will be found quite soon, according to Mr. Kimball."

"Mr. Kimball can't be sure."

"It's his job to be sure, isn't it. It's what his agency does."

"Cain worked for his agency."

"So does the solution to our problem. At least he will, presuming he passes the evaluation."

Alex stood silently for a minute, refereeing the internal debate she had every time she spoke with Gidden about these evals. Psychological evaluations for contractors and employees, anybody connected in any way with Gidden's primary program, whether they knew of their connection or not. Secrecy above everything else, although Elias Cain might have just made that irrelevant. Perfectly happy working in the Center's Genetics and Fertility Counseling Program, she'd never liked doing evaluations, least of all for the GreenSeed program.

This time she would refuse and make it stick.

"No," said Alex.

Gidden sat still, staring at her with unblinking eyes. Other men would stare because they found Alex's face and figure very attractive. Gidden stared only because that's what he did, seemingly without regard to what he stared at. "Please sit."

"I have work to do." Alex willed her hands apart, so that she wouldn't pick at her fingernails. Then she sat down. She stared at the polished desktop in front of Gidden, bare but for his computer and a single paper brochure, neatly folded and aligned with the edge of the desk.

"Who is it?" asked Alex.

"Duncan Stone."

A surprise. "I thought we cleared him. Is he—"

The intercom chimed. The admin sounded agitated. "Dr. Gidden, Senator Heidrick—"

Heidrick barged through the doors and marched to the desk.

"—just arrived."

"Senator." Gidden looked at the man who controlled his budgets. "I believe our meeting is—"

"It's now, Gidden," said Heidrick.

After a moment of unblinking eye to eye, Gidden said, without diverting his gaze, "Alexis, would you please excuse us."

Alex glared at Heidrick, then marched out the door.

Heidrick sat down, again disappointed that Gidden kept no liquor in his office.

"How much did he get?" asked Heidrick. He picked at miniscule bits of lint he imagined might be attached to his Brioni suit, perfectly tailored for his ample frame.

"I beg your pardon." said Gidden.

"Right," said Heidrick. Scientist or not, this guy should play poker. "What did Cain get. The data he stole."

Gidden blinked. "Excuse me, how do you happen to know of this?"

"It's why we invented NSA. They work for me."

Gidden waited a few moments. He'd only found out about this less than 24 hours earlier. "He has GreenSeed."

"How much?"

"It's encrypted. I'm told it's quite unbreakable," said Gidden.

"I heard the same thing about the IRS database two days before it got breached." Heidrick pretended to nonchalance and picked up a brochure, the only thing on Gidden's desk within reach. He leaned back in the chair and opened it. Something about a conference of the Association for Human Genetics, featuring Albert Gidden, PhD, MD, DrMed, DSc as Keynote Speaker. Why did Gidden attend these? It's not like he could mention anything that he'd really like to present. Heidrick tossed the brochure back on the desk. "How much?"

Gidden folded and carefully placed the brochure where it had been before Heidrick grabbed it. "Everything."

"Everything." Heidrick looked at Gidden, who averted his eyes. "You mean everything like experiments, subjects, recruits—"

"Yes."

"Staffing, funding, oversight?" asked Heidrick, his voice rising. "That kind of everything."

Gidden hesitated before answering. "Yes."

Heidrick's hand went to the knot of his necktie. Finding the knot in place and intact, as he always did, he lowered his hand and leaned back in the chair. "We knew it had to happen sometime, didn't we."

"No, of course not," said Gidden. "There was no possible way we could have anticipated Mr. Cain's action."

"We should have pulled the plug after Nangarhar. Cain, all of them."

"I am quite sure he cannot access any of it. He's quite

intelligent but he has no computational skills we're aware of—"

Heidrick held up a hand. Gidden wisely stopped speaking. Heidrick let the silence hang.

"And maybe he doesn't," said Heidrick, quietly. "I don't care. No more failures. Shred your databases. Everything. Shut it down. All of them."

Gidden leaned back in his chair. Any dismay he felt, he concealed. The senator had implied varied threats when he first heard about what happened with Gen 1, but he had never directly threatened to shut down the entire Arlington GreenSeed program.

"You can't be serious," said Gidden.

"Do I look like I'm joking?"

"What precisely do you mean when you say all of them?"

"Precisely, all of them."

"I think that's hardly necessary," said Gidden. He'd never imagined Heidrick would order the destruction of all three generations of GreenSeeds. "The risk is virtually nil that Mr. Cain can even open the data, much less understand it and there's certainly no risk that Gen Three—"

"All of them. No loose ends. Everything that smells like GreenSeed never existed as of ASAP. You have other things to do." Heidrick's ice blue eyes looked past Gidden at the scientists in the lab, hunched over their microscopes and workstations. He turned back to Gidden. "The Tampico work's not in your database is it?"

"It's completely separate," said Gidden. "We don't reference any of Dr. Perez's activity here."

Heidrick nodded his head. At least not everything had turned into stewed moose shit. "We should have done all of this in Mexico. Somebody does this kind of thing down there, nobody cares."

"Senator. Please."

"Gidden, do you have any idea what happens if DOJ sees any of this?" Heidrick hadn't seen eye to eye with any of the US Attorneys General, or anybody else in the Department of Justice, in the last three administrations. They all lacked a sense of humor and a sense of what it took to get things done, in particular that pernicious bastard, Wiggins. They just didn't understand what government was really all about. Once they started with their investigations they'd just keep going until they got a conviction or a dismissal.

"We wanted to help you do good science, good medicine. Maybe help the little people. All we got was man-made—" Heidrick stood up. "All we got's a mess."

He walked to the door then turned around and pointed a finger at Gidden. "Shut it down. That means now and that means everything. Including Gen Three."

— ALEXANDRIA

Milo walked alone on the street in front of the high school, carrying his lunch, looking for a place to sit. He weaved his way through groups of teenagers who joked, laughed and talked among themselves and not with him. Nothing new. Now at his third high school in half as many years, his mother hoped it would be the one from which he'd graduate.

"Hi."

Milo turned to the girl who had just walked up beside him, not knowing what to say.

"I'm Josie. From A.P. Algebra."

"Hi."

"Are you just in summer school?" asked Josie.

"Oh, like—yeah. Uh, I'm Milo," said Milo. "I mean, I'll start here in the fall."

"Cool. Do you—" Josie stopped in mid-sentence, looking past Milo. "Oh, great."

Milo followed Josie's eyes and saw Terence. Big, pale, with stringy hair, he looked as dense as the pavement on which he walked. He stopped in front of Josie, who didn't step back.

Terence looked at Milo and asked, "Hey, who's this?"

"What do you want?" asked Josie. She turned to Milo. "He's a loser who thinks he's cool."

"Shut up," said Terence. He pushed Josie.

"Loser meth head," said Josie. She pushed back. "What are you even doing here?"

"Hey," said Milo. "Why don't you—"

Terence slapped Milo's lunch to the ground and stepped closer.

"What did you do that for?" asked Milo.

"I felt like it, prick."

"You shouldn't, like, do that," said Milo, after a moment. He looked past Terence.

"Well, I did," said Terence. "Faggot. What are you going to do about it?"

Milo looked directly at Terence.

Terence saw Milo's face and immediately decided not to push him.

Milo stood for a moment, resisting his initial impulse. He didn't know what to do and he looked around and he saw people stop and turn around and look at him. He remembered what his mother had told him about keeping his temper and it confused him for a moment. He spoke softly. "You better pick it up."

Josie turned and stared at Milo. She heard more than a simple request in his words. So did Terence.

"Pick it up," said Milo.

After waiting a few seconds, Terence picked up the bag and handed it to Milo, then started walking away.

"Be seein' you around," said Terence, over his shoulder. "Milo."

Milo turned back to Josie and saw her staring at him.

"I should go too," said Josie. "I should go."

Josie walked quickly away, through the small crowd that dispersed because it had lost interest in watching two boys that didn't get into a fight. Milo watched her leave, then kept walking, alone.

— RESOLUTION SUPPORT AGENCY

The Suburban stopped at the back entrance of the government-issue building in Alexandria. Built of concrete, glass and steel, its architects neglected esthetics, favoring instead a blocky, government-ugly look inadvertently made popular in 1970s construction outside of Crystal City and the Washington, DC core.

Stone and Kimball got out of the Suburban, both reflexively looking around for anything that might want to shoot them. The area didn't warrant the caution, but battlefield habits fade slowly.

They entered the building that housed the Resolution Support Agency. A little-known federally funded agency, RSA resolved problems—with extreme prejudice—for other federally funded agencies. Senator Walter Heidrick was the chair of their oversight committee and Kimball reported to him directly to avoid confusion about whether any Administration staff knew or sanctioned what they did. Or if they even existed.

The elevator took them down to the basement. Like the third and fourth floors, it was a secure area to which none of the bureaucrats who occupied the first and second floors had access. Most of the people working at RSA knew little of what the agency really did and assumed it was something like Health and Human Services or Bureau of Land Management, but secret and slightly more exciting.

Most bureaucrats from one agency could be plugged and played into another and it didn't matter much what the agency did. Kimball made little time for his bureaucracy and remembered little of it besides the name of his finance manager, Mills, and that only because he had to meet with him about budgets every month. But Kimball knew the name, history, missions and military record of every one of his operators, living or otherwise. Including Stone.

They walked out of the elevator and down the hall. Kimball slid his card key through the reader and unlocked the steel door to the action range.

"What's this for?" asked Stone.

"Think of it as a second chance," said Kimball.

Stone followed Kimball inside.

The training pistols used lasers instead of bullets to mark hits on targets—not the same as what they carried on missions, but close enough to gauge reaction times, target selection and accuracy.

Kimball walked into the control booth, where he would run programs that would flash images and movies onto multiple projection screens. Anybody practicing could either stand at the firing line or walk through the range. Seasoned shooters from spec ops, FBI and SWAT teams created the scenarios that a trainer could present. Anything from straight target practice to mass civil unrest where shooting one or two bad guys in the throat could tame a mob.

Stone stood at the firing line and looked at the laser pistol lying on the bench in front of him. Did people actually forget how to shoot?

"Short course, urban, pistol," said Kimball.

"Really?" said Stone. "I'm wearing my big boy pants."

"Come on, Stone. I do this every night for shits and giggles."

Kimball rarely went active on RSA missions. He missed running ops in the field but standing orders precluded the agency director from getting in the line of fire. Years earlier he regularly went outside the wire with his spec ops teams in Helmand province—in violation of standing orders. That shortened his military career and explained his retirement with eagles instead of stars on his shoulders. Those had been the only orders he'd ever ignored.

Kimball dimmed the room lights and flipped a switch.

A frozen image of a crowded street appeared on a screen off to the side. Stone picked up the laser pistol and kept it at his side.

The frozen street image unfroze. A bad guy ran out of a crowd, carrying a pistol. He stopped, aimed. Stone quickly levelled the pistol and shot three times. The laser flashed twice on the bad guy's torso and once on his head. Another scene, a different screen, he shot two bad guys with laser hits executed just like in the text book.

Stone stepped inside the range, walked slowly, looked at nothing, focused on everything. The screen in front of him lit up. Three men walking towards him. Civilians. Stone kept the pistol at his side. Another three steps. Directly to his right a bad guy holding a hostage girl raised his pistol. Stone aimed. The image of the hostage registers behind his retinas and he freezes, then shoots. Two laser dots flash on the bad guy's face, one laser dot on the hostage's forehead.

Stone lowered the pistol, staring at the laser dot frozen on a forehead.

"Range is cold," said Kimball. He put still video images on the wall display by the booth. Red dots marked the laser hits on the bad guys. And on the hostage.

Kimball joined Stone at the firing line, then stared at the displays. He sighed loudly.

"So it's been a while," said Stone. He laid the pistol on the bench.

"Yeah." Kimball looked at the display, then at Stone, then shrugged. "Good enough for government work."

Stone hoped his relief wasn't obvious. "What's the mission."

"Somebody only you can get close to."

"Sounds like fun. Who?"

"After your psych eval," said Kimball.

"My what?"

"Psych eval. I believe I just said this out loud."

"What the hell for?"

"Upstairs. Pay attention, Stone."

— CONFERENCE ROOM, RSA

The man in front of Alex wanted to be there as much as she did. Vaguely familiar with his file, she focused on the iPad and scrolled between various dossiers. Stone looked bored, thus revealing his apprehension, and slouched in his chair across the table from Alex.

Alex stopped scrolling between files on the iPad when his photo appeared. Stone, in dress uniform and tan beret, wearing more medals than anybody she'd known with less than 20 years' service. She recognized all of the ribbons, including the Silver Star and Purple Hearts. She compared the man in front of her to the man in the photo. Except for the face and the hazel eyes, she noted little resemblance to the professional soldier displayed on the iPad.

Alex tabbed through to the next file. She read, "SOUTH ASIA SERVICE RECORD CLASSIFIED - REDACTED THIS FILE." 'South Asia', not just 'Afghanistan' or 'Iraq'. Stone had run missions where the US wasn't supposed to be. His records were need to know and apparently nobody thought she needed to know. She kept reading.

"You left the Army after your fifth tour of duty. Why?" asked Alex.

"It was an honorable discharge," said Stone.

"I see that. I want to know why."

"I'm not at liberty to disclose details. I spent some time in a hospital. Then I decided to leave."

"Friendly fire incident?"

Stone looked at Alex. How did that get in the file? On orders from so high up nobody needed to know, everybody from platoon leader to general staff had kept that quiet. "If that's what you want to call it."

"It says somewhere in eastern Afghanistan. The Arma mountains?"

"If that's what it says."

"Is there anything else?" asked Alex.

"I didn't like how something was handled, so I put in my discharge papers. That's when Kimball recruited me. Guess he liked my work from when I ran missions with Viper—with his teams a couple years earlier."

Alex scrolled to the next file, which contained a history of his girlfriends. No fiancés, no wives. Nothing longer than three or four months. Why would they capture this information, including photos, social security numbers, driver's license, associates, siblings, parents, grandparents, mother's maiden name?

His security clearance.

Alex wondered what her file contained.

Alex looked at the photos of the girlfriends. Young, sexy-pretty. How many had worked in strip clubs? He would attract these women. Handsome, in a kind of unwashed way, he seemed in good shape and still had all his hair, even though somebody with more scissors than skill had cut it.

"Missy, Terry Lynn, Jolene. Jodi, spelled with an 'i'," said Alex.

Stone looked up from the table top, surprised. Alexis Jones—Doctor Jones, as she had quickly corrected him—fixed him with her gray eyes and said nothing. Beauty and the beast, all in one package. Which, aside from the cold bitch part, looked pretty good.

"Nothing more than a few months. No lasting relationships. Is this about rejection or fear of commitment?" asked Alex. "Or is it something else?"

"That's kind of personal."

"This is a psychological evaluation."

Stone shifted in his seat. "Just—they didn't work out."

"Did you leave them?"

"Yeah, like any other non-crazy person would," said Stone. They were hot and nice enough provided you didn't mind clingy, whiny, needy zombies snoring in your bed. "Who else they find out about?"

"I only saw the last two years," said Alex. "Mr. Stone, sometimes relationships with mothers affect—"

"It didn't."

"You didn't give me a chance to ask the question."

"I didn't have a relationship with my mother. What else?"

Alex turned back to the iPad and scrolled through another file. Family, lack thereof. She saw a photo of Stone in high school, and another photo of a young woman, Margaret Stone—his birth mother. She read further, then looked back at him. His expression matched his name.

"What about your experience in foster homes?" asked Alex.

"Every one a great and wonderful childhood experience," said Stone. "My parents gave me up, I don't know why, and the world didn't care."

"Would you like to talk about that?"

"No."

"Why not?"

"I don't care either."

Alex typed in her notes about the half-dozen foster homes: "Says he doesn't care." With a regular counseling client she'd want to learn how the absence of permanent parents contributed to his fears of relationships. And the need for them.

"What scares you?" asked Alex.

Stone sighed. Loudly. He slid further down in the chair. "Is it just you don't like me?"

"It's not important whether I like you or not."

"So you won't go out with me?"

After a brief silence, "Do you want this mission, Mr. Stone?"

He blinked, hesitated, looked down at the desktop. "Yeah."

Alex saw a long moment of vulnerability. A crack in the armor made of...stone. Less firmly, she said, "Everybody is scared of something. Even highly decorated staff sergeants."

Stone relaxed a little. A flicker of a smile. "Needles. Drowning. Kick in the nuts."

"Missions?"

"No." Stone looked back at Alex. "Nothing like that. Doc, it's—maybe sounds lame—being average."

"Average," said Alex. "Do you mean undistinguished?"

"Yeah. Sure," said Stone. "Undistinguished. You live, you die, what. Everybody wants to do something important. Prove they deserve their place in the world."

— ALEXANDRIA

Milo sat on a bench outside the math department, studying polynomial multiplication. At least one problem would be on the next exam. Other students had long since left, enjoying the afternoon's freedom from classes and teachers.

He looked up and saw Terence standing in front of him.

"Hey, Milo," said Terence. "Prick."

Terence slapped the textbook Milo held to the ground.

"I ain't picking it up," said Terence.

"You better leave," said Milo, quietly.

"I ain't leaving either."

Milo stood up. "Back off."

Terence pushed Milo, who knocked his hand away. Terence threw a punch, more like a slap, at Milo's face. Milo grabbed his hand and threw a punch, more like a punch, which landed on Terence's nose. Milo grabbed Terence by the shirt and punched him again. And again. And didn't stop until Terence squirmed out of Milo's grip and backed up, followed by Milo who kept landing his fist in Terence's face.

Finally understanding he would not win a fist fight nor succeed at intimidating Milo, Terence broke away and ran. Milo chased him, only stopping when Terence disappeared around the building from which his math teacher emerged.

— CONFERENCE ROOM, RSA

"What do you think is something important?" asked Alex.

"Doc," said Stone. How to say this and not piss her off. "I worked lots of missions above your need to know. Some places, people know about, most places they don't. I made bad guys get dead. Now…"

Alex waited. "Now, what?"

"Now I'm a—" Stone managed a smile bereft of fun and friendship. "I'm undistinguished. I'm doing stuff that doesn't matter."

"Do you think working with Mr. Kimball is what matters? Doing that kind of work?"

Alex let the silence stand for a few moments.

"What do you want from me?" asked Stone. "What do you need me to say?"

"I want to know your commitment to your mission." Alex saw Stone look away as if she'd compared his manhood to an inchworm. "You worked missions for DEA, GRS, State Department, BATF. All good missions, except for what happened in El Paso. After that you separated involuntarily from RSA."

"You mean Kimball fired me."

"Yes. Mr. Kimball fired you," said Alex. "Is it still a problem?"

Stone hesitated. Blow it with this shrink and he'd go back to babysitting a rusty factory.

He'd hide nothing.

"You do a hundred things right, then you do one thing wrong and then you think you'll never get it right again. Kimball didn't fire my ass because I screwed up that mission. He fired me because I didn't show up for the next one."

"What will happen with the mission that Mr. Kimball wants to assign you?"

"It'll get done. I want back on the team. Most days I want it like nothing else," said Stone. "But here it is, doc. There's some days I think just take I-95 South and go. Florida, the Keys, just keep going, stay off the grid. Figure something else to do and stay the hell away from all the bullshit."

Stone leaned forward, looking down, as if he might find needed words on the tabletop. "And then I know that's not even in range. I need back in. After El Paso—I let it take charge. I have to—I'm telling you I can do it right."

She hadn't expected his honesty. Alex watched him. Charging a dozen Taliban machine guns took less courage than revealing his insecurity.

"It's the only thing I was ever really good at," said Stone. "Please. Doc, I have to get back in."

Alex saw a man in need. Of what she wasn't sure. Pride. Redemption. Justifying his existence. She didn't know if he had something to prove—maybe to the parents he never knew, maybe the girlfriends he feared would leave him. Or maybe he really just had to prove to himself that he wasn't...average. Stone had to get back to being part of something. Maybe something that, at least for him, was like a family. Up till a year ago it was RSA. Before that it was the Army. They'd given him structure, support, friends—they meant more to Stone than anything or anybody. Now he had nothing and nobody.

They'd vetted his file earlier and this interview confirmed their conclusions: a normal profile, but with risks that didn't fit what they'd expected. Even though nobody ever cleared 100%, once proven unreliable or unstable, the risk of another failure loomed large. But Stone had put himself in her hands, something no other eval subject had ever done. A remarkable sign of trust from somebody who hadn't had any five minutes earlier. That was a good leading indicator of commitment and reliability. Alex watched Stone, who only looked down at the table top.

"You may report to Mr. Kimball for your mission," said Alex.

Stone looked up. He took a moment and cleared his throat before saying anything. "Okay. Thanks, doc."

Alex heard her cell phone ring. "Excuse me."

She listened for a few moments, her expression changing to disappointment.

"I'm sure my son didn't start it—yes. Yes, I'll pick him up now," said Alex. She put the phone down and said to Stone, "Unless there's anything else, we're done. You may go."

"Okay." Stone stood up and nodded at her phone. "Hey, doc, don't worry. I was like that once and look how I turned out."

Stone watched her expression change from disappointment to dismay.

— DIRECTOR'S OFFICE, RSA

Anybody visiting Kimball's large office would immediately know he'd served in the Army. The American flag in the corner stood as straight as he did and the flagpole was topped by a gold spear point. A walnut-framed shadow box held a Ranger tab and insignia of rank including everything from a second lieutenant's bars to a full colonel's silver eagle, and ribbons from assignments in the Balkans, Africa and South Asia. Photos on the wall marked his field commands: in BDUs in Bosnia, desert camo in Iraq and Afghanistan. No photos of the Viper 20 meat-eaters he ran in the Helmand, since according to CENTCOM they didn't actually exist.

Used to the scenery, Clancy Ford, sitting across the desk from Kimball, ignored it. He normally sat one floor below Kimball's office, occupying one of the third-floor offices of a Senior Intelligence Officer.

"He's in his psych eval now. I figure he'll come back in," said Kimball.

"Why?" asked Clancy.

"I know what he wants and I'll let him think I'll give it to him."

"I didn't make myself clear. Why are we—check that—why are you bringing back a whiny broke-dick shitbag who forgot how to spell mission?"

"Did I request your opinion and up and forget I asked?"

"I excuse your lapse in judgement. Nobody expects officers, retired or otherwise, to use intelligence and reasoning in their decisions," said Clancy. He had no problem exchanging banter and bullshit with his boss and then challenging his decisions. He'd developed the habit as a staff sergeant after his third tour of duty, and refined it as a gunnery sergeant after his fourth tour. Smart lieutenants quickly learned to listen to him, thereby surviving their first tours. "You want me to repeat the question? I'll talk slow this time."

Kimball allowed a short smile. Clancy was one of the few people he always listened to, partly because of his long service in the Marines, partly because Semper Fi still mattered to him, and mostly because he was one of the smartest people in the building and knew the what and the why of the agency. Long before Clancy got his leg blown off, Kimball had heard about Clancy's work in Afghanistan, several times making good use of his systems in the Helmand. When they met for the first interview, Clancy wheeled himself in, arriving a half hour early and said he could do the job better than anybody else. Maybe because weeks earlier he'd been told that between his injury and his age, he'd never see a battlefield again and since he had his 20 why not take his retirement? Or maybe because he really was that good. Kimball quickly figured out that Clancy was motivated and smart enough to work at an agency that very few had heard of and whose work much fewer could even guess at. But Kimball didn't know whether he'd fit in because of recent life changes, like missing a limb and his employer of almost 25 years "suggesting" retirement. During the second interview Kimball asked whether Clancy thought "Marine" stood for "Muscles Are Required, Intelligence Not Essential," to which Clancy responded by asking whether Kimball knew that Army stood for "Ain't Really Marines Yet." Clancy arrived for work a week later, walking in on his new leg prosthesis.

"He gets the ticket for Cain," said Kimball.

"Stone must have recently pissed you off very much."

"Not recently."

"Maybe you want to borrow a rifle platoon from Sixth Marines," said Clancy. "Last thing I recall about Stone, he'll last about one minute with Cain."

"Way he was, sure. Maybe. I think he wants back in. He's a good operator if he wants to be. One of the best, he puts his mind to it," said Kimball. There were other reasons to bring Stone back, which Clancy didn't need to know.

"You want to give Cain some live fire practice, that's okay by me. It sounds like we're not voting on this. Or why am I here?"

"Sure we're voting. Today we're weighing the votes and I'm feeling fat," said Kimball. "Update the system. Stone's on the ticket for Cain. Log it as a GreenSeed. Now or yesterday would be very nice."

Clancy didn't smile. Something had always smelled bad about the GreenSeed missions and this unexpected addition only made it smell worse. "Yes, sir. Is that all?"

"Yeah," said Kimball. Clancy's face showed his disdain for the GreenSeed missions. Kimball didn't like them any more than

Clancy did. But RSA existed to eliminate targets, like terrorists and drug lords, that conventional methods, like arrest warrants and jury trials, couldn't. The people who authorized missions made GreenSeed fit RSA's criteria only by stretching them in very creative, borderline-illegal ways that only elected officials could comprehend. "We don't get paid to like it."

"Understood. Orders for RSA authorization will be available by 1500," said Clancy.

"Get armory and finance lined up. I'm sending him to you after I tell him about his mission."

"He doesn't know yet?"

Kimball smiled and shook his head.

"You think I'm going to cheer him up?" asked Clancy. Fat chance, but at least he'd get to make his own assessment of Stone, which as of the last time he'd seen him was well south of FUBAR. He stood up.

Clancy winced while getting to his feet—one of which was made of metal. Kimball knew better than to ask if he needed a hand. Clancy looked at Kimball and gave a short nod that said it didn't hurt much.

"Yeah, send him my way," said Clancy. "If he's dumb enough to stick around."

— MINERAL COUNTY, WV

Cain sat on a rickety wooden chair on the porch, reading the iPad. The chair creaked whenever Cain leaned back. He scrolled quickly through files until he found a folder named "Center for Human Sciences." He tapped it and watched more folders populate the display. He tapped on one and read the header: "Albert Gidden, PhD, MD, DrMed, DSc will headline the Association for Human Genetics Conference as Keynote Speaker. As Director of the Center for Human Sciences, he will address challenges faced by labs pioneering new genetics research techniques in the Mt. Olympus room at 9:00AM on…"

Cain browsed through the dozens of other folders. He opened a file and saw a photo of himself, taken about 20 years earlier, age 10 or 11. He opened another file and looked at a photo of a girl, titled "Annie Jane Cain." It must have been taken shortly before she dropped out of high school. She died before he got out of grade school and he remembered little of her except a gentle sadness.

The next file got him closer to what he was looking for. "March 17, 1984. GreenSeed program enrolled Annie Jane Cain into the GreenSeed Program...DNA reformation successfully completed ...GreenSeed Gen 1 Subject 2 Elias Cain born healthy..."

Cain stopped reading and went back to the photo of Annie Jane. Years of growing up without a mother, mostly without a father, then military service that took him from Fort Benning to dry, high parts of the world where he got to kill lots of people. Any resemblance to her that might have once existed had long since disappeared.

After reading his mother's file, Cain copied the data from the microSD datacard into the iPad's memory. After reading through the files, he put the iPad on the chair and went inside. Cain walked behind Jimmy Bob and stood silently for a few moments. Jimmy Bob had not cowered during the beating hours earlier and showed no signs of doing so now.

"You gonna git me a drink a' somethin'?" asked Jimmy Bob.

Cain leaned on the chair back and said, "Daddy, you kill Mama?"

"What the hell—?" said Jimmy Bob. He twisted around to face Cain. "Nobody never proved nothin'."

Jimmy Bob took Cain's punch across the jaw. Blood and a tooth fell out of his mouth and fear edged his voice. "Now you just listen here. That woman kept diggin' into my 'shine, wouldn't stop for nothin'. After all I done for the bitch—"

Cain grabbed Jimmy Bob by the hair and yanked his head back.

"What you doin' boy? God will—"

"God will worry about something else."

Cain grabbed Jimmy Bob's chin and pulled, twisting the old hillbilly's neck, slowly at first. Cain felt bones and ligaments and cartilage crackle. Jimmy Bob only groaned at first, then screamed until he suddenly sagged forward in the chair, limp, restrained only by the handcuffs. He wheezed, his breath shallow, and his head swung loosely on his chest. Cain unlocked the handcuffs and shackles and shoved Jimmy Bob onto the floor.

Cain leaned down and grabbed Jimmy Bob's collar and dragged him across the floor and out the door and across the porch and down the steps and around the trailer. Cain dropped him near the old fire pit.

It took just a few minutes to build the pyre, even less time to put the skinny old hound out of its misery. Shotguns came in handy that way. The batch of moonshine Jimmy Bob had just finished would help ignition, and the dead wood and dry brush would provide good fuel for the flames. Cain heaved Jimmy Bob onto the top of the wood pile, next to the body of the old hound, then stood still.

Fire.

Cain searched through Jimmy Bob's pockets till he found a matchbook, probably used for lighting propane burners under the moonshine pots. He lit one match, then ignited the entire book.

"Enjoy your 'shine, Daddy." Cain threw the matchbook onto the wood and waited. A small blue flame grew as heat met 180 proof vapor. The fire spread quickly, igniting the wood. He watched as the flames started to singe Jimmy Bob's coveralls and listened to the screaming for a few moments before turning and walking back to the trailer. The fire wouldn't smoke too much. The wood was dry and moonshine burned clean.

Cain leaned back in the rickety old chair, holding the iPad in one hand and a jar with a quarter inch of crystal clear 'shine in the other. The last time he'd visited there hadn't been anything like iPads or smartphones, not that anybody in these parts would have much use for them. He watched a video of Senator Walter Heidrick talking to other senators and Dr. Albert Gidden in a nice wood-paneled conference room, probably in some building that cost taxpayers plenty. Heidrick was one smooth-talking son of a bitch who could shit his pants and blame it on somebody else. Gidden didn't look too happy. Interesting video. Must have been taken a couple of months before Kimball recruited Cain—maybe six, seven months before his stint in Truesdale.

Cain watched the video for a few minutes, then stopped it. That's why Gidden didn't look too happy. Cain replayed the last 30 seconds.

"...it is unfortunate that we're finding out about this thirty years after we started the program. Obviously any discovery of these GreenSeeds jeopardizes the security and secrecy of this program and causes unnecessary damage to its oversight," said Heidrick. He shifted his attention from Gidden to Kimball, who sat next to another senator on the committee. "Therefore, Director Kimball of RSA has been instructed to limit our exposure..."

Government-speak for kill the bastards who might get in the way of re-election. The same bastards that Cain had finished killing as of one week earlier. He kept listening to Heidrick. "...he and Dr. Gidden have recruited a candidate who will take primary responsibility for the Gen Two GreenSeeds, a gentleman by the name of Elias Cain, whose background and military record uniquely qualify him to successfully complete this mission. He will terminate these GreenSeeds as early as is feasible with maximum containment."

"So that's who," said Cain. Heidrick ran the organization and had told Gidden to get Cain to kill the GreenSeeds who went a little crazy. Cain recalled the Greek myth of Kronos, the ruler of the Titans who devoured his children. He put the iPad down and stepped outside to look at the tall pines. He smelled the afternoon that late summer had not yet made too hot. He'd wondered, at the time, why Kimball picked him—they must have had plenty of good operators stateside so why bring him back from Jordan? Still no good answer to that question. He went back inside and sipped some 'shine.

None of those GreenSeeds had really challenged him. He'd been one of a very few outside the Marine Corps to train in the MCMAP—the Marines were very protective of their Martial Arts Program—and if there was somebody who could take him in hand-to-hand he hadn't yet met them. As one of five Rangers accepted into the program, he knew three from their class were still somewhere in South Asia and who the hell knew what happened to Duncan.

Cain remembered each of his targets, all second generation GreenSeeds. He'd quickly memorized their profiles so that he wouldn't be burdened with coded silver-inked paper files while hunting them.

Surprising what the legal system let walk around in public.

His first target, CHS File 2-3. Convictions for rape, aggravated assault, manslaughter and negligent homicide. First conviction at the age of 14. A second on multiple counts at the age of 15. After serving three years for voluntary manslaughter, he'd found his new calling peddling crank. He was a punk, big, strong, violent. Cain found him, picked a fight, then crushed his windpipe before he could grab the knife in his pocket. Cain walked away and the small news item only said some criminal died during commission of a felony, one of several in Baltimore that day.

Some dozens of people never knew how lucky they were when Cain killed his second target. CHS File 2-1. He broke her neck against the edge of her kitchen countertop just before she left her apartment, a Metro SmarTrip card in her hand marked with McLean station stamps. She had three gallon jugs full of gasoline packed into a rollaboard and a pocket full of rags and lighters. Cain figured she wanted to see what would happen to the Metro car if she lit it up at rush hour. Her only prior offenses had been arson of two neighbors' houses. Though they resulted in three deaths, she received no jail time. He spilled cooking oil on the kitchen floor so the news said only that she slipped and died in her home in an unfortunate accident.

The third target wore Nazi swastika tattoos and had a hobby of beating up the homeless in Park Heights. Cain relieved CHS File 2-4 of the steel pipe he was about to use on the old drunk and crushed the top of his skull. The old drunk nodded his thanks before asking for loose change. A reporter didn't think the dead body warranted any news coverage at all.

Cain's fourth target was the youngest, maybe 24 or 25. Tall and gangly, his only priors were assaults with deadly weapons…that happened to be guns. Four wounded in a library and he didn't have the decency to shoot himself in the head when the police arrived. His parents insisted he wasn't a bad kid. The courts believed them and their highly-paid attorneys and let him off with psychiatric counseling. Out on a million dollars bail after shooting two college classmates, one of whom died, they later found CHS File 2-6 with a bullet in his skull. The news item reported that he'd shot himself with his illegally-obtained pistol, which technically he did, though with Cain's assistance.

After reviewing the CHS File 2-6 history, Cain recognized the difference between law and justice, and that they converged only some of the time, frequently in conjunction with large sums of money changing hands.

The fifth target, CHS File 2-2, hadn't committed any crimes, or at least hadn't been caught. But apparently somebody thought he would get violent because of his GreenSeed heritage so Cain ran him over with a stolen car just outside the hospital where he was trolling for lawsuits. Cain left the car three blocks away, then walked back and checked to make sure the target hadn't survived. As a crowd gathered and mumbled about how life was so unfair, he watched the man lying dead in the street, face down in a puddle of blood as a TV news truck arrived to record something titillating for the 6 o'clock news show. According to the file, he hadn't done anything wrong, or at least he hadn't done anything illegal—since File 2-2 was a lawyer, he likely didn't know the difference, but that didn't mean he needed to be executed.

Cain started wondering about how people like Senator Heidrick got to decide who would die without the benefit of a jury or a judge or even any semblance of due process. Maybe killing people for other people without wasn't such a good idea, at least without knowing why. The dead people didn't bother him as much as the live people who ordered the missions. What made them so special? That led to more questions about what authority meant, and while stopping for a cup of coffee, he decided he'd visit Gidden, knowing Heidrick and Kimball would only respond with rudeness, incarceration, or all of the above.

One morning, early, Gidden discovered Cain sitting in his office and had asked "What in heaven's name are you doing in my office?" Cain had replied, "Good morning, sir. I just wanted to visit." Gidden wanted to know how Cain got in the office, past all the security alarms. Cain had simply responded, "It's my job, sir. I think I'm pretty good at it." When Cain asked why he'd been tasked with killing the GreenSeeds, Gidden simply told him, "You don't need to know." Cain disagreed and was pleased he'd copied what he needed from Gidden's computer onto his microSD datacard before Gidden arrived. He'd only met Gidden once before, at the mission briefing, and the second visit didn't improve Cain's opinion of him.

Killing the last target, Freddy, had been slightly more difficult than the others, since he'd had to get arrested in order to get close to him. Freddy, CHS File 2-5, had got in his car and ran it into a crowd at an outdoor shopping mall because he just wanted to kill lots of people. The news story reported three dead and 18 injured, but it never made national news because legally obtained guns weren't involved. A year into Freddy's 30-year stretch at the William G. Truesdale Adult Detention Center in Alexandria, they assigned Cain the file. Kimball arranged Cain's incarceration at the same prison and two days later Freddy was found in the showers with a crushed windpipe and a pencil stuck in his eye socket. Kimball had told him he'd get out on a mistaken identity, but another inmate fingered Cain as the killer. After not hearing from Kimball for a week, Cain decided he'd just get out on his own. Maybe Gidden mentioned his unscheduled visit, or his questions, or maybe Cain had just pissed them all off.

It didn't matter. When he heard about his transfer to a SuperMax he knew he had his opportunity. He didn't know what he'd do afterward but it probably wouldn't be working for the government.

It wasn't that his targets really had a reason to live. Except for maybe the lawyer, they were all vicious animals of man-made origin and who knew what went through their minds? They liked violence and killing only for the violence and killing, just like the terrorists and insurgents he'd hunted half a world away. But these targets hadn't learned to like it. It was just the way they were. And they were just the way they were because somebody made them that way.

Just the way somebody made him.

"Almost kin," said Cain, softly.

Cain finished the 'shine and felt the burn it left in his throat. He thought about Kronos and wondered if the ruler of the Titans looked anything like Gidden. He put the empty jar down and sat in place, motionless.

He'd just figured out why Kimball picked him. Because Heidrick told him to. Because Cain was one of them. GreenSeed. The files said Heidrick and his Senate committee and Gidden had watched all of them ever since they were born. After they saw some behaviors they didn't like—murder understandably being one of them—they ordered the deaths of the GreenSeeds and now they were almost done. That was why Kimball left him in

Truesdale—some newsman would report that a violent offender had been shot dead by a federal agent while trying to escape from a prison van driving to a SuperMax in Kentucky.

Cain turned on the iPad and looked for the GreenSeed files. He started grouping folders in new directories. It took him a few moments to remember how to encrypt the files, and then how to code instructions for automatic upload to a cloud server as soon as the iPad smelled wireless internet. After an hour, he finished and set down the iPad.

"For all the world to see."

— DIRECTOR'S OFFICE, RSA

Stone took a seat across the desk from Kimball. Kimball grabbed a remote control and clicked on the in-wall video display.

"Cartoons?" asked Stone.

"Something like that," said Kimball. He pressed a button on the remote control.

The herky-jerky images of combat video jumped onto the display. It could have been any dry, brown, arid plain in any dry, brown, arid country in South Asia. Lots of dust. It felt hot just looking at the video.

Not Peshawar. Not Quetta. Not Khost. Then Stone remembered it was somewhere in Iraq, a couple of months before that Marine helo went down, maybe springtime in 2005. Probably with Task Force North but he couldn't name the place or the map coordinates. After the second or third tour, they all tended to blend together.

The video abruptly steadied as the videographer hit the deck. A bullet-pocked brick house seen through clouds of smoke and blowing dust, unremarkable except for the three PKM machine guns firing through windows at anything outside. He heard no sound but Stone remembered the full-auto buzz of 7.62 millimeter bullets cutting through air.

"I think it was me with the camera," said Stone. He kept staring at the display.

The firing stopped. The gunners, with the less than adequate training provided to most insurgents, probably hadn't purposely timed the PKM barrel changes to occur simultaneously. A soldier in grimy desert camo ran to one of the windows and tossed a satchel inside the house. One second after running away, the image shook and smoke blasted out of the windows. The soldier strolled back to the bunker and threw two grenades inside. He stepped aside as they exploded and then walked toward the camera, a grin crossing his unshaven face.

"So? Elias Cain," said Stone. He'd shot that video because Elias wanted to send something to some girls back in the world. A buddy would do that for a buddy. "What."

"What do you mean, what?" Kimball turned off the display. "He's the mission."

Stone took a only a millisecond to understand that 'mission' meant 'kill Elias Cain'.

"Oh, shit."

"That's why they're called missions."

Stone remembered a friendly fire incident that wasn't so friendly and said, "Cain is generally hazardous to your health."

"Life is generally hazardous to your health. So what."

"What'd he do now?" asked Stone.

"He stole classified data, he is AWOL, and he is killing lots of people without permission. CHS File one-two, status immediate. You find Cain, retire his ass, secure the data." Kimball pushed a paper file titled "CHS File 1-2" across the desk. The silvery ink wouldn't show on photocopies and would disappear entirely four days after printing.

Stone declined to look at the file. "I want to do this, why?"

Kimball suppressed the urge to laugh. Some of the history between Stone and Cain was funny, provided you weren't Stone. He and Cain worked a mission years earlier in Nangarhar. A dusty, hilly pile of rocks in the Arma mountains of eastern Afghanistan, where Cain shot Stone twice in the ass. Cain got transferred to Amman, where he served as a field advisor to Jordan's counter-terrorist security forces. Stone got sent to a field hospital where he got two bullet holes in his butt cheek patched up. The chain of command was told that, essentially, it never happened.

"Nangarhar? He didn't want you dead. Still doesn't, probably. Maybe." Kimball pulled out a cigarette. "By the way, up till about 36 hours ago he worked for us."

"What?" Stone's crap detector started ringing. Very loudly.

"At ease, Stone." Kimball lit the cigarette and inhaled deeply. He slowly exhaled a cloud of blue smoke. "You're the only one who can get close."

"You don't know Cain."

"I know Cain and so do you. Better than anybody else among the living." Kimball took another drag. "You finish this, you're back on the team, full-time."

Kimball waited a perfectly-timed two second interval, then said, "And I mission-lock you for Salazar."

He and Stone looked at each other until Stone looked away.

"You remember Salazar, don't you?" asked Kimball. A taunt more than a question. "And his pal Guerro."

Without turning around, Kimball held up the remote and pressed the play button. He'd left nothing about this meeting to chance. Both of them knew hunting Elias Cain would make any rifle platoon think hard about how much gunship support they'd need.

A silent drone's eye view appeared on the wall display, which zoomed in on the parking lot of the El Paso warehouse. Stone watched it like a Los Angeleno ogling a freeway auto accident. The video showed Guerro packing Salazar into the semi-tractor cab while exchanging gunfire with Stone. Guerro jumped up into the cab and a cloud of black smoke blew out the exhaust pipes. As the semi-tractor lurched forward, Stone jumped on the running board, slipping but holding onto the frame of the open window, firing through the door. Guerro's arm whipped out the window and pounded Stone until he fell off. He rolled onto the pavement just as a black Ford Escape sped into the parking lot, skidding to a halt between the semi-tractor and Stone. A man in body armor jumped out of the driver's side and emptied his pistol at the departing semi-tractor, now speeding down the street. Another man got out of the passenger side and grabbed Stone.

"Maybe you remember that's Jaeger who grabbed you," said Kimball. "Yeah, he still talks about how he saved your ass. A lot."

The video showed Jaeger throwing Stone into the back seat of the Escape, then jumping in. After they sped off, nothing moved except for wind blowing dust across the asphalt, now empty except for Juan's mother holding the dead body that a minute earlier was Juan.

Kimball paused the video as Juan's mother turned her face to the sky, eyes closed and mouth locked open in a silent scream.

"That is what we call textbook FUBAR. Señor Guerro messed up your win streak. Sure as hell it would chafe my ass," said Kimball. He took another pull on his cigarette. "Come on, Stone, I know you want back in and I know you want Salazar."

"What if I do?" asked Stone, after a silence. He stared at the frozen image on the display.

"Like I said, you get your slot back and a ticket for Salazar." Cigarette smoke accompanied Kimball's words. Kimball actually did want Stone on another Salazar mission. Salazar and Guerro were the only targets they'd ever failed to kill—repeatedly. Maybe Stone could actually pull it off. Maybe it might actually work out.

Maybe.

Stone finally turned away from the display. "Guaranteed?"

"Sure. Guaranteed," said Kimball. He looked at Stone through the smoke curling through the air. "Absolutely."

— EL SAUZ, MEXICO

Rainless cumulus floated overhead, tinged pink by the late afternoon sun. Rocks and brown dust spread out on both sides of Highway 57, as far as anybody could see. Yucca and creosote nearly the same color as the dust grew on the plain, unspoiled by recent rainfall.

They'd followed the police car for almost two hours since leaving a small rundown house outside of Monclova. They'd waited down the street until they saw four men get into the Coahuila State Police car that had pulled up with the two female officers inside. Guerro recognized one of the four men as a Monterro gang member from the tattoos on his arms. As they drove away, Guerro told Tinto to follow the police car at a distance. Guerro knew they'd drive north, then stop to meet another Monterro that night, who would drive them to the border just south of Piedras Negras the next day.

Pedro had done a good job finding out the plan to import these *Musulmán terroristas* into the US. They were probably something like Al Qaida or these new ISIS *maniáticos* who chopped people's heads off on TV. Guerro told Pedro to make friends with one of the policewomen and maybe he would learn something. Women liked Pedro because of his good looks, charm, and because he was hung like a donkey. Pedro screwed that policewoman a few times and she started telling him how they worked with the Monterro gang. It was nice to see Pedro enjoying his job.

The Monterros had brought in maybe a dozen of these *terroristas* during the last year and she told Pedro how the gang gave them money to make sure nobody bothered them while they drove to the border. The same thing that other gangs had done until Salazar told Guerro to take care of business: they would hunt the terrorists, kill them and anybody with them, and spread their body parts in the desert. Now it was the Monterros. Different people, same job.

A friend would call once in a while and ask a favor. Friends did friends favors so Salazar would agree and tell Guerro to take care of it. They'd done this for their friend for almost 20 years and so far it worked out pretty well for Señor Salazar. They hunted *terroristas* or other gangs bringing drugs over the border and in return they got a call when police were ready to jump on them. None of them had gotten arrested by police or FBI or DEA or CIA or any of those *federale cabróns*. It helped grow their businesses in the US.

"Pedro, they going to stop soon?" Guerro turned around and looked at Pedro, sitting in the back seat of the Ford F-250 Super Cab.

"Yes, boss. It's going to be some shack off the highway, on the east side," said Pedro.

Guerro faced front and watched the police car driving a half mile in front of them.

The sun hung low in the sky when the police car pulled off onto a dirt road and stopped 100 meters off the highway, next to a Mazda sedan in back of a lone rusty metal building.

Guerro watched the building as they passed it and saw the officers and their passengers getting out. "Pull off up there," he said, pointing at the road in front of them.

Tinto drove the F-250 off the highway onto a dusty turnout a half mile north of the metal building.

Tinto and Guerro loaded their MP-5 submachine guns and Pedro picked up a pistol and a machete. They made their way south, walking well off the highway through the creosote and Spanish Dagger yucca. They stepped quietly as they drew closer to the building and knelt when they saw one of the police officers standing outside smoking a cigarette. They waited for a few minutes to make sure she was alone, then Pedro nudged Guerro and started walking towards her.

Esmerelda worked for the Coahuila State Police. The pay wasn't so good so she did only what other officers did and took money from gangs in return for things like escorting them, to avoid confrontations with the *Policìa Federal*. Of course, this was a valuable community service because nobody was better off when gangs and *federales* started shooting at each other.

"Hey, Esmerelda," said Pedro.

Esmerelda gasped and turned around quickly. Her hand went to a green-eyed golden angel on a yellow metal necklace.

"Is everything okay?" asked Pedro.

"Of course. Just like I promised you." Esmerelda smiled. She let go of the angel and pressed close to Pedro. He had given her money and promised to take her away, and what woman could refuse a man who looked like that? "All six are inside. Two Monterros have the guns. The other three men don't have any and they don't talk much. I think they like to pray a lot."

And then there was Esmeralda's partner who sat inside with the five men. Melosia, who always thought she was so pretty. *Puta.* She always got the men to look at her and was probably flirting with them all now just to have them smile and pay attention to her.

"Okay. That's good." Pedro turned around and waved.

Esmerelda watched Guerro and Tinto as they walked up. They were older than the Monterros and looked much more frightening, especially the big man with the scars on his face. And the other one—who would dye their hair red like that? Only somebody who would kill anybody who said anything about it.

"These are the guys," said Pedro.

Guerro looked at Esmerelda. From the size of her waist, she put too many tortas in that mouth every day. She had green eyes, brassy dyed blond hair and wore a cheap, gaudy gold-colored pendant around her neck. He watched her put her hand up to hold that green-eyed golden angel when he stared at it. Guerro nodded and turned to Pedro.

"She says it's all set up," said Pedro.

Guerro turned to Tinto. "Okay, let's go."

"Pedro, are we going now?" Esmerelda tugged on Pedro's arm. She didn't want to be around when those two men went inside the building.

"Not yet," said Guerro. He smiled and watched Esmerelda drop to the ground after punching her. Pedro taped her mouth and handcuffed her.

"Watch the door," said Guerro, to Pedro. He walked quietly with Tinto to the building.

The shooting took less than 20 seconds. As soon as they walked inside they opened fire, shooting in short bursts at each of the six seated around a table. They reloaded and walked inside. Tinto walked over to the Monterros, recognizable by their shaved heads and tattoos, and the pistols stuck in their belts. Neither moved and they bled from several bullet holes in their chests. Out of habit, Tinto shot each in the head a couple of times, then walked over to the *terroristas*. Guerro knelt next to Melosia. Her blouse soaked in blood, she took short breaths and stared at the ceiling. He ripped her blouse open and ran his hands over her body. She had nice skin.

"Too bad," said Guerro. Two bullet holes. She would die, but maybe not too soon. He leaned over and smelled her face and said, "Hey, you and me, we have a little fun, okay?"

Melosia looked at Guerro, then jerked her head to the side and opened her mouth, as if to scream. She froze for a moment, then stopped breathing.

Guerro stood up, disappointed. She was much prettier than Esmerelda.

"Hey, boss," said Tinto. "We got one still alive. Maybe not for long."

Guerro walked over and looked down at the *terrorista* who stared up at them. Hard to believe he could still breathe while bleeding from that many bullet holes. Guerro said, "Go get Pedro. I want to talk to this one."

After Tinto walked out, Guerro pulled over a chair and sat, staring down at the bleeding man.

"All those bullet holes, I think they got to hurt," said Guerro. He prodded one of the wounds with the silencer of his MP-5, pressing harder until the man screamed. "Yeah, I guess they hurt pretty bad. Hey, you ever chop anybody's head off?"

Guerro eased off and the screams stopped. The bleeding man probably didn't understand much Spanish and only looked up at Guerro's face. "I think we going to keep you around for a while," said Guerro. "You can watch the party, okay?"

"Hey, boss," called Tinto, from the door.

Guerro turned around to see Tinto walk in carrying the machete. Pedro followed him, dragging Esmerelda behind him, still handcuffed. Her face wet with tears and blood, she was naked from the waist down and her shirt had been ripped open. Pedro started partying without them.

Guerro walked over to Esmerelda. He slammed her against the wall and shoved his fingers in her mouth. She gagged and he pulled out his fingers, then slapped her.

"Hey, why you crying?" asked Guerro. He put his hand around her throat and squeezed. "We have a little fun, you and me."

— MINERAL COUNTY, WV

Cain sat at the table that held a rack filled with gray pipe bombs in various stages of completion. He glued an end cap onto the eight inch length of two inch wide schedule 40 PVC pipe. He'd set the kerosene lamp far enough back to avoid accidental ignition of the improvised explosives that had enough bang to destroy everything in the general area of the single-wide.

Four of the pipe bombs had small electronics boxes duct-taped to them, from which antennae sprouted. The rest had fuses. Half-empty boxes of stud hanger nails, PVC pipe end caps, PVC pipe glue and solvent, gunpowder cans, and diesel fuel littered the table top. Jimmy Bob was no stranger to improvised munitions, since he'd had a few neighbors happy to highjack his 'shine before he started using explosives as a warning device.

Cain inserted a fuse into the hole of the end cap and duct-taped a short loop of the cord to the pipe, then set it in the rack. Probably not as good as an M67 frag, but then he didn't have any grenades and not as good was better than none. He suppressed the urge to light one up outside and leaned back on the rickety chair, yawning. He didn't yet feel like sleeping, but the day's activities tired him enough that he didn't trust himself with assembling any more pipe bombs.

Cain picked up the iPad and re-started a video, turning up the sound. Another history lesson. An image of Dr. Gidden standing in a wood-paneled conference room appeared on the display, presenting to his Senate oversight committee. Senator Heidrick sat beside Gidden.

"We can only guess if these psychopathologies result from unexpected gene mutations that might have activated neurohormonal changes during adolescence," said Gidden. "Some GreenSeeds remain normal while most become ultra-violent murderers with a fascinating indifference to human life. Elias Cain was evaluated after the incident in Nangarhar, Afghanistan during which he killed 24 civilians and injured a fellow soldier who attempted to intervene. Our evaluation revealed no remorse, sense of guilt, or regret over the shootings…"

Cain heard a rumble of a big-engined pickup truck arriving outside. He turned off the lantern and went to the door. He cracked it open and saw the truck stop, its headlights still on. A man got out and walked around the front end.

Clem. He'd put on a few pounds in the last ten years. Or was it eleven. Cain remembered the date but not the year he'd shot Clem's brother, though he now didn't even recall why.

Cain quietly closed the door, stuffed a pistol in his belt and picked up the shotgun.

Gidden's voice droned on. "These violent episodes often occur suddenly, without warning and with surprising violence unusual even for—"

Cain turned off the iPad and quietly opened the door, walking outside. He leaned against the door frame and watched Clem, now joined by a large blonde woman, start unloading empty plastic gallon jugs. Time for a pickup—Jimmy Bob's moonshine.

"Hello, Clem," said Cain.

Clem looked at Cain and froze for a second before running to the truck cab. He might be able to grab his shotgun in the gun rack before Cain put two barrels of double-ought buckshot in his guts.

Cain dropped the barrel of the shotgun into his hand and fired both barrels from the hip. Clem dropped, bleeding. He gasped, trying to breathe. The woman with him stood still, an empty plastic jug in each hand, staring first at Cain, then at Clem.

Cain popped the shotgun open and plucked out the empty shells. He loaded another pair and flipped it shut. He walked over to Clem, who bled from 16 double-ought holes in his ample belly.

"You got fat, Clem," said Cain.

"You just go straight to hell," said Clem. He spit blood.

"See you there soon enough." Cain emptied both barrels into Clem's face. He turned to the woman. Cain heard the plastic jugs lightly thump on the ground.

"Hey, mister. I's just here to help out, you know. Just helpin' out." She started backing up. "I got nothin' against you. I don't even know who you are."

"Real sorry you had to see that," said Cain.

She moved pretty fast for a big woman, like she'd been shot at before. Cain pulled out his pistol and aimed, tracking her as she ran. He fired once. The bullet jellied her brain stem and she dropped in mid-stride.

Cain put the pistol back in his belt and stepped over Clem's body to look at the truck, a Ford F-150 SuperCrew. He popped the hood and looked inside. A big-ass custom engine. Nice. He went to the truckbed and looked inside the chromed steel toolbox. Level 4 body armor vest, ammo. And a very clean Smith & Wesson .500 Magnum revolver. Clem liked guns but never could shoot very well. He'd probably shot the revolver once and never picked it up again. Damn thing would kick like mule. The ammo measured a half inch wide by two inches long, including the 440-grain jacketed bullet that somebody had custom-loaded. Moving at around 1,600 feet per second, the slug would deliver over 2,500 foot-pounds of energy and nobody wants to be on either end of that.

But it might be fun to shoot. Now he just needed his first target.

— EL SAUZ, MEXICO

He finished with Esmerelda, for the moment, and picked up a machete. As the boss, Guerro didn't have to cut heads and hands off bodies, but he decided to chop off this *terrorista's* head, but without killing him first. After all, they did it on TV so maybe it was fun.

There was a lot of blood and screaming after he swung the machete the first time. It got stuck and the head didn't come off so he turned to Tinto, who was on top of Esmerelda, and said, "Hey, why didn't you sharpen it? This is going to take forever."

The screaming stopped before the head finally tumbled off the body. Guerro pulled Tinto off Esmerelda and handed him the machete. Removing heads and hands was work for Tinto and Pedro—they would leave the bodies in the shack, and scatter the heads and hands in the desert for the lizards and coyotes so nobody could identify the dead for a while. The chopping would be messy and take a long time and next time maybe they would remember to sharpen the damn machete.

They'd tossed the heads and hands into a large trash bag by the time Guerro stood up next to Esmerelda, her ankles and wrists still lashed to the table. He buckled his belt and wiped his hands off on a rag, then leaned over Esmerelda and stared into her bruised, bloodied face. She stared back at Guerro through green eyes swollen half-shut, her hair dirty and tangled and bloody.

"I told you we were gonna have some fun," said Guerro. He dropped the rag and picked up the MP-5. "I got to make a call now, okay?"

"My angel's going to come for you. She's going to be angry with you," said Esmerelda, her voice a hoarse whisper.

"We have some fun with her too," said Guerro. He yanked the green-eyed golden angel from its yellow metal chain around Esmerelda's neck and pocketed it. Maybe he could give it to one of the girls if Salazar ever let him have one for a while.

Guerro fired a bullet into Esmerelda's forehead, then said, "Hey, Pedro, take care of this."

Pedro walked over, carrying the machete, as Guerro walked out the door into the night's darkness. He pulled his phone out and dialed a number.

"Señor Salazar, you can tell our friend the job is done," said Guerro. "Tell him we always get the job done."

— DIRECTOR'S OFFICE, RSA

Early morning sunshine reflected off his office walls. Kimball kept the shutters open to let in light of any kind, natural or otherwise—a big change from Iraq and Afghanistan where his quarters had ¾" plywood nailed over windows to block both light and mortar shrapnel.

Stone and Jaeger stood in front of Kimball's desk.

"Stone, you clean up pretty good," said Kimball.

"When I have to," said Stone. He stood dressed in neatly pressed civilian clothes, his brown hair high and tight—cut by somebody who earned a good living by doing so.

"Jaeger's your backup—"

"Just me, this one," said Stone.

"Why," asked Kimball.

"Shit, fine with me," said Jaeger. "His funeral."

"Shut up, Jaeger," said Kimball. He looked back at Stone. "Any reason other than some weird desire for lethal injury?"

"Elias sees through armor and smells gun oil two klicks off. You send both of us, he'll know why we're there. We won't get inside two hundred meters."

"You know where to find Cain?" asked Kimball.

"I will," said Stone. "Just me, at least I get to talk to him. Probably."

"That it?" asked Kimball.

Stone glanced at Jaeger. "You don't send monkeys when you're hunting lion."

"You think you can take him," said Jaeger. He snorted. "Be my guest."

"You go, Jaeger stays. Get it done," said Kimball. "Nice, clean and quiet. No headlines. Got it?"

"Got it." Stone turned, then bumped Jaeger with his shoulder. Jaeger pushed back.

"Sorry. Oh, please excuse me," said Stone. He fingered Jaeger's gold cufflink. "Nice pressed suit. Going to a monkey dance?"

"Nice pressed shirt. Want me to wrinkle it?" asked Jaeger.

"Stone, why are you still in my office?" asked Kimball.

"Just see he doesn't pork too many monkeys." Stone walked out.

Kimball tapped a speed dial button on the desk phone.

Over the speaker: "Clancy. What."

"Duncan Stone's taking CHS File one-two," said Kimball. "He's visiting you after he signs his paperwork."

"So he's got a death wish. Fine. I'll set him up."

"Can you get armory to move fast? Usual battle-rattle."

"Done," said Clancy.

"He gets the new phone. In case I need to find him."

Kimball tapped the phone off.

"You worried?" asked Jaeger. It was too soon for an I-told-you-so smile.

"Not much. He's going nowhere except after Cain. I promised him a ticket for Salazar," said Kimball.

"Lying's a sin." Jaeger laughed.

Kimball didn't find it funny. "I have permission. I work for the federal government."

— Intel Office, RSA

Clancy Ford sat in his chair, a cane in easy reach. His prosthetic leg worked well, even though he still felt the phantom pain that had continued three years after the amputation.

Five large computer displays surrounded his desktop. Software manuals stuffed the shelves above which hung photos of him with his gun truck crew and with Harry Jones, Captain, USMC, deceased. A boxed American flag and a shadow box full of medals and his gunnery sergeant's stripes hung next to the photos. Clancy spoke into his cell phone.

"I was just looking forward to seeing them is all. It's been two months—fine," said Clancy. He didn't blame his ex-wife. It wasn't the first time his daughters wanted to do something other than visit their father. Who had run their lives like troops in a rifle company. "Just tell the girls...just tell them I love them. Yeah. Fine."

Clancy put his cell phone down next to the photo on his desk. It was a formal family portrait, back when he still had his leg and his family. Just now entering puberty, his daughters would soon start acting like women, behaving like babies and want even less to do with divorced parents. He didn't blame his wife for leaving. She'd never liked who she had to share him with. First the United States Marine Corps. Then Walter Reed. Then RSA. He spoke to her about duty and she always asked about duty to his wife and children. He knew he'd never had a good answer and it only got worse after his injury.

A knock on the door. Clancy turned around.

"Enter."

"Hey, Gunny. Been a while," said Stone. He felt like a new recruit in front of a drill instructor and didn't attempt a smile. The door swung shut.

"Yeah." Clancy looked Stone up and down. He'd cleaned up since the last time they met. Clancy used that very brief meeting to collect the phone and the pistols and nobody even pretended to friendship. He had little time and no sympathy for anybody who didn't do their job. Which Stone hadn't. Clancy formed his judgements quickly about everybody, and they were almost always correct. He had the benefit of over 20 years of commanding Marines and almost 18 years of being commanded by a strict father who had been one of the first African-Americans promoted to Sergeant-Major in the Marine Corps.

"Kimball brought you back against my recommendation," said Clancy. "As far as I'm concerned, this mission is a test. You read me?"

"Lima Charlie, Gunny," said Stone. Loud and Clear. He hadn't expected a pleasant, all-is-forgiven meeting. Everybody knew gunnery sergeants had no aptitude for such things. "I messed up. It will not happen again."

Clancy watched Stone's face. It had changed since a year earlier. None of that whiny, hangdog, woe is me crap painted all over it.

"All in?" asked Clancy.

"Yeah, I'm all in," said Stone.

"Okay." said Clancy, after a moment. He picked up a large envelope. He'd give him a chance. Especially considering Stone had pulled his ass out of very deep shit just over three years earlier. "You are now back with the good guys. You will not forget that."

Clancy handed the large envelope to Stone, who opened it. Papers with silvery ink, already starting to fade—his assignment—CHS File 1-2. And $5,000 in hundreds and twenties.

"Don't spend it all in one place. Mills wants receipts."

Clancy nodded at the Halliburton case laid on top of a stack of files.

"Your gear," said Clancy. He opened a desk drawer and pulled out a candy bar from a box, next to which lay a Beretta 92F, civilian version of the military standard M9 sidearm. He waved the candy at Stone. "Want one?"

Stone shook his head and opened the aluminum case. Two SIG P-226 and one P-250 sub-compact, all .40 caliber, as usual. Four magazines each and enough hollowpoints to inventory a small town's police force, plus a silencer. He worked the slide on each pistol and strapped on the shoulder holster, then attached the waistband holster, then the ankle holster.

"Still fits good," said Stone. He hefted the P-250 compact pistol. Bigger than the P-290 but probably easier to shoot.

"Phone's a little nicer. Built in GPS. It's always on when the phone's on. Not even you will get lost," said Clancy. "Your ride's downstairs. The beige Taurus."

"Beige Taurus," said Stone. He'd been thinking red Mustang. "Nice. I'll look like I'm dropping off kindergarteners."

"You're not here to pick up chicks. Stop your bitching and don't scratch the paint."

Stone nodded. "Thanks, Gunny."

"Don't thank me yet. Do your job and watch your six. This op's already messed up."

"Yeah." Stone grinned. "That's why they called me."

— CENTER FOR HUMAN SCIENCES

Kimball had just seated himself when Gidden pushed a folder across the pristine desktop. Before picking it up, Kimball noted the darkened, empty labs behind the glass wall. He took a few moments to scan through the papers in the folder.

"Gen Three," said Kimball. He looked up from the papers. "Heidrick know about this?"

"Of course. I certainly would not do this on my own initiative. These are his orders," said Gidden.

Kimball read further, noting Heidrick's electronic signature and verification proving origin and authenticity. "Yeah. All neat and authorized and everything. Why?"

"You don't need to know."

"Oh. I don't need to know." Kimball closed the folder and pushed it back to Gidden. He leaned back in his chair. "Now—I'm thinking maybe I got other things Stone can do. Maybe washing my car, cleaning my office, mowing grass at the Lincoln Memorial. Maybe fixing Cain and all your other problem children is somebody else's problem. How much don't I need to know now?"

"I quite understand, Mr. Kimball. Though perhaps you do not," said Gidden.

"No, I understand. Are we done?" Kimball stood.

"I trust you'll permit me to consult with Senator Heidrick before doing anything rash."

"Fine," said Kimball. It actually was not fine. Heidrick had chaired RSA's Senate oversight committee since before his appointment as director and he recalled each conversation being conducted with manners usually associated with the south end of a horse. He never could figure out how Heidrick kept getting re-elected. "Consult all you want."

— ALEXANDRIA

Stone drove the Taurus down the street. It had enough power to move around slow people, like anybody driving the speed limit. Cain wouldn't expect to see him in something like this. The last vehicle they'd ridden in had hillbilly armor and a ma deuce on top that was loaded with .50 caliber AP ammo.

He stopped at a red light. The day before, State Police found the prison van off a side road in Mineral County, complete with four dead bodies and Cain's prints on the steering wheel. He guessed Cain might be visiting family—or at least that's what he called them. Just after Ranger school Cain brought him out there on leave, thinking he might appreciate high quality 180-proof ethanol, known colloquially as 'shine. After meeting the people Cain termed 'family', Stone saw that good teeth seemed in short supply and left after deciding the local DNA pool was far too concentrated.

Stone thought he could still find Jimmy Bob's place—he recalled it was off some dirt road in the general vicinity of Knobly Mountain. He traced a finger over the map on his knees and read the names of small towns in the hills and valleys of West Virginia. He remembered the two-lane roads weaving through those hills, when, on an impulse, he looked up and saw a tall kid with dark, wavy hair walking down the sidewalk carrying a backpack on his shoulder two blocks away.

Somehow the kid stood out from the crowd of teenagers going to class. Something about him—he looked like somebody he met in El Paso.

More like somebody he shot in El Paso.

Stone didn't remember seeing his bullet punch a hole in the tall kid's forehead. He did remember Salazar dropping him on the ground. And the mother screaming.

It felt like his stomach contracted in on itself, the same feeling he had the first mission after El Paso, which was also the first mission he ever walked away from.

Stone turned his attention to the traffic light. He had cash and a car. It would take a couple days for Kimball to figure out he hadn't gone after Cain. They'd just get somebody else. It didn't matter who did it, as long as Cain got tagged before he took out too many more civilians.

The car behind him honked and Stone realized the light had turned green and traffic started moving. He hit the gas and peeled out of the intersection. Driving straight ahead, he'd wind up on Little River Turnpike, a faster way to get to I-66 and eventually to West Virginia and Elias Cain. Taking I-395 South would take him anywhere else.

Milo turned around when he heard tires screech. He saw a beige Taurus peel out of the intersection two blocks away. He adjusted the backpack on his shoulder and kept walking, alone among the crowds of teens going to their first class of the morning.

— MINERAL COUNTY, WV

Four hours after leaving Alexandria, Stone found the dirt road leading up to Jimmy Bob's trailer. He remembered the speed limit sign near the turnoff had more rusty buckshot holes than paint, but he missed it the first time since all the road signs had rusty buckshot holes.

Stone drove part way up the dirt road and parked. He'd walk the rest of the way. No sense advertising his arrival if Cain happened to be there.

He spotted the single-wide and hung back in the trees for a few minutes, watching the trailer and a real nice pickup truck, a tricked out F-150 SuperCrew. The truck's paint and polish, though dusty, contrasted with the mold and dirt on the trailer. Somebody was around and Stone wanted to find out who before moving closer. The mid-afternoon sunshine warmed everything up but it wasn't heat and humidity making him sweat.

Shadows got longer when Stone quietly chambered rounds in his pistols. His windbreaker mostly concealing his guns, he walked slowly around the trailer, making his way through weeds, past the pickup truck, noting empty plastic jugs surrounding the fire pit with burnt bones. Stone smelled charred wood and heard only flies and mosquitoes buzzing in the air. Nothing else moved.

When he heard the doorknob click he knew somebody stood on the porch and he hadn't listened as carefully as he should have.

"Duncan Stone. Well, hell," said Cain.

Stone waited for a moment.

No bullet. Stone turned around, keeping his hands away from anywhere Cain might think he had a pistol.

Cain stood on the porch, two pistols stuffed in his belt. He looked tired and Stone saw no humor, fun or friendship in that face.

"Elias," said Stone. He pasted on a smile, which lasted for less than a second. "How you doing?"

"Good. Great. Terrific. Been a while," said Cain. He put a hand on each pistol. "Still pissed about Nangarhar?"

"Naw, you know. What's a couple bullets between friends," said Stone. Now it was actually almost funny—a little bit—his buddy shooting him in the ass just because he tried to stop Cain from shooting any more civilians with the SAW. At least funnier than anything else at that moment. Cain kept his hands on his guns but cracked a smile.

"Sounds like things went off track a little, last few days," said Stone.

Cain stopped smiling. "That what Kimball says?"

"Things go bad for us all, one time or another." Stone wondered about stepping closer to cover, but decided not to move. "Guess you heard about—you know, guess you heard about me."

"I heard that kid took one in the face. You always were a good shot. No big deal."

"Yeah." Stone forced himself to show no reaction. "No big deal."

The sun dropped behind treetops but the late afternoon heat remained. Cain ignored the speckled sunlight on the wall of the single-wide, instead paying more attention to Stone's concealed pistols.

"Kimball fixed it so everything's good," said Stone.

"He said that?" asked Cain.

"Said I should give you a ride back."

"Where's your wheels?"

"Down the hill a ways."

"You could've just drove all the way up."

"Didn't know if this was still the family farm," said Stone. "We could even go now."

Stone saw Cain smile with nothing happy behind it. Neither man moved.

"Or what should I tell him?" asked Stone.

"I killed a lot of people without knowing why, Duncan. I'm done killing just because somebody else says I got to. Ever think about that?"

Stone knew Cain thought about a lot of things. No dummy, the little schooling he had never interfered with his education. In another world, Cain might have made a living publishing poetry instead of killing people.

It seemed seconds turned to hours and Stone wondered if he brought enough ammo.

"It's what we do, Elias."

Even the bugs stopped flying.

"Real sorry it's you," said Cain. "Nothing personal."

Stone jumped sideways and started firing at the same moment as Cain, his one pistol against Cain's two. They moved in tandem, mirror images in space, Stone through the weeds, Cain across the porch. Anybody nearby would have described a dull roar persisting for a few seconds, instead of individual gunshots. Bullet holes punctured the single-wide's wall, tracing the path Cain took as he ran.

Stone dove behind the graying trunk of a fallen tree just as his slide locked back. He dropped the magazine and inserted another, releasing the slide just as he heard the door on the single-wide slam shut.

Silence.

Stone breathed hard. Heart rate up. Fear? Panic?

Exhilaration.

It felt good to shoot at people again.

The door slammed open, then slammed shut. Stone popped up, pistol aimed at the trailer. He saw fuses burning on the two pipe bombs in front of the dead tree trunk and dropped back down. The explosions didn't sound as loud as he'd expected and only rocked the tree trunk a little. Nails from the bombs spattered the wall of the single-wide and the barkless gray wood he hid behind. The door slammed open again and he heard the report of two 12-gauge gunshots and the patter of double-ought buck slamming into the wood in front of him.

"Hey, I'm going to go kill Gidden," said Cain. He plucked the empty cartridges out of the shotgun, replaced them and snapped it shut. "Want to help?"

It sounded like an invitation to help fix dinner.

"What?" said Stone.

Cain spoke louder. "I said, I'm going to—"

"I heard you, damn it!"

"Mount Olympus. Dead gods. Come on. You in?"

"You crazy son of a bitch, what the hell—"

"Crazy? Yeah, shit, I guess," said Cain. He let loose with the shotgun, then cracked it open. "Sure. Maybe I'll run the asylum."

Stone popped up and fired at where he thought Cain stood. Six rounds smacked into the now-amply-perforated wall of the trailer. Stone dropped back down when he saw Cain level the shotgun at him out of the corner of his eye. More double-ought tacked into the tree trunk.

"I'm man-made, Duncan! Man-made."

Stone rolled out from behind the tree trunk, and got into a low crouch, looking over the sights of the P-226 to find Cain. He heard a truck door slam and turned to see Cain driving the F-150 down the dirt road. He aimed, then ducked when he felt the heat against the back of his neck, immediately followed by three loud explosions. It sounded like one pipe bomb, followed by a couple propane tanks, that exploded. The single-wide lifted off its foundation and burst open in a bright cloud of flame. As pieces of wall and patched roof dropped out of the sky Stone started running down the dirt road, following the dust raised by the F-150. Because of the ruts in the dirt road, Cain wouldn't go much faster than Stone could run, and maybe he'd only trail Cain by a couple hundred meters by the time he reached the main road.

Just another half mile till she'd turn up the long dirt road to her mama's house. She wore a loose faded print dress and fully broke-in leather combat boots. She walked along the side of the road carrying her bag of groceries and wearing the earphones she'd bought at the Walmarts. She'd listened to the same 10 songs the music player had when she bought it—too dang hard to get the thing plugged in to where it could get more songs. But she liked the music and at least she could get batteries pretty easy. Nobody had yet told her that listening with earphones with the volume turned up could hurt her ears.

She didn't hear the engine because she turned up the fiddle part so she kept walking and turned to cross when a big ol' pickup truck sped by, blowing her skirt up and the earphones out of her ears. She heard the heavy-breathing roar of the giant engine fade as it disappeared around a distant corner of the highway, and stood trembling for a minute, hanging on to the grocery bag and thinking what sum'bitch would speed like that on this old two-laner with regular folk walking along it.

She turned to start walking again when the brown Taurus raced past her, its engine sounding nothing like that big pickup, but there goes another sum'bitch speeding on this dang two-laner.

Stone caught up to within a few hundred meters of the F-150. He was surprised at the power of the Taurus—he drew closer, both of them passing slower cars and pickups on the old highway. They careened in and out of both lanes of traffic just in time to miss vehicles coming in the opposite direction. In a clear part of the highway, Stone shrank the distance between them as they both sped up.

He saw Cain drop something out of his window and wave. It smoked and bounced as he sped past it.

The pipe bomb exploded 100 feet in back of Stone. In his rear view mirror he saw the cars behind him hit the brakes and wondered how many would be involved in a pile-up. With the gas pedal fully depressed he pulled up alongside the F-150 and aimed his P-226. One shot and this could be over—except it needed to be his shot. When he saw the muzzle of the largest handgun he'd ever seen, it occurred to him that Cain figured out the same thing.

"Ah, crap."

Stone hit the brakes just before the .500 Magnum muzzle blast scorched his windshield. In the side view mirror he saw a telephone pole bounce and sway, held in place only by the telephone cables tied to its top crossbar. The half-inch wide 440-grain bullet blew the top 50 feet of pole clean off its bottom. He hadn't figured on Cain acquiring pocket artillery—that hand cannon would probably take out light armor at 100 meters. He sped up as Cain rounded a curve a half mile ahead of him.

The pipe bomb exploded 40 meters in front of Stone as he rounded the curve. Even Cain, improvised munitions expert, had a tough time figuring out how much fuse equals time and distance traveled while driving 90 miles per hour. Stone saw fragments speckling the windshield and he hoped the radiator hadn't taken too many hits. Accelerating through the cloud of smoke, he saw Cain's brake lights as he sped past. Stone looked in his rear view mirror and saw Cain pointing the revolver, and then the giant muzzle blast, a few milliseconds after which both rear and front windshields of the Taurus exploded into showers of glass. He hit the brakes and skidded into a half turn when he saw Cain accelerate. Stone hit the gas as Cain passed and rammed the front end of the truck, the grille of the Taurus hitting its front right tire and popping the hood. After his airbag deflated, Stone saw he didn't have a shot at the cab so he fired into the F-150's engine compartment.

Cain revved the engine and peeled out. Stone followed the truck, which wobbled down the highway. Stone guessed the crash had probably damaged the steering. When Cain skidded off onto a gravel road, Stone followed, knowing Cain wouldn't get far, at least in that truck. They'd driven into an old quarry where fine gray dust turned into thick clouds as they raced past scattered heaps of rock. He followed the dust swirls and jolted over the road that wound down to a flat, rutted area. Stone drove through a dust cloud just in time to see Cain smash into a pile of boulders.

Cain kicked the door open and rolled out of the truck, the .500 Magnum revolver in hand. Stone, bumping the Taurus over rocks and potholes, saw Cain aiming at him and twisted the wheel sharply. Cain was too good a shot to miss, even if he was aiming that small howitzer one-handed. For a moment he saw Cain's eye behind the sights, just over the muzzle, tracking him. He figured his time with RSA and everything else in this world was done when Cain shifted his aim and fired. The bullet shattered a boulder in a pile that Stone just passed.

He had no time to wonder why Cain didn't end him and pointed the front end of the Taurus at the F-150. Cain dodged just as the front end of the Taurus smashed into the truck's front quarter panel, sending both vehicles skidding across rocks and gravel. Unfortunately for Stone, his airbag had already gone off and the steering wheel rammed into his chest. Unfortunately for Cain, the impact slammed the F-150's rear end into his back, knocking him to his knees and dislodging the .500 Magnum from his hand.

Stone jumped out of the Taurus, slid over the crumpled hood and charged Cain, who reached for the revolver. When he saw Stone about to collide with him he knelt and twisted, falling backwards and flipping Stone over his head. Stone landed on his feet and reached for the P-226 in his shoulder holster. Just as he aimed, Cain chopped it out of his hands and in the same motion shot an elbow at Stone's jaw. Stone leaned back and grabbed the elbow, trying to twist it under and in back of Cain. It didn't work. No surprise. In the Marine Corps Martial Arts Program he and Cain regularly sparred and the instructors allowed that both of them were almost as good as real Marines.

They faced each other with open hands, motionless for a moment. After feinting low, Stone's uppercut hit Cain square on the chin. Aside from a split lip, Cain seemed unfazed. Stone back round kicked his right heel into Cain's midsection. Cain blocked the front kick and grabbed Stone's leg, then twisted and pulled Stone forward into his knee. He stepped inside and with a punch to the back of Stone's head, dropped him, then secured Stone in a choke hold. Stone put a hand under Cain's forearm to buy a few second's consciousness and bent forward, reaching for the P-250 sub-compact pistol in his ankle holster. Cain lifted Stone by his neck, straining against Stone's efforts.

"Everybody dies sometime," said Cain. "One, a hundred, a thousand people, what's it matter? Who cares?"

Stone struggled for a few moments, then sagged in Cain's grip, forcing the bigger man to slump over. Stone thrust up with his legs and twisted while knifing his hand between Cain's forearm and his neck. Stone spun away, rolled on the ground into a crouch, his P-250 in hand.

The bullet hit Cain off center in his chest. He staggered back against the truck's crumpled front quarter panel and slid down into a sitting position.

A short laugh, followed by a cough, followed by blood. Cain shook his head. "Only you, Duncan. I'd have killed anybody else."

"Sorry, Elias," said Stone. He kept the P-250 pointed at Cain.

"You don't even know what to be sorry about." Cain grunted, then nodded towards the F-150's cab. "It's okay. In there."

Stone watched Cain for a moment before opening the door. Cain appeared more distracted than in pain.

"In the bag. Give them the datacard, keep the iPad," said Cain. "But you look up Centaur...you look..."

Cain looked like he fell asleep, then started to wakefulness.

"Centaur."

Stone looked at Cain. Blood stained his shirt. His face pale, bloody froth covering his lips. Shot through a lung. What did they call that? A sucking chest wound, traumatic pneumothorax for short. Even Cain wouldn't last long.

"What are you talking about?" asked Stone. He turned back to the inside of the truck.

Cain watched him pull the bag out and toss it on the ground.

Stone opened the bag and rummaged through it. Lot of crap in there, most of it designed to explode or otherwise damage people and property. Then he found the iPad with the reader and microSD datacard attached. He looked back at Cain, who seemed to have trouble focusing.

"Centaur. Half man," said Cain. He watched Stone looking at the iPad. "For all the world to see. You should've helped me, you dumb bastard."

Stone found the remote control detonators in the bag when he felt the heel of a boot slam into his shoulder. He dropped the P-250. Knocked onto his side, he looked up in time to see Cain drag himself into the F-150 and start the engine. Stone grabbed for the .500 Magnum as Cain sped away and aimed at the back of the truck, which wobbled violently as it headed towards a cliff. He fired twice, surprised at the recoil. His second shot went high.

He saw the truck swerve, but not in time to avoid going over the cliff. It skidded over the edge in a billowing dust cloud and seconds later Stone heard a thump and a crash. Then an explosion. A surge of smoky flame flared upwards into the dusk.

Stone walked to the edge of the cliff and looked down at the burning truck.

"Damn it, Elias. What happened to you?" said Stone. He stared at the fire, hypnotized by the flame and smoke ballooning through the air. The tide of adrenalin receded and he felt weary, but in a way different from his other missions.

Killing a friend was more complicated than he'd expected. He remembered their training at Benning, and the missions in Iraq and Afghanistan and in other places the American military wasn't supposed to be. They'd pulled each other out of the shit for a lot of years, till Cain decided to put two 9 millimeter bullets in Stone's ass. Interesting personal histories get made when men help each other hunt other men and also when they shoot each other. He wouldn't forget Cain, or anything they'd ever done together.

Stone remembered the first couple of lines from a poem, Requiem, by Robert Louis Stevenson. He looked up and watched the first bright stars pierce a dark sky. He decided the rest of the short poem, which Cain had once read to him, didn't apply.

He looked up into the darkness, then turned and walked away from the cliff. He didn't turn or flinch when a second explosion thumped through the air.

"So much for clean and quiet."

— DIRECTOR'S OFFICE, RSA

Kimball rarely left before dark. RSA's business required all-hours availability and tonight was no different. Before sending Manson on his way he hoped Stone would call with news that he'd killed Cain and recovered the data. It was a long shot that it might happen that night but he could hope. He could also hope it was clean and quiet and nobody noticed anything—that this had never happened in the Agency's history didn't kill his hope that someday, on some mission, it would actually be executed that way.

"Tonight?" asked Manson. He slouched in the chair across the desk from Kimball.

Kimball nodded. "After you arrive at Biggs Field you head for Juarez. At 0700 you and Hargis liaise with Luis Lopez. Captain, *Grupo de Operaciones Tácticas.*"

"I worked with Luis before," said Manson. He and Lopez had worked two missions in Mexico, both targeting Salazar. The *Grupo* and RSA collaborated on high profile gang assignments when it was more explainable and convenient to have both the shooters and bullets made in America. The small Tactical Operations Group of the *Mexican Policía Federal* worked very similarly to RSA. Very clandestine, very unconventional and very operational, i.e. very lethal. Formed from the best officers and non-coms in the *Tercera Brigada de Policía Militar,* they took down gangs that conventional police forces couldn't—or wouldn't.

Everybody knew what the gangs did and who they were. Zetas ran cocaine and did a thriving business in extortion, kidnapping and beheadings. Monterros ran dope. Salazar's gang trafficked high-grade crystal meth and young girls across the US border.

Rarely did gang kingpins get arrested because nobody could prove anything. Massive amounts of cash bought the best lawyers, local police and judges. Cases got tossed out of court, evidence disappeared from police stations, and occasionally witnesses' heads appeared on street corners. After years of investigations, Salazar had still never seen the inside of a courthouse, let alone a jail cell. Local politicians and judges had enjoined the *Policìa Federal* from investigating Salazar in five states, and in Tamaulipas, State Police guarded his villas. Mexico's federal government called in the *Grupo* to solve problems like Salazar, just like the US federal government called RSA to solve problems like terrorists, nuclear materials smugglers, or criminal kingpins who never got served with arrest warrants.

"Breakfast at that same shithole in Obrera," said Manson. "Unless they torched the place for food safety violations."

"You want maybe the Four Seasons Hotel?"

"Sure. Thank you." Even though Kimball was once a bird colonel, Manson actually thought the guy was worth at least his skin.

"You just take a stupid pill?" asked Kimball. He liked Manson. Efficient, reliable, he executed his missions just like any seasoned operator who'd seen thousands of bullets coming and going. One of his best Viper 20 non-coms in the Helmand, Manson survived two lieutenants who didn't have enough sense to do what he told them. One of the best at finding his targets, Kimball brought Manson into RSA after his last tour and in the last two years he had not disappointed. "Your gear's already in El Paso."

"Orders," said Manson. He knew how to mix by-the-book with improvisation when the shit hit the fan, which meant every mission. For him, the by-the-book part always started with orders.

Kimball pushed the envelope across the table.

"If you do it right this time, maybe you won't have to go back," said Kimball.

"If you got good intel maybe we do it right," said Manson. He opened the envelope and took a quick look at the papers with the silvery print. As expected, the orders were the same as the last two missions in Mexico to take out Salazar, neither of which succeeded. He remembered El Paso as the only place where they came close, and then only because Stone ignored his instructions to wait for backup. "Luis'll be thrilled to see me again. Surprised he's showing up after the last couple missions. I'm pretty sure he could chase other gangs that are more shootable."

"Maybe he actually likes you," said Kimball. "He's doing it because he has orders and it's a mission. Which is the same as what you have. Why are you still sitting in my office? Plane's waiting at Quantico."

"They better have food. I don't mean peanuts," said Manson. He stood up.

Kimball's eyes went to the phone's display as it rang. He said, "Stone."

"Stone?" Surprised, Manson waited, his face asking if he could stay. Kimball nodded.

Kimball picked up the phone. "What took you so long?"

"It's done. I found the stuff," said Stone. "And I need a ride."

"What happened to the one we gave you?"

"It got—it doesn't work anymore."

That meant it was not clean and not quiet and there would be headlines. Kimball said, "That was a brand new Ford. Get Clancy to send somebody. You, in my office, tonight."

Kimball transferred the call to Clancy and hung up. He looked at Manson.

"Stone's back?"

"I figured it was time to get the band back together."

"He all in?"

"Just wrapped his mission. Cain. Took him one day."

Manson nodded. Stone took down Cain—and lived. Stone had always impressed him. Good shooter, good mission planner, good soldier. Until El Paso, he'd been a no-fail operator who always executed. "Maybe he wants to join me for tacos. All he can eat in Juarez."

"Thought's crossed my mind."

— ALEXANDRIA

Gunfire, explosions, and revving car engines reverberated in his ears, the rest of the world shut out for the moment. He focused on hunting the enemy with his squad, anonymously located in offices and bedrooms throughout the world. He'd need to upgrade the gaming console and the broadband if he expected to move up in the ranks of elite multiplayer gamers like his IronUprising teammate, SgtMax. Milo thought briefly about starting his homework, but it was only polynomial multiplication. He'd knock that out in a half hour after dinner. He triggered the antitank missile and watched it home in on its target, waiting for the explosion that would allow him and his team to move forward.

— Director's Office, RSA

Kimball watched the TV, phone at his ear, when Stone entered carrying Cain's bag and a grocery sack. The TV showed news footage of floodlit country roads littered with burnt pieces of PVC pipe and scorch marks on asphalt.

"Moonshine and a hill country feud may have caused a gunfight that ended in Johnson's Quarry," said an off-screen reporter. "Sheriff's deputies are now finding more bodies scattered in the hills around Knobly Mountain as fire still burns—"

Phone at his ear, Kimball turned off the sound with the remote control as the news footage shifted to a long shot of flames glowing through a dark tree line.

"Gidden, Kimball. Stone tagged him," said Kimball, into the phone. "Get over here now."

Kimball put down the phone and turned to face Stone. He pointed at the TV, silent for a moment.

"What happened to clean, quiet, no headlines?" asked Kimball. "For all this I could've just called in an air strike."

"Yeah, well you know that shooting and explosions and all the fire and shit, that was all Cain's idea," said Stone. He set the bag and grocery sack on the table.

"Where is it?" asked Kimball.

Stone opened Cain's bag and reached under the Level 4 tactical vest Cain had taken from Clem's truck. He unplugged the microSD datacard from the iPad card reader and put it on the table.

Kimball walked over and picked up the datacard. "He say anything?"

"Yeah, he said a lot of things and most of it was not complimentary," said Stone. "One thing he said, like—weird shit, I don't even know. Dead gods, something about killing Gidden. I think he said Mount Olympus."

"Mount Olympus?" said Kimball. He thought for a moment, shrugged, and stood up. About to walk out, he paused. That rang a bell. He frowned and sat back down.

Kimball leafed through his inbox and pulled out a brochure, titled "Association for Human Genetics Annual Conference." He opened it up and saw Gidden's photo.

"Albert Gidden, MD, PhD, DrMed—this guy have enough degrees or what—will present the keynote speech in the Mt. Olympus Room," said Kimball. He put down the brochure. "That's tomorrow."

Kimball grabbed the phone and punched a speed dial button. He waited, then said, "Kimball eleven bravo silvertower. Emergency code prima niner."

Ten minutes after calling, Kimball gave instructions to the Washington, DC bomb squad to search the entire Williamson Hotel conference center for IEDs, then hung up the phone.

"Nothing like a sense of urgency," said Kimball.

"Really?" asked Stone.

"No," said Kimball. Liaising with local authorities always took lots of time, especially for emergencies like credible bomb threats in the nation's capital. Good enough for government work. He stood up. "In the conference room. Wait for me."

— CONFERENCE ROOM, RSA

Stone dropped Cain's bag on the floor and the grocery sack on the table then sat down. He pulled out a new can of spray cheese and a pouch of real pre-cooked preserved bits of bacon from the sack. Time for dinner.

Stone hesitated while reaching for the bread.

Centaur. For all the world to see. What the hell was Cain talking about? Was he making poetry or just playing a few short of a full deck. Stone reached into Cain's bag, pulled out the iPad and plugged it in.

The display lit up and he tapped on the "Centaur" icon. He saw "DUNCANSTONE" in the user ID box and read the instructions. "Login?"

He stared at the display for a few moments then watched the field labelled "Login Password" as he started tapping on the keyboard with two fingers. 'Stone'. Nothing. 'Cain'. Nothing. 'Elias'. Nothing. He put down the iPad, and reached for the grocery sack. Then he decided dinner could wait and picked up the iPad and resumed tapping. 'Centaur', then 'Rangers', then 'moonshine', then 'Nangarhar'. The display stared back at him, unwilling to reveal any secrets.

— INTEL OFFICE, RSA

Kimball stood in back of Clancy, silently watching the drone's eye view of Cain's truck exploding and burning on one of the displays.

"Must have lit off some IEDs. He always did like blowing shit up," said Kimball. "I confirm Elias Cain retirement."

"I concur," said Clancy, watching the video.

Hearing a knock on the door, Kimball stepped over and opened it. Clancy turned to see Gidden standing in the doorway. He always reminded Clancy of a dead fish. Kimball pulled the microSD datacard out of his pocket and handed it to Clancy.

"Stone got this off Cain," said Kimball.

"Please check the data security," said Gidden.

Clancy plugged the datacard into one of the readers on his desk. Clancy worked his keyboard, interrogating its contents. The indicator light on the reader flickered green as instructions went back and forth between the datacard and Clancy's computer. The datacard contained the GreenSeed database that had been compressed and copied intact, with encryption and no-copy security. Without proper ID codes and voiceprints nobody could open it, and if somebody had, it would set flags that any engineer skilled in encryption algorithms could see.

Any engineer like Clancy. A couple of years after promotion to gunnery sergeant, he'd helped debug the electronic warfare systems on a new version of the Stryker-mounted MEWSS platform. The Defense Intelligence Agency noticed and decided to put his technical aptitude to higher and better uses. DIA put him through various technical schools that culminated in an engineering degree from Virginia Tech. They moved him from a combat battalion to the Adaptive Execution Office of DARPA, where he launched technology barely out of the lab into the Afghanistan battlespace.

"I confirm, it's the GreenSeed database," said Clancy. "Checking access flags now."

A stopwatch icon blinked as they waited for the verdict on the GreenSeed secrets. Windows flashed across the display and Clancy clicked them off almost as soon as they appeared. A log file appeared displaying a computer shorthand of Clancy's interrogation, each line making as much sense to a non-programmer as the US Constitution made to a senator.

Clancy cleared the display, then turned to Kimball. He paused before speaking.

"Yeah, good," said Clancy. "Intact encryption and no-copy code. Cain didn't open it. No way anybody saw it."

"The datacard, please," said Gidden. He extended his hand.

Kimball nodded at Clancy, who dropped the datacard in Gidden's hand.

Kimball and Gidden left the room.

"You're welcome," said Clancy, as the door closed. He turned back to his computer screens. "Choke on it."

— CONFERENCE ROOM, RSA

Kimball opened the door and saw Stone munching on a slice of white bread covered with orange stuff, white stuff and brownish stuff. He noted the can of spray cheese on the table, the open bags of taco spice and real pre-cooked, preserved bits of bacon, and said, "Stone, what are you putting in your mouth?"

"It's good. Piquant and savory," said Stone, pausing between bites. "Want me to fix you up one?"

"Jeezus, no," said Kimball. "Does that contain any actual food?"

"Suit yourself." Stone shook his head and took another bite of this delicious creation that just might get him on a TV food show competition.

"When you're done with that, you can go home," said Kimball. "We confirmed Cain's retirement. Come back Monday with your after-action. That means hard copy, not handwritten, and I need to see at least one complete sentence. Your new ride's downstairs."

The door hadn't quite closed, when Kimball reappeared with not quite a smile on his face. "Hey, Stone. You did good."

Stone stopped in mid-bite, then said, "Thanks."

"Yeah. Congratulations. You lived."

Kimball started walking down the hall with Gidden when his cell phone pinged. He stopped and read the text message.

"Bomb squad cleared the conference center. It's clean. Stone tagged Cain before he got there," said Kimball. He resumed walking, assuming that Gidden would follow him.

— DIRECTOR'S OFFICE, RSA

Neither said a word since entering the office, the late hour doing nothing to ease the tension. Kimball pulled out a cigarette.

"I prefer that you not smoke," said Gidden.

Looking back at Gidden, Kimball popped his lighter open and lit up, then exhaled a large cloud of smoke into the room.

"Stone cleaned up your mess pretty good," said Kimball.

"Yes, quite." Gidden looked at his phone as it buzzed. He read a text message and tapped out a short response before replacing it in his pocket. "When will the mission be completed?"

"I'm pretty sure I don't like the mission." Kimball dragged on his cigarette, seemingly intent on fumigating the office.

"Whether or not you like it has no bearing on whether or not you must do it."

"Okay, Gidden," said Kimball, after a silence. "I'm waiting for you to tell me what I need to know."

"Senator Heidrick will do the talking."

"Fine, when?" Kimball tapped ash in the ashtray, then sat back.

The door swung open and Heidrick, dressed in a tuxedo, stormed in. His aide waited outside. Kimball jumped to his feet and jammed the cigarette into the ashtray, extinguishing it.

"Senator—"

"Sit down and shut up. Gidden says I need to talk to you because you're refusing your orders. You want to tell me how this can possibly be true?" asked Heidrick.

"Sir, I'm not the one who—"

"Answer the question, damn it. I don't have all night." Heidrick leaned over, hands on the desk, and spoke as if to the subject of a Senate hearing. It pissed him off, spending his evening with the directors of the two programs that everybody but he could plausibly deny, in particular since they both seemed to be actively working hard to endanger that plausible deniability.

"Since you ask—" Kimball sat down and took a moment to recover from the surprise of seeing the chairman of his oversight committee a few minutes before midnight. "Sir, we process all kinds of bad guys, no problem. I get it. Here, I've got a mission to finish and I don't like it. Then Gidden says I have another mission, some third generation of his GreenSeeds. What I don't get is why I don't need—"

"You are not paid to get it and you are not paid to like it, you are paid to follow your fucking orders."

"Senator—"

"Get this. There are too many people above your pay grade touching this and none of us likes headlines. Therefore you will not screw this up."

"What he's asking me to do—"

"Shut up! Gidden is not asking you, he is telling you. Am I clear?" Heidrick straightened up and shot his cuffs. "God damn it, you get this done, Kimball, all of it. And keep it off CNN."

It took an hour for Kimball to calm down after Gidden and Heidrick left his office. He never expected anything amounting to mutual respect or good manners, and the senator didn't disappoint him. Heidrick had commanded a rifle platoon in Viet Nam and it remained a mystery why his troops hadn't dropped a grenade in his shorts at least once. Kimball briefly wondered what it would be like to frag Heidrick and smiled for a moment. These were the moments when he missed the relative simplicity of hunting and killing bad guys with guns. You hunt them, find them, and shoot them. No need to screw around with politicians that had more in common with loose cannons than the Afghan Army's first artillery battery.

He opened the file Gidden had given him two days earlier, then adjusted his computer's microphone. Reserved only for the agency director and the intelligence officers, none of the bureaucrats working in finance, IT or administration could access the Retirement System.

"Login Kimball eleven bravo silvertower," said Kimball. He waited a moment for the computer to verify his voiceprint.

The computer pinged, then responded in a female voice, "Kimball voiceprint confirmed, indigo fifteen. RSA retirement system ready."

"Originate retirement files, new portfolio, CHS Gen Three, all subjects, Gidden order lima hotel five. Activate." Kimball preferred speaking to typing, an activity at which he'd never excelled.

"Gidden order lima hotel five located. Heidrick authorization completed. Files three-one, three-two, three-three created in CHS Gen Three Portfolio."

"Confirm status immediate, all files. Authorization silvertower prime zulu, listprint local only, encrypt indigo fifteen lockout, Kimball eyes only." Higher data security didn't exist, and these GreenSeed files weren't anything he was proud to show anybody.

"Confirmed, listprinting now. Hardcopy expires in 72 hours."

Kimball watched the papers with silvery print pile up in the print tray: CHS File 3-3 covering up CHS File 3-2 which covered up CHS File 3-1. He picked up the phone and hit a speed dial button, expecting to leave a voicemail. To his surprise, Jaeger answered with a shouted hello against a loud thumping background of noise, known to some as dance music.

"Where are you?" asked Kimball.

"F Street. What's up?" shouted Jaeger. He sounded slightly intoxicated.

Kimball remembered Stone's comment about Jaeger and monkeys.

"I'm keeping you employed," said Kimball. "New gig, status immediate."

— PIMMIT HILLS, VA

Jaeger sat in the front of the black Suburban, waiting and yawning. Late night, early morning. Working 24-7 was okay, but Kimball could have picked a better time to start this mission. He'd had two hours between leaving the dance club and picking up the rig. After driving the half hour to this piece of Pimmit Hills suburbia, the clock read 6:00AM. Early, but surveillance always precedes action, and the surveillance part was one thing he wouldn't trust coming from anything but his own eyeballs. The Habits section of File 3-2 said this kid always went for his morning latte. The Locations section said he went to the coffee shop five blocks away from where he lived, seven days a week. Latte. At that age Jaeger didn't know what a latte was and wouldn't have cared.

Around 7:00AM he spotted Vernon Espinosa, CHS File 3-2, making his way down the sidewalk, earbuds firmly inserted and thoroughly engrossed with his smartphone. He paid little heed to moving cars, stop signs, stop lights or anything else relating to traffic control. In the space of two blocks, Jaeger saw the pudgy kid almost get hit by two cars, the drivers of which presumed he would stop at red lights. With any luck, some driver following normal rules of the road would do his job for him. Jaeger thought about getting a large cup at the coffee shop but started the engine and pulled away instead. Time to find out about CHS File 3-3.

— ALEXANDRIA

Late morning turned into early afternoon while he watched the dealer ply his trade. He seemed well-known to his customers who spanned the range of teenagers to people old enough to know better, but then stupid rarely respected age and vice versa. He looked back in the folder for Terence Maxson, CHS File 3-3. Occupation: part time high school student and full time crank dealer. Jaeger wondered why the cops hadn't picked him up already, since he was anything but subtle. He'd sit around on a bus stop bench, people would walk up to him, they'd walk into an alley, then they'd walk out. Terence even looked like the part of a big man dealer, and a cocky one at that. He wouldn't take long.

Jaeger put down CHS File 3-3 and picked up CHS File 3-1. He paged over to the Locations section. This one also attended night classes and hung out in Jones Point Park, right on the Potomac.

Jaeger pulled away from curb and headed east on Braddock, wondering who got all the information that populated these retirement files. RSA was a small agency by federal standards but Kimball had lots of other guys working for him, whether they knew it or not. Some of the intel looked like it came from FBI once in a while, Customs and CIA only sometimes, NSA most of the time. Amazing what you could find just by tapping into somebody else's data. How Kimball got it, Jaeger didn't care. He cared even less about the targets—as the enemy, their only purpose in life was to get killed.

He parked south of Old Town Alexandria and walked through Jones Point Park towards the river, under the Woodrow Wilson Bridge. Trees, grass, fields, a couple of docks for fishing rock bass, and the old white lighthouse they'd fixed up but wouldn't let anybody go into. He took two hours to walk through the playing field, the paths, and along the riverbank. He didn't see anybody matching the file's description. He paused by the lighthouse then resumed his leisurely walk. He walked to a bench and sat down, watching just a few people sitting around enjoying the breezes off the river that gave cooling comfort to an otherwise warm and humid late afternoon.

Jaeger spotted a tall kid sitting on the grass, reading a textbook. Caucasian, dark hair. Occupation, high school student. Might be him. He sort of matched the CHS File 3-1 description, but it was hard to tell with him sitting down. Jaeger had patience when it came to surveillance and the kid had to leave at some point. And if not, he'd go to the home address listed in the file's Locations section, but homes were usually hard to manage. Too many other people around and Kimball always said make it a clean job, which meant keeping it quiet and making it look like they had it coming.

Jaeger finally got a good look at his face when the kid stood up and looked around. He matched it to the photo of Milo Jones, CHS File 3-1.

Bingo. Three of three targets confirmed. After reading the Locations section of the file, Jaeger decided on a drive-by hit on the target at night, as he walked from a bus stop.

Jaeger went back to the Suburban. Most of RSA's business was done outside the US and it was nice to have all of these targets local for a change. This would be easy, since he could leave home, execute the mission, and arrive back in time for lunch. Things got lots easier when parachute drops, time zones and diplomatic cover weren't needed. He dialed Kimball and held the phone to his ear.

"What," said Kimball.

"I confirm ID and locations," said Jaeger. "With any luck, this'll all be done inside a week. Pretty easy. But I'm just kind of wondering."

"Wondering what."

"Never had all our retirements local."

"Yeah."

"And maybe they're younger than normal."

"Anything else?"

Jaeger paused for a moment. Somebody else wrote the mission. He just had to make it happen. "No."

"Good. Take the rest of the day off."

"It's dinnertime."

"So have dinner," said Kimball. "Start tomorrow. Use Woltz, Barrett. And Stone."

"Stone. Roger that."

— LABORATORIO DE ESTUDIOS GENÉTICA HUMANOS

Gidden buttoned his jacket after entering the marble-floored atrium. The air inside felt cold after the humidity and heat outside. Compared to London, Paris and Arlington, Tampico at least had the good weather and the warm waters of the Gulf of Mexico.

And now it had the only laboratory anywhere that housed a GreenSeed program.

"Good morning, Dr. Gidden, we've been expecting you," said the receptionist, with barely a hint of an accent. She smiled and waved at the two guards, who allowed Gidden to enter the inner lobby. "How was your flight?"

"Fine, thank you," said Gidden. Whenever Heidrick's office made his travel arrangements he avoided the usual burdens of customs, immigration and dealing with airports. He walked into the lobby with the receptionist, whose concealed sidearm seemed consistent with the guards' assault rifles. Security appeared only a slightly greater concern here than in most Federal buildings in Arlington.

"Dr. Perez will be here in a moment," said the receptionist, who took her seat at the security station.

Gidden nodded and looked around the lobby. Everything still looked as new and clean as it had 15 years earlier. When he stepped out of the limo he saw they'd finished building several additions, two of which looked almost like dormitories or apartment buildings. He found the detail of the tile and stucco construction beautiful, very much in keeping with the tropical climate, though perhaps too ornate for his taste. Dr. Perez had successfully developed an excellent lab, more than overcoming the initial concerns he'd had when Senator Heidrick arranged the first trip to meet with him. Gidden didn't think it possible to set up a world class genetics research lab in a minor city of a third world country, particularly when clean water and electricity were less dependable than officials' requests for bribes. A friend whom Senator Heidrick had known for years had introduced him to Perez. Following several meetings, Heidrick encouraged Gidden—strongly—to speak with him.

Dr. Perez explained his plans and understood Gidden's concerns. They'd read each other's papers over the years and Perez suggested that research conducted at the best institutes in Mexico compared with the likes of Delbrück Centre, Giessen, and Cambridge. Though much of the Mexican population lived in the third world, there existed an elite that functioned very much in the first world, and had made significant contributions to science beyond nachos and margaritas. Gidden finally agreed to establish a subsidiary GreenSeed lab in Tampico. It would be funded entirely by an outside investor and use the GreenSeed technology licensed from Gidden. It would reduce Heidrick's burden of concealing the GreenSeed budgets from federal audits while accelerating their research and clinical implementations. Gidden remembered that at the time, he'd held out little hope it would ever turn into anything resembling a productive lab.

Fifteen years changed many things, including his opinion of the

Laboratorio. Gidden turned around as he heard automatic double doors hum.

"Albert," called Perez. He walked through the doors into the lobby, wearing a spotless white lab coat over his business suit, and flashed a grin. His accent more German than Mexican, he said, "*Bienvenida a Tampico.* I believe it is almost six months, yes?"

"Gunther, it's good to see you," said Gidden.

Perez led Gidden through the double doors into a wide hallway. They passed immaculate glass-walled lab spaces where a dozen bunny-suited scientists peered into the large microscopes of ICellCo robotic workstations. A nucleic acid electroporation transfection system sat next to each workstation. Two long gleaming steel workbenches held orbital microplate mixers and Scilogex 3D gyratory rockers slowly stirring flasks half full of fluid. Stacks of Eppendorf incubators lined the far wall next to MagNA Pure nucleic acid purifiers. Gidden knew the lab had expanded into the new genomics tools but seeing the vast array of equipment, all installed since his last visit, surprised him. No longer a hidden subsidiary of the hidden GreenSeed program at the Center for Human Sciences, it was possible, even likely, that they would accomplish great things far beyond the GreenSeed technology that Gidden had first devised.

"Quite the investment in these last months, isn't it," said Gidden. "Most impressive."

"Yes, we have started working with the new toolkits," said Perez. "I think these open up opportunities we had not thought possible even a year ago. This is all in my report."

"I'll look forward to reading it."

"Your driver will take you to the Brisas hotel later. We have arranged the penthouse suite for you until your house is ready. I hope you will find it pleasant."

"I'm sure it will do."

"Your people arrive next week?" asked Perez. He considered Gidden a respected colleague, but not a friend. There was a distance within the perimeter of which this man did not allow him, or likely anyone. Did he ever blink his eyes? Perez imagined Gidden sitting on the balcony of his penthouse, overlooking the Gulf of Mexico on a sunny afternoon, fully clothed in his business suit and taking the sun as would a desert lizard.

"Yes, on schedule. Things were quite rushed," said Gidden. "As you can imagine, all of us were taken a bit by surprise at the sudden relocation announcement."

"Of course. But everybody will see their lifestyle improve immeasurably here. A dollar—or a peso, goes very far. They will quickly feel right at home. There are almost as many Americans in Tampico as Mexicans." Perez expected the new arrivals would find themselves frequently running into the numerous English-speaking expats in the stores and restaurants.

They would all be able to afford large, modern homes in gated communities with maids and cooks. Gidden would have drivers at his disposal, all of whom doubled as bodyguards. The threat of violence aside, the weather and affordability compared to Arlington eased the burden of relocation. In Tampico it didn't freeze and it didn't snow and he would never have to worry about driving on ice again.

Perez pointed at an empty long workbench at the end of the lab space. "We will put the ICellCo units from Arlington over there. We all look forward to your people joining us. I think we will find our productivity improves by having everybody in a single location. Do you agree?"

"Of course," said Gidden. He recalled his conversations about the relocation to Tampico, in particular, Heidrick specifying that it was not optional. The Laboratorio's facilities were much larger and well maintained—even the lobby would have likely passed an ISO 8 cleanroom inspection.

"My office will see to their welcome," said Perez. They stopped walking for a moment. "Albert, of course, you still retain full authority over the operation."

Gidden nodded and considered how much—or how little—authority, beyond scientific direction, he'd ever had. In Arlington, the Center's Genetics and Fertility Counseling Programs would continue without his oversight as would the Human Genomics Study Institute and the Genome Screening Program. Without doubt, Heidrick had already found an adequate administrator to replace him. Those who fulfilled the requisite checkboxes for gender, preference, race, age, political reliability, and who had some sort of degree from at least some sort of college in anything but science and who wouldn't know DNA from RNA would doubtless be selected. Ability had become optional in hiring—as well as electing—high level government bureaucrats. A pity it hadn't happened before, since Gidden had never found administering what he considered "minor science" programs interesting. Absent GreenSeed—indeed now it had never existed—they didn't need him to oversee the other programs. He wondered how much longer they would exist, since their only purpose was to masque the true target of the federal funds: his GreenSeed program, also known as "something for the little people," courtesy of Senator Walter Heidrick.

They turned down a hallway that looked more like a private bank's entryway than a lab. Perez opened a door into a suite of offices and they walked to the back, past well-dressed men and women sitting in hardwood cubicles. They smiled and waved at Gidden and Perez as they walked past. A woman stood as they approached.

"Good morning, Adelita," said Perez. "You remember Dr. Gidden."

Adelita smiled. "Good morning, Dr. Gidden, it is our pleasure to have you here," she said, her accent all but undetectable.

Perez took Gidden through a large, carved wooden door, into a corner office. Its windows faced onto the new buildings located beyond a manicured courtyard, and its furnishings brought to mind the ornate, slightly overstuffed styles of Gainesborough and Chesterfield.

"We have arranged to make this your permanent office. I hope you find it satisfactory," said Perez.

"Yes, it will do just fine."

"Your staff will have the leisure of gradually integrating. You, my friend, unfortunately are not so lucky. We have much to do. Tonight we have a dinner with the Governor of Tamaulipas. It is a political meeting of course, since he is a very good friend of our investor but at least we will enjoy a very fine meal." Perez closed the door behind them. "It is a kind of ritual gift exchange with the politicians. We give them money and in return we have few regulations and no inspections to contend with. It is different from what you are used to."

"A bit, perhaps," said Gidden. Because he'd hidden GreenSeed in the Center for Human Sciences, Senator Heidrick had shielded them from the massive regulatory burdens that increased employment of consultants advising how best to amass large piles of paper. Even though not technically illegal in the US, human genetic experiments were best kept far from the public's awareness.

"I will leave you to arrange your things. Adelita will assist you," said Perez. "Shall we meet for coffee later?"

"Yes, that will be fine."

Perez left the room, allowing the large wooden door to slowly close of its own weight. Gidden sat at the computer and opened the login screen. He typed "gidden p15C" into the first box, "green$eed#@80" into the second box, and tapped the audio file icon when the third box appeared.

"Login Gidden prime fifteen chelsea," he said.

A moment passed, until the computer responded. "Gidden voiceprint confirmed indigo fifteen. Read-write file access enabled. Welcome back, Dr. Gidden."

It was always good news when technology worked the first time. Working in Tampico thus far had much to recommend it.

Gidden had little to organize until his office materials arrived. He opened a file on the computer and re-read the report he'd received from Perez a day earlier. He'd found what he'd expected. Dr. Perez's team had expanded use of single guide RNA sequences, non-viral plasmid transfection tools, and the Cas9 enzymes and dCas9 repressors.

The theory and science seemed sound. Though the new technologies achieved results similar to the techniques he'd developed, they promised to greatly improve yields and productivity and expand the range of genetic modifications they could make. Of concern was the paucity of experimental work conducted, or at least described, regarding experimental outcomes with these new tools. He appreciated more than anyone else the penalties for insufficient experimentation prior to clinical practice. Gidden picked up the phone and waited a moment for Perez to answer.

"Gunther, I read your proposal about modifying the GreenSeed technique. It's quite good," said Gidden. "Might I suggest a meeting with your investigators?"

— 3RD FLOOR, RSA

Alex saw Clancy limping down the hall and walked over to him, smiling.

"Clancy, I haven't seen you forever," said Alex. She put a kiss on his cheek.

"Hey, Alex. How are you? Hey, how's your boat?" asked Clancy. A rare smile appeared on his face.

"The boat." Alex grinned. "Well, we're still working on it, a lot. But it's nice having something for Milo and me...you know, something we did with Harry. You'll be on the first cruise when she's ready. With a little luck we might sail the River Festival."

"Count me in," said Clancy. They'd worked on that fugitive from a salvage yard forever. He remembered seeing it a couple of months earlier, when he, Alex and Milo had dinner together in Old Town. It looked exactly the same as it had a couple of months before that. "You really think you'll ever take it out on real water?"

"Well, if it's a really calm day and if things are working really well and she's really seaworthy," said Alex. She gave a short laugh. "Maybe."

"A landing craft it's not," said Clancy. He'd never considered rivers real water. He liked the sea. The smell, the salt, the waves. He cracked another smile. "So rivers are good, but technically it's not seaworthy—riverworthy maybe, but that's okay. Really."

"Well, good. Milo might even let you drive."

"Deal," said Clancy. "How's Milo doing?"

A pause. "He's fine."

"Good." Clancy saw Alex look away. "That's good, right?"

"It's still hard for him," said Alex. The years since her husband's death had been at least as hard for Milo as for her. To have a father, and then to lose him. He'd become more isolated, and though they weren't his fault, the fights...she was certain Harry's death was the reason. Almost certain.

"I wish I could say he'll get over it." Clancy knew nobody ever gets over it. Including him. It was his mission, running the gun truck on a recce that tested some new electronic gear, some of which was for detecting IEDs. It didn't work and it cost him his leg, his team, and his commander. "We lost a lot of good Marines over there, but Harry, he was the best."

They both searched for words to fill an awkward silence, but neither could find any. Alex saw Clancy still wore a shroud of guilt from that mission, unchanged from when they'd attended her husband's funeral. She'd stopped saying there wasn't anything Clancy could have done, worried that he might let slip that maybe there was because his team and his commander died and he didn't.

"Haven't seen you around for a while. What brings you over?" asked Clancy.

"Filing a report. I just cleared one of yours for the CHS project."

Clancy thought for a moment. "Duncan Stone. Sure. He just wrapped the mission last night."

"That was fast," said Alex. "Good. I had some doubts."

"Yeah. He had some issues here a while back." After a pause, he said, "Guess you should know. He was at Musa Qala."

Alex hadn't seen anything like that in Stone's file and hid her surprise poorly. "He was a Marine?"

"No, but he should've been. He got his Silver Star pulling our butts out of the shit. He's the one who got Harry on the medevac."

— ALEXANDRIA

Alex walked out of the RSA building and wondered how she happened to evaluate the man who tried to save her husband's life three years earlier. Was there really something like a cosmic interconnectedness? Or a mystic synchronicity of humanity? Her thoughts took her back to her college years, when things like mystic, cosmic and synchronicity seemed as natural as eating. Everything was possible, including that she might save the world, and it only got more hopeful after Dr. Gidden helped her and she delivered Milo as a healthy, normal baby boy. It was before Harry, when she and her son lived in a cramped studio apartment with neighbors helping out when she was at class or working at the restaurant to pay the rent. The intervening years, the day-to-dayness of getting past tragedies big and small, had since drained her belief in cosmic or mystic anything.

"Hey, doc," said Stone.

Surprised, Alex redirected her eyes from the pavement and saw Stone standing in front of her. Cosmic interconnectedness suddenly felt way more possible than 10 seconds earlier.

"Oh," said Alex. "Hello, Mr. Stone."

"Just call me Stone."

"Not Duncan?"

"Yeah, please don't."

She looked at Stone and saw somebody much different than the burnout who sat in front of her a couple days earlier. She noted brown hair neatly cut, face clean shaven, well dressed in unwrinkled clothes that fit instead of a baggy uniform that hid what now looked like a well-kept physique.

"I guess I clean up pretty good when I have to," said Stone, looking at Alex looking at him. He smiled.

"Oh, no, that's not—what I mean is congratulations on your mission," said Alex.

Stone's smile disappeared. "Thanks."

"Did I say something—is something wrong?"

"No. Just the mission—Elias—he was a friend." Stone looked away, failing to understand why he'd just said that to her. "Once."

"I'm sorry. I didn't know."

"It's okay, Elias was a lot of other things too. It's what I do," said Stone. He wondered what to do, then what to say, then just waved. "Nice seeing you."

"Here." Alex pulled a business card out of her purse and wrote a phone number on the back. Stone took it and looked on the front: "ALEXIS JONES, PH.D – GENETICS & FERTILITY COUNSELING, CENTER FOR HUMAN SCIENCES."

"My cell number. Please call me if you want to talk," said Alex. She smiled. "It's what I do."

"Sure. Thanks." Stone turned to go, then stopped. He turned back to Alex. "Hey, doc."

— CRYSTAL CITY, VA

Military in uniform mixed with millennials in business suits, all getting a late afternoon caffeine fix in one of the many coffee shops off Crystal Drive. Conversation buzzed, most of it about things not top secret. Stone looked at those officers dressed in various flavors of camouflage battle dress uniform and wondered where the battle was. It seemed ordinary service dress would do in an area generally free of gunfire.

Stone turned his attention back to his coffee. It was very good coffee, so said the barista. A luxury he hadn't enjoyed for about a year.

Alex smiled as she watched him stir sugar into the brown brew, then taste it…then add a little more sugar…then taste it again, like he was creating the perfect cup. She took her coffee neat, the stronger the better.

Her smile faded a little, as she watched two second lieutenants at the next table attentively listening to a gunnery sergeant expounding at length about his beloved Corps and the meaning of Semper Fi. She remembered Clancy before he lost his leg and she her husband. Both had lighter spirits then, before Musa Qala changed their world.

"Sometimes I think it's all he has," said Alex. "His work. Belief and faith that he's doing the right thing. Clancy once told me that's why he enlisted. It's why he keeps doing what he does."

"Everybody's got to believe in what they do, right?" asked Stone.

"There are very few fortunate enough to do what they believe in," said Alex. She stopped watching the Marines and looked at Stone. "That's why I cleared you."

"What do you mean?"

"You believe in the work you do. You do what you believe is important. There's not many who can say that about their jobs. I think that's why you won't forget your friend—Cain—and you won't let him get in the way of anything. I think you will honor him that way."

"Honor him. I like that. Not sure I know exactly how it works, but I like it," said Stone. He and Cain shared an honor among men who helped each other hunt and kill other men. He remembered every time they went outside the wire that trust was always given and never betrayed. At least not until Cain shot him in the ass. That day was the beginning of the end. Stone filed his discharge papers when they told him only that Cain was being transferred, which meant he wouldn't receive any disciplinary action for purposely shooting a fellow soldier. Stone figured his butt cheek was worth something more than that. Better to remember everything before Nangarhar than anything after. Stone smiled. "I tell you what, Elias was one high-speed motherf—I mean, he was the best operator I ever ran with. We always wondered whether we'd make it back without bleeding too much but we always liked showing up for work."

Alex followed Stone's look to the coffee shop entrance. A man, his hair cut high and tight, took two tries to pull open the glass door with the forearm prosthesis attached to his right elbow. He'd refused to use the power switch or his other hand. On his third try, he opened the door and walked in. Stone followed him to the counter and handed the clerk a five-dollar bill.

"Coffee's on me," said Stone, to the man.

Surprised, the man looked at Stone for a moment, then failing to remember him, said, "Thanks, but I can—"

"That's an order, one jump chump to another," said Stone. He patted the man on the shoulder, then walked back to Alex. He sipped his coffee then mixed in another 1/8th teaspoon of sugar.

"Do you know him?" asked Alex.

"Not exactly." Stone didn't look up from his coffee. "His tattoo. Airborne. Some guys in my squad—just like him. Looks like he's maybe getting some help at Walter Reed."

Alex looked at the man at the counter, ordering coffee, starting to make his way in a world in which his future had changed. She knew the feeling.

"You didn't have to do that," said Alex.

"Actually, yeah, I did."

The man came to their table and paused.

"Excuse me, sir. Thank you. Did we serve together?" he asked.

"I don't think so. And it's not 'sir'. I worked for a living," said Stone.

The man grinned and left after shaking hands.

"You known Clancy for a while?" asked Stone, after stirring a few more grains of sugar into his coffee.

"Yes." said Alex. "He told me you served together in Afghanistan."

Stone nodded. "Can't really talk about it much."

"My husband was Harry Jones. Musa Qala."

It took a second for Stone to remember the Marine captain he pulled out of the gun truck.

"Captain Jones?" What were the odds. "I'm sorry. We tried—"

"I know. Thank you for that," said Alex.

It was a recon maybe 10 klicks outside the town weeks before First Battalion, Second Marines went in. Stone accompanied the patrol while attached to the Afghan National Army commandoes in the trailing Humvee. The Marines were testing new gadgets when the IED detonated. The MaxxPro gun truck's armor prevented its total destruction from the buried mortar rounds but the explosion threw the truck 50 feet off the road and onto its side. Moments after Stone and his driver pulled Clancy, Captain Jones and two other Marines out, flames had fully engulfed it and started cooking off ammo.

"'Thank you' sounds like too little," said Alex. She looked into her empty coffee cup. "I know it was dangerous, what you did. I just don't know what else to say."

"No need to say anything. It's just what we did. Any of them would have done the same for me," said Stone. The burns had long since healed and 'dangerous' in Afghanistan was all relative anyway.

"I don't think they award Silver Stars for nothing." Alex remembered what her husband did to earn his. They often arrived together with a Purple Heart.

"Yeah, well…" Stone looked away. "That's just what happens when you hang out with the wrong people."

They listened to the buzz of conversations and Stone tinkered with his coffee. Alex watched him and finally laughed.

"May I get you another cup to go with that sugar?" asked Alex.

"No, it's just—when it's just right there's nothing like it—" Stone looked at his coffee and laughed.

Alex brought two fresh cups.

"Hey doc. You know—"

"You can call me Alex."

"The other day—you asked about commitment. You were right to ask," said Stone. He opened a fresh sugar packet.

"Because of El Paso?"

"This job, you're either all in or you sign out. After I—after what happened, I stopped showing up. Kimball signed me out."

Stone put down the sugar. "I knew he did the right thing but I was still pissed."

"Are you okay with that?" asked Alex. "You're going back to work with him now."

"He gave me a second chance. I told him I didn't like the mission. It was Elias and I didn't like the idea it was either him or me walking away. I was more than a little worried maybe he'd be the one walking. But I took the mission and I got it done. I earned my way back."

"Is it what you want?"

Stone smiled. "Still the doc."

Alex smiled. "Just a friend."

"What I want? It's all I know." His smile faded. Stone added a little sugar to his coffee and stirred, seeking the right mix of sweet and bitter. "Sure I want it. I knew as soon as the shooting started."

— ALEXANDRIA

Jaeger watched Terence walk out of the alley, stuffing cash into his pocket. A few seconds later a man walked quickly out of the alley and down the street. Right under a streetlight at a bus stop. He still wondered why the cops hadn't picked up this punk. How many people had he killed with the crystal meth he sold? It wouldn't matter after another few minutes.

A bus stopped and picked up the only person waiting, leaving the street empty for the moment. He nodded at Barrett.

They'd worked together on a few missions. Barrett had just finished his tours in Afghanistan when Kimball recruited him. He qualified Expert with rifle and pistol and everybody liked working with him since he was quiet, competent and followed orders.

Barret looked young. Dressed in expensive street fashion-grunge clothes, he looked like somebody from the 'burbs who liked getting high on weekends, and might soon like getting high every day. He walked over to Terence, who turned away from him.

"How good's the ice?" asked Barrett.

Without turning around, Terence said, "Why you askin' me?"

Barrett snapped out crisp hundred-dollar bills and tapped them on Terence's shoulder. Terence glanced at the cash, then turned around.

"Mexican," said Terence, quietly. "The best, real clean."

"Quarter ounce."

"Four hundred."

Barrett nodded. Terence looked around then walked into the alley. Barrett looked at Jaeger, then followed Terence.

"Cash," said Terence.

"Let me see it," said Barrett. He fanned the bills.

Terence brought out a small baggy containing chunks of milky white crystal. He looked up and saw Jaeger standing next to Barrett, then stuffed the baggy back in his pocket.

"Who're you?" demanded Terence.

Jaeger put his gloved hand around Terence's throat and squeezed his carotid arteries. Terence struggled only for a few moments before dropping. Barrett already had his rubber gloves on and a small case open by the time Terence hit the ground. Jaeger rolled up Terence's sleeve and saw the tracks.

"Lot of mileage on these veins," said Jaeger.

Barret filled a syringe from a small bottle while Jaeger tied a rubber tube around the target's arm. It didn't take long for Barrett to find a vein and he just hoped it wouldn't collapse from all the heavy use. He jabbed the needle in and injected 20 milliliters of near-pure methamphetamine. Jaeger released the rubber tube and stood up.

Terence's eyes bulged open. He gasped, choking and convulsing as his eyes rolled back. Barrett and Jaeger stepped back just in time to avoid the vomit and watched Terence shudder, then fall over, the needle still in his vein.

Jaeger took the cash and the ice from Terence's pockets and left him lying in the dark, among the trash and dirt and vomit. Jaeger and Barrett walked out of the alley and headed to the black Suburban parked two blocks away.

"Who says you can't cure stupid," said Jaeger.

— CRYSTAL CITY, VA

Alex and Stone walked slowly on the sidewalk, among a thinning crowd in the pink-tinged light cast by overhead streetlamps.

"It was crazy," said Alex. "I was working, going to school, and here, me, a young single mother. Too young, maybe."

"Maybe," said Stone. He remembered some of the girls in his high school. "Not that unusual."

"I really wanted children. Justin said he wanted kids too and he seemed like the right guy. Then I found out I had..."

"What?"

"Oh," said Alex. She shook her head and stopped chattering for a moment. Some memories of those years were best not shared. At least not yet. "Just that after I got pregnant, you know, he decided being a dad and 18 wasn't for him."

Stone barely remembered age 18, since some of it was spent in Basic Training and the rest in what seemed like a dozen Army schools. What he did remember excluded a desire to have kids. "Go figure."

"Boys." Alex laughed. "It made me grow up real fast. I thought I wanted something, and then I got it and didn't know what to do with it."

"Be careful what you wish for?"

"I wouldn't change anything. Things work out. After I had my baby I set my priorities. My son, my education, my career. There were times when I didn't know if I'd make it, when it just seemed like it was too much. Then luck or fate, something would happen. Something would come into my life to make it okay."

"Luck and hard work. That's what makes success. Some football coach said that," said Stone. "Something like that. Sounds like it paid off for you. You got a family, a good job. Sounds pretty good to me."

"I fuss too much about little things when I should be grateful for what I have. I like my job. Genetics counseling is interesting and lets me put both my degrees to good use. But sometimes I get assigned evaluations for the—for Dr. Gidden's other programs," said Alex.

Stone saw the brief frown when she mentioned the 'other programs'. "Or for guys like me?"

"No, not—well, yes. I didn't want to do your evaluation, but then look how things turn out," said Alex. "The Center isn't where I want to be forever and—oh! Listen to me yak. I've had way too much coffee."

Stone remembered she had four cups to his two. With that kind of coffee he should have wondered why she wasn't bouncing on the sidewalk.

They stopped walking when they reached Alex's car, a Camry.

"Do you like boating?" asked Alex.

"Boating. Yeah, I mean, sure, who doesn't like boating?" Stone hadn't been in a boat since before arriving in South Asia and it was by choice. "Boating, you know, that's good."

"We're—my son and I are fixing up an old cabin cruiser. It's kind of a—it's been through a lot, but the motor usually works."

"Usually works. Good. Does it also usually float?"

Alex laughed. "Yes, it usually floats. Maybe we can go some weekend. I mean after I get it fixed up."

"It got a life raft? You know, in case there's a problem with the floating part and you have to abandon ship."

"I don't think it has problems like that. We'll float just fine."

— PIMMIT HILLS, VA

Vernon Espinosa waddled down the sidewalk towards his morning latte, watching a video on his phone about an interesting experiment. Early morning brought little traffic, and he didn't notice the weather-beaten old Corolla parked at the corner, its engine running.

As he stepped into the crosswalk against the red light, the Corolla's engine revved, then died. The noise of the engine revving passed through his earbuds and Vernon looked up and saw the driver staring at him. He kept walking past the car and didn't stop until he heard the engine rev again. He turned to see the car speed towards him, then jumped onto the sidewalk just as the car raced past, missing him by inches. Twenty meters away the Corolla skidded into a U-turn and stopped, facing him. Vernon pulled out his earbuds and flipped off the driver. It was probably one of the seniors on the lacrosse team. They were all assholes.

Vernon heard the engine rev and it seemed very loud for such a small car. He hesitated for one second. The Corolla's tires screeched as it sped towards him again and he started running. His hesitation made no difference in the result of the collision. The front fender caught him in the back of his knees and flipped him up over the hood and off the right front quarter panel. The impact at 40 miles an hour broke bones in his back and arms and legs, but none of these injuries were fatal. Vernon lay on the pavement and wondered why he didn't hurt. Only when the Corolla's tires rolled over his chest did he experience a crushing sensation that quickly gave way to pain. He struggled to breathe and tried to reach for his phone, only to discover the only thing in his body that still worked, for a brief moment, was his voice screaming.

Jaeger parked the Corolla 10 blocks away. Empty streets didn't mean nobody saw the kid get run over. He put his gloves in his pocket and walked another two blocks to the parked Suburban. He opened the passenger side door and got in.

"Done?" asked Barrett.

"Done," said Jaeger. "One to go."

— DIRECTOR'S OFFICE, RSA

Stone wondered if Kimball lived in his office. A little before 6:00AM and here he sat clean-shaven, fresh suit, ready to go. Maybe he kept clothes in the closet. Probably next to his guns, a Colt .45 ACP doubtless among them. Kimball qualified as pistol Expert early in his Army career with the M1911A1 and re-qualified late in his career with the 9 millimeter M9. Stone had seen Kimball shoot the Beretta quite well, proving old dogs can learn new tricks even if they don't like them.

"I thought I had till Monday," said Stone.

"Who asked you to think," said Kimball. He pulled out a cigarette and looked for his lighter. "You back Jaeger. Tonight. He's got the file."

"Jaeger. I'd rather bite my—"

"This sound like a suggestion?"

"You told me I get Salazar—"

"Not if you don't un-ass yourself out of here and get with Jaeger."

Stone sat formulating his response when better judgement started him walking out.

"Hey, Stone," said Kimball. "Wish you could have had till Monday."

Stone didn't stop walking.

Kimball found his lighter, then threw the unlit cigarette in the ashtray. He didn't need to like his orders, he just needed to execute them.

— ALEXANDRIA

Alex welcomed the coffee Milo had made, not having slept much the night before. She wondered why she'd invited a man she'd just met a couple of days earlier for a ride on a boat that she was still fixing. She also wondered how that man, of all the men in the world, was the man who had tried to save Harry. Maybe that explained the 'why' but only some kind of synchronicity in the world could account for 'how'.

After placing Milo's sandwich in the refrigerator, she turned on the small TV on the kitchen counter and switched to the morning news. Greeted by a mugshot of Terence Maxson, she turned up the sound. The TV switched to a shot of police cars, parked in front of an alley.

"...cause of death apparently an overdose of methamphetamine," said an off-camera reporter. "Unlike the street drug he allegedly sold on the streets of Alexandria, it appears to be medical grade and police are investigating this as a possible homicide. They're asking anybody with information to contact the Alexandria police department..."

Alex turned down the volume when Milo walked in.

"Hi, Mom," said Milo. He went to the refrigerator and pulled out his neatly wrapped sandwich, then turned back to Alex. "Is everything okay?"

"There was just something on the news," said Alex.

Milo walked to the door. "I'll be home late. Class at NOVA."

"Milo, be careful," said Alex.

He gave her a 'what?' look and said, "Yeah, like, whatever. Bye."

Alex turned back to the TV after Milo stepped out the door, then gasped at the photo on the screen, which was then replaced by a head shot of the reporter standing in front of an ambulance. She turned the volume up.

"…in other news, Vernon Espinosa, a young Pimmit Hills teen, was found dead in his suburban neighborhood, apparently a victim of a hit-and-run before this morning's rush hour. Police are looking for any information about—"

Alex punched the TV off and sat down at the kitchen table. Another coincidence? She knew about Terence and Vernon, only because she once had clearance to look at anything in the GreenSeed database. None of the GreenSeed families knew any of the others. Terence and Vernon didn't even know they were GreenSeeds and probably didn't know each other, unless it was incidental, maybe from school. Vernon wouldn't use meth, but as smart as he was, he was absent-minded. She knew his medical history included broken bones from running into doors and falling down stairs while not paying attention to where he was going. And Terence—if somebody didn't kill him first, he was on a fast path to killing himself. Not just using meth but dealing it brought risks along with the high.

Two in less than 24 hours.

They were just kids.

She picked up the phone and punched in a number.

"Clancy, it's Alex."

— MARINE CORPS WAR MEMORIAL

Morning sun had dried the dew off the grass in Arlington. Clancy limped with Alex past the statue. They paused for a moment and Clancy looked up at the flag, barely nudged by a slight breeze. He didn't visit the Memorial often, since memories years old remained fresh.

"It's the GreenSeeds," said Alex.

"What about them? The mission closed two days ago," said Clancy. He paused and thought about security clearances. "You're the client. I guess we can talk about it."

"There's a Gen Three, teenagers. They don't have any of the problems that Gen One and Gen Two did. They're not like Cain or any of the others."

"Okay. So?" asked Clancy.

"Clancy, I'm worried. They found two of them dead this morning."

They stopped walking. Clancy remembered watching the news. "Those kids? One guy was a street dealer, I think some kind of meth. Fast ride to the morgue with that stuff. Don't know about the other one."

"They're saying both might be homicides," said Alex.

"With the dealer, go figure, sure." Clancy thought for a moment. "Two of them inside 24 hours—can't be coincidence. How many of these Gen Three are there?"

"Three," said Alex. She hesitated. Clancy worked for RSA. RSA maybe killed Terence and Vernon. He didn't need to know about Milo. Not yet, if ever. "I don't know what goes on with GreenSeed anymore. They only call me when they need an eval. Clancy, with these missions, do you know if RSA—"

"Hey, this is my unit," said Clancy. He suppressed irritation. To somebody like Alex what they did wasn't pretty but she had to know it was necessary—and killing kids wasn't necessary. "It's not even an option. If somebody took them out—I'm just telling you, it's not us. We don't do kids. No way in hell we ever take a mission like that."

— ALEXANDRIA

Stone read File 3-1 while riding in the back seat of the black Suburban. Jaeger drove and Barrett rode shotgun—appropriately named because a short-barrel pump 12-gauge resided under the passenger seat.

"I don't like it," said Stone. He leafed quickly through the file, looking for the missing parts.

"You don't get paid to like it," said Jaeger.

"Bullshit. Some high school kid. Why's he—"

"He's a mission. We get it done tonight. Kimball says he's bad news," said Jaeger.

"Doesn't sound like bad news to me. Should be local police working it. This got stink all over it," said Stone. "Why—"

Jaeger slammed on the brakes and pulled over to the curb.

"Hey! You in or not?"

Stone took a deep breath and made sure his hands stayed occupied holding the folder. "Where's the photos?"

"In my pocket. You're just backup."

"So now I don't need to know what he looks like? You want me on this gig or what?"

"Kimball wants you on this gig! Get this clear. You work for me. Got it?" Jaeger pulled away from the curb and kept driving.

"How lucky am I."

"Just do what I tell you to do," said Jaeger.

Jaeger stopped next to a parking garage. He turned to face Stone.

"Me and Barrett'll do the heavy lifting on this one. You hold at Jones Point Park and I'll let you know if you can be useful," said Jaeger.

Barrett handed Stone a walkie-talkie.

"Closed commo tonight. Radio check at nineteen hundred, channel 16," said Barrett.

"Get going, Stone," said Jaeger. "Do what I tell you and we're all happy."

"Hey, Jaeger, your anti-asshole medicine stopped working." Stone got out and slammed the door.

— MARINE CORPS WAR MEMORIAL

Clancy hadn't actually checked to see if RSA had any more GreenSeed missions. Very few missions went active that he didn't know about and he hadn't even heard of Gen 3.

"Maybe there's somewhere else you can work," said Clancy. "This whole GreenSeed thing. I don't like Gidden, I don't like that he's in charge of your agency and I don't like the idea of you working there."

"It's complicated," said Alex. She took a step away from Clancy. "Ever since Dr. Gidden helped me—I can't explain, but I can't just—"

"I don't give a damn what he did." Clancy stepped in front of Alex. "I promised Harry—look, I'm just telling you, there's stuff happening there that's messed up."

Alex turned away. CHS always seemed strange to outsiders—sometimes ominous if they personally met Dr. Gidden. As gifted as he was, he unnerved anybody who didn't know what he'd done for medicine, since much of the scientific work the Center had done never made the news.

"It's all I know." She turned back to Clancy. "I'm sorry. I didn't mean to accuse you—RSA of anything with those kids. I know you wouldn't be part of something like that."

— INTEL OFFICE, RSA

"Login Ford niner mike silvertower." Clancy looked at the bank of displays on his desk, focusing on the one that accessed the RSA retirement system, a euphemism for system-that-keeps-track-of-sanctioned-assassinations. He'd set the voice for female, as did most of the system's male users.

"Ford voiceprint confirmed indigo twelve. RSA retirement system ready."

Clancy remembered the keyword. Simple, same as the client agency acronym. CHS. Center for Human Sciences. Director Albert Gidden, who usually looked like he had too much sex with cadavers. Clancy had done his research when the first missions were assigned to RSA and found most CHS programs seemed legitimate, like the counseling division, where Alex worked, or the testing services, or the genetic research programs. But something about the GreenSeed Program just smelled bad. A very secret government research program needing retirements? And it bugged him that now Alex thought it possible that RSA would start killing kids. The other GreenSeeds—those were proven threats and if they didn't take them out more civilians would get killed. That's why RSA existed. Do things quietly that other agencies couldn't or wouldn't, quietly or otherwise. But RSA doesn't do kids and after a quick check he'd reassure Alex with a clean conscience.

"Query. CHS portfolios, detail, retirement files, Gen Three," said Clancy.

"Query rejected. Indigo fifteen required. Lockout set."

"Logoff," said Clancy. Indigo fifteen? Nobody at RSA had indigo fifteen clearance except Kimball and that was only because he was the Director. And nothing was lockout-protected from intel officers. Except, now, these CHS missions, all of which were GreenSeeds.

Clancy hesitated, then, on another display, opened up several windows. One after another, they showed long lines of code. After scrolling through them, he sat staring, not having found what he looked for. He looked at his watch. Two hours already burned looking for a back door to the system that the designers intentionally neglected to include. A candy bar for lunch would have to do.

— DIRECTOR'S OFFICE, RSA

"Activate retirement file, CHS Gen One portfolio—"

Kimball stopped speaking and sat in front of his computer screen, unlit cigarette in hand.

"Waiting," said the RSA retirement system. "Log off in sixty seconds."

Kimball heard a nagging quality in the system's female voice and had lately thought about changing the settings. It was pretty easy to do. Too bad he couldn't have changed the settings on any of his ex-wives.

He stared at the display, doing nothing. He'd never had much use for the Bible, or religion of any kind, but he'd been raised with it and a lot of people he grew up with took it word for word. He remembered something about God testing Abraham, by telling him to kill Isaac. Wasn't that in Genesis? Abraham passed the test and Isaac got off lucky when an angel of God showed up.

After waiting 59 seconds, Kimball said, "Activate CHS File one-one. Status immediate. Authorization silvertower prime zulu, listprint local only, encrypt indigo fifteen lockout, Kimball eyes only."

The printer churned out the paper printed with silver ink custom-made for federal agencies engaged in protecting secrets or killing people. The top sheet in the paper tray showed "CHS FILE 1-1."

Kimball put down the cigarette, concluding that no angels of God would appear in his office that day. Or ever. He ignored the file papers and looked out the window at the late afternoon light painting the buildings across the boulevard, then dialed his phone and waited for Jaeger to pick up.

"Yeah," said Jaeger. His voice sounded tinny over the phone's speaker.

"CHS File one-one is now status immediate," said Kimball.

"And the hits just keep on coming."

— JUAREZ, MEXICO

It didn't take long to load everything back on the truck. Crystal meth didn't take up a lot of space and they hadn't uncrated the rock when the call came in. Guerro stood by the grimy window of the tin-walled warehouse and looked outside for anything that might want to shoot at him. He saw nothing except the sunbaked hardpan parking lot, littered with broken wood pallets and rusty trailers.

"Tinto, go start the truck," said Guerro.

"What about the boxes?" Tinto pointed at the pallets lined up on the warehouse floor. Colorful boxes, each half full of powdered laundry detergent, sat on the pallets. They would have had the meth crystals, already in plastic bags, put into the boxes, then sealed for transport over the border. They'd already paid off the women who would have done the work and told them to leave and be quiet. None needed to be reminded what would happen if anybody spoke to the *federales*. Besides, the money was good, the work was regular, and they'd just gotten paid to leave without doing anything.

"Señor Salazar says to leave them. Nobody outlawed washing clothes," said Guerro.

"Okay, boss," said Tinto. He stuffed two pistols in his waistband and walked outside.

Guerro heard the engine of the truck turn over. They'd move the crates back to the storage unit by the airport, then take the next flight home. The crank peddlers across the border would have to wait a little longer for this rock.

Guerro took a last look out the window and, still seeing nothing unusual, walked out to the truck. He got in the passenger seat and turned up the air conditioning.

"Let's go," said Guerro.

"You get a call or something?" asked Tinto. He drove slowly over the broken parking lot, then sped up as he turned onto Magneto Road.

Guerro turned and stared at Tinto.

"What, I say something wrong?" asked Tinto.

Guerro got the call an hour before. He knew when that phone number appeared on his phone it was Salazar's friend calling in with a warning they were going to get arrested or shot at. Sometimes they had plenty of time to get lost. Sometimes, like that time in El Paso, they had only maybe a couple minutes. Their friend usually just said when, where and who, and then hung up. This time they had two days and it was the *Grupo* and some *Americano federales* coming after them in Juarez. Somehow somebody found out about this rock and this warehouse, even though they always changed where they did the packaging. Usually Salazar was pretty careful about talking on phones, but anybody could get careless and say something and then everybody knows about it, especially with all those *Americano* electronics all over the place.

"Why you asking that kind of question?"

"Hey, nothing, boss. Just asking, you know? Forget it."

"Yeah, forget it," said Guerro. Only he and Salazar ever talked to their friend and that was the way everybody wanted to keep it. It was one of the favors that friends did for friends.

— INTEL OFFICE, RSA

"And the back door is now..." Clancy hit the return key. "Open."

The nerve of system designers, not including a back door. Every system had one, or should. And now the RSA retirement system did. The hardest part wasn't building the back door, it was making sure nobody knew it existed.

Within minutes he sat staring at CHS File 3-1, unsure of what he looked at. He re-read it. Then he waited, doubting he'd read anything correctly, so he re-read it a third time.

Why hadn't Alex told him?

Photos of Milo appeared, one looking like it came from the Department of Motor Vehicles, and the others looking like they came from traffic cams. He read the file contents: CHS File 3-1-status immediate…Milo Jones, age 16…mother Alexis Jones, PhD…father Harrison Jones, CAPT, USMC…

Retirement Authorization by Senator Walter Heidrick.

Clancy scrolled down the file to the mission staffing section: "Jaeger M, Barrett J, Stone D."

Clancy sat back in his chair, disbelieving. He leafed through the other two files, which were each marked "retirement concluded." Jaeger and Barrett killed those two kids. He read File 3-1 again and authenticated the electronic signatures and the authorization by Heidrick. He'd just assumed his government would not order the deaths of teenagers who had done nothing wrong. He'd just assumed he worked for the good guys.

Up until that moment it always seemed like a good assumption. Clancy leaned forward onto the desk and put his face in his hands.

Taking out human traffickers, terrorists, drug runners, rich mad dog mass murderers, anybody who had the money or the brains to beat the system using the system—that's why they created RSA. Killing—murdering—teenagers was not.

Clancy never before wondered about why RSA did what it did. He'd never had to, at least until Kimball agreed to execute the first GreenSeed missions. Clancy hadn't liked those any more than Kimball did but they both understood them. Then Cain. He hadn't liked that but he understood when somebody starts freelancing his own hits, they have to take him out. But now these kids. Milo. How did Kimball think killing kids was a good idea?

How did anybody think it was a good idea?

It then occurred to him that good and bad don't matter to big organizations because they have no capacity to understand the difference. They do whatever they want and he shouldn't be surprised since the federal government was the biggest organization that had ever existed.

He checked the door then punched a number into his cellphone. "Stone D" appeared in the display.

— JONES POINT PARK

Stone heard the ring from his phone and the buzz from the walkie-talkie at the same time. He turned off his phone and turned up the volume on the walkie-talkie. Jaeger's voice came through with a raspy overtone of static.

"Radio check," said Jaeger.

"Copy radio check," said Stone.

"Don't do anything till I tell you. Out."

"Go take a Midol. Out." Stone dialed down the volume on the walkie-talkie and tossed it back on the passenger seat. Jaeger's voice irritated him at least as much as Jaeger did.

Stone put his phone in his pocket without turning it back on.

— VERITAS, TIDELOCK MARINA

Alex had never stepped onto any kind of watercraft before meeting Harry, who grew up sailing all kinds of boats. The thing he liked most of all about the Marines were the amphibious operations and he didn't care if it was an AAV-7 or a Zodiac boat. Shortly after the wedding, they'd purchased the Veritas, a Matthews 38 cabin cruiser that hadn't seen a paintbrush in decades. The Sterling Petrel engine started working—some of the time—after welcoming its first oil change in recent memory, and when they'd patched and coated the hull, they found the boat floated reliably. Only the bridge woodwork, galley, and cabin remained to be finished.

As she sanded the wood panels on the bridge, she remembered when she almost sold Veritas after Harry died. She thought it would see better days in the hands of somebody with more skills, time and money, but Milo had enjoyed working on it with his stepfather and she decided to keep it. Together with Milo, she'd spent parts of most weekends and many evenings making it what she expected would be seaworthy.

Whether sanding, cleaning, varnishing or painting, the corners were the hardest. Bits of decrepit varnish found a way to stick and she welcomed the phone call, an excuse to take a break from working the deck with a folded corner of sandpaper.

She looked at the phone display and answered.

"Hi, Clancy. What's—"

"Alex, take Milo and get out of there."

Alex knew Clancy had little capacity for making jokes, bad or otherwise.

"What's wrong?" asked Alex.

"It's us doing the Gen Three. Milo's next. It's above my clearance—I'll try to explain later," said Clancy. "You get Milo, you get out of town and I mean now. Get all the cash you can, don't use credit cards and keep your cell phones off."

Alex stared out the windows, silent, not knowing what to think, not having anything to say. Had Clancy just said they were hunting Milo? Had he just said they were going to kill him?

"Alex!"

"What—how—Clancy, how do you—"

"Get Milo and get going. Get a new cellphone, stay mobile and call me in twelve hours. Avoid the city if you're driving, or even better, use your boat if you can. I'll figure something out."

Alex put her phone down, fighting a surging panic. She remembered the same feeling when she heard Harry had been wounded, and took deep breaths to try to slow her heart down, to think clearly. Get Milo, get out of town, stay mobile. And stay on the boat and don't drive in the city. And keep the phones off. And get cash. And hurry.

She picked up the folded corner of sandpaper and looked at the dust on the deck. Leaving it like that didn't seem right, not with the humidity. When would that get cleaned up? When would they finish the sanding? She looked at the sandpaper, which trembled, because the hand holding it trembled. She dropped the sandpaper and picked up her phone and punched in Milo's phone number. Her hands stopped shaking enough so that she got it right on the third attempt.

"Pick up, Milo, pick up," said Alex. She listened to the ringing on her phone.

— NORTHERN VIRGINIA COMMUNITY COLLEGE

Milo walked alone down the well-lit sidewalk on Dawes Avenue. Night classes at NOVA just ended and students and teachers started on their way home. He switched his phone on as he walked to the bus stop on King Street. It pinged at him and he looked at the display. Three voicemails from Mom. She probably had the phone in her back pocket and butt-dialed him.

Even though the display didn't signal arrival of any text messages, he looked anyway. None. Not that many people would text him besides Mom and maybe Uncle Clancy. Maybe he could have gotten Josie's phone number if that asshole, Terence, hadn't butted in. Maybe he could talk to her again...sometime. Maybe after the next algebra class. He put the phone back in his pocket and stood at the bus stop, not noticing the black Suburban that had parked down the street. He looked at his watch. About another five minutes for the next bus. He looked up and saw the overcast. Earlier they said there might be thunderstorms and he hoped the bus would arrive before it started raining.

His phone rang. The display said "Mom." He answered, expecting to hear only background noise or the TV.

"Milo!"

"Hi, Mom."

"Where have you been? Why didn't you call me?"

"I told you I had class at NOVA tonight," said Milo. Why was she mad at him? "I'm on my way home."

"No, Milo, come to the boat now."

"Okay." Milo saw the bus slowing as it neared the stop. "But like, why?"

"Milo, please. Just come to the boat."

He stepped back as the bus stopped and put away his phone—he'd take the 15B bus instead, which fortunately would arrive in about two minutes.

Milo wondered why he had to go to the boat. It was too late to do much work, especially on a school night. Maybe they'd go out for a late dinner in Old Town. He liked going to the restaurants on King Street and it was just a few minutes from the marina. There was that burger place and the Lebanese place where Harry always used to take them.

Or the Italian place that was Uncle Clancy's favorite. Maybe they could go there.

As Milo boarded the 15B, the black Suburban turned on its lights and pulled away from the curb.

— ALEXANDRIA

Jaeger followed the bus, which stopped every few blocks even though few people boarded or exited. Barrett, riding shotgun, alternated between looking at the bus, to make sure Milo hadn't exited, and the GPS display that showed a slowly moving dot labelled 'Jones M'.

As the 15B drove past Braddock Road without turning, Jaeger said, "He's not going home."

Barrett grabbed the folder and examined the Locations page, then zoomed out the GPS display and overlaid the bus routes onto the map.

Barrett traced the 15B's route and looked back at the file. "They got a boat. Tidelock Marina. That's got to be where he's going."

Jaeger picked up the walkie-talkie. "Stone, no-go your location."

— INTEL OFFICE, RSA

Bits and pieces of fragmented text files scattered across two of Clancy's displays, hacked from the data he'd downloaded from the microSD datacard that Stone recovered from Cain. He saved it onto his servers after Kimball gave him the datacard only because it felt like pissing on Gidden's shoes without him knowing. Now he figured maybe it was just intuition at work.

Another display showed a drone's-eye view of a black Suburban driving down King Street; it found the vehicle when Clancy coordinated the GPS signals from Jaeger's phone with the street map and assigned an NSA tasker to do a flyover. The map next to the video window showed scattered dots labelled 'Jaeger M,' 'Barrett J,' 'Jones M,' and 'Jones A.'

Clancy opened the drawer and pulled out the Beretta and his car keys. He stood, unsteadily, and tightened his prosthesis, then stuffed the Beretta in his belt. A computer alarm pinged and he turned to the display that flashed the notification and clicked on it, then read the message that appeared.

"CHS File one-one," mumbled Clancy. He opened the file and stared at the display. After re-reading the document, he shook his head and stared at the door. "Shit, what's next?"

One surprise after another and none of them good.

He looked back at the displays then limped out the door, dialing 9-1-1 on his cell phone.

The operator answered immediately—must be a slow night in the 'hood.

"Nine-one-one. What is the location of your emergency?"

"Hey, there's this black SUV going south on King, right around Rosemont," said Clancy.

— KING STREET, ALEXANDRIA

Intent on following the bus, Jaeger didn't notice the police cruiser's U-turn two blocks behind him, therefore he didn't know that the two officers observed him slowing behind the bus each time it slowed and sped up from a bus stop. There were still people walking in Old Town and the stop signs, stop lights and bus stops slowed their progress. At the end of the line, near the Torpedo Factory Art Center, all the passengers stepped off the bus.

As Jaeger pulled over into a loading zone, Barrett compared Milo's photo to the tall kid in a windbreaker with a backpack slung over his shoulder.

"Target confirmed," said Barrett. He looked down at the GPS and saw the dots labelled 'Jones M' and 'Jones A'. No 'Stone D'.

"Hey, it's not seeing Stone. Isn't he supposed to be—"

"Ping him," said Jaeger. He'd told Stone to get to the Tidelock Marina 10 minutes earlier. "He better be here."

The police cruiser parked behind Jaeger and turned on its flashing blue and red lights.

Jaeger looked in his mirrors at the cruiser.

"Shit. Call it in to Stone. He's up," said Jaeger.

"He can't ID the—"

The officers emerged from the cruiser, hands on their pistols.

"Call it in, damn it."

Barrett picked up the walkie-talkie. "Stone, what's your location?"

No answer. Jaeger and Barrett looked at each other for a moment, then checked the side view mirrors. Two cops. Did the city need ticket money that bad? They'd only parked in a loading zone and it was late at night.

The walkie-talkie crackled for a moment, then, "Stone. I copy. I'm at the south end of the Tidelock parking lot."

"You're up," said Barrett. He spoke quickly. "Target approaching, main entrance. Male Caucasian, five foot ten, slim build, wearing a windbreaker and carrying a backpack. He's going to one of the boats. Take him out after he boards."

"Roger that," said Stone.

Barrett turned the volume down and dropped the walkie-talkie on the floor.

Jaeger opened his door as he saw the cop walking up.

"Sir, stay in your vehicle," said Officer Davis.

"Okay, fine with me," said Jaeger. He closed the door. "What's the problem?"

"Sir, we have a nine-one-one call about somebody in a vehicle like this brandishing a firearm. Any weapons in there?" asked Davis. He peered in through the window, shining his flashlight in the front seat.

"Obviously there's been a mistake," said Jaeger.

Officer Hansen walked to the passenger side and shined his flashlight on Barrett, then in the back. He spotted a long black case on the back seat. "Please roll down the rear window, sir."

As Barrett turned, his jacket opened.

"Gun!" said Hansen. He'd just spotted Barrett's shoulder holster with the full-frame SIG P-226 pistol.

Both officers stepped back and drew their sidearms.

"Out of the car now. Slowly," said Davis. "Hands."

— TIDELOCK MARINA

It hadn't taken long for Stone to drive to the marina. He'd parked in the far corner of the half-empty parking lot and just waited till Jaeger called him, recalling Clancy's words two days earlier. He understood the assignment for Cain. Nobody but him could have gotten it done. But this assignment was messed up. Why take out a kid? Most likely it was a job for local police. Or the truant officer.

Or maybe the kid really was a badass problem requiring forcible removal from this world. He remembered suicide bombers in Kabul coming in all sizes, shapes, and ages.

Stone saw movement at the main entrance to the parking lot. Through the ATN monocular night-vision scope he evaluated the tall male Caucasian walking quickly past parked cars. Backpack, windbreaker, slim build, nobody else around. He couldn't see a face but everything else matched Barrett's description. And he didn't know what the target looked like anyway.

The target walked onto the dock, then onto the deck of an old beat-up boat. Stone put down the monocular and pulled out his P-226. He'd cleaned his weapons hours after last using them and now he smelled the familiar, comfortable aromas of solvent and gun oil. He chambered a round in the pistol and screwed on the silencer. He reached for the door when headlights illuminated the interior of the car, as a minivan drove into the parking lot. Stone took his hand off the door handle and raised his cell phone to his ear, pretending to listen.

The minivan drove to the entrance of the dock and stopped. A middle-aged couple got out and proceeded to carry boxes and bags to a large cabin cruiser. Different people, different location, and he might have thought they were running cocaine. These two were just stocking their boat for some party cruise. He hoped they'd be lucky enough to get gone by the time he had to start shooting.

— VERITAS, TIDELOCK MARINA

Cans and jars sat on the small galley table, next to the crumpled front page of the newspaper from two days earlier. She'd rushed to pack a few things from her apartment and she'd used the paper to pad the box of plates. She stood staring at the half-filled cabinet, a jar of mustard in hand, wondering how she would explain to her son why they needed to escape from their life in order save his life.

Where would she begin? With Justin? She wasn't much older than Milo when she and Justin shacked up and that wasn't something she wanted to share with Milo, at least not yet.

But hadn't that started everything? After she'd run away from home, she found Justin and with the flush of teenage hormones, decided they'd have a baby. It would make the perfect family that she'd never had and things looked hopeful and happy. They got jobs, made enough to keep them going and the future seemed ready to fall into place. Until the miscarriage. After losing the baby, Alex wanted nothing more than a baby and she asked the doctor about tests, to see what she needed to help with another pregnancy. Because she and Justin didn't have much money, she got referred to a government clinic, which they assumed was like any other clinic.

Alex remembered her first meeting with Dr. Gidden, surprisingly comfortable with his sterile, detached demeanor. She remembered him almost like a really smart uncle whose personality was not to have a personality—it took years of working with him for her to develop misgivings about him. At the time—she was 17—she didn't know anything about the tests they performed, mostly because nobody spoke to her about them. Then they presented the unfortunate findings that said any baby she would have would likely not live long after birth. She was one of the few unlucky women who had bad genes, something called mitochondrial DNA disorders. But they could help her. They were experts in fixing bad genes and her enrollment into Dr. Gidden's program seemed like a gift sent from heaven—he promised he would help her have a healthy, normal baby and they would even pay for everything. She would have jumped at the offer even if they had explained everything that would be done to her and asked for informed consent. After Justin and she went through the arduous in vitro fertilization procedure, he suddenly decided he just didn't want to be a dad at age 18, partly convinced by his parents who lured him back home by giving him a new car.

Pregnant, almost age 18, she found herself alone, and the only people who helped her were at the clinic where Dr. Gidden worked.

She gave birth to her baby, alone. And raised him, alone. And she met Harry who helped her raise him and then Harry was killed. And now she and Milo were alone and the people she worked for were trying to kill Milo. How would she explain it all? What would Milo think about it?

What would he think about her?

Footsteps on the deck jolted her out of her memories and back into the galley.

"Mom, it's me," said Milo. He walked in and slung his backpack onto the bench.

Alex put the jar of mustard down and gave him a tight hug. Milo didn't know why. He looked at the jars and cans and jugs of water stacked in the small space and asked, "What's all this?"

Alex sought a sequence of words she hoped would both explain things and make everything okay. She found nothing.

"Mom? Like, what's going on?"

"Sit down. Please," said Alex.

"What's wrong?" Milo sat on the bench.

"Let me have your phone."

"I'm not over on data or anything."

Alex turned their phones off and left them both on the table. She leaned on the table and stared at the crumpled newspaper and her hands smoothed it out. Maybe it could reveal what she would tell her son. She only saw the photo of Cain and the headline staring back at her.

"Something happened...where do I start?" Alex sat down. "Something happened a long time ago. Before you were born."

— ALEXANDRIA

Clancy parked his van and watched the police speaking to Jaeger and Barrett, both handcuffed. Three police cars with flashing blue and red lights attracted a small crowd of people walking out of restaurants and bars. Slow night, no football, or people just wanted to see some guys get busted. He wondered how long it would take the cops to get the order to release their detainees.

Clancy allowed himself a smile. Jaeger shouldn't get so pissed. He might find himself locked up just for being a prick. Though getting handcuffed for no good reason looked like a good reason to get grumpy. Barrett seemed to handle it a little better and just leaned against the Suburban. Clancy looked for Stone. Maybe still in the rig?

— TIDELOCK MARINA

Stone watched the couple cart box after box from their minivan into their cabin cruiser. Still no sign of any other movement or people. From his car seat he'd see the target walking off that boat unless the kid decided to swim away in the middle of the night.

No indication the target would do that.

And no indication the target wouldn't. What if the target figured out he was a target?

— VERITAS

"Even before you were born I loved you. And nothing—nothing will ever change that. But I have to tell you some things. It might be hard for you to understand," said Alex. It was certainly hard for her. "We need to leave here, now. We have to go."

"Leave where?"

"We're going away. From Virginia, from everything. Just for a while."

"Like…what? Why?"

"When—before I was pregnant with you, I had genetic problems that could make my children die very young."

"Oh. You mean, like birth defects," said Milo. What did that have to do with moving away? He didn't have birth defects.

"Yes. And you don't have any because Dr. Gidden helped me—helped us. He developed a new technique, like a treatment, to help people like me who had these problems. Not exactly experimental—"

"Experimental. You mean like—" Suddenly aware that his mother was telling him something she didn't want to tell him, Milo asked, "What do you mean?"

"He said he could make you normal, Milo. And healthy. They did some things so that I could have a healthy baby. They tried some genetic modifications, replaced some DNA—"

"Genetic modifications," said Milo. He studied those in A.P. Biology. He knew what those were. He read about them on the internet. Was that even legal? "So it was experiments. On you. And me."

"No—no! Not really experiments. I don't know how it works, but you were just as natural as any other baby. And you're just as natural and normal as anybody now."

Milo stared straight ahead and remained silent. Alex saw him thinking about what he just heard, trying to figure out if it was good, bad, or something not worth thinking about.

"I'm sorry. I should have told you sooner. I guess I thought maybe it didn't matter. GreenSeed—it's what they call it. It was— it is just another medical technique," said Alex. "It was really nothing new. It's just like getting any other kind of treatment."

Milo seemed not to listen and Alex didn't blame him.

"So—I mean that's weird," said Milo. "I'm a—what does it make me?"

"It doesn't make you anything. You're a normal teenager and you're healthy. That's all."

"So, why are you telling me this now?"

"We're not the only ones who had this treatment. There are others like us," said Alex. "Kind of like us."

Milo waited to hear more about the others like him—kind of like him. When Alex said nothing more, he asked, "Mom, who are they?"

"They're really not like you. There were experimental cases before—long before me—us." Alex picked up a jar then put it down, and willed her hands not to touch each other, not to pick at her fingernails, not to fiddle and fold the wrinkled newspaper or anything else in front of her. "But they had some problems. With some of these other children, and they're all different from you— some of them—many of them, when they grew up—"

Alex's will failed and her hands yielded to their impulses. They picked up the newspaper and started folding it and unfolding it.

"Mom, what did they do?" asked Milo.

"They started killing people."

"Who were they?" asked Milo, after a silence. He spoke quietly. "Who did they kill?"

"It doesn't matter—"

"Why?"

Alex saw Milo start looking around the cabin hoping for answers to questions, only some of which he'd formulated. Not finding any, he would get confused, then he would get anxious, then he would get angry. She unfolded the newspaper and put it on the table.

"They're not important and—"

"Am I going to kill somebody?"

Alex froze, then said, "No—of course not! They were just— something went wrong with them. Mistakes were made and their treatment didn't work well. They were a little—they weren't right. They started killing just to…"

Alex's eyes looked down and she saw the wrinkled front page of the newspaper. She saw the headline and the photo of Elias Cain. She quickly looked away as Milo's eyes came to rest on the photo and he read the headline about the guy who killed that shopping mall murderer in the jail.

Milo remembered that shopping mall from over a year earlier. He thought it was weird that this guy just decided to run over a lot of people one day. Just to kill them. He remembered that news because they said he had all kinds of video games, some of them just like the ones Milo played.

"Like that guy who hit those people with his car," said Milo.

Alex didn't answer.

Milo's eyes opened a little wider. His mother's silence confirmed what they had done to him was worth thinking about, and it was not good and it was probably bad. "I'm just like—"

"No!" said Alex. "They told me you're not like that. I know you're not like that. You don't have these problems. Please listen to me."

"Then I don't get it. Why do we have to go away?" asked Milo. It was so confusing. He looked away from Alex.

"We just have to. The people who—some people think you

might be dangerous. They just need some time to understand that you're just a normal boy."

She watched his expression turn from confused to anxious, and then to angry.

"Milo, listen to me!" said Alex. "We just have to go away till they understand."

"I'm just a bad experiment. That's why nobody likes me. All the fights. I'm—"

"Don't!" Alex leaned over and held his face in both her hands. "It'll be okay, I promise it'll be okay. You are my son, you are not an experiment and stop saying that."

"Why?" Milo stared at Alex as if at a complete stranger, then knocked her hands away. He jumped to his feet. He stopped moving for a moment. He didn't like getting confused and angry and this usually just made him angrier. "What am I?"

Alex stood and put her arms around her son. She'd witnessed his rage only a few times before and hoped it would quickly pass, as it usually did.

Milo pushed Alex away and turned around. Alex fell against the wall, surprised. Milo stood, breathing hard.

"What am I? When does it start?" asked Milo. "When do I start killing everybody?"

"Milo—"

"When does it start?" Milo shoved cans and jars off the table and slammed it with his fist. "Look at me! What am I?"

Alex stood in front of Milo and spoke softly. "Stop it now, Milo. You are my son."

The rage drained. Alex waited to take a deep breath.

Milo picked up the cans and jars from the floor and started neatly stacking them on the table.

"We have to go, Milo."

Milo kept stacking the cans and jars on the table, slowly, one by one.

"Just tell me why," said Milo. He put the last can in place.

"Because," said Alex. She took her deep breath. "Otherwise they'll kill you."

— TIDELOCK MARINA

Stone got out of the car, quietly pressing the door shut, and walked quickly across the parking lot as soon as the minivan drove off. He paused and sidled up to the parking lot fence when he saw the target emerge from the boat and walk along the dock, stopping at one of the benches next to a wooden boat locker. The target stood for a moment, then sat down. Good news—he hadn't yet figured out he was a target. This would go quickly—two in the back of the head, pick up the shells, walk away.

Stone quietly stepped from the fence to within six feet of the bench and raised the pistol. Any closer, he might get chunks of bone and brain on him and at this range pointing was almost as good as aiming. He'd be two for two since Kimball brought him back and he'd soon get his ticket for Salazar. He started squeezing the trigger when the target turned around.

Reflex moved his arm up and his finger off the trigger. All that training about don't aim at anything you don't wish to destroy. The last time he'd seen that face was in El Paso, with a .40 caliber hole in its forehead.

What was that face doing on his target?

He heard somebody else jump on the dock, then shout. He glanced away from the target and saw Alexis Jones, PhD standing, then breaking into a run. She looked scared. Stone's brain went into overdrive for a moment. What was she doing here? Why did she run towards his target?

"Stone!" said Alex. "Stop!"

Alex ran to Milo and shoved him behind her.

"Alex, get away—"

"He's my son! Please."

Stone hadn't thought of anything to say except 'get away from my target who's about to get dead.' He immediately decided that wouldn't sound good under the circumstances.

"Mom, what's—"

"Milo, stay behind me," said Alex. She started backing them away from Stone, back towards the Veritas. "Stone, you can't hurt him. They made a mistake. It's a big mistake. He's not like Cain."

Not like Cain.

What?

Stone stared at Alex and the boy she kept behind her. He recognized the target. It's the tall kid with the dark hair in El Paso. Except he didn't have the bullet hole in his face. And he's standing behind Alex. And he's her son. And they're going on her boat—with the engine that usually works. This all was perfectly reasonable except for the part about the kid being minus the bullet hole in his face and, of course, being Alex's son.

Good and wonderful. What's next? Stone found out when he heard an engine and tires rolling on asphalt behind him and quickly turned, lowering the pistol to his side. He watched the van pull up.

Clancy leaned out the window and said, "Hey, Stone!"

"What—Gunny?" said Stone.

"Clancy!" said Alex.

"Mom?" said Milo. "Hey, Mom. What's going on?"

Stone looked at Milo, Alex and Clancy. He tried to remember if, at some point, in the preceding 10 minutes, he'd stepped off the earth and into a different world where all of this might make sense.

"Just slow down a minute," said Clancy. "Let's slow this down."

"What the f—"

"It's okay. Mission's closed," said Clancy. "Give me the pistol."

Stone hesitated. He'd never finished a mission without finishing the mission. For sure he'd never heard of 'closing' a mission.

"Stone," said Clancy. "Gun."

Stone handed over the pistol. He looked at Alex and Milo.

"The other two," said Clancy.

Stone pulled out the other two pistols and put them in Clancy's hands.

"We never kill missions like this, Gunny."

"We never had missions like this. Come on, get in," said Clancy. He waved Alex over as Stone walked around to the passenger door. "Alex, can your boat move?"

"Clancy," said Alex. She brushed her hair back with shaking hands. Wasn't she supposed to call Clancy? But not for 12 hours. "I don't know what we—"

"It's okay. It's okay. Listen up," said Clancy. She didn't look like she was listening. "Alex! You have to listen up. Now, tell me, can your boat move? Does the engine work?"

"The engine. Yes," said Alex. "Yeah, it usually works. We have to go. We're going to go on the boat. I think we have gas in the tank. Or we can get some."

Clancy saw she was on the verge of losing it. Who wouldn't. Thirty seconds ago she was a half second away from seeing her son's brains on the dock. He waved Milo over.

"Hey, Milo. This is pretty scary shit, huh?" said Clancy.

"Like, yeah," said Milo.

"I know," said Clancy. Milo didn't look like he was scared. Maybe he just didn't get how close he was to being killed. Or maybe he did and he just locked up. He'd seen kids not much older than Milo do that when they took hostile fire for the first time. Milo needed specific instructions on what to do, to get him off thinking about getting killed.

"You and your Mom, you get on the boat and get going. Get that engine going, get the boat going. Get out of here. Do you understand? Can you do that?"

"Yeah."

"Okay, tell your Mom to call me in 12 hours on a pay phone or something. You keep your cell phones off. Keep out of sight. Got it?" asked Clancy.

"We'll be okay, Clancy," said Alex. She shivered in the evening's warmth and her voice sounded tentative and she put her arm around her son's shoulders. "Milo and I will take Veritas and we'll leave. We'll be okay. I'll call you in 12 hours."

Stone watched Clancy talking with Alex and Milo like he was an uncle or a brother. How did that make sense? He saw Clancy's face as Alex and Milo walked towards their boat and then it made all the sense in the world. Clancy had served with Alex's husband. The captain that Stone pulled out of that gun truck in Musa Qala.

Small world, but it was still a world where missions mattered. Why had Clancy just made a target an ex-target?

Clancy watched Milo and Alex walk down the dock. Alex's words, meant to be reassuring, weren't. He wanted to go with them, but he needed to get this fixed permanently and not get them killed in a gunfight he couldn't win.

— ALEXANDRIA

Clancy drove west on Duke Street, he and Stone staying silent during the few minutes it took to get to Business Center Drive. Clancy slowed down as they rolled through the deserted warehouse area, trailers lined up in the parking areas like tanks waiting for Desert Storm. He didn't know how the night would end, but witnesses were unnecessary if not dangerous, regardless of the outcome.

"So he's Alex's son," said Stone.

Clancy pulled over and stopped. A long train rumbled past on the tracks, its horn silent. Small raindrops started spattering the windshield.

"Does it matter?" asked Clancy.

"That the only reason the mission's dead?"

Clancy stayed silent. Stone noticed the Beretta in Clancy's left hand, its hammer cocked but not aimed at anything. Yet.

"Who killed the mission?" asked Stone.

The rumble of the train evaporated into the night, leaving silence in its wake.

"This is us, Gunny. This is what we do," said Stone. "Figured you'd know that better than any of us."

"Jaeger and Barret took out two kids yesterday. They didn't do anything except get born. Neither did Milo," said Clancy.

Silence hung heavy in the van.

"Go after him, you go through me," said Clancy. "I've known Alex and Milo a lot longer than you."

Stone saw Clancy holding the pistol, now pointed in his general direction. Stone nodded. "Okay."

After a moment, Stone grabbed Clancy's throat in a backhand choke hold and snatched the pistol away in one quick motion. He released Clancy's throat and racked the slide, ejecting a round. The pistol was ready to shoot.

"I screwed up once, I'm not doing it again," said Stone. He pulled the key out of the ignition.

"You're not going after him."

"Don't make me shoot a cripple," said Stone. That boat probably hadn't left the dock. He could still finish the mission.

Clancy waited barely a second before punching Stone in the

mouth. "That why you came back? Kids and cripples?"

Stone backhanded Clancy in the face.

"This is a mission—"

"He's a kid!" said Clancy. "He hasn't done a God damn thing and they want to kill him. This is not what we do."

"Get out."

"No." Clancy had no time to tell all the secrets and Stone wouldn't believe him anyway. "After him, who else?"

"You think you can stop me?"

They challenged each other with their eyes, until Clancy looked down. Ten years earlier, before age and injury slowed him, he would have taken Stone. He wrapped his hands tightly around the steering wheel.

"Maybe not," said Clancy. "You want back on the team so God damn bad, start here."

"Don't push me," said Stone.

"You think I'm scared of you? You want to go out and kill kids, start with me."

"You think I won't end you?" Stone put the muzzle of the Beretta inches from Clancy's head.

"Okay. Then Alex gets a bullet. Then Milo. That sound like a good mission to you?" said Clancy, quietly. He turned his head to face Stone, his hands in a death grip on the steering wheel. Dead or alive, he would at least buy Alex and Milo a few minutes. "That's what you do? Go ahead. Be brave. Be a hero. Finish your mission."

Stone watched Clancy sit calmly with a 9 millimeter bullet 12 inches from his face. He watched the gunnery sergeant he'd pulled out of the burning gun truck years earlier, as calm now as he had been then. Stone remembered Clancy ordering him to clear out his team and his captain first. He didn't do it because he figured he'd bleed out anyway and it wasn't because he wanted to die. It was because he was a Marine and Semper Fi meant something. It meant everything. Stone looked at the prosthesis Clancy wore as a replacement for his leg and knew part of Clancy died in that gun truck alongside his Marines and his captain. The part that lived now sat next to Stone, risking everything and getting ready for the last bullet because that was the only thing he could do for the last people in his life.

Clancy didn't move and just stared out the window at the darkness. Larger raindrops started falling, beating a steady cadence on the roof and on the windshield.

— VERITAS

Her fear subsided as the engine finally coughed smoke and kept sputtering instead of dying. She flicked on the running lights and waved at Milo, who cast off the lines and unplugged the power cable.

They slowly backed out of the slip. She remembered the last time they'd taken Veritas out. The engine had barely worked and it took them a half hour to get it running well enough to get to the dockside gas pump. She'd packed the picnic lunch for the three of them: Harry, Milo and her. Manchego cheese, Serrano ham, fresh rye and the pasta salad made with aged balsamic vinegar as thick as maple syrup. Harry's request, for a last family time together just days before his second deployment. She remembered cruising on that summer afternoon, the breeze slowly blowing off the Potomac, the three of them pretending not to remember where Harry would soon go.

She hadn't made a picnic since.

Alex shifted gears and slowly motored forward, through the channel, past the other boats tied up to their moorings, most of their windows dark.

She watched Milo neatly coil the lines and stow them. He joined her in the cabin, and they stood silently together, watching the darkness outside. She moved the throttle forward a little, hearing the engine's dull rumble increase. It seemed to run smoother after warming up.

"Where are we going?" asked Milo.

The engine died without warning, simply stopping and leaving only silence as Veritas slowed in the water.

— KING STREET

Officer Davis got off the radio and looked at Officer Hansen, shaking his head. Four concealed handguns, a full auto 5.56 millimeter rifle with silencer and night-vision scope, and a sawed-off shotgun. No permits, no licenses, no BATF, no nothing. Up till five seconds ago, he figured this was a textbook-clean stop for multiple weapons violations and they'd get credit for the collar. Davis walked over to Jaeger, who stood next to the Suburban. He still looked pissed. Davis wanted to book him just for being an asshole, but that was still not illegal.

"You're free to go, sir," said Davis. He unlocked the cuffs and nodded at Hansen, who returned the pistols to Jaeger and Barrett.

"Thank you," said Barrett. He checked the magazines in both pistols before holstering them.

Davis and Hansen waited until the Suburban drove off.

"With that much hardware and ammo, I got a dollar says something's going to happen," said Hansen. "We follow them?"

"No frigging way," said Davis. "We are hands off in no uncertain terms, know what I mean? I got my ears burned for calling this one in. They got friends in high places I don't even want to know about."

— INTEL OFFICE, RSA

Almost shooting somebody—especially on purpose—is worse than just bad manners. They hadn't talked much during the ride back to RSA and both remained taciturn during the cautious walk from the parking garage to Clancy's office. Stone heard Clancy grunt as he stepped down from the van onto the pavement. Clancy had never complained but Stone guessed his leg still hurt. He'd always resisted the urge to help Clancy, knowing his gesture would be greeted with a less than appreciative response.

Clancy sat with Stone at his desk, watching a short video on one of the displays, one of the many files he'd hacked from the datacard. He'd watched it already but Stone hadn't and anybody assigned to kill somebody else should know why.

Clancy turned down the sound as the title, "3-Parent

Mitochondrial DNA Replacement," rolled off the screen and the animation started playing. It showed a needle piercing the cell wall of a human ovum, and removed a blob, labelled 'maternal nucleus.' Then it injected that blob into another human egg labelled 'donor egg.' A sperm cell attached itself to the cell wall of the donor egg and the single cell turned into two cells, then four, then eight. The ending title scrolled down the screen, "Mitochondrial DNA Replacement Will Prevent Incurable Genetic Disease." The entire video lasted less than 35 seconds, matching the attention span of most elected officials.

"Some presentation Gidden made over 30 years ago. He invented this technique and showed the video to a bunch of senators. That's how he got his funding. He bypassed every other federal agency and started doing all his experiments without anybody's permission except his Senate committee. He called it GreenSeed," said Clancy. Never one to hold a grudge, it still felt awkward speaking to the man whose finger, just minutes earlier, was a quarter inch away from putting a bullet in his brain. "I read where everybody else in the world who did this got shut down. I think they called it cytoplasmic something instead of three-parent mito whatever."

"So, yeah," said Stone. He rubbed his jaw and tried to sound matter of fact. He kept his eyes on the computer display, trying to figure out how to politely converse with the man he'd just insulted by almost shooting him in the face. "I mean, he was trying to cure genetic disease. What's wrong with that?"

"Sure, sounds like a good idea." Clancy shook his head. "Typical government program. They try to do something right and it turns to shit. Gidden tried to cure birth defects and got man-made killers instead. All because of some stupid side effect nobody saw coming."

"Side effect," said Stone. "Sounds more like a main effect to me. You're saying that's why they're targeting these GreenSeed kids?"

"They're just the latest. Cain executed the missions to take out the other GreenSeeds. They picked him because he was one of the first."

"What—Cain was one of them?" asked Stone. He thought about Nangarhar and the civilians Cain machine-gunned to death.

"Anything they can do to fix them?"

"Everything I saw says no."

"What about Alex's kid?"

"There were three teenagers in Gen Three. Jaeger and Barrett already took out two of them and you were supposed to finish Milo," said Clancy. "No loose ends is what they said. Supposedly there's nothing wrong with them but they're taking them out anyway. This cover-up makes Iran-Contra look like Beavis and Butthead."

"Cover-up?"

"They're saving senators' asses. That's why Heidrick's erasing all the evidence," said Clancy. "With extreme prejudice."

"Heidrick." Stone looked blank. "Heidrick who?"

Clancy looked at Stone. Did he live under a rock? Heidrick's name came up at least once in every other news headline. "Heidrick, the senator who chairs more committees than God. And who's had the most federal investigations since Abscam. You need to get out more."

"Yeah, so why's he—hey, how the hell you know all this?" asked Stone.

"I bugged Gidden's office and I tapped that datacard you got from Cain," said Clancy. NSA was good at cracking data, but he could—in fact, at DARPA, he had—shown them a few things about breaking encryption. "I never trusted that Limey prick. He got kicked out of England for doing this DNA gene changing shit. Now he and all those cake eaters are getting away with stuff nobody else can because they work for the government."

"We work for the government," said Stone.

"We're the ones doing the real work." Clancy didn't smile. "And maybe it's starting to be a problem."

"Nothing good about this," said Stone.

"It gets worse," said Clancy, looking uncomfortable. He looked away from Stone.

"What."

"Just…" Clancy wanted to say something, but how to say it. Atypically for a gunnery sergeant, he searched for a kind way to say something unpleasant. "There's this other thing—your file just went active. Status immediate."

Stone looked at Clancy, waited for the smile that would give away the joke. Then Stone laughed. "Are you on crack? Where did you—"

"Hey!"

Stone stopped laughing for a moment but still wore a smile that verged on a chuckle.

"Look at me." Clancy pounded the desktop. "Look at me! Do I look like I'm joking?"

Stone lost the smile. There was such a thing as taking a joke too far. "What the hell."

"No loose ends is what Heidrick said," said Clancy. "Cain tags Gen Two. You tag Cain. They tag you. This was their plan from the get-go."

"Bullshit. There's no way. Why would they—"

"Shut up and listen. The reason is there's this—there's something else," said Clancy. He looked at the computer display. "You're one of them. You were the first. Gen One, subject number one. Cain was the second. You and him..."

Stone's defocused look made Clancy think he didn't hear anything he said, much less believe any of it.

"Stone. Did you hear me?"

"Yeah. I heard you," said Stone. This went way beyond funny. It was like some cheap horror movie where daddy got a chainsaw and started going after the kids. "Where do you think this shit up?"

"Nobody could make this up." Clancy tapped on his keyboard. Three large windows appeared on the displays. "That stuff on that datacard. Everything you ever wanted to know about GreenSeed."

Stone looked at the displays. His eyes immediately went to a photo of a young woman. She seemed vaguely familiar. The caption under it read "Margaret Stone, 1983."

"That's your mother," said Clancy.

"I never had—" Stone turned to Clancy. "That's my mother?"

Clancy scrolled down and started reading aloud from a scanned image of a typewritten report. "GreenSeed Program Summary Log. December 22, 1983, Margaret Stone enrolled in the GreenSeed Program. Referral made from the Community Physicians Clinic in New Freedom, Pennsylvania. Maternal family history of CAC deficiency reported on screening. IVF and DNA reformation successfully completed by A. Gidden. Fertilized ova reinserted into subject. Normal gestation of a single ovum completed and live subject GreenSeed One born healthy and named Duncan Stone. Margaret Stone discharged after—"

"Stop reading," said Stone. He stared at the photo of Margaret Stone, and then his eyes started looking at the information about GreenSeed, Margaret Stone, Duncan Stone, DNA transfer... It all faded into words and pictures and none of it seemed real. He looked away.

Kimball brought him back to take out Cain and now he wanted to kill him just to clean up some senator's mess. So much for being back on the team.

Stone remembered what Cain said, then laughed at nothing funny. "I just killed the guy who was more family to me than anyone else."

He didn't know how much time had passed when Clancy next spoke.

"Hey," said Clancy. "I'm sorry."

Stone leaned forward and planted his face in his hands. "Maybe this makes perfect sense on another planet."

"Yeah, except for we're still on this planet."

"And look at you, you dumb jarhead son of a bitch," said Stone. "You're buddies with a man-made killer."

— TIDELOCK MARINA

Jaeger stood on the dock under the light, alternating his stare between the file and the empty slip where the file said the mother's boat should be. The boat that didn't work and couldn't move. No boat, no target, no Stone. He looked at Barrett, who only shrugged. Jaeger pulled his phone out and dialed Kimball.

"Done?" asked Kimball.

Jaeger didn't need to see Kimball to know he wasn't happy. Maybe the call he'd got earlier from the Alexandria police set him off.

"Not exactly," said Jaeger.

"That's usually a no," said Kimball.

"We tracked them to the mother's boat but we had to send Stone when we were—when we got stopped. Boat's gone, Stone's gone, no target, no nothing. GPS can't find them."

Jaeger heard Kimball getting much less happy during the momentary silence when it occurred to him what might have happened—or at least what he hoped would sound believable.

"So, I was thinking—I mean it might be that Stone finished it," said Jaeger. "He took them both out, got on the boat, headed out on the river to dump—"

"Or—or it might be that he got a date with Cinderella and is about to get lucky," said Kimball. His voice got very loud. "Jaeger, you find Stone and you find that goddam target and I don't mean tomorrow."

— INTEL OFFICE, RSA

Stone felt ready to leave. Enough news, enough surprises. GreenSeed. Man-made killer. So what. Most guys in 75th Rangers were man-made killers if you put them in the right place at the right time and said "light 'em up!"

Except they weren't born that way—unless their names were Cain and Stone.

"I didn't give you any good news," said Clancy.

"I'm not blaming the messenger," said Stone. After a moment he turned to face Clancy. "Listen, Gunny, sorry about, you know—"

"Forget it. I'm used to people pointing guns at me."

Stone checked his pistols and holstered them, then didn't move.

"What," said Clancy.

"He knew."

"Who?"

"I should've known Elias knew all about this. He knew he was part of this GreenSeed thing. When he gave me that datacard he said he put it all online. Something—some file called Centaur."

"I figured he might have done something like that. The web, cloud, some private data server. I looked around for a while but couldn't find it. You get a chance to look at the file?"

"That iPad knew how to find it. Somewhere on the internet, but I couldn't figure out how to log in," said Stone. "Wonder why he named it Centaur."

"It's a Greek mythical creature. From Homer. The Odyssey," said Clancy. He spun around and did an online search, then pointed at the display, which showed a drawing of a Centaur and a description. "Says it's half horse—"

"—half man," said Stone. He turned away from the display. "I always knew Elias was different. Real smart but real different, poor dumb bastard. He said I should've helped him," said Stone. "He was right. I should've done something."

"Nothing anybody could've done. He's—he was what he was. All the way from the time he was born."

"Like me." Stone spoke like he'd just heard he had Ebola and would soon infect everybody around him. "Just like me.

"Maybe. I don't think so. He was never the type who's dumb enough to run into a burning gun truck that's about to explode. You, however," said Clancy. "Are dumb enough."

"Thanks."

"Let me say it so a grunt like you can understand. I don't buy it," said Clancy. "Sure, Cain was off the reservation. Way way off. Maybe some of those other GreenSeed people were too. They maybe messed up on some of this GreenSeed stuff, but not Milo and not you."

"How do you know? You some kind of scientist?"

"I served in the Marine Corps of the United States of America for over 20 years and they saw fit to promote me to Gunnery Sergeant. I commanded men in combat and I know people. I know who will choke and I know who will fight and I know nutcases from regular joes I can drink a beer with. In spite of your very poor judgement in joining the Army instead of the Marines, I believe you are fit to have a beer with me. Cain was not."

Stone stayed silent.

"Would I spend my valuable time explaining all this shit to you if I thought you're same as Cain?"

Stone shook his head. "But why—"

"Do not ask why, you'll only hurt yourself and your country. I don't know why," said Clancy. "I ever steer you wrong before?"

Clancy didn't sound convincing but it was better than if he said Stone was four short of a six-pack and needed to die quickly. "Okay, Gunny. I hope you're—"

They heard a card key slide through the lock. Clancy pointed to the wall next to the door. Stone moved behind the door as it opened, his pistol in his hand.

Kimball stood in the doorway.

"What's up. Kinda late," said Clancy. He yawned. "Just about to roll out of—"

"Sleep tomorrow. We can't find Stone. Track him, find him. Call me when you get him," said Kimball. He left, leaving the door to shut by itself.

Stone holstered his pistol, wondering only for a moment if he should have shot Kimball. Probably not. RSA was staffed 24-7 and it would attract attention. And the body count would be too high. And Kimball might just be the only person who could fix the situation.

"You better get out of here," said Clancy. "Give him a minute to get in the stairwell."

Clancy's phone buzzed. The display showed "Alexis Jones."

"Yeah," said Clancy, into the phone. After a moment, he shut his eyes and said, "Okay, stay there and keep your phones off. Wait till I get there."

"What happened?" asked Stone.

"That broke-dick fugitive from a scrap heap's busted. They had to tie up at the end of the dock. I got to go," said Clancy. "Hey, your phone off?"

"Yeah, all day. We used this," said Stone. He showed Clancy the walkie-talkie.

"Jaeger's GPS can find you when you're phone is on. It's set to broadcast your location to anybody who wants to know and right now I'm pretty sure Jaeger wants to know. Lose it. Go."

Clancy extended his hand. Stone shook it.

"What about them?" asked Stone.

"I'll figure something out. You need to get gone. You're a target."

"So are they. Difference being I know how to be a hard target."

"This is on me. I owe Harry," said Clancy. "You don't have to help them."

"Well, actually, I kind of think I do."

"Stone—"

"I'm all in, Gunny. Way I see it, I'm sort of related to the kid."

— WASHINGTON, DC

Barrett looked at the GPS when it pinged. A dot labelled "Jones A" flashed onto the display and he zoomed in for the detailed coordinates.

"Hey," said Barrett.

Jaeger grunted, not moving his eyes from the road in front and the rear view mirrors. Who knew if the cops decided to follow them.

"Looks like the mother's at that marina," said Barrett. "At least her phone is."

The dot on the GPS display disappeared as suddenly as it had appeared.

"Or was."

Jaeger pulled a U-turn at the next intersection. It was late and they'd just got their first break of the evening.

"What's ETA their location?" asked Jaeger.

"Looks like about 25 minutes," said Barrett. "If she's with the target what do we do with her?"

— TIDELOCK MARINA

Clancy stopped near the main entrance to the marina. Stone opened the door only when he didn't see any sign of Jaeger's Suburban.

"Just get them off the grid for a while. I'll figure something out," said Clancy. He looked at the man who an hour earlier decided not to shoot him in the head. "Hey, Stone. Thanks—"

"Forget it. I got it covered," said Stone.

"I know," said Clancy. He grinned. "And smile, otherwise you'll make her nervous. The man-made killer thing, you know?"

— VERITAS

Alex stood up when she heard footsteps on the deck. She stood between Milo and the cabin door as it slid open, her eyes immediately focusing on the pistol held by the man who had tried to kill her son barely hours earlier.

"What's that for?" asked Milo, pointing at the gun.

Stone looked at Alex. "Visitors?" he asked, quietly. His eyes moved around the cabin, looking for anything that might reveal the presence of somebody else on the boat, in particular, anybody who might want to shoot them.

"Only you," said Alex. She hoped her voice didn't betray her fear of the man with the gun standing in front of her.

He waited a moment, listening, then holstered the pistol and slid the cabin door shut.

"Clancy told me what's going on," said Stone. "It's okay."

"Where is he?" asked Alex.

"Fixing this," said Stone. "I'm getting you out of here. Let's go."

Alex didn't move.

"If I was going to make you dead, it'd already be done," said Stone. "We don't have a lot of time. Get your stuff."

Milo moved out from in back of Alex. "Why's he telling us what to do? Like, wasn't he going to shoot us?"

"I was actually only going to shoot you."

"Oh, like that makes it better. Why do we—"

"Clancy found you, they will too. Just a matter of time, which for you is running very short," said Stone.

"Hey, who are you anyway?" asked Milo. He stepped towards Stone. "We don't know you. Why would you help us?"

Alex put a hand on Milo's shoulder. "Milo, please—"

"Hey, kid. I'm the only thing between you and bad guys with guns," said Stone. "Maybe you want to get your ass in gear and do something that keeps you breathing more than temporarily."

— TIDELOCK MARINA

"No time to dress it up," said Jaeger, switching off the engine. "Rifle."

Barrett moved into the back seat and uncased the AR-15. Its full length bull barrel, night vision scope and laser targeting made it one of the best weapons for accurately shooting people in the head at less than 100 meters. From where Jaeger had just parked, near the main entrance of the parking lot, Barrett's field of fire covered everything from the dock to the other entrance. Nobody would get out that they didn't want getting out.

He scanned the area with his night vision ocular and ranged the dock. Nobody around, normal for the late hour.

"Range, 70 meters," said Barrett.

Jaeger looked through his ocular and nodded. "I confirm, 70 meters."

Barrett put down his ocular. No need to make any sight adjustments. He folded down a bench rest, then snapped on a silencer and loaded a full magazine of hollowpoint 5.56 millimeter ammo. At this range his second shot would be redundant. He pressed the switch of the laser and played the red dot on his hand. Everything ready. He only needed targets.

"Bogeys," said Jaeger. Through the ocular he saw the fuzzy, grainy image of three people emerging from a boat at the far end of the dock. He saw the man look around, then beckon to the other two. They started walking down the dock towards the parking lot. Barret had his eye focusing through the 12x night-vision rifle scope.

"I confirm target, file three-one," said Barrett. He'd memorized Milo's photo the day before. "I see target plus two. I make one female and—Stone."

"Stone?" said Jaeger. The magnification of his ocular wasn't enough for him to make a positive ID. He thought for a moment. He had orders for only two of them, but he couldn't risk leaving any of them in condition to speak with police—not after Alexandria's finest detained them that evening. "Take three-one out. Then Stone. Then the female."

"Roger that," said Barrett. He switched the AR-15 from safe to semi-automatic, then looked away from the scope, at Jaeger. "Say again?"

"Target order. Three-one. Stone. Female," said Jaeger. "Stone is file one-one, target status immediate. Confirm."

Barrett paused, registering the instruction to assassinate a fellow assassin. "I confirm."

He put his eye to the scope and tracked his target, then switched on the laser and put his finger lightly on the trigger.

Walking on the dock, Alex noticed a box sitting on the deck of the large cabin cruiser and wondered why the elderly couple who owned it might have left it there. She didn't know them well since they hired people to take care of their boat and she remembered they'd hosted parties on the Potomac several times earlier that summer. Maybe someday she and Milo might do the same.

Milo dropped one of his textbooks onto the dock and bent over to pick it up when Alex saw the red dot waver only slightly on the cabin cruiser's hull. Some new kind of alarm system?

Fiberglass splinters edged the hole that suddenly appeared in place of the red dot. Stone quickly turned, hearing the dull thud, which sounded like a 5.56 millimeter bullet hitting soft cover.

"Get down, get down!" said Stone. He pushed Milo to the ground then tackled Alex as nine more holes thudded into the hull. The red dot disappeared.

"What did you do that for?" asked Milo.

Surprised, Alex looked at Stone, who lay on top of her. Their faces inches apart for a moment, he rolled off her and looked around, pistol in hand. Alex said, "Stone, what are you—"

"Stay down, somebody's shooting," said Stone. From his prone position he looked for the source of the bullets and saw nothing except for Milo getting to his knees.

Stone low-crawled towards Milo as Alex stood up.

"Milo, get down!" said Alex. She saw the red dot wavering slightly on Milo's chest. "Milo!"

Alex ran past Stone to Milo and pushed him to the deck. A small hole replaced the red dot that momentarily painted her backpack.

She dropped face down onto the weathered planks of the dock, her eyes closing to half open and focusing on nothing. Three more holes appeared in the cabin cruiser's hull in a tight group, in back of where Alex had just stood.

"Mom?" said Milo. "Mom."

Stone saw the dim muzzle flash of five more shots that splintered the dock two feet away. He knew generally where the shooter was. Too far for accurate pistol work, but they had no cover and needed to get out of the kill zone. Stone thought he counted 19 rounds. The shooter had to reload if he followed procedure—nobody ever loaded 20 rounds in a 20-round magazine—and if Stone had counted correctly. He jumped to his feet, aimed and shot the magazine empty, then dropped down to the deck. Good thing the shooter hadn't used a 30-round mag. Lights appeared in windows and portholes of boats along the dock.

He turned to Milo. "Okay, we're going to have to—what happened?"

He saw Milo staring at the blood slowly starting to pool underneath Alex. Stone looked around and saw the wooden boat lockers. Nobody would consider those hard cover but at least they'd be out of sight. He grabbed Alex's backpack strap and dragged her across the dock.

"Come here, kid. Stay down and—hey, get over here!" said Stone. He had already started pulling Alex's backpack off when Milo dived beside them. Stone rummaged in the backpack and found a scarf, which he folded and pressed onto the bleeding wound in Alex's back.

Alex struggled to grasp Stone's hand.

"Hey, Alex, you're going to be okay," said Stone. He had no idea if she would or wouldn't, but it was what everybody always told him whenever he'd got shot.

"Please," whispered Alex. "Don't let them kill my son. Please…"

"Milo," said Stone. He looked at the teenager's white face getting whiter and knew he registered little, if anything. He took Milo's hand and put it over the folded scarf. "Milo! Hold this."

Milo complied, but said nothing.

Stone heard bullets thump into the plywood on the opposite side of the locker. Something inside was stopping them from coming through. He jumped up and emptied another magazine at the dim muzzle flashes. As he dropped back down he heard the buzz of 5.56 tearing through air above his head. More thumps— and a crack as one of the bullets shot through the locker six inches away.

Stone saw Milo start shaking, his face contorting, looking like people who get pushed way too far way too fast. He heard sirens in the distance.

"Hey, Milo!" said Stone. Milo's hand, shaking, touched his face as if checking to see if it was still there. This was a confused, pissed off kid getting more pissed off and getting ready to do something stupid. "At ease, Milo."

But Milo was a kid, and he was confused and he had no clue what 'at ease' meant. Stone grabbed him just in time to keep him from jumping up and charging the enemy like in the movies or video games, thereby solving the shooter's problem. Stone pulled Milo down and put his arm around his shoulders very firmly to keep anything else stupid from happening. He put Milo's hand back over the scarf.

"Okay, Milo. This is not good. Okay? Nothing good's happening now. But we're here and I have to make the bad guys stop shooting. Keep your hand here. You have to take care of your mother," said Stone. "Milo! Can you take care of your mother?"

Stone felt Milo relax. "Can you—"

"Yeah, I can take care of her," said Milo. As quickly as the rage in him rose, it subsided.

The sirens sounded louder.

"Help's almost here. Take care of her."

Stone reloaded his P-226 and pulled out his P-250. He rolled out from behind the locker, chased by bullets splintering the wood on the dock. He sprinted an erratic zig-zag towards the muzzle flashes and saw a silhouette of a large SUV. No surprise that it was a Suburban. Stone broke right off a left zig and took a knee. He fired both pistols at the silhouette and hoped he'd convinced the occupants that it was a good time to leave. Otherwise he'd receive the business end of at least one 5.56 millimeter bullet.

Barrett ducked as he heard .40 caliber slugs hiss past his head and punch through sheet metal. If he'd got a piece of Stone it wasn't much judging by the return fire, probably because Stone ran a lot faster than any white guy should. Jaeger started the engine. He heard the sirens sounding very loud, almost like cops pulling into the parking lot.

"Pack it up," said Jaeger. He spun his tires and skidded a U-turn away from the dock, watching flashing lights reflect off windows.

Barret packed the rifle in its case, prudently hunching down in case any more bullets came his way. He'd noted six bullet holes in the roof over his head—Stone must have mis-guessed the range and aimed a little high. He rolled up the rear windows as Jaeger slowed down and drove past Stone's car, out the side parking entrance.

Seconds later the first police car sped into the parking lot through the main entrance, sirens blaring and its spotlight illuminating most of the area that, fortunately for Stone, excluded the part where he stood. He holstered his pistols, and looked back at the boat locker. He saw Milo peek over the top of the locker, then wave at the police, then duck back down. The police car screeched to a halt and played its spotlight across the dock.

Two pistols, five empty magazines, and ample gunshot residue would not support any explanations an investigating officer would find reasonable. Stone watched police approach the boat locker, pistols and shotguns in hand, then walked quickly in the dark to his car.

— ALEXANDRIA

Stone forced himself to drive at 37 miles per hour, exactly two miles over the speed limit. Police cars sped past him in the opposite direction, lights flashing and sirens screaming as they approached, then passed him. He saw the I-395 onramp sign and changed lanes. I-395 South to as far as he could go and let somebody else worry about this clusterfuck. He stopped at the red light a block from the onramp. Cops would take care of Milo. Alex, if still alive, would get to a hospital. They'd tell the cops everything. They'd get put in protective custody and it's not his problem anymore.

Except as soon as this appears on the police blotter, Kimball finds out. Guys in suits arrive and take custody, and nobody ever hears of them again. The word would get out they're in witness protection in a secure, undisclosed location—code for they're buried in an unmarked hole somewhere in the Alleghenies. He'd seen that drill before.

He'd done that drill before. It worked really well.

And he'd promised Clancy.

Stone hit the gas and cut a U-turn across four lanes against a red light, then turned on his phone and dialed a number.

"Clancy," said Stone.

"You got them?" asked Clancy. He sounded stressed.

"Alex got shot. Cops are on scene. I think it was Jaeger. They were waiting for us at the marina."

A silence before Clancy spoke. "Is she—"

"I don't know. I'm guessing five-five-six, about 70, 80 meters," said Stone.

"Where's Milo? Is he—"

"Last I saw he didn't get shot. He was with Alex. Find them, okay? Let me know."

"I'm on it. Call me in one hour."

"Roger that." Instead of hanging up he said, "Hey, Kimball still in the building?"

"Probably," said Clancy. "Hey, if you're thinking about—"

Stone hung up and turned the phone off.

— INTEL OFFICE, RSA

Clancy opened his desk drawer and pulled back the slide of his Beretta. Round in the chamber. How many times had he already checked? He turned back to his computer and typed in the search criteria: "60 minutes, Tidelock Marina, female gunshot victim, destination hospital, status." He hit the enter key then turned to the display with the GPS map. The scanner search program would take a few minutes to return the results and he needed to find the black Suburban that contained the night's shooters. He saw the dot moving away from Tidelock Marina at two miles over the speed limit, with the labels "Jaeger M" and "Barrett J," when he heard the card key slide through the lock. Whatever happened to a polite knock on the door?

"You find Stone yet?" asked Kimball, before the door had opened all the way.

"Maybe he'll find you," said Clancy.

"Yes, no, what. Where's Stone?"

Clancy forced himself to remain calm. "You mean file one-one?"

Kimball blinked hard. "How'd you find out?"

Clancy shrugged.

Kimball hesitated, then stepped inside the office and let the door swing shut. For a moment it almost appeared he was at a loss for words.

"Yeah." Kimball stared over Clancy's head for a moment, not willing to have their eyes make contact.

"He's a target. Same as any other," said Kimball. Another moment. "No. He's not, is he."

"Why are we doing this?" Clancy looked at Kimball, tie still tied, suit still pressed, standing in front of Clancy's medals and the American flag on the wall.

"What do you mean, why?" asked Kimball. Now he looked directly at Clancy, surprised at the question. "What—Jeezus, it's a mission."

"This isn't even close."

"This is what we do. You ought to know."

"Me? Bullshit," said Clancy. "This is not what we do."

"If you look at our orders it is. Now find me Stone." Kimball turned to leave.

"Why we killing our own? Kimball! You know this is not what we do. Why are we killing—"

"Damn it!" Kimball slammed the door with his fist. More quietly, he said, "This is what we do. This mission will be executed in accordance with our orders, with you or without you. Think hard."

Kimball flung open the door and walked out.

Clancy pulled his hand away from the desk drawer handle. He leaned back in his chair and rubbed his leg. Somehow that tingling just never went away. He turned to look at the photo of his crew on the wall, standing next to the MaxxPro gun truck. He wished he could travel back in time and get to a place where things were simple: find the enemy, kill the enemy. Outside the wire at least you had a general idea who the enemy was. He didn't move his eyes from the photo. He'd give anything now to have those jarheads still walking around—he'd tried to give everything then, when the IED exploded, but that hadn't been good enough and it was his crew and his commander that died and it wasn't a very good God who'd left him alive after that. And now he'd probably just signed his exit papers from the last job he'd ever have serving his country.

Except it just became abundantly clear that this job was not serving his country.

He limped over to the wall and pulled the shadow box of his medals and the boxed flag off the wall and brought them back to his desk. He tried to arrange them near the photo of his daughters, but after testing several configurations he just stacked everything on the desk, less a shrine and more just a pile of stuff and used-up memories.

— TIDELOCK MARINA

Officer Davis approached the boat locker slowly, shotgun raised.

"Police! I need to see hands," said Davis. "Now!"

He watched one bloody hand rise from behind the boat locker. Somebody huddled behind it started shouting. "Hey! It's my Mom."

Two more police cars skidded to a stop just in front of the dock, their headlights increasing the candlepower bathing the area.

"Davis, I'm behind you," said Officer Hansen. Walking quickly over, he kept his shotgun aimed at a point just above the boat locker. Anybody standing up suddenly might not live to regret it. "Check it out."

"Don't move," said Davis, walking around the boat locker, the muzzle of the Mossberg 500 aimed in front of him. He saw more than a dozen bullet holes in the locker. Somebody really wanted to shoot whoever was behind it. Over the front sight he saw a kid, one hand in the air, the other hand pressing on a scarf on a woman, face down in a puddle of blood.

"Anybody else here?" asked Davis. He raised the shotgun's muzzle and waved off Hansen.

"I don't know," said Milo. "Hurry, my Mom—"

Davis turned to the police swarming the area. "I need an ambulance. Civilian down, major injuries. I need paramedics now!"

Several officers starting checking the boats tied up at the dock as Officer Bradley hustled over with the first aid kit.

Davis stood with Hansen, both watching Bradley start working on the victim. "You think those guys we stopped have anything to do with this?" asked Hansen.

"We can't even ask," said Davis. "Better call in detectives. Hey Brad, you need a hand?"

Bradley looked up and shook his head. "She's got a pulse and she's breathing. Where's the paramedics?"

"On the way," said Davis.

Bradley had eased Milo's hand off the scarf and pressed down on a roll of Celox combat gauze he'd slid over the entry wound. It seemed to work here as well as it worked for the medics in Iraq. The victim breathed and had a heartbeat. All good, considering the injury. He just had to make sure none of that changed by the time the paramedics arrived.

"Hey, kid," said Bradley. "She's going to be okay."

Alex opened her eyes, which had trouble focusing on Milo.

"Milo. I love you," she said. Her voice was hoarse and barely audible. "Go. Don't get found."

"Must be confused," said Bradley. He turned to Milo, who no longer kneeled beside him. "That's normal when—"

Bradley looked around and saw only police. "Hey, Davis. Where's that kid?"

— ACTION RANGE, RSA

Kimball encouraged all the operators to get as much practice as they could at the range—it was cheap, excellent training, considering there was no live fire. He stood at the firing line, rolling his shoulders, to loosen knots that invariably accumulated during his 14-hour days. He'd get a few active shooter scenarios in. It helped keep his skills up, and he liked it in a relaxing, kill-the-bastards kind of way.

The timer pinged and the first images flashed on the large screen in front of him. He picked up the laser pistol and watched the images change, almost like he was an actor in a movie. A man stepped out from behind a building, walking away from him. The man turned and Kimball saw the pistol in his hand. Kimball fired and the hits registered as red dots on the screen, two in the head, one in the throat. He walked into the range and faced the next screen, where images of a desert village showed only an empty street, until three masked men walked out of a building with AK-47s. When one of them aimed at Kimball, he quickly fired. Two seconds, three hits center of mass. Another two seconds, three hits in the head. Perfect score. Another man walked out of the building and Kimball shot him once in the head. The man was unarmed with his hands in the air, and except for the economy of shots, it might have occurred in any neighborhood where distinguishing criminals from victims is difficult.

"How many times you kill the good guy?"

Kimball turned and saw Stone standing by the control booth. He considered his employee's marksmanship and recent absence from duty before moving.

"Why are you here and not doing what you are supposed to be doing?" asked Kimball.

"Figured I'd come down before bedtime. Just for shits and giggles," said Stone. "File three-one. Why?"

Kimball walked back to the firing line and put the training pistol on the bench. He kept his hands in front of him and looked at Stone. Behind him, the images switched from a desert village to a sleazy urban neighborhood with two hookers and their pimp walking down the street.

"Son of a dead war hero. Probably a good kid. Nice mother. Hell, she even works for the client," said Kimball. He sighed. "Orders come down and sometimes we don't like them and it's shitty but we follow them. Same as Kabul, Fallujah, anywhere."

"His mother just got shot."

"Life's hazardous to your health," said Kimball. "Sometimes nice people get hurt."

"How's that kid a threat to national security?"

An image of a young boy wearing a bomb vest replaced the image of the hookers on the screen behind Kimball. Only the reflected light from the screens illuminated the range.

"He going to blow something up?" asked Stone. "Maybe go after the President? Take down some computers or steal secrets?"

"Don't know, don't care, doesn't matter," said Kimball. "Maybe you want to tell me why we're really having this conversation."

"I don't like being ordered to kill some kid who hasn't done anything," said Stone. "And somehow, having my own file makes me think maybe I'm not wanted so much around here."

Kimball took a moment before speaking. So much for top secret. "Clancy tell you?"

Stone stepped out of the booth towards the firing line. Kimball saw the P-226 in Stone's hand.

"I was thinking you'd say not to worry, it's all just a big mistake. Everything went FUBAR, client got out of control, but we're much better now. Something like that," said Stone. He watched Kimball's expression. "Nothing?"

"No. Wish I could say I was sorry and mean it."

"Good and wonderful. Who's next?"

"Jeezus, you know better than that."

"Little guy doesn't matter now, is that it?" asked Stone.

"Little guy never mattered," said Kimball. "I'm surprised I have to explain this."

"I'm surprised too, but only because people I work for are trying to kill me. I know, it sounds petty and selfish," said Stone.

"Nothing personal."

"How'll this look when it's on the front page of the Post?"

"Who would believe a disgruntled employee who was fired from his job? And who also has multiple arrest warrants for murder?"

"I don't have any warrants."

"In the unlikely event you survive the next six hours, you will. Maybe we throw in drug trafficking. We are limited only by ourselves and our creativity."

Stone didn't doubt Kimball. Stone nodded towards the door. "Let's go. We have to fix this."

"No," said Kimball. "We don't."

Stone didn't actually expect Kimball to make excuses or let anything interfere with a mission. Kimball would always keep trying to convince you he was right while he continued to do whatever he'd set out to do, including shooting you if that's what the mission required. Before Stone could move, Kimball twisted around one of the barricades on the firing line. As he raised his P-226, Stone saw Kimball's pistol and very little else of him that was shootable. Stone moved behind another barricade.

"I'm reporting a safety violation, Kimball. No hardware on the action range."

"So what," said Kimball. "I'm about to permanently rescind your range privileges anyway."

"Don't make me kill everything."

"Tell me something scary. This only ends one way."

"Not with your bullet," said Stone.

"Right." Kimball listened, hoping to hear Stone move. Weird how Stone just showed up at the range. Guys like him could easily disappear off the grid fast and forever. He didn't stop by just to get himself off the kill list—he wanted to keep the kid and his mother breathing and who knew why. Not that it mattered. "Go tell your mother. Or somebody else who cares."

Stone heard the acoustics in the room change—Kimball started moving. He looked out from behind the barricade and saw Kimball sidestep quickly into the range, pistol aimed. Stone stepped back and ran behind the firing line away from Kimball, who shot three bullets into each of the barricades as Stone passed behind them. Stone spun around the last barricade in a low crouch and aimed. The image on the screen inside the range changed again, this time to a mother holding her child. Stone saw the image and froze for a moment, then looked for Kimball.

Out of sight, still somewhere near. Whoever made the first move would take the first bullet. Stone shot out the projectors that cast images on the interior screens. Bullets tore through the image of the mother and child, shredding the screen, until Stone shot that projector dark, removing the last bit of light from the room.

"Thanks for everything, Kimball," said Stone. He'd already started moving towards the door before he'd shot out that last projector. Reflecting on the events of the preceding three minutes, Stone concluded that, in retrospect, this was the best possible outcome of his visit since he wasn't dead or bleeding.

How had this seemed a good idea an hour ago?

"We're not done," said Kimball.

Stone heard Kimball's words as he slammed the heavy door to the range shut. Stone took Kimball at his word. They wouldn't be done until one of them stopped breathing.

— BENSON-PHILIPS FACTORY

The ticking never bothered him before. The cheap clock, cracked plastic and all, and who even knew if it told the right time? Stone sat in the room, on the ragged couch, his face illuminated only by the glow of the iPad display. He didn't know why he'd come back to the factory and he couldn't stay long. This room and the rest of the factory almost certainly had their place in his retirement file's Locations section.

He'd learned many things that night, which he could have blissfully gone the rest of his life without knowing. At least he'd learned about centaurs. Stone typed in 'halfman' in the password field, then tapped the display.

He read the contents of the window that appeared. "Centaur login accepted—GreenSeed Found." A new popup window appeared: "Duncan, if it's you reading this, I'm dead and you're not. It was nothing personal. Maybe you want to let the whole world know. Elias."

The popup window disappeared and a series of file folders populated the display. Most of the files had "GreenSeed" in the filename. Some files had photos on the icons. He recognized Cain, Milo, Alex, but most people were unfamiliar to him. One file had his photo on it, taken just after high school. Another had a woman's photo on it, taken just after high school, the same one Clancy showed him earlier. Margaret Stone. He tapped that file and watched as it opened.

A brief history of GreenSeed Subject 1.

The file said they recruited Margaret Stone after her second miscarriage. Pregnant and married at 17, accepted by GreenSeed at 18, divorced at age 20, institutionalized for depression and substance abuse at 21. Then only "lost to follow-up" and nothing.

Another file listed the six foster homes in which they'd deposited Duncan Stone for 14 years. He starred in football and wrestling and his grades were sufficient for him to graduate high school. He dodged juvenile detention six times for fighting. Army enlistment after graduation. Stone read a brief summary of his Army service record, excluding details of assignments but including all of the Army schools he'd attended and results from many tests, most of which he didn't remember.

Stone looked at the photo of Margaret Stone again. Enlarged it on the iPad display. A normal high school photo of a normal high school girl who happened to have given birth to him. The photo triggered no memories and Stone didn't know what to feel or think. Foster homes and foster parents had come and gone. He barely remembered what made one different from another and had not kept contact with any of them. Long before departing the last one he'd pushed away any thoughts of parents, never thinking about who they'd been, or what happened to them, or why they had sent him away.

Now, Margaret Stone. A photo. Her history. Her child. That he'd had a mother who gave birth to him—a real mother—still remained only an abstract thought represented in words and a photo on a mobile computing device. She was still less than gone. She never was.

Stone turned off the iPad and stared at the floor of the small room. At least this place seemed familiar, normal, almost comfortable. He held the iPad and resisted the temptation to turn it back on.

How could you suddenly miss somebody who never was?

Sudden silence brought Stone back into the small room. The clock stopped ticking. He wondered how long it had pushed its hands in an endless circle before losing the will to keep time— before it decided to just quit.

Stone walked out of the room.

— ALEXANDRIA

Few cars populated the roads. In the small hours of the morning, most people on the street either were victims or victimizers, and police would look for anything out of the ordinary. Stone drove at exactly two miles over the speed limit— that was about as ordinary as it got, so the RSA procedure manual instructed for ops executed in the US.

Stone turned his phone on and called Clancy.

"I found Alex. She just got out of surgery," said Clancy. His voice sounded strained, or maybe it was just the phone connection.

"Where?" asked Stone.

"Alexandria General."

Stone made the next right turn. He'd get there in 10 minutes.

"She's back in her room—I think 51-101. Fifth floor Intensive Care Unit. Nicked her lung but they patched her up. Guess it wasn't so bad," said Clancy.

That could mean anything. Clancy had also said the damage to his leg 'wasn't so bad'.

"She got lucky," said Stone.

"Bullet went through books and sandwiches in her backpack."

"Milo with her?"

"No. Police reports say he took off. No sign of him," said Clancy.

"I guess that's good. As long as they didn't find a body."

"We had a lockdown tonight, maybe couple hours ago. Security had alarms going, then they said it was just a drill. You find Kimball?"

"He's still the good soldier. We work around him or over him," said Stone. "Any ideas?"

"Working on it." Clancy's hesitation before speaking told Stone he had no ideas.

"How do I find Heidrick?"

"Why do you want to find him?" asked Clancy.

"I want to make a sizeable campaign contribution."

"He's a US senator. I don't think you want to go there."

"There's a lot of things I don't want. Most of them I learned about tonight."

Stone heard worry in Clancy's silence.

"Do I have anything to lose?" asked Stone.

"Hang on," said Clancy. "He's making a speech tomorrow for some food bank. Convention center. Not too much security there. We can make it work. Where do we meet?"

"Yeah," said Stone. "So I was thinking maybe you want off the grid for a while. Best if I run solo since—you know, I might have to move quick or something."

"Hey! Don't worry about me, jump chump—"

"Help me out, Gunny."

"You're the one who needs—"

"Just get me Heidrick," said Stone. Maybe he should have

picked his words more carefully. Never question a gunnery sergeant's abilities no matter the extent of his injuries, past or present. "What you're doing now is the best thing you can do. Maybe see if you can find Milo."

"You mean stay out of the way."

"You're the only guy I trust. I got nobody else. Please."

"Yeah. Sure," said Clancy. But Stone was right, since people he thought he trusted a day earlier were trying to kill him. And it wasn't like he could outrun Stone—or anybody. "You need anything else?"

Stone thought briefly about asking if Clancy could find anything about Margaret Stone. Maybe he could look in some government file and find information that Stone couldn't. Like if she was still alive. Or if she had another family. Or if she remembered her first child. He then wondered what to do if Clancy found that information.

"No. I'm good," said Stone. He saw the main tower of Alexandria General up ahead.

"Call me when you need a Marine to bail your sorry ass out."

"Roger that. Thanks, Gunny."

— INTEL OFFICE, RSA

Clancy put down his phone. He could've helped but he didn't blame Stone for not wanting a broke-down old warhorse slowing him down. Even though a one-leg Marine is better than a two-leg anything else.

He stared at the box of medals and at the American flag. At the photo of his daughters. None of it belonged to him anymore.

Clancy picked up the photo of him and his team and Captain Jones, all smiling in front of the gun-truck. They took that photo in the Helmand two weeks before they got hit by the IED and a month after he'd brought two new systems for field testing. One picked up radio chatter and the other was supposed to help detect IEDs. The engineers in the lab told him they were ready and Clancy believed them. One system worked well. The other killed everybody but him. Nobody ever said he shared any blame for that. Everybody said nobody could have done anything different.

It didn't matter. He'd put the systems in the truck and said "move out" and that meant he was the only one who got his people killed. Whatever it took, he'd never let anybody down again.

He looked back at the display. The code he'd spent the last couple of hours writing only needed activation. It would probably piss off lots of people, mess things up for a while. A day earlier the notion wouldn't have occurred to him and he still didn't want to do it. But, like Stone said, there's a lot of things he didn't want and most of those he'd just learned about.

What Cain had done with the GreenSeed data—that was really what set everything off. Stone, Milo, Alex, all getting ready to get dead and, knowing Heidrick, Kimball's ass was in the crosshairs too. Data was the only thing that could save any of them.

Clancy tapped the enter key on his keyboard and pulled open the desk drawer. A window opened on the display with a countdown timer: "AUTO-UPLOAD READY—HIT ANY KEY TO ABORT." Copies of everything would get hidden in so many places nobody would even imagine how to track them all down. He just hoped the right people would figure out how to find the gigabytes of data soon to stream out to the cloud.

The timer started rolling. Clancy sent his email, then pulled the Beretta out of the drawer and watched the timer change from 00:57 to 00:56 to 00:55.

All ready to rock and roll.

— ICU, ALEXANDRIA GENERAL HOSPITAL

Alex drifted between waking, sleeping, and dreaming, most of the latter verging on nightmares. She wore an IV line in her arm, a pulse oximeter on her finger and an oxygen cannula in her nose. Wires snaked out from under her gown to the overhead monitor, which beeped softly with each heartbeat and showed tracings of the electrocardiogram and pulse oximeter. She heard the door softly open, then quietly click shut. She did not stir, did not care, did not look to see who just walked in.

"It's me. Stone." He sat in the chair next to the bed.

"Milo," said Alex. Her voice sounded hoarse, dry. "Where's Milo? Is he—"

"He's okay. He took off. How you doing?"

"I'm okay. Sore."

Stone listened to the slow beeping from the monitor. He'd arrived wanting to make sure she didn't wind up in some hole or landfill. And maybe find out something about who—what he was. Or not. She knew about GreenSeed and she knew about Cain. Maybe she knew something about him, and if she did, would she want him around?

"Did you know—this thing about me. One of Gidden's—"

"How did you—did Cain tell you?" asked Alex, surprised. She forced herself awake.

"Sort of," said Stone. "So I get it if you don't want me around Milo. Or you."

"Why do you say that?"

"I'm like him. Cain," said Stone. "Man-made."

"No, not man-made. You had a father and a mother, like everyone else who's ever been born," Alex turned her head and looked at Stone. "Your mother was a good person."

She listened to his surprise in the silence and darkness of the room.

"How…"

"I work for the government. We love our paperwork." Alex laughed, then stopped, quickly learning that laughing after lung surgery hurts. "I knew about you. I knew all of the GreenSeed families. Dr. Gidden and me. Besides him I was the only one who had access to all the data until I left GreenSeed. Until Cain took it."

"Am I…" Stone stopped talking. He didn't know how to ask the question.

"You're not like Cain. Or the other GreenSeeds he had to…the ones he had to stop." Alex struggled to speak even as the sedatives and painkillers conspired to make her incoherent.

"How do you know?"

"The genetic profiles. Behavior histories and tests starting in junior high. With all the tests and schools in the Army you never even noticed all that—all the stuff we collected about you."

"Then…I'm—"

"Yes."

"Why did Cain go wrong?"

"Dr. Gidden changed the technique. Cain and Gen Two didn't work out. Gen Three did. And so did you," Alex coughed, then groaned.

"Sorry. Don't talk. It's okay." He hoped believing her would turn out okay. It would be nice to be normal. He would even take undistinguished.

"You're just like Milo," said Alex. She turned her head away. "I told him. He was so angry. I tried so hard to be a good—"

"He's going to be okay—"

"They told me they'd leave all the normals alone. They told me you and all the Gen Three—all the normals. They told me they'd—" Alex wheezed, then remained silent.

The monitor beeped faster.

"I just went along with everything," said Alex. She put her hand to her face. "Stone, I should have done something, but Milo—I should have told somebody but I didn't. I should have done something—"

"No, it's okay, Alex. Listen, you have to—"

"No. I know them. Gidden, Heidrick, all of them. They lied. They broke their promises. Everything we did...all for nothing. I'm so sorry, Stone, I'm so sorry. They won't stop till they kill Milo, all of us."

Stone hesitated, then tentatively, he took her hand in his. She squeezed and he squeezed back.

"Hey. I mean, me and Clancy, we got this handled. We'll get you and Milo on your boat, and maybe by then that engine'll even work."

"I wish I could have met you before. I wish we could have had that boat ride. Take care of Milo. Go with him, please make him safe."

"I'll get us all safe."

"Goodbye, Stone."

She closed her eyes and released his hand. Stone sat for moments in the darkness, then disappeared as quietly as he'd arrived.

— ALEXANDRIA GENERAL HOSPITAL

On his way out, Stone walked through the ambulance entrance as the guards and nurses were distracted with the arrival of another gunshot victim. He walked through the parking lot towards the garage, head down, phone to his ear waiting for the call to start.

He'd got inside and up to Alex's room way too easily. Notable absence of any police stood out in his mind. Had somebody already put a call in to the watch commander? He'd seen The Godfather too many times to expect that hospitals were safe places for shooting victims.

Just calling the cops would result in nothing, especially if their absence resulted from a phone call by somebody working for Kimball or Heidrick. But a response to a dangerous criminal threat, including gunfire, would get the attention of too many people for it to get covered up or ignored, at least for a while. He stopped walking near a grassy strip next to the parking garage.

"This is nine-one-one. What is the location of your emergency?" The 911 phone lines were busy. It had taken two minutes for them to pick up.

"Hey, I'm at Alexandria General. They got this patient here, Alexis Jones. The guy who shot her, he's here. I think he's going after her again. I seen him in the parking lot," said Stone. He hoped his faked Brooklyn accent would pass, at least over the phone.

"What is your phone number?"

"Hey! Hurry, the guy—he's got a gun!"

Stone pulled his P-226 out and fired three rounds into the grass, then another two, hanging up just as he fired the last shot. He holstered the pistol, then stepped inside the parking garage as a hospital security car sped around the corner.

He heard the sirens just as he got into his car. By the time he turned out of the parking garage he saw the police cruisers, lights flashing, race to the emergency entrance at the same time as a black Suburban slowly drove away.

— WASHINGTON, DC

Locked in morning rush hour traffic, just where it backed up on Minnesota Avenue SE, Stone inched his car up to a smoky old pickup truck with a Maryland license plate. The truck bed brimmed with old lumber, a battered wooden chair and remnants of a plastic table. At the Pennsylvania Avenue intersection, Stone waited until the light turned green, then dialed a 900 number on his phone and tossed it under the plastic table in the truck bed.

In the stop and go of the morning crowds of cars, he let the old pickup move ahead of him. The fat hairy guy driving it didn't bother to use his signals as he turned onto Pennsylvania Avenue, into the lanes for the onramp to northbound Anacostia Freeway. Stone turned right onto Pennsylvania, losing sight of the old pickup in his rearview mirror.

He checked the cell phone he'd bought at the liquor store, which still needed another half hour before it reached full charge. Earlier that morning he saw that Clancy had sent him an email. He'd read it later. Nothing more Clancy could do for them now.

— DIRECTOR'S OFFICE, RSA

Swapping bullets with Stone the previous night just pissed him right off. This was his ground and Stone walked right in without anybody thinking to stop him. Which was mostly because Stone worked there and nobody had announced that he had just turned into a target. As Kimball walked out of the elevator, cell phone to his ear, he waited for Jaeger to pick up his call. Jaeger didn't like early mornings but since Kimball had only slept three hours he just didn't give a crap. The sun had barely risen over the horizon when he stepped into his office.

"I'm at security. On my way up," said Jaeger.

"You're almost late," said Kimball, into his phone. At least Jaeger had enough sense not to sleep in after missing two targets in one night. "Get your ass in here—"

Kimball stopped and turned around as his office door clicked shut.

"Good morning," said Clancy. He sat on the couch by the

door, holding his Beretta. "Hands."

Kimball put the cell phone down on the desk without hanging up and showed his hands.

"Gun and everything," said Kimball. He spoke loudly, hopefully loud enough for Jaeger to hear over the cell phone. "Clancy, I believed you were smarter than this. I am disappointed."

"Makes two of us."

"You tell Stone?"

"Our own people," said Clancy. He sounded tired. He'd sleep after he made Kimball fix this mess and he didn't care if it was in a jail bed. "Milo, Alex, Stone. Even Cain. This isn't us. Rescind the orders."

"That isn't how it works."

"It is now. I'll want to see confirmations from DOJ." Clancy waved the Beretta at Kimball. "Otherwise nothing'll work out for any of us."

Kimball sat down. He looked at his phone and saw a blank display. Jaeger had hung up.

Kimball started typing. "Put it down, Clancy. This does not end well."

"I don't care. I'm done."

Kimball heard the cardkey slice through the reader and saw the doorknob turning.

Clancy turned to the door as Kimball said, "Yes. You are."

The door swung open and Jaeger stood in the doorway, pistol in hand, with two security guards behind him. The door hung silently between Jaeger and Clancy, motionless for a brief moment before it wanted to swing shut. Kimball locked eyes with Jaeger then turned and looked at Clancy. Jaeger nodded, then quickly turned to the door and started shooting through the heavy wood. Clancy started firing as Jaeger's first bullet splintered through the door and struck the American flag standing in the corner. Splinters and dust filled the air as hollowpoints shattered the door and walls. Jaeger took a step back as three rounds hit him. Clancy didn't notice the bleeding until after the third bullet hit him in the chest. He stared at the Beretta's slide as it locked back and dabbed at the blood on his shirt with his other hand. He stared at his hand as Jaeger's last bullet punched through the door and knocked the

American flag onto the floor. Clancy slumped over, his pistol dropping to the ground, followed by a drizzle of thick blood from his mouth.

Jaeger dropped his magazine and loaded another when Kimball said, "Cease fire, cease fire! God damn it! Get the medics."

Jaeger moved around the door and saw Clancy, unmoving. He holstered his pistol and peeled squashed hollowpoints off his body armor. He'd have big bruises within the hour, if not a broken rib or two.

"Damn it." Kimball walked over to Clancy and knelt beside him.

Clancy's eyes opened halfway. His voice a whisper, he said, "How—how'd we get like this?"

"I do not know," said Kimball.

Clancy exhaled and did not take another breath.

Kimball stood up and turned to Jaeger, angry because the man who just saved his life just killed his friend.

"I'm okay," said Jaeger.

"So what," said Kimball. "Get to work."

— JEFFERSON DAVIS HIGHWAY

"Get onto the 695," said Barrett. He looked out his window at the tall buildings bordering the highway, pleased that he picked up the GPS signal. He watched the dot labelled 'Stone D' on the display as it moved onto the Anacostia Freeway across the river. "He's moving northbound on 295. He was probably hanging out in his old neighborhood. Wonder why they didn't pick him up."

Kimball had assigned one of the B teams to stake out Stone's neighborhood. Most of them still rookies, they would be able to recognize Stone if he showed up at any of the obvious places, like at the room he rented.

"Because he wasn't there. He's not stupid," said Jaeger. He accelerated out of the intersection and cut across onto the onramp. It would take at least an hour to catch up to Stone with morning traffic bunching up. But as long as that phone stayed on, they'd find him, no matter how stupid or smart he was.

— LABORATORIO DE ESTUDIOS GENÉTICA HUMANOS

Their presentation ended and Gidden waited for the associate scientists to leave his office before saying anything.

As the door closed, he waited a moment, then said, "Your adoption of CRISPR is coming along nicely, isn't it."

"Yes, thanks to the extraordinary effort of our staff. We also conferred at length with Dr. Ma and Dr. Pande about implementation and their contributions proved quite helpful," said Perez. "Of course, we mentioned nothing to them about GreenSeed."

"Of course," said Gidden. He had written several early papers about some of the precursor science for CRISPR, a technology to make precise permanent changes to the genomes of living cells. Ma and Pande, both capable scientists, had reviewed many of his papers and both could certainly help guide a lab about how to integrate CRISPR into their genomics programs.

"Do you have questions about our deployment?" asked Perez, after a silence.

"Permit me to speak directly. Your science is fine," said Gidden. "Your experimentation is not."

Perez leaned back in his chair. "Oh?"

"There is so little of it. Your team is moving far too quickly to clinical implementation. I don't believe they understand what they are getting into."

"And what is that?"

"Gunther, you are not working with a zebrafish or some newly found strain of archaea. The DNA transduction techniques you propose are too new—unproven—for clinical use. You have no data to support such implementations for GreenSeed."

"It may seem that way. We do things differently here than in the US."

"You are doing things differently than in any research institution anywhere in the world," said Gidden, quietly. "We made mistakes in the early years of GreenSeed, some of them quite terrible. I don't wish to see them repeated here."

"We must take a more aggressive approach than perhaps you are used to," said Perez. "Are there risks? Of course. But we are willing to pay the price if we can accelerate the GreenSeed timelines. Albert, it is possible we can cut years off each subject's maturation cycle. Is this not worth the risk?"

"It is not you who pay the price for a failure, is it? Certainly not the kinds of failures that we—that I had at the beginning of GreenSeed. You must understand—"

"I understand quite well!" More quietly, Perez said, "Yes, I do understand your position. I might say the same things if I were you. You had little success with your GreenSeed Gen two clinicals and you blame this on inadequate pre-clinical experimentation. I disagree. You could have discovered the faults in the technique only by doing what you did in the clinical phase. You judge your own work far too harshly."

"We have had to terminate all of the GreenSeeds."

Perez nodded. He knew the history of the Gidden's GreenSeed program in Arlington.

"It is most unfortunate. But you could only know the result of the mutations by observing the subjects' behaviors. No experiments would have warned that technique caused the mutations or that these mutations caused undesirable behaviors," said Perez. He walked to the window and stared at the new buildings across the courtyard. "Your first subject was normal but your yield was very low. You changed your technique and your yield increased but it induced harmful mutations so you changed your technique back. Your next subjects were normal but your yield was very low again. You must change as the data change."

Gidden remembered each subject of each of the three GreenSeed generations. He lost the first 47 embryos of Gen 1, and then Martha Stone delivered the first live subject. Duncan Stone's genome tested negative for harmful mutations and for the genetic disease proteins that would have killed him by the age of 18 months. But a success rate of one in 48 was not acceptable given the money expended, as Senator Heidrick often reminded him. He altered the GreenSeed technique to increase yield and, to satisfy Senator Heidrick's demands for faster results, cut back the pre-clinical experiments. To his relief, the next Gen 1 subject was also successful and he decided to use that same technique for Gen 2, ignoring unforeseen changes in Elias Cain's genome that he hoped would prove insignificant. He closed the Gen 2 series after six successes and only 12 failed embryos. As he planned Gen 3, his post-natal genome testing of the Gen 2 subjects revealed mutations in the CDH13, ADRA2b, and MAOA genes, the same as he'd observed in Cain's genome. He didn't know what, if anything, would happen as a result of the mutations but, ignoring Senator Heidrick's requests for more GreenSeeds, he changed the technique back. Only three out of 31 Gen 3 embryos survived. Although post-natal testing showed negative for harmful mutations and genetic disease for the Gen 3 subjects, he stopped GreenSeed clinical implementations in Arlington when he started suspecting the consequences of the genetic mutations in Cain's genome and dedicated his research to developing a new, safer technique.

"We must move ahead, we must learn, and we must continue to move ahead," said Perez. "Failure is a necessary part of success."

"Not in a clinical program. Not with human subjects. We were not willing to accept that. What was done was done, but we cannot accept propagating risk to more subjects."

"The question is what you are willing to accept then, is it not," said Perez. He turned away from the window and faced Gidden. "We are willing to accept more, perhaps, than you."

At Heidrick's insistence, Gidden had allowed GreenSeed to continue in Dr. Perez's Laboratorio, which delivered very good success and high yields with their continuing modifications to the Gen 3 technique and ever-improving genetic editing tools. Tampico grew while Arlington languished.

"You saw our early results," said Perez. "We had some failures and we quickly terminated them. It was not pleasant, but it was expected and, for us, it was acceptable. In return, we have shown many, many successes."

"I only encourage you to take time to study potential outcomes before moving to clinical phase," said Gidden. He now understood who ran GreenSeed and it was not its discoverer. Perez had done him the courtesy of listening to him, and would proceed with his GreenSeed program as if he hadn't. Scientific capability had again surpassed the wisdom with which it is employed.

"More time." Perez smiled at nothing funny. "Yes, that would be a welcome luxury. But I am reminded, often, that more time is the one thing I do not have."

— L STREET NW, WASHINGTON, DC

Stone had angled the passenger side rear view mirror so he could see people approaching from the rear, then got into the back seat. Heidrick had a nice limo. Bar, complete with ice. Remote control television. A bunch of switches that probably controlled traffic lights. The driver remained in his seat, not that anybody outside could see through the tinted windows, and even if they could, they wouldn't see the duct tape connecting both his wrists to the bottom of the steering wheel. They might notice the tan colored tape covering his mouth, which Stone had applied just after tasing him. Inducing compliance usually proved easy with 50,000 volts.

Heidrick's keynote speech to some local food bank lunch fundraiser must have run late. Rich people paid plenty for box lunches just to hear Heidrick talk about food bank assistance for inner city families. And to get a photo posing with one of the most powerful politicians in the country. And, of course, the charitable deduction.

Stone saw Heidrick walk through the convention center's large glass double doors, towards the limo. As he got closer, Stone saw his irritation, probably because the driver had not emerged to open the door for him. Or maybe Heidrick just walked around pissed off all the time. Stone slid across the leather seats to make room as the door opened.

"Damn it—" Heidrick stopped in mid-sentence when he saw Stone, who gestured at the still-open door with the P-226, silencer attached.

"Inside, please. Close the door," said Stone.

Heidrick got in and gently closed the door, immediately recovering from the surprise of seeing somebody only vaguely familiar occupying his limousine. And pointing a pistol at him. He looked at the back of the driver's head. "What happened to my driver?"

"Napping. I'd talk to him about that. Can you raise the partition?"

"That depends on why you—"

"Raise the damn partition. Lock the doors."

Heidrick flipped switches on the console. The locks clacked

and the dark glass partition hummed into place. His finger lingered over the console, until Stone nudged him with the muzzle of the silencer. Heidrick then recognized the man with the gun, feeling like he'd known him since he was a kid. He'd last seen his file when Staff Sergeant Duncan Stone's discharge papers appeared on his desk. That was when he told Kimball to get Stone on the RSA team ASAP. After Cain had his mad minute in Nangarhar, he and Gidden determined to keep both their Gen 1 GreenSeeds under close supervision. Who knew what Elias Cain or Duncan Stone might do when suddenly deprived of the military structure and order they'd known for all their adult lives?

They might want to point a pistol at a sitting US senator.

"Kimball's team. Duncan Stone," said Heidrick. "What can I do for you?"

"Well now Senator, it's nice of you to ask. There's actually quite a bit you can do."

"Some things are simple, other things aren't."

"Murder's simple, probably like lots of things when you get elected," said Stone.

"I'm afraid I don't understand what you mean."

"Yeah, you do," said Stone. "Lie to me again, I'll hurt you. Here's the deal. You're going to fix some things and I'm going to let you keep being a living US senator."

Heidrick sat still, then smiled. A well-practiced reflex for all elected officials when caught in a lie. "Would you like a drink? You have a gun, I have a bar. Bourbon?"

"GreenSeed. You authorized the retirements. Call Kimball off."

The liar's smile vanished and Heidrick's hand hesitated as he reached to open the bar. Heidrick's smile quickly returned and he grabbed a tumbler and the bourbon.

"What do you think you're doing?" asked Stone.

Heidrick filled his tumbler.

"Anything I want. Mr. Stone, you want to talk about GreenSeed. We thought it was something good until it turned into something bad. You want to fix things, that's something we had to fix and there's a price to be paid. It's unfortunate. It's regrettable," said Heidrick. He stopped smiling. These people had no idea. They'd never heard about Dr. Kligman and his human experiments with dioxins at Holmesburg Prison. Or Dr. Saenger's lethal whole body radiation experiments in Cincinnati. Or Sonoma State Hospital's experiments on those retards. Or Tuskegee, or Guatemala City, or Avon Park, or St. George and the nuclear bomb test fallout. Or all the other human experiments in the US, most of which weren't public yet and might never be. "But it's nothing. Lots more people had it worse than this. It's nothing."

"How do you figure murder's nothing?"

"Murder? No. Sometimes little people have to take a hit for the team, for the greater good. For the good of the country." Heidrick took a sip. "Here's a little secret. We take care of the little people. We protect this country and we keep this country going. We are the government and we do what needs to be done and none of you have any idea of what that really means."

It sounded like a bizarro world election commercial. Stone wanted to laugh. And shoot Heidrick in the face. "Yeah. You're from the government and you're here to help. How the hell do you even know what the greater good even is?"

"You tell me. You picked us. You elected this government. We do what you ask us to do. The deal is we let you sleep at night, keep some nickels in your pocket, maybe even get pork chops at Sunday dinner, but you damn well better jump when we holler. Little people do what we tell you and sometimes it's going to hurt. It's your government at your service. You can thank me later."

Stone tapped the silencer against Heidrick's temple. "How about I thank you now?"

"That supposed to scare me?"

"Call Kimball off. We walk away, you walk away," said Stone. He saw Heidrick smile, then shake his head, as if pitying somebody too dumb to know he was a dead man who still happened to have a pulse.

"Mr. Stone, I worked Khe Sanh, Cambodia, Santiago. Places you don't even know about. I've been shot by guys one hell of a lot tougher than you."

"I don't care. Neither does this gun."

"You won't use it. You still think you're one of the good guys."

"You still think that's why I won't shoot."

"There's too many of us. If it's not me, it's somebody else." Heidrick tossed back the bourbon and smiled and shook his head and pitied this little man and all the little people, not for their lot in life but for their hypocrisy and naiveté. "We are the government of the United States. How do you imagine somebody like you can change a God damned thing?"

The government of the United States.

Stone looked out the window at the crowds walking on the sidewalk. How had this ever seemed a good idea? Heidrick wouldn't call Kimball off. Even if he did, how would he know Kimball would stay called off. And even if he killed Heidrick there would be another senator or congressman to take his place. He should have known more people than just Heidrick had their hands in this. In everything. Government at your service.

Heidrick faced Stone. After a moment he pushed the gun away with his finger. "Sure you won't have that drink? Or shoot. I'm running late."

Heidrick refilled the tumbler and pressed a button on the console. A red light next to it flashed.

"You have about forty seconds. Is there anything else?" asked Heidrick.

Stone looked out the rear window and saw a black sedan speed around the corner onto L Street. He could easily shoot Heidrick and get into the crowds before it pulled up behind them—Stone guessed it contained two Homeland Security agents who probably had no idea what to do once they arrived. Either Heidrick had more balls than the NFL or he just didn't care whether he lived or died. He moved the pistol back to Heidrick's head.

"Then we're done," said Stone. Shooting Heidrick wouldn't fix anything but it would make him feel a lot better.

Or not. Killing an unarmed sitting US senator, especially without orders, had never been made a part of his training. His finger did not push against the trigger and the pistol did not shoot a bullet into Heidrick's head.

Stone stuffed the pistol under his windbreaker and opened the door. He stepped into the street just as the crowd from the fundraiser stepped into the crosswalk. Then he turned back to Heidrick. It occurred to him that Heidrick might not care whether he lived or died but he probably did care about getting re-elected. And about not going to jail for ordering the murders of US citizens to cover up GreenSeed. And maybe that would get them safe.

"GreenSeed, Senator. I have the data. Everybody's going to know."

Heidrick hesitated, then laughed. "Who would believe you?"

Stone hesitated, then slammed the door and joined the crowd as the sedan pulled up behind Heidrick's limo. He waved at the two men inside. In two minutes he'd be wearing a hat and a different jacket and sitting in a Green Line train to somewhere else.

The agents from the sedan tapped on Heidrick's door. Heidrick unlocked the doors and pointed at the driver's seat. He had two phone calls to make that couldn't wait. He decided to call Jepson at NSA after he calmed down, since he'd need to collect his thoughts in order to properly explain exactly what files he needed NSA to find.

Heidrick dialed Kimball's number and tossed back his bourbon, calmly waiting until Kimball answered, while the agents untaped his driver from the steering wheel and called for another limo.

"I just had an unscheduled meeting with Duncan Stone." Heidrick spoke quietly—loud histrionics and cursing never sounded intimidating over a phone. "Kimball, listen carefully. You handle this now and you handle it right. I don't expect to have another conversation with you about this."

He put the phone down and poured another shot of bourbon. Even though it now presented the biggest threat to his office and possibly his freedom, he'd never regretted approving GreenSeed. It wasn't like he was the first to ever authorize trying to improve the genetic quality of humans. And given the state of all the little people, a quality improvement was certainly wanting. They'd known it a century earlier. Heidrick remembered studying the Buck v. Bell case in law school—as Oliver Wendell Holmes most eloquently stated in the Supreme Court's 8-1 decision: "Three generations of imbeciles is enough." Over 60,000 women had undergone compulsory sterilization as a matter of law in 30 states starting in 1907, including Carrie Buck in the Commonwealth of Virginia. That was one way to improve the population. Fix it so retards and other undesirables couldn't breed. Heidrick remembered the case when he authorized funding for the Center for Human Sciences and hired Gidden. If everything worked out, GreenSeed would be something good for the little people, and, even though he probably wouldn't live to see it, something that would be good for government.

But now it had just turned into a raging shitstorm that would drown them all unless he did something about it. Heidrick tossed back the bourbon and put the glass down, then dialed the personal cell phone number of NSA Assistant Deputy Director Jepson.

— HIGHWAY 3, MARYLAND

Four hours in traffic. Another hour shaking down a nasty drunk fat guy. And nothing.

Jaeger watched the old pickup loaded with crap drive off. A fat hand at the end of a fat arm emerged from the driver's side window and extended its fat middle finger.

They'd tracked the phone in the truck bed and finally caught up with the truck at a rest stop. They'd flashed badges and shook the fat guy down, only to learn he'd gotten lost because of the cheap gin he'd drunk for breakfast. He had no idea there was a phone in his truck bed, but then seeing it, wanted it and got nasty when they wouldn't let him have it. Jaeger grabbed the phone, gave the fat guy a twenty and told him to shove it up his ass.

He pulled out his phone and called Kimball.

"It wasn't him," said Jaeger.

"It's luck. His is good and yours is bad," said Kimball. "Forget about looking for Stone. Find the kid. You find the kid, you find Stone."

— ORCHARD STREET

Finding a crappy neighborhood in Baltimore wasn't hard and Orchard Street, a few blocks north of Lexington Market, would do. Stone didn't worry about running into any of Kimball's people since nothing in any federal database would indicate he'd ever come here. For good reason. He'd picked it at random and it made burned out parts of Detroit look hospitable.

He couldn't go back to his apartment—Kimball would have eyes all over it, just like Alex's boat, her apartment, the marina,

Milo's school, anywhere any of them had ever been. Stone had called Clancy from a pay phone in a gas station just after leaving the factory. No answer. He waited and called again. No answer, again, and he wondered what Clancy was up to.

Stone felt disconnected from everything and he had the strange sensation that 'future' was a term that might not apply to him for much longer. After leaving the gas station he drove to Fairfax and pulled his paycheck out of an ATM, stuffing the twenties in his pocket. Just before dawn he arrived in Baltimore and parked the car on the street in the Ellwood Park neighborhood. He left the car keys on the dashboard and guessed a half hour would see it in possession of somebody else.

Two blocks away, Stone saw his new ride parked in an alley lined by garbage cans, graffiti, and barbed wire. The weather-beaten Chevy Impala probably once belonged to somebody in the suburbs, but as rust and miles accumulated, it got sold and re-sold, finally winding up in the inner city, its last stop before the scrap yard. After swapping license plates, Stone drove it to the Medical Center parking garage on Martin Luther King Jr. Blvd and parked near the shiny Beamers and Benz's in the Physicians' Parking area. If anybody had to pick a car to break into, it wouldn't be the rusty Impala.

Walking away from the Medical Center, Stone passed steel grates defending ground floor windows and doors of apartment buildings, liquor stores, pawn shops, and a couple of sordid strip joints that nobody would mistake for gentlemen's clubs. Aromas floating out of small, greasy restaurants smelled delicious and belied their grubby storefronts. He kept walking till he found a dark brick building off Orchard Street with a dirty sign advertising rooms for rent. The place smelled of cigarettes, sweat and bleach and the old guy behind the bulletproof glass didn't like being awakened. He grunted at Stone only after re-lighting a cigarette butt and sucking down a lungful of smoke. Resentment faded as he snatched up Stone's twenty-dollar bills and shoved a key under the thick glass barrier, probably wondering why a young white guy rented a room for a week and not an hour.

Stone walked up the creaking stairs, doubting he'd stay long. He just needed space to figure out what to do and maybe get some rest. He tossed his bags on the table and lay down on the bed, neither inspecting nor caring about the cleanliness of the bed covers. The last 24 hours had shorted him on sleep, and exhaustion saturated his bones.

Kimball wouldn't find him here. At least not if he left before a drone or a traffic camera or a cop's dash cam picked him up on the street. He had a good two days, maybe three, with a little luck. Stone wanted to keep his eyes closed for at least one of those days. Sleep sounded good but sure as hell Kimball wasn't getting any. And if Kimball wasn't, neither was Jaeger, or Barrett or any of the other operators who by now had new orders with Stone's name on them. Stone wondered how long Alex had till Kimball figured out a way to pull the police detail out of the hospital, and how long Milo had till Jaeger found him. The kid wouldn't know to stay the hell away from wherever he'd ever been.

Stone opened his eyes. He might have two or three days but Alex and Milo didn't. They were just hours away from a dirt hole somewhere in the Alleghenies.

It wouldn't be the first time he'd made sleep wait.

— JONES POINT PARK

He walked through the trees, avoiding the paths and trails. Stone could see well enough in the evening's darkness and had trained in enough environments to move silently, whether on smooth pavement or through thick leaves. He remembered this park as one of the locations in Milo's file. Jones Point Park covered several acres south of Old Town Alexandria and Milo could be anywhere. Or nowhere.

Under the bridge, among the massive concrete pylons? He'd have to take his chances with the junkies who camped there between fixes. Even with all the information contained in the retirement files, sometimes they could use more detail. Stone crossed Jones Point Drive and walked under the Woodrow Wilson Memorial Bridge. He strolled around the massive bridge supports and saw there wasn't much to hide behind. When he walked out from under the bridge he looked across the playing field and saw the lighthouse.

No sign of Milo. Stone walked south, through the woods on

the east side of the playing field to the lighthouse. Ignoring the notices that said it was closed to the public, he tried the door on the newly rebuilt porch and found it was open. He waited for a few minutes, listening.

The evening wind gently nudged pre-autumn leaves across the grass. He heard the big semi-tractor diesels and small motorcycle gas engines on the bridge, and the hum of boats motoring out of Hunting Creek into the Potomac. Nothing that would suggest anybody nearby. He walked around the lighthouse and the shed, both looking prim and well-kept now that they'd completed the exterior repairs and reconstruction.

Flashlight in one hand, pistol in the other, he ducked his head inside the lighthouse. Not a sound, nobody there. He played the flashlight across the room. Apparently the reconstruction hadn't included the interior of the lighthouse. Bare wood planks on the floor and nothing to suggest habitability. For being 160 years old, Stone guessed it looked okay. He checked each of the four rooms and found a similar state of disrepair, but the front room facing the Potomac contained more than only spider webs and dust. He found two blankets in the corner, and two grocery bags, one filled with empty soda cans. The other contained empty bags of chips and not just the ordinary kind. These were made from three different kinds of potatoes and lightly dusted with truffles and sea salt and a blend of organic European herbs. Stone checked one of the empty cans and found remnants of wet soda on the rim. Somebody parked their ass here recently.

He flicked off the flashlight when he heard footsteps, first on the gravel path outside and then thumping up the porch steps. Stone flattened himself against a wall and waited. By the sound of the heavy footsteps, this was somebody who didn't know how to move quietly or didn't care. He waited until that somebody walked to the opposite side of the room before turning on the flashlight.

Milo turned around and squinted as Stone flashed the beam into his eyes. He carried a plastic grocery bag.

"Who's that?" asked Milo.

Stone aimed the beam up onto his face for a moment, then turned off the flashlight. "Anybody with you?"

"No." It took a moment for Milo to recognize Stone. "How did you know—"

"Anybody outside?"

"No. There's usually nobody around at night," said Milo. "Do you know—have you seen my Mom?"

"She's in the hospital. She's okay," said Stone. "What is this place?"

"It's just someplace. Like for when—what's it to you?" Irritation replaced fear in his voice. Milo put down the grocery bag.

Stone wondered how often he'd sounded like a belligerent prick when he was a kid.

Maybe Milo came to this place to get away from people when they weren't nice to him. Probably because of the belligerent prick thing.

"How did you get in?" asked Stone.

"They had a crappy lock on the door."

"Let's go."

"I want to see my Mom now," said Milo.

"Well, you can't see your Mom now. Come on."

"No."

"It's not a request. Move out." Stone started walking out of the room.

"Hey, you can't tell me what to do."

Stone turned back to Milo. "You're right. There's bad guys with guns out there, so at your funeral I'll just tell your Mom I couldn't tell you what to do. Probably be a closed casket. Head shots get real messy so you want to take the bullet in the forehead. See you at the morgue."

Milo stared at the floor, then spoke softly. "What about my stuff?"

"Take one bag. Move quietly."

Milo picked up the plastic grocery bag and followed Stone to the door opening onto the porch. Stone cracked it and looked outside, waiting for a few moments.

"Why are you doing this? You don't have to help us," said Milo.

Stone kept looking outside, then turned to Milo. "Actually kid, yeah, I do." He pushed the door open and stepped outside, listening. He heard nothing but wind and traffic.

Stone stepped silently down the porch stairs and, avoiding the gravel path, started walking on the grass towards the trees to his left. He heard Milo thump down the stairs then step on a twig. He wondered if boaters on the Potomac heard it snap. A herd of goats in heat would be quieter. He grabbed Milo's arm.

"Quietly, please" said Stone. "Like you're walking on eggs."

They walked under the cover of the trees, the Potomac on one side and a walking path on the other. Between the evening darkness and the underbrush they'd stay out of sight of anybody more than 10 meters away, at least until they had to cross under the bridge. If Jaeger's team figured out where Milo was, that's where they'd wait for them. They'd wait behind the bridge supports or in a shooting position in the bridge understructure. He and Milo would take the long way by walking along Mt. Vernon Trail, then taking the Parkway overpass across the freeway, and then walking on Church Street to the car parked near the school. Longer, but safer.

Stone stopped and held up a hand. He heard Milo stop behind him. He pointed to the ground and kneeled. He listened.

Wind. Traffic.

Footsteps.

"That old lighthouse is the only place around," said Barrett. He walked less than 10 meters from Stone and Milo, on the paved path that edged the trees. "Unless he's camping."

Stone couldn't see who accompanied Barrett, but he heard at least three sets of footsteps. He looked back at Milo and put his finger to his lips.

"We just stay on this path, we run right into it."

"Woltz, through the trees," said Jaeger. He pointed towards the bridge. "Barrett, on the field. Go."

Stone heard Woltz walk softly on dry leaves under the trees. Woltz moved quickly but carefully and quietly, not more than five meters away from where they kneeled. Stone listened to Milo breathing harder and faster and concluded Milo would soon run. Loudly.

Milo stood up. Stone reached out to him but Milo took a step directly onto a dry branch. Woltz heard the loud crack and stopped walking. He switched on his flashlight, passing the beam across tree trunks, underbrush...flashing across Stone and Milo. Woltz saw their faces for a brief moment as the beam passed off them onto tree trunks. He quickly aimed the beam back where it had flashed across Stone and Milo, just in time to see them running away.

"Hey!" said Woltz. He turned to the path and saw Jaeger running towards him. "Got them!"

"Go, go, go!" said Jaeger. He turned and shouted, motioning follow me. "Barrett!"

Jaeger and Barrett ran parallel to the path, close to where they knew Woltz had seen Stone and Milo. Woltz ran through the trees, hoping to keep up in the darkness.

Stone heard Woltz coming after them and knew Jaeger and Barrett started flanking them. The water was on their left, Woltz was behind them and Jaeger and Barrett were on the path to their right. They could only run forward, towards the bridge. Stone knew that, which meant Jaeger knew that.

Milo tripped over a tree root and stumbled to his knees. Stone grabbed Milo and hauled him to his feet, barely breaking stride. He looked back and saw Woltz's flashlight about 30 meters behind them—Woltz had no need to hide and closed the distance fast. Another minute and he'd start shooting. Woltz knew how to work the smart end of a pistol and Stone worried Milo would take the first bullet.

"Keep running." Stone turned and pulled out his P-226.

He aimed into the dirt and fired three times, then caught up with Milo. He grabbed Milo's arm and they weaved a zig-zag between the trees. He heard voices shouting by the basketball courts under the bridge, then a siren starting in the distance.

Stone heard gunshots behind them. Woltz. Bullets thudded into the tree trunk they'd zagged around. Through the trees in front of them he saw a lighted road, Mt. Vernon Trail, which ran alongside and below the bridge. Two more gunshots. Stone heard the bullets hiss past at eye level. He pushed Milo to the ground and stopped behind a tree. He aimed at the flashlight, then adjusted his aim as it kept moving towards him. Stone shot three times.

The flashlight stopped moving, then fell to the ground. Too bad. Woltz was a good operator. Just not good enough that evening.

Stone grabbed Milo and they ran across the Mt. Vernon trail, under the bridge and across the parking lot. Stone holstered his pistol just before two police cars sped into the parking lot. Stone and Milo headed towards the trees on the north side of Jones Point Drive.

Stone waved at the police cars. One of them skidded to a stop by Stone and Milo. Officer Davis leaned out the window and looked at them. He stared at Milo. Something familiar about the kid? Was he—

"Hey!" said Stone. "We heard gunshots. Somewhere over on the field back there."

"Okay, you and your boy take off," said Officer Davis.

"There's a couple guys running on that path. Big guys. Don't know if they had the guns," said Stone. He pointed behind them, at Jaeger and Barrett, who had just emerged at the other end of the parking lot. "I think that's them."

"Go!" said Officer Davis. "Get out of here!"

Stone watched the police car speed towards the other end of the parking lot, just as Jaeger and Barret faded back into the trees.

"Let's go. Just walk now. Enough running. For a while," said Stone. He looked at Milo, who still carried the grocery bag. "Hey, why are you still carrying that?"

Milo looked down at the bag. "It's got Cokes and some chips."

"Oh, good. For a minute I thought it was something important." Stone didn't think Cokes and some chips, no matter how organic or gourmet, were worth taking a bullet. The kid had a lot to learn and Stone hoped he'd live long enough to study the first lesson.

— KING STREET

They might have had some fun in Old Town Alexandria that night, except they figured they should avoid the men trying to kill them. Milo watched the people on the sidewalks as they moved slowly through the traffic.

"That guy," said Milo, quietly. "Who was shooting at us. Is he, like, dead?"

Stone decided not to answer. If he had a way to get out of the park without shooting Woltz, he would have taken it. He didn't like killing Cain and he liked killing Woltz even less. But when guns came out, Woltz knew he had the same chance of walking away as Stone did. That evening, Stone got to do the walking.

As they inched forward in traffic, Stone glanced at Milo, who stared straight ahead. Killing other people is difficult to explain to teenagers. Only a little older than Milo when he'd enlisted, Stone never thought too hard about it until his first tour in Iraq. It's never so simple as point a gun and pull a trigger, at least not for him. Maybe that's what made him different than Cain and some of those GreenSeed nut cases.

Milo stared at a crowded hamburger joint as they drove past, then started rummaging around in his grocery bag.

"Want a Coke?" asked Milo. He opened a can and offered it to Stone.

"Thanks," said Stone.

Milo opened a can for himself. "Are you, like, some special forces guy?"

"Not anymore." said Stone, though he remembered everything he'd learned from all the Special Operations schools. Sniper school. Jump school. Ranger school. Unconventional warfare. Survival, Evasion, Resistance and Escape. Spec ops taught skills that shaped new instincts to execute missions, kill people, destroy things and survive.

Milo had none of the above.

"Kid, here's what's happening," said Stone. "We got a good chance to get safe, all of us. I do—I did this kind of thing for a living. I can keep us a couple steps ahead of them, but you need to work with me. You listen to me and I can take care of you. Thing is, it's dangerous."

"I'm not scared."

"I know. And that's good," said Stone. "That's real good. Except being scared usually helps you survive when people are trying to kill you."

"Maybe I'm a little scared," said Milo. He stared at the Coke in his hand, relieved that being scared was okay. "Where are we going?"

"We're getting out of town for a while. Until we can get all this fixed."

"But they're trying to kill me."

"They're trying to kill us," said Stone. "We're kind of the

same."

Milo looked at Stone, then said, "We are?"

"Your Mom said she told you about the—that DNA thing."

"Yeah." Milo looked out the window. "She told me. Some weird test tube experiment."

"Not really. Same thing happened to my mother. And me," said Stone. "Guess that makes you and me a little bit special."

Milo watched a group of teenagers, three girls with three boys, walking on the sidewalk. One of them must have told a good joke since they all laughed.

"I'd rather be like, just normal, you know?" Milo kept watching the teenagers. "I don't want to be special."

"There's lots of things we don't want but shit happens," said Stone, a little irritated. Then he remembered that many teenagers have a paranoid belief that everything in the world conspires to keep them from being happy. Although government men with guns kept trying to kill this teenager for the last two days.

It's not paranoid if they're really trying to kill you.

"We're who we are. We just have to deal with it," said Stone.

"Whatever." Milo spoke softly. "Why did she even do it?

"Some weird thing about mothers," said Stone. "They want their kids to be healthy and normal and other crazy shit like that."

They stopped at the red light. A crowd of people crossed in front of them, some hunting for a restaurant, some looking for the next bar, some just enjoying the evening. A young couple walked past, the mother carrying a baby.

"I never knew them, but I had a father and mother and so do you," said Stone. He looked at the mother and her child. She reminded him of Margaret Stone, just as she looked in the only photo he'd ever seen of her. "Sounds like normal to me."

The light turned green and Stone slowly pulled away from the crowd of normal people who went their different ways. "Maybe someday you tell me what it's like to have your mother around. She took a bullet for you."

Milo stayed silent and looked away from Stone, out the window, worried that the man who just saved his life would see tears only as weakness.

They drove past a Mexican fast food place. The smell of tacos wafted into the car.

"You hungry?" asked Stone.

"What?" asked Milo. He looked at the Mexican restaurant. "I guess."

Stone pointed into the back seat, at a grocery sack. "Grab that bag. Let's fix you up some tasty, healthy stuff. Almost organic."

Milo grabbed the bag and opened it. He pulled out a half-empty bag of white bread, sachets of mayonnaise, sugar and taco spice. He held up the spray can of cheese and the bag of bacon bits.

"You mean—like this stuff?" asked Milo.

"Yeah. You spray that cheese on the bread with some mayo, then sprinkle on the sugar and that taco spice, then the bacon," said Stone. His salivary glands started working. "I'll tell you how to do it. You have to get it on nice and even otherwise it might taste funny and—"

"It's okay. I'm really not hungry." Milo put the food back in the bag. "But thanks."

"Okay," said Stone. "You want to fix me up one?"

Milo looked at a Lebanese restaurant as they drove past. Stone turned left onto Union Street, where traffic thinned out. They'd soon leave Old Town behind.

— CONSTITUTION AVENUE, WASHINGTON, DC

Lit up for the evening, Lincoln looked troubled, as if worried about his government of the people, by the people, and for the people.

Sitting in his parked limo, Heidrick turned away from the marble statue and re-filled his tumbler with bourbon, neglecting to offer Guerro anything.

Kimball had failed and there was far too much at stake to allow that to continue. He needed more reliable resources—people who didn't worry about US laws and proper authorizations getting in the way of what should have been a couple of simple, no-frills assassinations.

"Señor Salazar asks me to send his thanks," said Guerro, after a long silence. He placed a thick envelope on the seat between them. It was the first time Guerro had ever met their friend, and neither he nor Salazar knew why he was summoned on such short notice.

Salazar had packed a hundred $100 bills into an envelope together with a thank you card as simple good manners. It was proper to bring something when visiting a friend, especially one who had just warned them about Juarez and saved them and several hundred thousand dollars of crystal meth from capture.

Heidrick looked at the envelope and gave a short laugh. The cash was nickels and pennies compared to campaign contributions. In Spanish, he said, "Keep it."

"Senator—"

"Forget it," said Heidrick. Put a nice suit on a thug, you have a well-dressed thug. These guys only knew how to say thank you with dollars or whores—which usually worked well enough for his colleagues. "Keep waxing Johnny Jihads, everybody's happy."

Heidrick made deals with Salazar's organization of a nature much different from NAFTA. Oversight, political correctness, and accountability requirements made US interdiction efforts directed at Islamist terrorists at the Mexican border largely ineffective. When dozens of illegals cross into Arizona and Texas every night, it didn't take a genius to figure out that's the easiest way into the country. When Heidrick received intel about terrorists coming into the US, like from Syria or Lebanon, he'd call for "a favor." Over the years, Salazar's people got good at finding the gangs who moved terrorists across the border and Salazar would do Heidrick the favor by putting Guerro to work. They would find the terrorists, kill them and scatter their body parts across dry swaths of Chihuahua and Coahuila, well away from the US border without DOJ interfering. And without having to answer all kinds of awkward questions that had nothing to do with national security and everything to do with politics. Which normally Heidrick wouldn't mind if only they were his kind of politics.

Friends did favors for friends. As long as Heidrick got what he wanted, Salazar could do business wherever he wanted, whenever he wanted. Salazar would receive advance warnings of assassination and arrest attempts, including those that agencies like RSA planned. Which sometimes Heidrick would initiate when Salazar's cooperation seemed to wane.

"I'll need you to do something for me," said Heidrick. "Cleaning up a mess."

"Of course. Señor Salazar has instructed me to do whatever we can for our friend. What do you need?"

"Insurance."

It took a moment for Guerro to relate their friend's use of the term, 'insurance', to their specialties of killing people and importing methedrine and young girls. He most likely did not mean the drugs or the girls.

"Ah, yes, of course." Guerro laughed. He and Salazar had never before considered themselves to be in the insurance business. "Where?"

"Get your people here now. Lots of them." Heidrick handed over an envelope. Guerro opened it and found documents to get people quickly past customs and immigration. Heidrick had provided these before.

"Who will be insured?" Guerro smiled, proud to use this new American slang.

"You've met one of them before," said Heidrick. "El Paso."

Guerro stopped smiling. He suppressed the reflex to touch the newer scars on his face. "Of course, we will do this. It will be easy. I was not impressed with him."

"Neither were your guys in El Paso. If I were you, I'd get impressed real soon." Heidrick sipped at his bourbon, resisting the urge to toss it all back. "Bring a crowd."

— ORCHARD STREET

The night air cooled the sidewalks. Stone and Milo walked from the parking garage to Orchard Street, past neon-lit storefronts and restaurants.

Milo slowed as they walked past a strip club, his attention diverted to a girl who lingered by the open door. She displayed ample expanses of skin, advertising the goods and services for sale inside. She was prettier than Stone would have expected, given the likely class of customer on this street.

Stone gave Milo a push from behind before she could do anything but smile and lean over to give the white kid a better view.

"She was, like, really nice looking," said Milo, looking back at the stripper, who gave him a smile and a wave.

"Yes, she was," said Stone. Some things didn't change with each generation, including teenage boys staring at half-naked—in this case mostly-naked—women. "That's a good place to burn lots of cash and catch something that only injections can cure."

Milo kept looking back at the stripper while they walked away. "What kind of injections?"

"The kind that really hurt."

Stone kept Milo moving down the street, until they turned into the apartment building and walked up to the room.

Once they stepped inside, Milo kept standing, wondering if there was a dirt-free surface on which he could sit. "I mean, is this safe?"

Stone drew the frayed curtains closed. He pulled out his pistols and set them on the table, then pulled off his holsters.

"Probably safer than that strip joint," said Stone.

He watched Milo eyeing the pistols and asked, "You ever shoot one before?"

"Not a real one," said Milo. "I mean, on the video games I shoot all kinds of guns. So I kind of know how."

"These might be a little different," said Stone. He picked up the P-226, pulled out the magazine and cycled the round out of the chamber. He handed it to Milo, who held it like it was made of gold.

"It's not as heavy as I thought," said Milo. He stared at the weapon.

Stone pointed out the levers. "This is the slide release. You push this down and it releases the slide, which chambers a round if it's got a loaded magazine inside. This is the decocking lever. It drops the hammer without firing a round."

Milo turned the pistol over, then hefted it. "Where's the safety?"

"No manual safety. If you see a safety on a firearm, never trust it."

"But—"

"This is real stuff, kid. Rule number one. Never point this at anything you don't want to kill. Rule number two. Treat every firearm like it's loaded, because chances are good that it is. Rule number three. Keep your finger off the trigger until you're ready to shoot, because when you pull the trigger, gun goes bang and someone's going to die."

"Are there other rules?" asked Milo.

"Yes," said Stone. "Go ahead, try aiming."

Milo held the pistol with his right hand, aimed it at one of the cracks in the wall, and closed his right eye. Stone put Milo's left hand in place over his right hand, cocked his elbows, and tapped his feet into a modified Weaver Stance.

"Maybe you want to close the other eye instead. It makes aiming a little easier," said Stone.

"Oh. Yeah," said Milo. After a few moments, he handed the pistol to Stone. "That's cool."

"Maybe sometime I'll give you a shooting lesson," said Stone. He sat down in the armchair.

"Really?"

"Just don't shoot anybody before I train you," said Stone. With luck, neither of them would have to shoot anybody anytime soon, but only if their luck changed for the better.

"Thanks, Mr. Stone."

"Sure." Stone saw Milo smile for the first time. "Just Stone. Without the 'mister' part."

"Also, thank you for, like, helping me and my—my Mom and me," said Milo, correcting himself. He sat down on the chair next to the table. "We'll be okay, right?"

"Yeah. We'll be okay."

Milo looked like he didn't quite believe Stone. "What are we going to do?"

"We stay here for a couple days."

Milo looked at the streetlight shining though the seams and ragged holes in the curtain, then back at the pistols. "I didn't even do anything to them."

"It's not anything you did," said Stone. "We just became inconvenient. The government did some things that got screwed up, then they did other things to cover them up. Then those got screwed up and now if anybody finds out, some powerful people will get in trouble. Now they're trying to kill anybody who's part of it. If we're dead we can't tell anybody."

"Maybe we should tell everybody about it now."

"The problem is getting everybody to believe somebody like me, or you, or even your mother. Even if people did believe us, it wouldn't stop them from coming after us."

"Why not?" asked Milo.

"We—they know how to do this. They'd say I'm a killer running from police, that you're lying to protect me, maybe that we're all on drugs. Then we'd disappear and people would maybe ask questions for a couple days and then nothing else would happen."

"Besides Uncle Clancy, who can help?"

"Can help? Lots of people. Will help? Nobody," said Stone. Especially since Kimball had probably already issued warrants for his arrest to all the police departments on the mid-Atlantic coast. He waved at the bed. "You want to get some sleep?"

"I wish I had my computer," said Milo. He leaned back in the chair. He didn't feel like sleeping and wondered if he'd need injections if he touched the bed. "I was going to play IronUprising tonight."

"Some kind of video game?"

"There's people all over who log in and play. It's a totally steamin' game."

"How do you play?" asked Stone.

"You sign in and everybody has their own character. Then you have to fight battles and get stuff to win."

"Are you the good guys?"

"We're the rebels who have to stop the all-powerful coalition from enslaving the citizens. But it's not really a coalition, it's only what they call it because it's really just a dictator with a big army who's fighting all the rebel teams."

"Sounds like the history of the world to me," said Stone. He leaned back in the armchair.

"It's really cool. The graphics are awesome and you have a headset to talk with your team so you can help each other win battles. You get points for each battle you win, and you can buy or trade stuff, like health or ammunition or guns or secrets to the dictator's fortress so you can win more battles. Whoever overthrows the dictator wins the game."

"Then what happens?"

"Then it's finished. You buy a new game and start all over."

"That's a pretty good racket if you're selling the games," said Stone. He closed his eyes. "How do you pick your team?"

"That's why you have a headset. You talk with other players. You find other people for your team and you trade stuff. Sometimes you can get somebody who switches sides from another team."

"Why would somebody switch teams?"

"Sometimes they find out their team is actually fighting for the coalition and so they're not allowed to overthrow the dictator. That means they can't win."

"And that's when they want to switch," said Stone.

"Yeah. It's like you trade stuff to get them on your team. It's really complicated. A lot of trading, a lot of action, and there's a lot of strategy. It's so fun." Milo stared down at the tabletop. "I guess I'll have to wait before I get to play again."

"You'll play again, Milo. Soon," said Stone. It would help to have a team bigger than him and Milo. If only he could find some people that suddenly found out they were actually fighting for the all-powerful coalition. Too bad he didn't have stuff to trade, like health or ammunition or guns or secrets.

Or maybe he did. Stone opened his eyes.

— DIRECTOR'S OFFICE, RSA

"Zulu check-in. Niner tango twelve." Kimball heard the beeps as the system confirmed his codes and voiceprint. He waited while satellites completed their connections and confirmed identities. He watched the display on his office phone and saw "PB16" appear, code for confirmed connection.

"Zulu check-in confirmed," said Manson. "Status, please."

It was good satphone link. Calls to Juarez usually didn't sound this clear.

"Status abort. You and Hargis are recalled priority one, effective now. Do you copy?"

"I copy and confirm," said Manson. "How'd you find out so fast?"

"Find out what?" asked Kimball.

"Luis had a camera dropped inside that warehouse last night. Nothing except for a couple thousand boxes of laundry soap. Cleaned out everything else, like he knew we'd show up. He got lucky again."

"I could use that kind of luck," said Kimball. Every time they launched an op against Salazar he was ready. This time he was ready days before they even arrived. Once is lucky. Three times is very lucky. Five times is not lucky, it's getting information they weren't supposed to have.

"It won't be easy to get Luis onboard again. Our cred's done nothing but shrivel into a little dried up turd ball," said Manson. Meat-eaters want meat and they lose interest when there's none to be had. This was the third mission he'd worked with the *Grupo de Operaciones Tácticas* and the results hadn't changed: Salazar not available for killing. "We out of here today?"

"Grab your last taco, you're coming back home. Biggs Field. You fly out tonight. We have local business and Jaeger needs adult supervision."

Kimball put the phone down. He rubbed his eyes. Nothing had gone right since he didn't remember.

He did remember. Since Stone retired Cain. In another place and at another time Kimball would wonder about whether they hunted the right people. At this place and at this time his current employer didn't allow that luxury. Kimball figured Heidrick had him on a short list of soon-to-be-former federal employees if he didn't execute his mission in a matter of hours, not days. Even as a fresh-out-of-the-academy second lieutenant, he knew mission failure is leadership failure. Time to get the A team onboard, and get eyes on every conceivable place Stone might hide. As much as he didn't like Heidrick, he wouldn't blame him for stringing his ass across all the fence posts in Virginia if success didn't find this mission soon.

— BENSON-PHILIPS FACTORY

Stone estimated the range at 100 meters. The light pole held the surveillance camera 30 meters off the ground, so the bullet would drop by a little over five inches. He leaned against the fence in the brush at the edge of the parking lot, out of sight from the road, and aimed the P-226 through the chain link at the camera. This would be a tough shot on a good day. As the sun peeked over the horizon, he fired and heard a satisfying ping. The camera shuddered and stopped rotating. The lens fell to the ground.

The security company still thought he worked for them so there wouldn't be anybody around—at least anybody who was supposed to be there. He'd waited two hours, watching and listening and seeing nothing. Nobody surveilling the place, except maybe by drone or, more likely, just these cameras. Stone unlocked the gates and drove inside, noting the new "SALE PENDING" stickers on the For Sale signs. He parked in the back next to a rusted pile of scrap metal. He pulled Cain's bag out of the back seat, leaving the neatly wrapped laundry bundle that sat next to it.

Stone walked into the loading area and quickly aimed his pistol at the surveillance camera, shooting it clean off the mount. Kimball eventually would have somebody check the video feeds—he was too good to ignore the obvious just because it was obvious, but Stone figured by the time Kimball learned he'd killed the cameras he'd get everything set up without Kimball knowing anything.

Stone picked up the bag and walked past the forklift and around the power hammers, the press brakes, the lathes, the presses. This place had once hummed with people using machines to create things from steel sheets and pipes and bars. It now sat doing nothing except collecting spider webs and dust, waiting for something to happen. He stopped next to the 500-ton punch press and set the bag down. After making nightly rounds for seven months he didn't need what little daylight passed through the grimy skylights to find his way.

Kimball was the only one who could get Milo, Alex and Stone off the retirement list. He just needed a reason to abort the GreenSeed missions. Something conceptually easy since there were just two targets left—three including Alex. But this meant Kimball needed a reason to disobey orders, which required something drastic, probably approaching the Biblical. Stone could give him that reason but only if Kimball's team didn't shoot him in the head before he could explain.

Maybe he could phone in, but Kimball would just trace the call and talk only long enough to lock his location, and then Stone would start running again. Visiting Kimball at his office? Since their last meeting resulted in doubled-up surveillance and security, he wouldn't get inside the building. Intercepting Kimball at home, on his way to work? That was his ground, way too public, way too hard to attack and way too hard to get away.

Stone needed a meeting on ground that he knew and could stage the way he wanted, to both keep Kimball engaged and himself alive. Stone walked slowly through the wide corridor, looking around the large presses. He looked around the factory floor. It had to be in here. Stone had nothing if this didn't work.

He stopped near a 50-ton cornice press, one of five along the wide central corridor. Not knowing the layout of the factory floor, whoever showed up with Kimball would take the wide corridors since these had good visibility and allowed both maneuvering space and hard cover behind the heavy equipment. Stone opened the bag and pulled out one of the pipe bombs with the remote detonator. He duct-taped the bomb just inside the control panel, so that the blast would shred whoever stood within 20 feet. He did the same to the press at the other end of the corridor.

Stone walked to the back of the factory floor, past the 500-ton punch press and through the wide door leading into the back room that housed the machine shop. No other exits in this room. Anybody coming or going went through this door. He looked around and saw the steel rack over the doorway, now empty. Maybe it once held a ventilator or fan of some kind. He walked out the door, crossing over a long gutter covered by a rusted steel grate that led to a floor drain. Empty metal cabinets flanked the doorway, their doors having long since been re-purposed for something else.

Stone hoped he wouldn't have to use the bombs. But then he'd also hoped being targeted for death was a minor mistake easily fixed.

— DIRECTOR'S OFFICE, RSA

Jaeger stood in front of the desk while Kimball sat in his chair, massaging his forehead and eyeballs.

"Nothing from TSA. If he's moving, he's not using an airline," said Jaeger.

"He doesn't have to use an airline. He can drive. Walk. Or even just not move," said Kimball. NSA made him wait hours the night before patching through their video feeds. Anybody who remotely resembled Stone that any of the thousands of cameras recorded would be profiled and processed over to RSA's consoles. Clancy would have made it happen inside an hour.

Kimball walked to the window, past the bullet holes in the wall and the shot-up American flag. He stared at the early morning sun painting the street. "Maybe he went to Florida. Maybe he's working on his tan because I don't have anybody around who—"

"I did what I what I was supposed to—"

"Please do not speak or do anything stupid for one hour." Kimball stared out the window. Stone was doing a damn good job of protecting the kid. He'd do the same for the mother and himself and probably in that order. Stone had asked who's next just before they tried to shoot each other in the action range. Kimball wondered if Stone knew the mother's retirement orders just came through. He must have taken it into his head that he liked the kid, otherwise he would have finished the mission and Kimball wouldn't have to eat this gigantic shit sandwich by himself. Or maybe Stone wanted to pork the kid's mother, or maybe he got religion when he found out he was next. Or maybe something got into him and he just wanted to do what he thought was right. Naïve, dumb bastard. In their business, doing what's right meant doing your job, which meant following orders.

Kimball watched an ambulance speed past on the streets below. Heart attack, auto accident, fell off the ladder, gunshot, knifing. At this hour it could be anything. Somebody getting the fast ride to some emergency room at the nearest hospital.

The kid's mother was still at Alexandria General. They hadn't found the kid but he'd stick around till his mother was okay. And Stone would stick around to make sure nothing happened to either of them.

Stone and the kid hadn't gone anywhere. They'd wait till the mother got out of the hospital. Certainly she'll meet up with Stone and her kid somewhere. Manson could track her, then they bring in the team to take care of business.

"He's close," said Kimball, to the window. For the first time in days, he saw a shred of a chance at finishing this mission.

"Maybe he—"

"I said do not speak," said Kimball. "I believe I said this out loud."

Hearing a knock, Kimball looked at the splintered door.

"Yeah!" said Kimball. "Come."

A uniformed guard carrying an MP-5 opened the door to let in the Admin, who carried a tied up laundry bundle. He set it on the conference table.

"Courier delivery," said the Admin. "We scanned it. Just clothes."

After the Admin left, Kimball walked over and looked at the bundle. No stranger to dry cleaning, Jaeger recognized that it came from a commercial laundry.

Kimball pulled out a knife and flicked open the blade. He cut the strings and opened the bundle. Stone's dry-cleaned security guard uniform lay in the paper wrapping, his name badge pinned to a note. Jaeger walked over as Kimball opened it: "See you around. Stone"

"Guess he didn't go back to his old job," said Jaeger.

"Jaeger—" Kimball faced Jaeger, then looked back at the uniform in the wrapping paper, at the note in his hand, then back at Jaeger. Kimball had checked the feed from the Benson-Philips factory the day before and the cameras showed the place was empty. And that was yesterday. "That's the first smart thing you've said—ever."

Kimball went to his computer and brought up the NSA video feeds and archives. The console on his display allowed him to look at archived files and real time images from any of tens of thousands of cameras in the country. He selected the archive for the Benson-Philips factory from a week earlier and fast-forwarded until he saw Stone idly driving a six-ton forklift in circles on a dusty floor. Kimball stopped playing the file after he watched Stone park it by the loading door. He remembered watching this just before they'd picked up Stone. Kimball selected the real time video console and selected the live feed from the Benson-Philips parking lot. Nothing. A message indicating 'no connection' appeared. Kimball selected the live feed for the Benson-Philips factory floor. Again, 'no connection'. Yesterday the video feeds worked. Today they didn't.

Kimball sat down. "Time to gun up."

"Stone?" asked Jaeger.

"An invitation," said Kimball. Stone set it up in that factory, on his ground. Maybe Stone knew Kimball had to finish the mission and bet big he'd have to show, but it didn't matter. There was no way Kimball would take a pass. If this went down the way it smelled, anything subtle wouldn't work: they'd use body armor and carbines. Kimball would personally run this op and make sure it got done. And there might even be a chance that it would get done clean and quiet. After retiring Stone, the kid the and mother would be easy. "Level four and five-five-six. Get Manson. We run this tonight."

Kimball dialed his phone. One of Heidrick's aides answered and recognized Kimball's voice.

"Tell the Senator I found him," said Kimball.

— HART SENATE OFFICE BUILDING, WASHINGTON, DC

The voicemail system would automatically forward his instructions and the address of the Benson-Philips factory. Sometime in the next 10 minutes he'd get a call back, if everything worked normally. Heidrick slipped his cell phone in his coat pocket and walked across the atrium, barely glancing at the monumental black sculpture, Mountain And Clouds, that filled it. He'd always thought it looked like a 50-foot high blood-sucking spider and hadn't any idea why Senator Brady went out of his way to raise private money for it. Regardless of whether you liked the result, spending the public's money is what the Senate does. And does very well, particularly when there's lots of commas in the numbers. Heidrick smiled, remembering the quarter trillion dollars of overhead cost that got loaded into that national health plan. Even Dirksen would have been impressed.

Kimball said he found Stone and mentioned a time and place, and the expected result of their impending meeting. Heidrick put even money on whether Kimball would make it out alive. He'd seen really good operators and counted both Kimball and Stone among them. This would be a good fight—but only if Stone and that Gen 3 kid and his mother got retired—and that result was by no means guaranteed.

Heidrick felt his phone vibrate. He answered it and heard Guerro say only, "Your insurance is ready," then hang up. Message sent, another received. Guerro would make sure the result happened. Señor Salazar had sent Guerro and a large contingent of his *soldados*. A favor for a friend, and their deal would continue. Heidrick thought about all the trade legislation crap he'd listened to for days. Those committees could take a lesson from him and Salazar, except for maybe the assassination part: they'd done their deal quickly and without several thousand pages of posturing, hot air, and horse shit.

Before he put his phone away another call came in. He recognized the number: NSA Assistant Deputy Director Jepson. Heidrick walked towards an empty corner of the atrium and held the phone to his ear.

"Have you found anything?" asked Heidrick.

"It took some hunting," said Jepson. "We found it. You'll never guess where."

Having just ordered the murders of three US citizens by Mexican gangsters, he didn't feel like guessing anything. "Jepson. Where?"

"Resolution Support Agency."

"Are you joking?"

"No sir. We had to use the same searchbot we used on the phone company to find it. Some user named Elias buried it behind the RSA firewall in three distributed compressed directories on their cloud server. This guy's good, but not good enough to hide anything from us."

"What's the status of the files?"

"Will you confirm your order?"

"Shred them," said Heidrick.

"Done."

"Jepson, there's going to be a leadership change at RSA. I'll need you to put in a total database lockdown. Midnight shutdown. Close everything till you hear from me."

Heidrick put the phone in his pocket and started walking back to his office. One way or the other, RSA would change within a matter of hours. He'd have to get with the RSA bureaucrats—probably that finance manager, Mills—while everything else ran its course.

A legislative aide from the Economic Policy Committee walked past and waved. Heidrick didn't remember her name but recognized the face. Pretty enough to look pleasant but not enough to entice any of the committee's senators into an affair.

"Good morning, Senator," said the aide. She smiled, nervous and giddy at her proximity to one of the most powerful people on Capitol Hill.

Heidrick waved back and smiled. "Yes, it is."

— ALEXANDRIA GENERAL HOSPITAL

The Charge Nurse hadn't guessed this patient was a VIP. She stapled a copy of the letter to the discharge orders, then handed the letter back to the man in the suit, a very handsome Mr. Pedro Vasquez. His visitor badge matched what the Discharge Planning department had told her earlier.

She walked him into Ms. Jones' room, where her patient sat in a wheelchair, then turned to the police guard at the door. "We're discharging the patient now."

The patient looked tired but antibiotics, painkillers and sedatives do that to people.

"Ms. Jones, it must be nice to have important friends," said the Charge Nurse. She patted her patient on the shoulder. Not everybody had a limousine sent for them by a senator, no less than Senator Heidrick himself. She smiled at Mr. Vasquez. He was tall and good-looking and half the unit's nursing staff found reasons to stand in the hallway, staring at him like sharks eyeing seals. "I'll wheel her down to the lobby with you, Mr. Vasquez."

"Please call me Pedro." Pedro liked dressing in suits and someday hoped he'd trade his guns for neckties permanently. A move up in Salazar's organization would suit him fine.

— ORCHARD STREET

Sometimes SWAT teams moved silently and invisibly, without people noticing. This was not one of those times. Maybe it was just Baltimore or maybe it was just because its SWAT teams were overworked. As he walked down the street, Stone noticed the large unmarked step van pulling into a parking lot long before the crack dealers on the corner did. He saw the undercover cops in each of the three cars parked across from the apartment building and dismissed the possibility they'd arrived for somebody else. What had Kimball put in the warrant to get this kind of attention, and which traffic camera had finally picked him up? He thought he'd get at least another day without getting found. No sign of any RSA teams so Kimball had no idea he was here. Yet.

Stone walked around to the narrow alley leading to the unused back exit of the apartment building, which he'd unlocked the day he'd arrived. He walked inside and quickly up the stairs, then unlocked the door of the room and walked in. Milo sat at the table, a now-empty bag of chips in front of him. Milo had followed Stone's instructions: he'd stayed put, kept the door locked and the curtains closed.

Stone moved the curtain aside and looked down into the street. No movement. Stone hoped Milo could have stayed in the apartment until after he'd had his conversation with Kimball, but if SWAT grabbed him, he'd get turned over to Kimball today and dumped in a hole tomorrow.

"We have to go now," said Stone. He handed the grocery bag to Milo. "Quietly."

He led Milo quickly out of the room, down the back stairs and out the back exit.

Stone saw the man at the end of the alley, where it intersected St. Mary Street, and kept walking towards him. He had undercover all over him. Stone guessed they had about two minutes before SWAT engulfed the apartment building. Both men looked at each other, the undercover cop processing whether or not the man in the alley fit the arrestee's description in the warrant, which made no mention of a kid. Stone waved and smiled. Having Milo with him threw the cop off for the half-second it took for him to get close.

"Hi, I'm Jim Smith. This is my nephew," said Stone. The introduction surprised the cop for a second. "I seen you around here before."

The cop hesitated, then decided Stone looked like somebody he should probably arrest. He pulled out his badge and reached under his shirt. "Baltimore P.D. Hold on—"

Stone head-butted the cop and quickly put his thumb and forefinger over the cop's carotid arteries. It took five seconds for the man to go limp and drop to the ground. Stone kept pressing for another 10 seconds, then dragged him to the wall and sat him up against it. He figured they had one minute left.

Milo stopped walking when he saw the badge and now stood, frozen in place, surprised that Stone had attacked a cop and that it took less than 10 seconds to disable him.

Stone turned to Milo and said, "Let's go."

"Is he—I mean, did you—"

"No, and if we don't get out of here now, he'll let us wear his handcuffs. Just walk like we're on the way to the store," said Stone. They walked to Eutaw Street, then headed north to the Medical Center parking garage.

"Where are we going?" asked Milo.

They turned into the parking garage and started up the stairwell.

"You ever see a factory?"

— BENSON-PHILIPS FACTORY

The parked van waited in the far corner of the parking lot, well away from the closed roll-up door on the side of the factory. Everything looked deserted. Manson sat in the driver's seat and resisted the urge to light a cigarette, just as he had for the last 15 years. His eyes flicked between the factory building and the parking lot entrance.

"Company," said Manson. He saw a Suburban drive through the open gate and rested his hand on his pistol when he saw its headlights.

"Looks like Kimball." Hargis, in the passenger seat, looked through his night vision ocular at the approaching black SUV.

Manson put his phone on speaker when it chimed. "Yeah."

Kimball's voice sounded tinny over the phone's speaker. "It's us, black Suburban. We're pulling up behind you. Finger off the trigger, please."

Manson moved his hand away from his pistol and watched in

his rear view mirror as the Suburban pulled to a stop behind the van. He waited till he saw Kimball exit the back seat, then opened his door.

Kimball walked up to him as Jaeger and Barrett got out and started unloading duffel bags from the back of the Suburban. They left empty body bags inside.

"Anything?" asked Kimball. He looked around the parking lot, saw the shot-up surveillance camera, then looked at the building.

"Nothing in four hours. Anybody's in there, they been there a while. Some old piece of shit car's parked in the back lot. You got hardware?"

"Yeah, Manson. We got hardware." Kimball lit a cigarette. "We even got ammo."

"Orders," said Manson.

Kimball handed over an envelope. Manson pulled out papers and started reading.

"Target, Milo Jones. A kid," said Manson. He turned to Kimball with a look that asked if he needed to know why.

"A future extremely serious problem, who won't be in about an hour," said Kimball. "And Duncan Stone."

"What?" asked Hargis. He'd worked with Stone and liked the guy. And didn't want to trade bullets with him.

"Duncan. Stone," said Kimball. He dropped the cigarette and squashed it with his boot.

Manson quickly leafed through the papers and found Stone's retirement orders. He read through the file.

"Problem?" asked Kimball.

"You going to tell me why?" asked Manson, still reading.

"No."

Manson looked at Hargis for a moment. They both shrugged. Manson nodded at the factory. "Anybody else in there?"

"Maybe. Only we walk out," said Kimball.

"They got anything we should know about?"

"Assume same as what we have. Probably still has his forty-cal, maybe he found a five-five-six somewhere."

"Let's go," said Manson.

Hargis and Manson walked over with Kimball to Jaeger and Barrett. They all put on Level 4 body armor vests and slipped the ceramic plates into the front pockets—the protection against rifle bullets. They buckled on pistol belts. Manson was happy to see plenty of ammunition. When running Viper 20 missions with Kimball he shorted his MREs so he could carry another dozen mags. There was no such thing as a tasty MRE or too much ammo.

Kimball cycled a round into the chamber of his pistol and waited for the others. They'd carry CAR-15s with EOTech red dot optical sights and 20-round mags in addition to sidearms. As per their routine, they took the time to check their weapons, working the bolts and checking the chambers. Jaeger and Barrett seemed pleased. It wasn't often they used carbines, which proved far more accurate than pistols at target distances over 10 meters. Hargis plugged a magazine into his CAR-15 and listened while he chambered a round. He'd done this enough so he could tell by feel if it worked. So could Manson, who found the action on his carbine slightly sticky, nothing anybody who hadn't shot a couple hundred thousand rounds or so would notice.

"You give me a dry weapon?" asked Manson. He opened the receiver and pulled out the bolt.

"Jaeger," said Kimball. Everybody in the world knew the CAR-15 liked lots of oil. Apparently except for Jaeger.

Jaeger tossed a bottle of gun oil to Manson. "Drown it if you want."

Manson squirted oil onto the bolt like barbecue sauce onto ribs. He slid the bolt back in and cycled it, still unhappy. He finally stuffed a magazine in and chambered a round.

"They're zeroed at fifty," said Jaeger. He switched on the EOTech on his CAR-15, as did the others, each looking through the red dot sight. Just like old times.

"We just going to walk in?" asked Manson.

"We were invited," said Kimball.

Manson looked at the steel roll-up door on the side of the building and didn't see any way to open it. "What about the front door?"

"What about it?" replied Kimball.

"You figure it's wired?"

"I think we go hard and fast." Kimball nodded at the roll-up door.

"You bring a key?"

Kimball nodded and started walking towards the building. After a moment so did everybody else. They spread out as they approached the roll-up door.

"Barrett," said Kimball.

Barrett slung his carbine and reached into his satchel. Det cord, detonator—it was a big door but nothing a little Primacord couldn't blow through. He'd tape the det cord in three tight, concentric man-sized rings at the right side of the door. They'd be inside in 90 seconds.

Before he unreeled the det cord the door started slowly rumbling upward. Barrett jumped to the doorframe, out of direct line of fire from inside.

"Key not needed," said Manson. He joined the others by the doorframe and waited till the door fully opened, then glassed the inside with his night-vision ocular. Darkness, nothing moving. He sliced around the corner and crouched inside. Hargis did the same on the other side, looking around with his ocular.

"I got nothing," said Hargis.

Kimball walked inside and stood straight. "Stone!"

Jaeger and Barrett crouched by the forklift.

Silence.

"Stone!"

"Kimball," called Stone, from somewhere inside. "You need to talk to me—"

Jaeger loosed a barrage in an arc around the factory. Ricochets bounced and sparked off heavy steel. Empty brass bounced on the cement floor. He dropped the magazine and reloaded.

Stone felt the sting under where his vest stopped a ricochet bouncing into his back. Too many hard surfaces in this place. Bullets would bounce all night, hopefully not into his skull. He stepped out from behind a large generator. From his dark corner he had a clear line of sight to Kimball, his crew and the wide open roll-up door. They were probably all wearing Level 4 with rifle plates so his .40 caliber pistol wouldn't do anything more than piss them off. Time to even up teams a little. It was way too far for reliable pistol work but he braced himself and aimed the .500 Magnum revolver, then fired five rounds. Each thunderous shot flashed brightly and echoed loudly in the enclosed space.

Hargis dropped his carbine, then fell forward, leaving a bloody mess on the wall behind him. The others had already dropped to one knee, carbines aimed into the darkness.

"Hargis bought it," said Jaeger.

"Kimball," called Stone. He flexed the pain out of his hands, then reloaded the revolver, hoping he wouldn't have to shoot it again. "You really need to talk to me. Stand down."

"One out of five, Stone? You're losing it," called Kimball.

"Was that a yes?" asked Stone.

"You invited me," said Kimball. He waved at Jaeger and pointed towards a corner of the factory floor—go left—then waved at Barrett—go right. They maneuvered down the corridors, past large equipment, looking for a target. "So talk."

"You really do want to listen." Stone heard men moving and stepped quietly to the breaker panel and opened the box. As he closed the main breakers, he heard the hum and whine and hiss of motors and hydraulics of metal presses and mills starting up. Two dusty incandescent bulbs high overhead flickered on, replacing the total darkness with a simmering dusk. Several presses and mills started cycling automatically, stamping pointlessly on nothing just because they were set that way when their operators, pink slips in hand, left for the last time.

As the heavy equipment buzzed and bashed, Manson looked at Kimball, who waved at him—move out, straight ahead.

"I'm giving you a chance to walk away," said Stone.

"Sure you are. In case you didn't notice, you are right next to being dead," said Kimball. He stood briefly and saw Jaeger and Barrett, who both signaled they couldn't locate Stone. He waved at them—keep moving. "Where's the kid?"

Stone knew the inside of the factory floor better than he knew his two room apartment. He looked down his sight lines and listened through the din of the presses and mills. Something—somebody close by moved. Stone stopped breathing for a moment and listened for footsteps or a brief irregularity in the sounds of heavy equipment reaching his ears. Stone looked, saw maybe a shadow moving past the 200-ton presses. Maybe nothing. He looked down the corridor at a 50-ton cornice press and saw a glimmer—light from the overhead bulbs reflecting faintly off a shiny metal surface. None of the factory's equipment had any kind of shine to it. Too far for pistol work, and Stone pulled out the detonator for the pipe bomb he'd taped to the press and pushed the button.

Nothing. He should have checked the detonators' batteries. He'd have to use the old fashioned way.

Stone aimed the revolver at the glimmer and fired twice. Bright flashes lit up the interior of the factory and the roar of the gunshots reverberated. In the flash of the second shot he saw Barrett fall backwards as the .500 Magnum slugs blew out his chest cavity.

Ricochets pinged all around Stone and he looked at his left arm when he felt a sting. A ricochet hit his bicep. It probably had bounced off a couple hard surfaces and lost most of its energy before ripping through his sleeve and cutting across the skin.

"Kimball! You're starting to piss me off!" said Stone. He listened for a response that didn't come.

Kimball hand-signaled to Manson and Jaeger—keep moving…cover fire.

As Manson let loose controlled three-round bursts, Jaeger sprayed bullets in front of him. Stone kept his head down and peered between the equipment. He watched Kimball sprint across the factory floor, heading towards a press to which he'd earlier taped a remote controlled pipe bomb. Kimball would flank him and in a matter of seconds he'd get caught between three guns. Stone reached for the detonator and flipped up the thumb safety. He put his thumb on the firing button, then flipped the safety back down. Wrong guy in front of the bomb. He needed Kimball still breathing and able to operate a computer and make phone calls.

The gunfire abruptly stopped. Magazines hit the concrete floor, bolts closed and Jaeger and Manson were ready to rock and roll again. Kimball had figured out his location and probably started coming around his left flank.

"Hey Jaeger, you pork any monkeys?" called Stone. He ran towards the back of the factory floor, not bothering to silence his footsteps.

"I'm gonna kill the kid, Stone. And I'm gonna hurt you bad before I kill you," said Jaeger. He moved to where he heard Stone running, carbine at his shoulder.

Stone ducked around a press and opened the .500 Magnum's

cylinder. Two live rounds left. Then he'd only have his P-226 and he doubted the .40 hollowpoints would penetrate the body armor they undoubtedly were wearing. He'd have to take head shots. On moving targets. In the dark.

Things could be worse but he didn't know how.

Milo huddled in the darkness, on the floor next to the couch, the hood of his windbreaker pulled over his head. He'd seen the clock that didn't work, just like all the other stuff in that factory. Stone had put him in here, saying it was the safest place and keep the door locked and not to worry. Now Milo stared at the locked door, which did little to muffle the shouts and sounds of gunshots coming from outside the room. He hugged his knees and tried to make himself smaller. He'd read where bullets could easily go through doors and according to all his video games they could go through walls too.

The gunfire stopped. Then the shouting stopped.

The doorknob started rattling.

Stone heard the snick of a CAR-15 firing pin not hitting a primer. No gunshot and Stone got to keep breathing for at least one more second. He spun around and saw Manson, close enough that he should have smelled his breath, pulling the charging handle on his carbine. Stone grabbed the barrel and pulled hard. Manson pulled back on the weapon then pushed forward, his forehead smashing into Stone's. Stone dropped the revolver and twisted the CAR-15 out of Manson's grasp. Stone smashed Manson's jaw with his palm and the bigger man fell back as Stone pulled his pistol. Manson recovered quickly and front-kicked the P-226 out of Stone's hand, then launched a side kick into his mid-section. Stone fell back and stumbled, landing on his butt, making Manson's back round kick miss his head. He pulled the P-250 from his ankle holster and fired twice. Squashed bullets bounced off body armor as Manson fell back gasping. Absorbing 700 foot-pounds of energy from the rounds would distract anybody but Manson had the presence of mind to pull his pistol and fire. The first bullet had the desired effect of getting Stone to keep his head down. The second bullet hit Stone in the middle of his body armor vest. He fell back, dropping the P-250 and rolled to the ground, towards the revolver. Stone grabbed it and slammed the cylinder closed. He aimed and pulled the trigger twice, the hammer falling on spent rounds.

Manson pointed his pistol in Stone's general direction. He fired again, the first round going wild.

Stone pulled the trigger again. Another empty chamber.

Manson took his time. He aimed one-handed since at this range, against a sitting target who had an empty pistol, a head shot was a done deal.

Unless the sitting target had a .500 Magnum that still held two live rounds.

Stone barely heard the gunshots. Blinded by muzzle flash for a moment, he dropped the empty revolver and groped for any pistol that might be within reach. His ears ringing, Stone listened for anything that might be trying to shoot him. He blinked and as his night vision slowly returned he saw Manson lying in a pool of blood, the body armor shattered by two .500 Magnum slugs.

Stone became aware of a sensation between a bee sting and a deep bruise in his leg. It didn't feel like he'd been shot, so it was probably another ricochet. He pulled a Celox gauze out of its sachet and stuffed it over the wound.

"Manson's down, Jaeger," called Stone. "You're next."

Stone stuffed his pistols back in their holsters and picked up Manson's CAR-15. He'd have a better chance taking Jaeger with the carbine than with a pistol. Even if the bullets didn't go through the body armor they'd knock him down with body shots and he'd have a better chance at a headshot with its optical sight. He ejected the misfed round, then grabbed more magazines off Manson's vest. You could never have too much ammo. Especially when you're hunting men who are hunting you.

"Come on, Jaeger," called Stone. "You and me!"

Stone pulled himself to his feet and crept past the presses and saws and power hammers, listening for Jaeger. He heard nothing except the yammer of heavy equipment cycling and humming. Until two gunshots reverberated from the hall by the loading area.

The doorknob flew off with the first shot. The second shot shattered the lock work and swung the door inward. Kimball slammed the door open and leaned against the door frame, pistol aimed at anything in front of him. He swept the room with his flashlight and spotted the kid.

Milo jumped at Kimball, who easily backhanded him down to the floor. Milo scrambled to his feet, then stood still as he faced Kimball's pistol.

"I'm sorry, kid," said Kimball. He was surprised. He looked at a teenager, one who looked like any of millions who went to high school, ate burgers, and prayed the girl they asked to dance would say yes. He was just a dumb, scared kid who stared at the pistol aimed at his face. "It's not my call."

Kimball watched the teenager's face transform as emotions washed across it. Fear. Anger. Defiance. Kimball had known them all and remembered when he'd gotten pushed around, just like every kid got pushed around at one time or another. Too bad this one just got pushed for the last time. Kimball saw surrender on Milo's face.

"Just—please," said Milo. He closed his eyes. "Don't shoot my Mom. Please."

Kimball stared at Milo. If he was a punk, or if he screamed or attacked or begged or did anything but plead for his mother's life it would have been easier.

This was just a kid. Dumb and scared and still standing up, getting as ready as he could be to take a bullet.

Kimball holstered his pistol, then punched Milo, who collapsed onto the floor. This kid would still get pushed around for a while.

Stone walked quickly and turned the corner into the loading area. Jaeger stood facing away from him at the entrance to the hall. Stone didn't have a problem shooting somebody in the back, especially when they were trying to kill him. He aimed the CAR-15 and put the EOTech's red dot on Jaeger's center of mass. Jaeger made a good, big target.

Snick.

Jaeger's ears heard the sound of a firing pin not hitting a primer, over the din of all the equipment in the factory. Stone dropped the carbine and grabbed his P-226 as Jaeger spun around and aimed his CAR-15. Stone fired three shots and threw Jaeger off balance as two rounds hit his body armor and the third sliced through his ear lobe.

Jaeger aimed again and fired two three-round bursts, which hit Stone center of mass. As he fell back from the impact, Stone's next three shots bounced off steel beams supporting the ceiling. Stone staggered, gaining his balance only for a brief second, then fell face forward onto the concrete floor.

Jaeger ran over to Stone and prodded the motionless body with his boot. Six rounds center of mass. He wasn't going anywhere. Too bad he didn't have time to deal some serious hurt on him before ventilating his chest.

"Jaeger!"

Jaeger turned around to see Kimball dragging Milo, nose bloody and hands ziptied together, out of the hall onto the factory floor. He slung his carbine and mashed a wad of Celox gauze onto his ear.

"Manson?" asked Kimball.

"No," said Jaeger.

Kimball pushed Milo onto the floor and stood still for a moment. He'd lost good people. In this business he'd lose people, sometimes sooner, sometimes later, but he never liked it and never got used to it. That night the wrong people were dead and he had one too many live bodies—who happened to be a target. It would take a lot of work, imagination and cash to fix this and make it all in the past.

The factory smelled like gunpowder and blood. It couldn't just be a clean, quiet op.

Kimball shook his head. "Too damn many headlines."

Jaeger nodded at Milo. "He coming with me?"

Milo watched Jaeger and Kimball speaking, then saw Stone lying on the concrete. He looked back at Kimball.

"I got him," said Kimball. "Get Stone in the van. Everybody. We got serious cleanup to do."

"What about we burn the place."

"I said get the bodies in the van." Kimball looked at Stone, lying face down, motionless. "All of them. We don't leave our own."

"Roger that," said Jaeger. His ear started to feel like somebody had run it through a food processor.

Milo jumped to his feet and charged into Kimball, knocking him down, then started running. Jaeger took two long steps and grabbed Milo's arm. He threw him down onto the floor and aimed his CAR-15.

"Wait!" said Kimball. He regained his feet and stepped towards Jaeger.

Two gunshots.

Jaeger staggered forward as bullets hit his body armor. He spun around and took another on the front panel of his body armor, then stumbled as he took a round in his leg. Jaeger and Kimball rolled behind a rack holding rusty sheets of quarter-inch thick steel.

Stone stood up from his kneeling position, dropped the magazine from his P-226 and loaded another. He looked slightly better than a dead person but felt much worse.

"Hey, Jaeger. Who taught you how to shoot?" said Stone. He coughed and looked for a target. He saw none and backed behind a press. "Come on Jaeger! You want to deal some hurt? I'm still waiting."

Jaeger turned to Kimball. "That dumb son of a bitch doesn't know how to die." He stuffed another Celox dressing on the bullet hole in his leg.

"You're his new teacher," said Kimball. "Get it done."

Kimball looked around for Milo. Nowhere to be found.

"Get it done!" said Kimball. He had to find the kid. He didn't know what he was going to do but one thing certain as birds shitting on clean cars, that kid couldn't walk around telling everybody about his adventures with grown men shooting each other. Kimball ran through the saws, presses, and lathes looking for him. Nothing.

"Hey kid! You're better off with me than Jaeger. Come on out," said Kimball. He listened for a few moments, then heard what he expected. Nothing.

Jaeger listened to Kimball moving behind him. He should have just shot the kid like he was supposed to.

"Come on Jaeger, this ain't no monkey dance!" called Stone.

Jaeger looked from behind the press. He saw Stone turn a corner and run towards the back end of the building. He looked like a one-legged chicken running from a hatchet.

Stone, exhausted, stopped at the back wall near the wide doorway. His ribs hurt, making breathing hard. He limped inside the dark back room and leaned back onto the workbench. He couldn't see far outside the doorway but heard Jaeger's heavy footsteps coming towards him.

Stone saw the muzzle flash but didn't hear the gunshots. He felt the impact of another three rounds on the front of his vest and fell back against the workbench, then slid to the floor. Another couple thousand foot-pounds punching into his Level 4 vest knocked the wind out of him and dialed up every single pain receptor in his chest. He dropped his pistol and saw Jaeger in the doorway, aiming his CAR-15 at Stone's head. Jaeger wouldn't miss a head shot at this range. Struggling to breathe, Stone reached into the pocket of his vest.

Jaeger had his EOTech's red dot on Stone's forehead but didn't focus so closely that he missed Stone pulling the detonator out of his vest pocket. Instinctively, he looked up and saw the pipe bombs taped to a metal rack above the doorway. He quickly backed away, out of the room and onto the factory floor, his carbine never leaving his shoulder. Stone must have thought he was stupid. Joke's on him.

"Welcome to the monkey dance," said Stone. He flipped up the thumb guard and pressed the detonator button.

The yammer of the equipment behind Jaeger continued uninterrupted by the explosion.

As Jaeger squeezed the trigger he felt his feet leave the floor and a vast wave of heat wash over him. For a moment he wondered if he'd loaded some new kind of ammo but the sensation of hot metal shards tearing upwards through his body led him to conclude that Stone had detonated a bomb under the drain on which he'd stood a couple dozen milliseconds earlier.

Stone watched Jaeger land against the side of the 500-ton punch press. Bleeding from everywhere, Jaeger leaned against it, grabbing for anything to keep from crumpling onto the floor. He struggled to stand but slipped and stumbled into the wide bed of the press. He writhed, turned himself over, then lay motionless and stared up at the 28-inch wide die mounted on the ram. Stone wondered why Jaeger didn't do something, then decided that Jaeger couldn't move because he took most of the shrapnel in the pipe bomb that Cain had so thoughtfully crafted. Stone leaned heavily back against the wall. He dropped the detonator, then looked up and saw machine screws embedded in the wall two feet above his head. Just as well he was on his ass when the pipe bomb exploded. Still struggling to breathe, he loosened his vest then opened its front flap and pulled out the large cracked, bullet-pocked ceramic plate that stopped nine 5.56 millimeter bullets. Stone gulped in air and felt his ribs move in ways that nature had not intended. He groaned and wished breathing was optional.

Stone's shirt, stained with blood and sweat, stuck to his skin. He picked up his P-226 and, holding his ribcage, hoisted himself off the ground. He walked over to Jaeger, who opened his eyes but didn't move. Stone guessed he took shrapnel in his spinal cord, along with just about everywhere else, since more of his blood was outside his body than inside.

Stone aimed his pistol at Jaeger, then lowered it. Jaeger would never shoot anybody again. He turned around.

"Stone," said Jaeger, in a harsh rasp, all that remained of a voice. "Not like this."

Stone turned and faced Jaeger. "I don't even like you."

Jaeger only wanted what he'd want. Stone hesitated, then punched the big green switch on the press. It hummed, and for the first time in years, cycled, flattening the top half of Jaeger.

"Nice pressed shirt, my ass," said Stone.

He walked to the breaker boxes and shut off the power. The saws and mills and presses stopped their restless activity as quickly as they'd started and who knew when anybody would give them power again. Stone listened to the silence and heard nothing except the ringing in his ears.

Just another day in paradise.

He limped to the loading area, holding his pistol, then moved down the hall, only intermittently using a flashlight to make his way. No sense being more of a target than he already was. He saw the open door missing its doorknob and looked into the room. No signs of Milo or Kimball.

He walked back to the loading area and listened. Nothing. The only other people inside the factory besides him had stopped breathing. Too many bullets, too much blood. That all of them knew bad things happen when men hunt men didn't make Stone feel better. They had all once served together and he'd just taken their lives.

And for what.

When Stone walked out of the loading door into the parking area he saw Kimball standing behind Milo, next to the black Suburban. Anti-freeze and oil puddled underneath it and under the van, rivulets streaming past Kimball's boots like wrong-colored blood in a psychedelic abattoir. Their cracked front grilles were each punctured by two holes approximately .500 inches in diameter.

"And here I thought you forgot how to shoot," said Kimball. He nodded at the puddles. "You find a fifty cal or something?"

"Yeah," said Stone.

Stone returned Kimball's stare. They looked at each other in the dim light of the parking lot's only functioning overhead lamp. Kimball held his pistol at his side with one hand and Milo in front of him with the other.

"You thinking about maybe walking away?" asked Kimball, after a silence.

"Actually, no," said Stone. "See, I'm having this trust issue right now. The guy who hired me just tried to kill me. I'm not feeling the love."

Kimball rolled his eyes. "Did you just O.D. on stupid pills? Stone—Jeezus, you know how this works."

"You mean as in now I shoot you in the face?"

"I never liked any of this, retiring you least of all. It's just—it's the mission. Nothing personal."

"Yeah, I know. That's one reason I haven't killed you. Something I really need you to understand, Kimball," said Stone. He nodded at Milo. "The only other reason you're standing is because he's standing. Nice to see he's still breathing."

Kimball nudged Milo. "Got to give him credit. He tried to drive the rig out of here. Too bad you need an engine without holes shot through it to make it go."

"You and me have to talk."

"Sure we do. Whatever you think you have to say, might as well say it now."

"Think we can do that without pulling a trigger?" Stone nodded at Kimball's pistol.

"You tell me," said Kimball.

Milo sneezed through his bloody nose and Stone pointed at

him.

"So why's he still breathing?" asked Stone.

"I like working with disadvantaged youth. And he's standing right here," said Kimball. He gave a brief smile as he nudged Milo. "El Paso, Stone. Maybe you like this kid better."

"How do you think this is a good mission? All you're doing is covering Heidrick's ass, which is going to be plenty pissed, the mess you made here. What makes you think you're not next?"

"He's a U.S. senator and a close personal friend. That all you got?"

"Really?"

"Doesn't matter. We follow orders. We're not required to like them," said Kimball.

"Pay attention to who's giving the orders. Any of this make sense to you, like it's for protecting the country? Even a little of this sound wrong?"

"Haven't thought about it."

"None of this even makes sense on another planet. Murdering U.S. citizens on U.S. territory—how's that going to sound to a grand jury?" asked Stone.

"Heidrick's calling the shots. If this is all you got, we talk about how to walk away."

"You're not as smart as you look. To him you're just little people," said Stone. He pointed to Milo. "Same as him, same as me, same as everybody. He'll hang you out to dry as soon as somebody figures out these missions are all GreenSeed."

"Not going to happen. GreenSeed, whatever, they're missions. Duly authorized."

"They're murder. Heidrick giving the orders doesn't make it legal."

"Sure it does," said Kimball. Or maybe not. The GreenSeed missions—Cain's targets didn't need RSA. Local law enforcement and any District Attorney with some balls could have handled them. They could have figured out how to keep it all quiet. And legal. Then Cain. Then Gen 3—the kids. But what law stated that orders issued and authorized by US senators had to be legal anyway? Kimball had only disobeyed orders once, by going downrange with his Viper 20 teams. That cost him a star and another couple years of command. He had no intention of disobeying another order.

Kimball glanced at Milo. So he disobeyed orders twice. It didn't seem like it would matter past the next few minutes anyway.

"I got all the GreenSeed data," said Stone.

"Sure you do," said Kimball. He exchanged stares with Stone. "Nobody's got it."

"Clancy probably told you that and you probably thought he wasn't lying," said Stone. "Cain put it all on the internet. Some cloud thing. Easy to find once you know how."

"Bullshit."

"Clancy showed me how. I'm sending it to CNN first. Then the Post, New York Times, National Enquirer, whoever else. It goes in 24 hours whether I'm around or not. Somebody'll print it and it'll cost him votes. When Heidrick sees it you get blamed and how much you want to bet your autopsy happens about the same time the second headline breaks."

"Nice try," said Kimball. He pushed Milo. "What do you want to do about this?"

"There's this video of Heidrick and you at his sub-committee meeting. Maybe you remember him telling you to use Cain to kill the GreenSeeds," said Stone. He watched Kimball blink. "And then there's all the dead bodies."

"This all you wanted to tell me?" asked Kimball. If Stone had what he said he had it could hurt Heidrick. But it was all circumstantial, something plausible deniability could easily handle—no hard evidence to hang him. Like many politicians before him, Heidrick had got himself out of much worse in his career.

But it would make him angry. Powerful men who are angry make problems for those who made them angry, in this case Kimball. At best his career was over, maybe some criminal penalties. At worst, his ex-wives would stop getting alimony.

Stone watched Kimball's face. Now they had something to talk about. "Maybe you got a way out."

"Maybe."

They stood staring at each other.

"You want me to tell you or not," asked Stone.

"Speak."

"Let Heidrick take the hit," said Stone.

"Fine with me." Kimball almost laughed. "Except I doubt he'll agree with your suggestion."

"You and me need to work together. It means we stop shooting at each other."

"Why are you and me talking if you already got the data?"

"The GreenSeed data gets him in trouble. Bad P.R. Best case he gets kicked out of office but it doesn't get him indicted. Only pissed off enough to do nasty things to you."

"I agree."

"He gave you the retirement orders. Documents. Authorizations. E-signatures. Hard evidence that gets indictments. He goes to jail, he can't touch you or any of us," said Stone. "With all the dead bodies, what do you think the Attorney General will do with source files and authentications for all these retirement orders? That and the GreenSeed data—any of it goes public, they'll have to indict even if they don't want to."

"The A.G.? Not a problem." Wiggins would sell his ass for a chance at convicting United States Senator Walter Heidrick. It would also mean Kimball had to do some things not very short of mutiny. "What do you want?"

"I want us to keep breathing. You put in the RSA files, I put in the GreenSeed data and we both start working for Justice Department. You're connected. You can get to people before getting killed. I try it, I might not get there without bleeding. Plus maybe they think you're more credible than me."

"You're saying we go state's evidence. And I willfully disobey my orders," said Kimball.

"You want to maybe think about who's giving the orders? Or maybe you figure Heidrick won't throw you under the bus."

Is it still mutiny if your superior officer is about to hang you while committing crimes against your country and its citizens? Kimball decided not to think hard about it.

"I got people I can call," said Kimball. Not that he would take any enjoyment from seeing Heidrick in jail. Not too much anyway. The harder part would be keeping the rest of RSA's activity secret, but that could be handled with DOJ since they were one of RSA's client agencies. Kimball released Milo. "Stone, you're slightly smarter than I thought you were."

Stone nodded at Kimball's pistol. "Cut him loose."

Kimball laid his pistol on the ground and cut Milo's zipties. Milo eyed the pistol as he rubbed his wrists.

"Now apologize," said Stone.

An apology. What next. Kimball shrugged. "Sorry, Stone."

"Not me, you dumbshit, to him."

"Oh." Kimball turned to Milo. "Sorry, kid. Nothing personal."

"Like, what?" demanded Milo. He looked at Stone. "Nothing personal?"

"Yeah, it actually wasn't," said Stone. He turned and walked towards the corner of the building. "Let's go."

"Where we going?" asked Kimball.

"To a car that has a functioning engine attached. Unless you want to walk out of here."

Stone felt like napping for two or three days, but he turned and started walking towards the corner of the building, to the beat-up Impala parked in the back lot. Milo zipped up his windbreaker and stepped alongside Stone.

"Hey, Stone, thanks for helping me," said Milo.

"It's okay, Milo," said Stone. "We're going to be okay."

Stone and Kimball froze when they felt the muzzles nudge against their skulls. Two men had stepped away from the wall as they turned the corner and a third grabbed Milo's collar. Headlights from three trucks parked near Stone's beat-up Impala flashed on.

"Señor Stone, maybe you remember me."

Stone couldn't see who spoke until the man walked closer.

Guerro. With new scars. Probably ones earned from the last time they swapped bullets. When had these guys shown up?

"Hey, you know, you *federales* talk too much. I hear all the noise and all the shooting when we come here, so we wait. Then the noise and the shooting stops." Guerro paced back and forth in front of Stone. "Then you talk and talk and talk and I keep waiting some more. I keep thinking maybe you kill each other and make things easy, but no, you do not do this for me."

Guerro turned and waved. "Tinto!"

Tinto walked over and searched Kimball, then Stone. He quickly found Stone's P-226.

"*El tiene otro*," said Guerro. He has another. Guerro

remembered El Paso very well.

Kimball remembered Guerro. He'd issued five retirement orders with his name on them, none of which they'd successfully executed.

Tinto found the other P-226 in the belt holster and held it up. Guerro nodded and his men walked Kimball, Stone and Milo towards the trucks.

Tinto set Stone's pistols on the hood of the new Ford F-350.

"Who is this boy?" asked Guerro. He nodded at Milo.

"Some dumb homeless kid," said Stone. "You can let him go."

Guerro stepped in front of Kimball and checked his ID. "So you are *el jefe de los federales.*"

"You're making a mistake. I have twenty men three minutes from here," said Kimball. "If you cooperate—"

Guerro laughed. "I do not think so. Señor Kimball, you are the reason I am here. You are not good at your job so your boss must demote you. Him and me, we have been very good friends for many years."

Kimball understood two things at that moment. Heidrick had set him up. And Heidrick had fed Salazar and Guerro information about Kimball's raids for at least two years. That was why they never got to Salazar. Kimball guessed they had three minutes to figure out a way not to get killed.

Guerro stepped in front of Milo and checked his face, then looked at a photo. Guerro raised his hand. "Pedro!"

A back door to the Dodge Ram 2500 opened and Pedro got out, dragging Alex behind him. He grabbed her arm when she stumbled and yanked her to her feet, then marched her over to Guerro.

"Mom!" Milo took one step before the man standing behind him jerked his collar.

"Milo!" said Alex. Pedro pulled her back as she moved towards Milo.

"Mom, I'm okay," said Milo.

"Alex," said Stone. "How the hell did she—"

"Heidrick. He set us up," said Kimball. "He must have told Guerro about her and the kid."

Guerro stepped in front of Stone and grinned. "A homeless boy. Not for too long, yes?"

"Nice scars," said Stone. "It's a good look for you."

"Yes, a good look for me." Guerro kept grinning, then patted Stone's cheek. Then punched him. "You are not so tough and not so smart."

Stone wiped blood from his mouth. "This time I will hurt you."

Guerro punched Stone again, knocking him to his knees. He grinned and sighed. "I do not think so." He turned and walked away, nodding to Tinto. "*Ahora*."

Tinto started screwing a silencer onto his MP-5 as the men standing behind Kimball, Stone and Milo backed away.

"Milo!" Alex looked at her son, terrified.

Stone, still on his knees, looked at where each of Guerro's men stood.

"Milo, I'm sorry! I love you, Milo." Alex struggled to get away from Pedro, who pushed her to the ground.

Guerro walked over to her. He grabbed her hair and pulled her head back. "I think maybe I keep you for a little while. We have a little fun, you and me."

Alex slapped Guerro. He grabbed her throat and held her for a moment, then pushed her away. He laughed and nodded at Pedro. "She is a wild one. I think we gonna have a lot of fun."

Stone reached for his ankle, but stopped and looked around when he heard Milo shout.

"Hey!" Milo grasped Kimball's pistol with both hands. "Freeze, you assholes!"

Guerro stopped and turned around. Everybody looked at Milo, surprised. His windbreaker unzipped, he'd just pulled Kimball's pistol from his belt and aimed it at Guerro.

Stone grabbed the P-250 from his ankle holster and shot Tinto once in the face then fired once into the heads of the three men who just backed away from them. Kimball started moving after he saw Stone draw his pistol and grabbed the MP-5 from Tinto as he dropped.

"Get down, kid," said Kimball, as he shot three-round bursts at the men surrounding Guerro by the trucks. Two men dropped as Guerro ran behind his Ford F-450 and kneeled by the front tire.

Pedro grabbed Alex and held her by the throat in front of him, a human shield. He watched Stone with one eye, the other half of his face shielded by Alex's head. He moved slowly backwards into the glare of the Dodge Ram's headlights. He pointed his pistol at Stone and fired wildly.

"Mom!" said Milo. He took a step but Kimball pushed him down while shooting at Guerro and the last two of his men, stitching 9 millimeter holes into the bodywork of the F-450.

Stone, still kneeling, aimed at the half a face that Pedro exposed. He waited, then aimed again. Then he fired twice. Alex stood frozen in place, illuminated in the headlights, her hair spattered with blood. Her eyes stayed open, staring directly ahead and she started to tremble as Pedro fell limply backwards.

Guerro nodded at the last two of his men, also crouching behind the truck, and pointed at Alex and Milo. Both men nodded and started circling around the backs of the trucks. Guerro pulled out his pistol and stood up, firing at where he thought Stone stood.

Stone had rolled to his right and jumped to his feet, looking for another target. As Guerro's bullets ricocheted off the factory wall, Stone fired. Guerro took a bullet in his shoulder and looked around as if a bee had just stung him. Stone ran towards Guerro, shooting until his P-250's slide locked back. He dropped the compact pistol and reached for his belt holster.

Empty. He looked at his pistols lying on the F-350's hood, then at Guerro.

Just like Jaeger, Guerro could take a beating and bullets and still keep going. Bleeding from his shoulder, he only looked pissed off. Guerro raised his pistol and fired. The bullets went wild, mostly because his arm contained a .40 slug that interfered with its motor nerve impulses.

"Hey, Stone!"

Stone turned his head and saw Milo tossing Kimball's pistol at him. Stone caught it and fired as he levelled it. Guerro moved out from behind the truck, breathing hard and shooting. Both men emptied their pistols without hitting each other. They charged and collided, Stone falling back from the impact of what felt like a very large defensive end. He rolled away just as Guerro jumped for him and heard Guerro land face first on the asphalt. Stunned, Guerro scrambled to his hands and knees. Stone kicked him in the ribs, lifting him off the ground and rolling him onto his back. Stone dropped, leading with his elbow into Guerro's chin then battered his face with his fists.

Milo turned back to Alex, only to see through the glare of headlights one of Guerro's men appearing out of the darkness, aiming his MP-5 at him. Alex jumped to her feet, grabbed at the weapon and promptly took a punch in the face. She fell to the ground, bleeding. Milo tackled the man and both fell to the asphalt. The wind knocked out of him, the man struggled to recover his submachine gun but found his arms pinned by Milo, who straddled him and stared into his face. In a rage, Milo punched the man, just once, as hard as he could. The man's head rolled to the side and he stopped moving. Milo turned and saw Alex struggle to sit up, stunned, blood covering her face.

Milo turned back to the man and, seeing him start moving, punched him once more. He felt something in the man's face crumple under his fist.

Milo punched him again. And again. Then, in a rhythm, one fist, then the other. Milo's knuckles started to hurt so he aimed for the man's throat, which felt better. He heard somebody far away call out his name as he continued his rhythmic hammering of a bloodied human.

"Milo!" screamed Alex. Terrified, she watched her son batter a now-helpless man to death—in the same detached, methodical way that a GreenSeed like Elias Cain would use.

"Milo, stop it!" Still dazed, she struggled to stand. "You're not like that!"

Almost hypnotized, Milo continued the pounding after the man lost consciousness, until he heard a burst of gunfire behind him.

Milo stopped and turned around. He saw Kimball standing next to a man lying on the ground. The last of Guerro's crew, his chest bloody, courtesy of Kimball's marksmanship. Kimball slid a new magazine into his MP-5. Milo stared at Kimball, registering no emotion.

"Get off him, kid," said Kimball. "Get off. You don't want to kill him."

Milo looked down at the bloodied man he straddled, whose swollen face appeared halfway between raw and medium rare. He looked at his hands, and opened and closed them and felt the blood turning sticky. He jumped off the man and stood, breathing hard. He looked at the man's face, then at all the bodies lying on the ground. He realized that all the accumulated bullets and blood and bodies didn't just happen inside a computer, and real people who had lived minutes earlier had really just died.

Milo looked back at the man lying at his feet gasp for breath, then stop moving. Milo looked at the man's eyes, which now only stared half-closed at nothing. Milo turned to Kimball, wanting to ask but not daring. Kimball took one look and shook his head.

Milo looked back at the man, at another real person who had really just died. He tried to remember what he'd done, how it felt. Had he enjoyed it? Was beating the life out of a man fun? Milo started trembling, fearing that the men who failed to kill him that night had allowed a monster to wander free. What would that monster do next?

Milo looked at his mother.

Alex stood up. She hadn't seen her son cry in years.

Milo started screaming, only stopping when Alex ran to him. It was not something a GreenSeed would do. She hugged him very tightly and gave thanks that all she heard from her son at that moment was despair.

"Milo," said Alex. "You're not like that. We'll be okay."

Stone had put his forearm across Guerro's throat and leaned on it, pressing until the bigger man stopped moving. Stone eased back and looked at Guerro lying under him, eyes closed and motionless.

"Hey! A little help here." He heaved himself to his feet, having little energy for anything but breathing. He turned around and waved at Kimball, unaware of Guerro opening his eyes.

Kimball turned around and only had time to shout, "Behind you!"

Before Stone could turn back, he felt a large fist slam into the side of his head. He stumbled and turned around just in time for a blood-covered Guerro to pick him up in a bear hug and slam him into the ground. Stone wondered if any of his ribs remained unbroken. Not that it mattered. They couldn't hurt any worse.

Guerro saw Kimball aiming the MP-5 and started running. Kimball fired in several bursts but missed. He wished he had a carbine—he'd never much cared for submachine guns.

Guerro slid into his F-450 and gunned it. Engine roaring with every one of its 440 horsepower, it lurched forward through smoke that smelled of burning rubber. He yanked the wheel over as the tires grabbed onto asphalt and steered the truck towards Stone, who jumped to his feet and dodged. He timed his move almost perfectly so that Guerro only grazed him with the front quarter-panel. Stone bounced off and rolled to his feet.

"Get them out of here!" said Stone.

As Guerro skidded a turn and sped back towards Stone, Kimball grabbed Milo and Alex and ran them over to the Dodge Ram, saying only, "Hug later!"

Kimball piled Milo and Alex into the front seat of the truck and stood next to the driver side door, watching Guerro. They waited for Kimball to tell them what to do.

"Don't wait. You guys take off. Get out of here!" said Kimball.

Milo, in the driver's seat, wiped his eyes and reached for the ignition switch. He found no key inside it.

"There's no keys," said Milo.

"Find them!" said Kimball. He'd already turned around to look for Guerro, and saw the truck speeding towards Stone.

Kimball aimed, pulled the trigger of his MP-5 and noticed that no bullets came out. He looked around for another magazine.

Stone ran to the F-350. He grabbed his guns and turned to see Guerro speeding at him. Raising both pistols, he fired. Guerro sped up as fractured white spots spattered the windshield. Bullet-proof glass. He'd need something a lot bigger than a .40 caliber bullet. Stone dodged away as Guerro's F-450 rammed the F-350 he'd just stood in front of. Sheet metal and steel frames shuddered from the impact. The F-450 pushed the smaller truck across the asphalt until Guerro hit the brakes.

Stone dropped his empty pistols and watched as the conjoined Ford trucks skidded to a halt. He ran towards the corner of the factory while Guerro shifted between forward and reverse, gunning the engine as he rocked back and forth until he disengaged from the F-350. He swerved into a turn, chasing Stone.

Skidding around the corner, Guerro saw Stone run inside the large open door of the factory and hit the brakes. He had no thought of his injuries or his dead men—only that he hadn't finished what he was told to do. If he failed and came back to Salazar alive, he might not remain so for very long, even in spite of his long years of service. Señor Salazar and the government these *federales* worked for were not so different.

Guerro loaded a fresh magazine into his MP-5. He would finish the boy and his mother and then *el jefe de los federales.* Then he would kill Stone. It would not take long and he would save the best for last.

Kimball watched the truck turn the corner and speed towards them.

"Now's a good time for those keys, kid," said Kimball. He worked the cocking handle of the MP-5, hoping Guerro wouldn't figure out that the magazine was empty.

Milo kept searching for the key, in the glove compartment, under the seat, between the seat cushions. He kept looking at Alex sitting in the passenger seat, pale, bruised and exhausted. She flashed a smile at him.

"We'll be okay, Milo," said Alex.

Guerro hit the brakes 20 meters away from where Kimball stood. He waited and watched from behind the bullet-proof windshield, this *federale* holding the MP-5 at his side. Maybe this would be like the old movies. Two gunslingers in a gunfight in the street. Except this time they would use MP-5 submachine guns instead of Colt .45 revolvers.

By now this *federale* would have tried to shoot him, if he could. Guerro smiled. These three would be no trouble.

Still breathing hard, Stone ran inside the factory, past the forklift, and stopped next to Hargis's blood-stained body. He rolled the body over and grabbed the CAR-15, sticky with congealing blood, correctly believing Hargis wouldn't need it anymore.

Looking at the door, Stone worked the carbine's charging handle and found it moved too easily, not engaging the bolt. First Manson's weapon and now Hargis's? Good enough for government work, but not for Kimball's team. Stone took a look and found the reason for the malfunction. The .500 Magnum bullet that killed Hargis had first gone clean through the carbine, leaving a hole slightly larger than a half inch extending from one side of the receiver to the other. Stone dropped the weapon, then pulled Hargis's pistol out of its holster and grabbed spare magazines. Not much use against up-armored vehicles but something equals better than nothing.

Stone leaned against the forklift to catch his breath. He felt exhausted and he hurt. A lot. Looking back on it, maybe the night watchman gig wasn't so bad.

He heard a roaring engine outside and headed for the door, cycling a round into the pistol. Just before running through the roll-up door, he hesitated, then stopped, then turned around.

Guerro worked the cocking handle on the MP-5. He watched the *federale* raise his weapon and move away from the truck that the boy and his mother sat in. Guerro smiled. If this man had ammunition he would have fired. Now he was only an easy target. A brave man, if incompetent.

Kimball watched Guerro lower the driver's side window. At this range there wasn't much time and hopefully the kid would find the key. Then he wondered if he even knew how to drive. What he wouldn't give for more ammo. Or a dozen grenades. Or an air strike. Kimball kept his eyes on Guerro until he saw something come around the corner that made no sense.

Guerro aimed his MP-5. He paused as he noticed the *federale's* face. Why did he look so surprised?

The impact slammed Guerro against the door as the truck skidded sideways. Stunned, he didn't hear the crash of metal on metal.

Stone put the forklift in reverse and pulled away from the truck. He hadn't knocked it over, but then up-armored trucks are much heavier than normal. As he backed up, he searched for the lever that raised the forks—all he'd ever done was drive the thing in circles. He looked up and saw the truck speed away. Where the hell was Guerro headed? Stone pressed the accelerator pedal and drove as fast as the forklift would go.

Guerro skidded into a 180 degree turn and sped straight towards Stone. An interesting game of chicken and it wasn't clear who would survive, if anybody. Guerro pointed the MP-5 out his window and started shooting. Stone didn't worry about getting hit until bullets started sparking off the driver cage and front frame. Stone found the lifting lever for raising the forks and pulled it in the correct direction. The massive carriage moved up the mast, surprisingly quickly given its size and weight. The heavy steel forks reached chest height, barely clearing the hood of the F-450 as it smashed into the forklift. At the closing speed of 50 miles per hour, the crash rocked the forklift but did not push it backwards. The truck's back end bucked and raised up because of the impact of the collision and the massive steel forks pinning down the front end.

In addition to plowing twin gashes across the top of the truck's hood, the forks punched through the bullet-proof windshield into the seats of the truck cab, in one of which sat Guerro. He hadn't felt the impact of the crash and didn't remember if he felt the steel slide into his chest. He stared down at the black-painted fork, silently appreciating its mass and immovability. Not knowing if he felt any pain, he tried to move his hand, the one that might still hold the MP-5. He still had killing to do. He would shoot Señor Stone first and then he would shoot *el jefe de los federales*. Then he would kill the boy. And then he would have some fun with the woman.

Surprised that the warm summer night had grown so cold, Guerro watched shadows grow in front of his eyes. He wondered why his hand did not move, or his arms, or anything. He raised his head and for a brief moment, just before the shadows closed everything to darkness, he saw only the angry golden angel with the green eyes, who did not come to take him to heaven.

Stone stared at the forks and the shattered windshield of Guerro's truck and turned to step off the forklift. He'd earlier thought his ribs couldn't hurt more and discovered he was wrong about that when he felt the collision with Guerro's truck, and again as he staggered onto the ground. He pulled out the pistol and limped to the cab of the truck, looking for any movement behind the shattered windshield. It looked like neither the truck nor its occupant would move again.

He stepped to the driver's side door, pistol aimed at Guerro, who sat motionless with his head bowed and eyes half-open. When Stone opened the door, he saw the massive steel fork implanted inside Guerro's chest.

Everything he ever learned about first aid did not apply to that injury.

Stone looked at the forklift, then back inside the truck. He saw a small pendant hanging on a chain from the rear view mirror, a golden angel with eyes painted green. Maybe Guerro put it there for good luck, in which case, it didn't work very well. Stone walked away, towards Kimball, who stared at the forklift and the truck and the dead man inside.

"Didn't know you could drive a forklift like that," said Kimball.

"It's going to need paint," said Stone.

Kimball looked at Stone, standing bloodied, sweat-stained, grease-stained and dirty. "Jeezus, I've seen dead guys who look better."

Holding his ribs, Stone coughed and tasted a little blood. "I blame you."

Stone walked past Kimball towards Alex and Milo.

Alex stepped out of the truck and walked to Stone. She dropped the rag with which she'd wiped blood from her face and stood in front of him for a moment, then wrapped him in a hug. Stone wheezed as he heard what might have been his last unbroken rib crack.

"Sorry," said Alex. She smiled and released Stone.

"Didn't hurt," grunted Stone. He took small breaths very carefully. "How the hell did you get here?"

"His men showed up and told the hospital that Senator Heidrick booked a nursing home for me. I thought the insurance company kicked me out of the hospital and Gidden asked Heidrick to do me a favor."

"Really? So after being hunted and shot and almost killed—and none of this by mistake—that just made lots of sense to you," said Stone.

"At the time nothing hurt and everything seemed fine. I was pretty drugged up."

"How about we leave." Kimball turned and listened to the sirens that wailed in the distance. "Unless anybody feels like spending time with police? Anybody?"

Stone, Alex and Milo stared at Kimball.

"I'll ask it differently. How about let's go. Now."

Kimball walked to Milo, still sitting in the truck searching for keys. Kimball reached into the visor and pulled out the key fob. "Hey, kid. In case you ever want to steal a car. Sun visor."

— SHEPHERD PARKWAY

Kimball drove the Impala out of the parking lot, down the street and onto the Parkway, slowing to five miles over the speed limit as a line of police cars raced past, lights flashing and sirens blaring. Stone rode in the passenger seat and Milo and Alex sat in the back seat. Kimball would have preferred driving one of Guerro's trucks, except for the bullet holes and smashed sheet metal that could attract unwanted attention from the police. He rolled down the window, to let fresh air drive out the smoky exhaust smell that infused the Impala's interior.

Milo sneezed.

"Hey, kid," said Kimball. "You okay?"

"Hey, asshole," said Milo. "Stop calling me kid."

"Milo," said Alex. "Manners."

"This thing smokes like napalm on cowpie mountain," said Kimball. "Did it ever get anything like maybe a smog inspection?"

"I don't know," said Stone. "It's stolen."

Kimball checked his rear view mirrors, then asked, "Any bodies in the trunk? Might be nice to know in case we get pulled over."

"I never checked."

Kimball drove them over the Woodrow Wilson Memorial Bridge, then made his way north on Patrick Street.

Milo pulled Cokes out of the grocery sack and handed one to Stone as they drove through Alexandria.

"Thanks," said Stone, taking a sip. Warm Coke was better than no Coke—but not by much. "Hey, Milo, next time can you fix it so they're cold?"

After a silence, Alex laughed first.

"I think it's your move," said Stone, to Kimball.

"I know the SAC at the Washington Field Office," said Kimball. "He owes me from Bosnia. I hope he remembers."

"You going to call him now?" asked Stone. He worried only a little. FBI Special Agents in Charge could help, provided they first agreed not to throw him and Kimball in jail.

"We did a couple gigs for him two years ago. I'll call him in a minute." Kimball turned onto the street fronting the RSA building.

"Why wait?"

"It's against the law to talk on a cell phone while driving."

"Right. I keep forgetting, breaking the law's a bad thing," said Stone.

Kimball switched off the headlights and parked a block away from the RSA, watching for anybody who might be expecting them. They saw no signs of anybody for several minutes. Under pink-tinged streetlights shining over empty sidewalks, traffic lights cycled red to yellow to green.

"Cain was smarter than all of us," said Stone, quietly. "One thing he told me, he didn't want to keep killing just because somebody told him to. He had the right idea."

"Sure he did. Stone, what the hell else would you do?" asked Kimball. He laughed.

Stone looked at Kimball as he poured the rest of his Coke into Kimball's lap.

"Hey! Shit," said Kimball. He looked at his wet crotch. "You just had to do that."

"Actually, yeah, I did. Nothing personal."

— RESOLUTION SUPPORT AGENCY

No cars moved on the street in front of the RSA building. Stone saw no sign of anybody ready to take them into custody or shoot them. Kimball stepped to the side of the car, pocketed his phone and slid into the driver's seat, waking Milo and Alex.

"Your buddy remember Bosnia?" asked Stone.

"He didn't need to," said Kimball. "Couple agents are on their way."

"Who they coming for?"

"Thank me later. I got us immunity."

"Immunity's good." Stone sounded relieved. Kimball wasn't such a bad guy when he wasn't trying to kill you. "I guess your buddy wasn't too pissed you woke him up."

"Not after I mentioned Heidrick. Minimum, he gets indicted on RICO, murder, conspiracy. One second after he gets our stuff, the Attorney General's going to party big," said Kimball. "They're arresting Heidrick tonight."

"Where?"

"His place. Georgetown. We're going to visit before they show up."

"Visit," said Stone. "Now? Why? It's two in the morning."

"There's no traffic."

"I'm tired, I hurt, I'm wounded—I might even be dead. Just let your FBI pals—"

"Couple cracked ribs and you think the world's ending," said Kimball. "Grow a dick and stop whining. Don't you want to watch FBI agents arrest a senator?"

Stone felt exhausted. Everywhere in his body that had a nerve ending ached. He looked around at Alex and Milo sitting, tired, in the back seat, then thought about watching Heidrick get handcuffed. "Want me to drive?"

— Q STREET NW, GEORGETOWN

The brick four-bedroom probably rented for at least $12,000 a month, give or take a few hundred. Stone thought for that much money they could have put in a better alarm system and decent locks. He led the way through the back door into the downstairs kitchen.

Kimball closed the curtains and turned on the light as Milo, yawning, sat down at the breakfast table. Alex admired the hardwood cabinets, the glass tile backsplash, and the granite slab countertops. Kimball pulled his cell phone out and dialed. They heard a cell phone ringing upstairs.

"Senator, please join us," said Kimball, into his phone. "In your kitchen."

They heard bumping, then somebody thumping down the stairs.

Stone put the iPad on the table and put his hand on his pistol. Alex sat next to Milo. Kimball leaned against the wall near Stone.

Heidrick walked in, wearing a silk bath robe over his pajamas. He looked unhappy. Four people who should be dead appeared very much alive. And in his kitchen.

Kimball nodded at the chair by the table. "Senator, thank you for joining us. Please have a seat."

Heidrick watched Stone unholster his pistol and place it on the bar by the kitchen counter. After only a brief hesitation, Heidrick put on a smile. "Would somebody care to make coffee?"

Alex went to the large coffeemaker and puzzled over its operation.

"Just press the big green button," said Heidrick. "It's hooked up to water and the beans take about a minute to grind. I hope you like Jamaican Blue Mountain."

"Sit," said Kimball.

Heidrick pulled the chair away from the table and sat down. "Do you have any idea what time it is?"

"Yes."

Kimball let silence sit in the room.

"Would you mind explaining yourself?" asked Heidrick.

"Yes."

"Cut the crap, Kimball. Who do you think you're talking to?"

"Somebody who the Attorney General will enjoy indicting. I believe you and he have met."

"He's got nothing," said Heidrick.

"He'll get something soon," said Stone. He held up the iPad. "Want to hear about it?"

"Hear about what?" asked Heidrick.

"GreenSeed." Stone sat down at the bar and smiled at Heidrick.

"Greenseed." Heidrick returned the smile and leaned back. "As a matter of fact, I would very much like to hear about GreenSeed. Please. Go on."

Stone tapped on the screen of the iPad. He watched the display, then frowned and tapped on the screen again. Then he just stared at it.

"Stone," said Kimball. He stepped next to Stone. "Please show the senator."

Stone showed the iPad to Kimball. A window was open on the display, which read, "File Error: GreenSeed Not Found – Centaur Not Available."

"Lose something?" asked Heidrick. He waited a long moment for them to understand that what they thought they had no longer existed. "You have nothing, Mr. Stone. Did you really think we'd never find them?"

"Doesn't matter," said Kimball. "I have the RSA files."

"You do? I think you're referring to the RSA database, which I instructed NSA to lock down as of midnight. Kimball, I've shut down your agency effective immediately because unauthorized activities conducted by rogue operators on your orders jeopardize national security and the public's safety," said Heidrick. He enjoyed watching Kimball's and Stone's faces as they discovered what NSA had done to help preserve its government. "Of course, the contents of the database are top secret. But I think you knew that."

"Maybe you know a guy named Guerro. He a friend of yours?" asked Stone. He kept working on the iPad. "We just met him. He's got a half ton of steel stuck in his chest"

"Four witnesses here," said Kimball. "Ready to testify to attempted murder and conspiring with known violent felons."

"Presuming you survive the evening outside of jail, who would believe you? Disgruntled employees with outstanding arrest warrants. A punk drug pusher. A vengeful mother. Who cares?"

Kimball looked at Stone, who continued staring at the iPad, then back at Heidrick. "Do you really think you can get away with this?"

"I already have," said Heidrick. "Is that coffee ready yet?"

A hum and a hiss filled the room as Alex pressed the big green button. Hot water got hotter and coffee beans turned to dust.

Kimball thought he had his problem solved just a few hours earlier. Now it appeared his problem just solved him. He'd never liked all this electronic data and email crap. He'd never had a problem with paper files and it wasn't as easy to steal them or make them go away and at that moment he sure could use a couple hard copies of everything in the safe under his bedroom floorboards. Heidrick was about to get away with it. All of it. At best, the rest of them would be jailed for some kind of "threat to national security" that NSA or CIA would soon uncover about them. At worst they'd never be heard from again.

"I was hoping this would have been over by now," said Heidrick. He yawned. "We could wait till a decent hour, but since you were rude enough to wake me, I'm sure we can arrange something else for right now."

"Maybe I can arrange something like they just find you on the floor. Self-inflicted gunshot wound," said Kimball. "There's getting away with it, and then there's getting away with it and living. Do you think there's anybody in the world that would give a damn?"

"Do you think I believe somebody like you would shoot somebody like me?"

"Easy to find out," said Kimball.

Heidrick laughed. "Who would authorize that mission?"

Kimball walked over to Heidrick, and stood over him, silent. Heidrick stopped laughing.

"What you want and what you'll do are two different things. You know how this works, Kimball. This time your ass is at the hard end of my boot."

Alex stopped tending the coffee maker and walked over to Milo. She looked around at Kimball and had the feeling that she and her son were about to witness at least one homicide.

"Stone," said Alex, softly. She kept her eyes on Kimball, who kept his eyes on Heidrick. "Can you do something?"

Stone, busy working on the iPad, held up a finger. "Wait one, please."

"I don't care how it happens, you're not getting out of this house a free man. Dead maybe, not free," said Kimball, more quietly than Stone or Heidrick had ever heard him speak.

Stone leaned back in his chair and looked up from the iPad. "Hey, Kimball."

Kimball didn't turn around. After a long moment he said, "Yeah."

"A lot of your stuff you thought was secret isn't anymore. Courtesy of Clancy Ford," said Stone. "I just read this email he sent me."

"What do you mean?" Kimball turned to face Stone. "Clancy's—"

Stone tapped the screen of the iPad. Gidden's voice blared from the small speaker. "—some GreenSeeds remain normal while most become ultra-violent murderers—"

Stone tapped the screen again and showed the iPad to Heidrick. A freeze-frame from a video remained on the screen that showed Gidden speaking in a wood-paneled room to a group of men that included Heidrick.

"You should lose some weight. The camera adds five pounds," said Stone. He set the iPad on the desk.

"Clancy uploaded everything to a dozen different locations on the internet. Including three of DOJ's cloud servers," said Stone. "I think I'll send something to CNN. It would make some reporter's career move a hell of a lot quicker."

"So?" asked Heidrick. "Let them report."

"When I said everything, I meant everything," said Stone.

"What do you mean, everything," asked Kimball. It seemed that electronic data and email weren't quite as bad as he'd thought one minute earlier.

"GreenSeed, RSA, everything," said Stone. He pointed at Heidrick. "He thought we had nothing. He's wrong. I can also play videos where he authorized the murders of all the GreenSeeds. And the orders you got that have his authorizations. FBI gets—"

"It won't matter. What do you want, Stone?" asked Heidrick. This would take much longer to fix than he'd thought before going to bed. "You're just little people with guns."

"What I want, Senator," said Stone. He picked up his pistol. "Is to shoot you in the face."

Stone walked over to Heidrick and stood in front of the sitting US Senator.

"But," said Stone. "I'm cutting back on the ultra-violent murder thing."

"You're amusing," said Heidrick. He stood and faced Stone, nose to nose. "I believe the coffee's ready. Have a cup?"

"Thanks, I will," said Stone. He holstered his pistol, then put his fingertip on Heidrick's throat and pushed him back down into the chair. "Let's drink to jail food. Maybe pork chops for Sunday dinner," said Stone. "You're still pretty, for an old guy. Maybe an ass raping every day or two. You might learn to like it."

"He's a six-term senator. He's got lots of practice," said Kimball. "But not on the receiving end. Yet."

"All you've done is sign your own warrants," said Heidrick. "Little people with warrants go to jail."

Alex put large cups of coffee on the bar.

"Everybody in this room except you has immunity. Enjoy your coffee, I'm expecting special agents in a couple minutes," said Kimball. He looked at his watch, then shook a cigarette out of a crumpled pack. "Maybe we can find you a good husband in

Leavenworth."

Heidrick stood up again. Stone pushed him back down in the chair.

"Get your hands off me," said Heidrick. He twisted away and looked up at Stone. "You're just a man-made killer, Stone. You were born in a test tube. How's it feel?"

Stone looked over at Milo. "I wouldn't know."

Kimball lit his cigarette.

Alex put a sugar bowl on the bar beside the cups of coffee. Stone ignored the sugar and picked up a cup of coffee. He took a sip, nodded, and took another sip.

"Wow, that's really good coffee. Us little people pay for it?" Stone poured the coffee into Heidrick's lap. "Nothing personal, Senator."

— E. BARRETT PRETTYMAN COURTHOUSE

Heidrick walked down the steps of the courthouse and past the reporters and the cameramen and the miscellaneous other sons of bitches. He ignored his aide who held the door to his limousine open for him, thinking only of the indignities publicly served to him that morning. Wiggins hadn't bothered to show up, instead delegating the prosecutorial role to some fourth level attorney who probably just passed the bar the previous month. This would be all over the news by noon. They'd say the Attorney General would finally get his conviction, even though he didn't bother to attend the hearing for the great and mighty Senator Walter Heidrick.

Campaign contributions would dry up, voters would stop calling, he wouldn't be able to bully votes for his bills, and his elected colleagues would condemn him for doing bad things that weren't half as bad as what they didn't get caught for. He'd be a pariah, an exile. Again.

But just for a little while. In a year or two he'd beat this just like everything else DOJ dug up and it wouldn't matter. Again.

Heidrick didn't look out the window at the Capitol as the limo turned onto Constitution Avenue. He didn't comprehend the likes of Wiggins and his DOJ lackeys. An Attorney General should know better. He and his people obviously didn't understand that they were all part of the same government. They didn't understand that government by necessity and intent served itself, existed for the benefit of itself, and generously rewarded those who nurtured and grew it. Wiggins and his ilk believed that government should serve the people. They also probably read poetry, and believed in fairness, freedom for all, and the Constitution. How did meddlesome, naïve, fairy tale assholes like that even get into government?

Heidrick straightened his necktie and flicked on the intercom. "Kevin, get going."

"Where are we going, sir?" asked the aide.

"My office." Heidrick still had work to do. "Where else."

In other countries they call it a regime. When the regime changes, the government changes. In the land of the free and the home of the brave, the names change and the people change, but, like its bureaucracies that get created and never destroyed, government does not change. It just gets bigger.

— DIRECTOR'S OFFICE, RSA

It almost looked like a few dozen rounds had never been fired in his office. The GSA contractors took their time patching the bullet holes and installing a new door but didn't excel at either. As mammoth as the General Services Administration had gotten, you'd think they could find somebody who could patch drywall without getting spackle all over the carpet. Given the cost, he'd expected something more than the ass end of mediocrity.

He'd had a light schedule since Heidrick's indictment. Some things go quickly, like when people who pissed off other people got caught doing something bad. For years, political pundits had said it was just a matter of time till Wiggins would find the proper tools with which to nail Heidrick. It now appeared those tools would be Edward Kimball and Duncan Stone, now living at the beck and call of the Attorney General, who had made it clear that immunity can be revoked if he didn't get what he thought was proper cooperation. The names may change but you always have to kiss somebody's ass.

Kimball had only spoken with Stone at Heidrick's hearings, and then only briefly. He didn't blame Stone for the cold shoulder, especially after he told him what happened to Clancy. Nobody liked how any of it turned out, but for Kimball, Clancy's death was the greatest tragedy.

Kimball looked away from the news on television as an Admin ushered in more workmen, who walked over to the flag. After staring at it for a moment, they unceremoniously started wrapping the tattered stars and stripes around the pole.

"Leave the flag," said Kimball.

He turned back to the television as the workmen left. The press had been remarkably cooperative and suppressed the bulk of the data in the RSA database—thus he still had a job, at least for the time being. They were not so generous with Heidrick. Kimball turned up the volume when he saw Heidrick's face on camera, looking like he'd just walked out of a Senate hearing where he'd reamed somebody's ass, instead of having just turned over his passport and posted a one million dollar bond. Kimball wondered which Fortune 500 CEO put up bail as a favor to their friend. Or maybe it was Salazar. The camera cut to a reporter.

"New allegations not only of murder and conspiracy, but also of government-funded human experiments have been exposed by the FBI and Attorney General Wiggins' special investigators," said the reporter. "Senator Walter Heidrick, at whom these allegations have been leveled, says he will demand a full Senate investigation—"

Kimball turned off the television.

— VERITAS, POTOMAC RIVER

Milo steered the Veritas carefully, maintaining their position in the line of boats that loosely formed the River Festival flotilla. Alex and Stone sat on opposite sides of the boat near the stern, the American flag fluttering between them in the cool afternoon breeze. Billowy cumulus clouds floated overhead, threatening thundershowers and casting quarter-mile wide cloud shadows on the river.

Stone pleasantly surprised Alex when he accepted her invitation. An afternoon cruise on the Potomac, a last chance before the weather turned cold. DOJ lawyers had kept Stone busy so Alex hadn't talked to him much after Heidrick's first arraignment. Weeks passed, during which she'd hoped for maybe a coffee date or even just a phone call and Milo had asked if they'd ever see him again. She had to tell Milo she didn't know. She didn't tell him she knew Stone had problems with relationships and trust, in that he had none of either, and who could blame him. People he'd trusted hid things from him and lied to him and then they tried to kill him. And most of those people worked for the federal government of the United States of America. He would be a prized permanent counseling client if she ever went into private practice. Alex looked over at Stone and watched him watch the river.

They looked up when they heard the rumble of Sea Stallion helicopters rising from the Marine Corps Air Field-Quantico, and watched them pass overhead. As the beat of their rotors faded in the distance, Alex stood and looked at the buildings on the Marine Base and then back at the Potomac.

"Milo," said Alex. "Please slow her down."

Milo steered out of the flotilla, heading towards the bank on the Virginia side of the river. When they could see the Marine Corps University at Quantico, Milo idled the boat.

They'd attended Clancy's funeral at Arlington National Cemetery weeks before. They'd listened to the rifle salute and watched the flag presented to his ex-wife. They watched her leave the grave, alone and dry-eyed, still jealous of the careers, far worse than any mistress, that took her ex-husband away from her long before his death. Stone and Alex and Milo had taken their time, waiting until the rows of gray shadows from the rows of white tombstones lengthened across the grass. They left fresh flowers at two graves that day.

On the boat, they had nothing but memories to honor their friend. Alex stood next to the American flag. Stone joined her.

"I promised Clancy the first boat ride," said Alex. Her eyes were wet.

"He would have had fun," said Stone. He remembered Clancy as his friend, a man of honor and fidelity, one of a very few whom Stone never regretted trusting.

Stone looked at the distant flag waving over Quantico. Clancy gave far better than he ever got from his employer. Would any of them wind up any better? It was hard to know. Clancy believed in his country but people like Heidrick called the shots and they only believed in their government. It didn't help to know that, despite its many flaws and failures, his government was still better than any other in the world.

Heidrick called them all little people, the great unwashed masses who needed to be governed. He had it all wrong. They were just regular people who had dreams and only wanted what had been promised to them. Clancy gave everything he had to make sure promises to him and to Alex and Milo would be kept.

Why were those promises so hard to keep?

"Anybody want to say anything?" asked Stone. He had to clear his throat, but had nothing else to say aloud.

Alex stared out across the Potomac, wanting only to speak her few words without crying. She couldn't say nothing about the man who was more family to her and Milo than anybody else.

"Clancy was the best friend—" Alex found speaking much harder than she'd expected. "He gave us—we're going to miss him."

Alex put her hands over her eyes and said nothing more.

After a few moments she nodded at Milo, who slowly steered Veritas to rejoin the other boats that had already turned around and headed back upriver.

They heard the wind and the water and boats and birds. Alex and Stone exchanged no words. Alex listened for a skip in the beat of the engine that thankfully never came. Stone watched as they passed the Benson-Philips factory, no longer a derelict building. In the distance, he saw trucks and cars filling its parking lot and the walls wore a coat of fresh paint. It gave work and hope to dozens of citizens who likely never thought of themselves as little people.

"Milo, everything okay?" asked Alex.

Milo turned to them, smiling, and waved. He seemed absorbed in driving the boat and enjoying the day. He looked forward to their picnic, which they'd enjoy later after docking, though without the benefit of the spray can of cheese Stone had brought. It had somehow wound up in the water along with the rest of that grocery sack's contents. "Yeah, I'm good."

Milo returned his attention to the river ahead.

"He's a good kid," said Stone. He watched Milo. "Lucky to have a mother like you."

"I'm the lucky one," said Alex. "I worry. I hope I can give him enough so he'll be okay."

"Both of you will be fine."

Alex and Stone looked at anything except each other.

A large cabin cruiser with a family picnic on the stern deck passed by and the children waved at them. Stone waved back and found it hard to look away. They all seemed happy. Parents had their kids. Kids had their parents. After they docked the boat they'd go home together, probably have dinner together. Maybe tomorrow one of those kids might play soccer or football and his parents would watch him and cheer for him. He didn't know what any of that was about but it all seemed like a good thing.

Stone kept watching the cabin cruiser as it pulled away from them.

How could you miss something you never knew?

"You get wrapped up in the day to day of things. Work, stuff, the next big thrill. Doing something you think is important." Stone nodded at Milo. "Easy to forget what matters."

They passed under the shadow of a tall cloud that threatened rain.

"Sometimes I wonder, you know, what it's like? Have a mom, a dad watch me, maybe playing football, winning something. Anything. Or just—I don't know," said Stone. "Make them proud."

"You missed out on a lot. And so did your mother. I'm sorry," said Alex. She watched Stone looking at the family on the cabin cruiser. What he said didn't surprise her. She'd expected it, even hoped for it, if not then, perhaps at another time. She saw a hard man, with very few people in his past. Maybe he looked for somebody in his future. Alex didn't know who, but she'd ventured a guess. Being able to connect with one person can lead to connecting with another.

Alex pulled a folded paper from her pocket and handed it to Stone. He saw the name, "Margaret Stone" on the front and opened the paper. The breeze made the paper flutter, like it wanted to fly away from him. He saw an address, somewhere in West Virginia, and refolded the paper. He stared at it until they passed under the Woodrow Wilson Bridge.

He put the paper in his pocket.

"How did you find her?" asked Stone.

"It took a little digging," said Alex. She smiled, then looked away. "I work for the government. We love our files and we love our paperwork."

Stone gave her a brief smile, then asked, "Why?"

Alex considered the tall cloud above them, and decided it didn't know if it wanted to rain. She looked at Stone.

"Mothers expect to be around while their children grow up," said Alex. "I'm guessing she didn't think she had lots of choices then. A girl thinks she wants things and then she gets them and she doesn't know what to do. She was told things. Promises were made, and maybe they weren't kept. None of us walked in her shoes."

Stone didn't know why he suddenly remembered the young boy with his mother arriving at a bus stop in the early morning. They didn't look like they had much, but that kid sure as hell never got shorted kindness or love by his mother. She would have done anything for that kid. Just like Alex did for Milo.

"A mother's love can look like a lot of things. She had to do what was best for her child, no matter how much it might hurt her. Or him," said Alex. "Only she would know."

"She was just regular people, wasn't she."

"I think she was a good person."

"I wonder if she knows about me," said Stone. "I hope I wouldn't—I hope she wouldn't be disappointed."

"I don't think she would be. Maybe you could find out."

"I guess maybe I could, you know, look her up."

"I guess maybe you could." Alex took his hand in hers.

The air warmed a little as they passed from under the shadow of the tall cloud. Milo slowed the boat as they neared the entrance to the marina, leaving the other boats in the River Festival to travel upriver to their own moorings.

"And here we are," said Alex. She and Stone looked up into the sky and they both felt the warmth of the sun on their faces.

Alex tapped the hull of the Veritas. "I told you we'd float just fine."

The drone flying overhead recorded images of the boats cruising on the Potomac and immediately transmitted the data to several agencies, where it would be stored forever. A large luxury yacht motored into its view, moving alongside the regatta of smaller boats. Anybody querying the image would learn the yacht's name was Senate Seat and find its registration under the name of a closely-held Bermuda corporation that had lots of cash and little else.

— SENATE SEAT, POTOMAC RIVER

The yacht barely slowed as it passed the flotilla of smaller boats, rocking them with its bow wave and wake. Senators and lobbyists crowded the decks, the latter inevitably cozying up to the former in a display of dignified enticements, inducements and ass-kissing. Bundles of cash changing hands were the only things missing, but only because wire transfers between Bermuda bank accounts were so much more convenient.

Senator Heidrick wore the only necktie on the yacht and he stood at a table, drink in hand. A folded newspaper lay on the tabletop. Ever since his first arraignment, fellow senators greeted him warmly, wished him well, and left him standing alone at parties, tainted as he was by the specter of indictments, many of which, this time, promised a guilty verdict.

Heidrick watched Salazar walk up, arm in arm with a stunning young woman. Her long dark hair fell over her form-fitting white dress, far too short and far too snug for the event, thus eliciting stares from everybody aboard, heterosexual or otherwise. Heidrick didn't resent Salazar for agreeing to testify against him—he'd gotten immunity and Salazar had to do what any man had to do to keep his business going. But that drug lord/human trafficker/murderer didn't have to show his face in this crowd and pretend he was as respectable as everybody else aboard.

"Senator Heidrick, I do not think you have met Catalina," said Salazar. He smiled and nodded at the exquisitely gorgeous girl next to him, who only smiled demurely. It had taken some time and work and money to turn the raw beauty who had shown up over a year earlier in El Paso into this elegant young lady. Her charms would easily earn him a million dollars a year for at least another 15 years.

"My pleasure, miss," said Heidrick. He smiled at her. He could admire a nice piece of ass as well as anybody else on the boat, even though he didn't indulge in the same kinds of extra-curricular activities that his colleagues did. He turned away. "It was nice meeting you."

Salazar shrugged. He and Catalina walked away. Salazar had made his point. He walked free in the US, without fear of arrest while this senator might soon go to jail. Weeks earlier, Señor Wiggins had said that Heidrick had played him and promised immunity in return for his testimony. And doing business would be even easier than when he worked for Heidrick. They must want to put this senator in jail very badly.

Salazar spent the rest of that afternoon renewing relationships with several other senators and congressmen. He might need to buy their assistance when the *Americano federales* decided they didn't need him anymore. It was just a matter of time until having these new friends would pay off, and introducing Catalina helped him make friends very, very easily.

Heidrick watched Salazar and Catalina walk over to Dr. Perez and the girl on his arm, who looked like she could be Catalina's sister. Perez didn't have immunity but then he didn't need it, since he ran a respectable genomics laboratory. Anybody who knew Salazar was his investor or that Salazar had introduced Heidrick to Perez also knew enough to keep their mouth shut.

Heidrick finished his drink and left the glass on the table. He picked up the newspaper and walked across the deck to the hardwood railing. He stared down at the motley collection of boats they passed on the river. He wondered where to put the newspaper. Perez had given it to him earlier, after extending his greetings and regrets at the terrible things the US government was doing to the good senator.

Heidrick thought he saw Stone on one of the boats. He turned his back to the river and the boats cruising around in that sloppy fleet. The newspaper said it was the annual River Festival, sponsored by the city of Alexandria. Good. Keep the little people happy.

Perez had pointed to a front page article with the headline: "U.K. Parliament Legalizes Human Embryo DNA Modification." Perez didn't mention whether Gidden had read that news story. Gidden was too chicken-shit to show his face here after turning state's evidence. He'd better be careful what he said, since the people Perez worked with didn't have the same sense of humor and forgiving personality that Heidrick did. If he just stuck to the science, Gidden would do fine in Mexico. He wouldn't move back to England just because they legalized what he'd been doing for decades.

It would only be a matter of time till some ambitious congressman put up a bill for legalizing human DNA modification in the US. Anybody could then get into the business of editing people in a street corner shop and nobody would worry about it. Legal or not, it didn't really matter, at least not for Gidden and not for Perez. Nobody could do anything about the GreenSeeds they manufactured in Mexico anyway, but at least nobody would wonder why all of Salazar's girls looked so much alike.

GLOSSARY

.338 Lapua Magnum – a high-powered rifle cartridge with a lethal range of 1,500 meters and a bullet having a maximum diameter of .338 inches.

.40 caliber – a pistol cartridge with a bullet having a maximum diameter of .40 inches.

.500 Magnum – a pistol cartridge considered to be the most powerful in the world, having a bullet with a maximum diameter of .50 inches.

'shine – slang for moonshine, i.e. homemade alcohol, usually illegally distilled.

3-Parent Mitochondrial DNA Replacement – any of several in vitro fertilization techniques, which combine genetic material from a human ovum that carries faulty mitochondria, with genetic material from a donor ovum's healthy mitochondria. The resulting embryo carries nuclear DNA from the mother and father and mitochondrial DNA from the donor, and is thought to help prevent debilitating inherited diseases. The United Kingdom legalized the technique in 2015 and the US FDA is reviewing it (as of 2016).

5.56 millimeter – a rifle cartridge with a bullet having a maximum diameter of 5.56 millimeters; the 5.56x45mm cartridge is commonly used in the AR-15 series of rifles and carbines.

7.62 millimeter – a rifle cartridge with a bullet having a maximum diameter of 7.62 millimeters; the 7.62x39mm cartridge is commonly used in AK-47 assault rifles and other automatic weapons deployed by Soviet Bloc forces and their clients.

9 millimeter – a pistol cartridge having a bullet with a maximum diameter of 9 millimeters.

AAV-7 – acronym for Amphibious Assault Vehicle, a tracked, armored vehicle for transporting personnel and cargo from ship to shore and inland objectives.

After-action (report) – a report often filed after a military or clandestine mission.

AP ammo – Armor Piercing ammunition.

AR-15 – standard assault rifle for the US military and widely used by US police SWAT teams, most often issued for the 5.56x45 millimeter cartridge.

BATF – acronym for Bureau of Alcohol, Tobacco and Firearms, an agency in the Department of Justice that enforces laws regarding firearms, explosives, tobacco, and alcohol.

Beretta M9 (92F) – standard 9 millimeter sidearm for US military forces.

Cake eater – derogatory slang referring to politicians.

CAR-15 – designation for the carbine (short barrel) version of the AR-15.

Cloud – refers to cloud computing, a technology for distributing computerized data storage and processing at locations other than where a user is located.

Colt .45 ACP – a pistol cartridge having a bullet with a maximum diameter of .45 inches, which was standard for US military sidearms until 1985.

CRISPR – an acronym for Clustered Regularly Interspersed Short Palindromic Repeats, an increasingly popular, easy-to-use technology to make permanent changes to the genomes of living cells, including those of humans.

DARPA – acronym for Defense Advanced Research Projects Agency, which commissions advanced technology research for the Department of Defense.

Det cord – also known as detonation cord or primer cord, it is used as a fuse to detonate explosives, or as a cutting charge on thin or relatively weak structures.

DOJ – acronym for Department of Justice, which includes the FBI and the Office of the Attorney General.

E-8 pay grade – Master Sergeant or First Sergeant in the Army and Marines.

EOtech – a brand of optical sights used on rifles, carbines and pistols.

ETA – acronym for Estimated Time of Arrival.

Five-five-six – nomenclature for a 5.56mm weapon or ammunition.

FUBAR – "fouled up beyond all recognition," or more commonly, "fucked up beyond all recognition."

Full bull – military slang for a full colonel.

GRS – acronym for Global Response Staff, a unit of the CIA that provides armed support for its clandestine operations.

Grunt – military slang referring to an Army infantryman.

Heckler & Koch MP-5 – a widely used automatic submachine gun made by the Heckler & Koch company.

Helmand Province – the largest of 34 provinces in Afghanistan, located in the south of the country.

Hollowpoint – a bullet having a cavity in its tip to enable greater lethality.

IED – Improvised Explosive Device, a "homemade" bomb often manufactured by insurgents in South Asia by assembling a detonator to artillery shells or other explosives.

ISO – acronym for the Switzerland-based International Organization for Standardization, which defines standards and specifications for products and services, and creates full employment for consultants.

Klick – slang for kilometer.

"Leg" – military slang for non-Airborne infantry.

Level 4 body armor/tactical vest – Level IV is the highest rating for personal body armor and has been shown to stop rifle bullets.

Lima Charlie – military phonetic alphabet for "loud and clear."

M1911A1 – refers to the ".45 Auto," the standard semi-automatic sidearm in .45 ACP (Automatic Colt Pistol) caliber issued to the US military until 1985.

M67 – explosive fragmentation grenade having a kill radius of five meters.

Ma deuce – M2 Browning .50 caliber heavy machine gun, in use since 1933 and highly effective against personnel and lightly armored targets.

MaxxPro – a version of the Mine Resistant Ambush Protected (MRAP) class of armored vehicles, designed to withstand IED explosions of up to 15 pounds of explosive.

Meat-eater – special operator working in South Asia.

Moonshine – homemade high-proof alcohol, usually illegally distilled.

MRE – acronym for Meal Ready to Eat, which are dehydrated rations issued to troops in the field.

PKM – a belt-fed machine gun firing the 7.62x54 millimeter cartridge (longer than that used in the AK-47), in common use in Soviet Bloc forces and their clients.

Primacord – a brand of det cord.

SAC (FBI) – acronym for an FBI Special Agent in Charge, usually a senior agent in command of a field office.

SAW – acronym for Squad Automatic Weapon, referring to the M249 light machine gun that shoots 5.56x45mm ammunition.

SD Card – a Secure Digital non-volatile memory card, available in several formats including microSD, for storing digital data.

SIG P-226, SIG P-290, SIG P-250 Sub-compact – semi-automatic pistols manufactured by the SIG SAUER company, all of which are available in several calibers including 9 millimeter and .40 caliber.

Smith & Wesson .500 Magnum Revolver – a 5-shot revolver manufactured by the Smith & Wesson company, the ammunition for which is considered the most powerful for pistols anywhere in the world, with a muzzle energy of up to 3,000 lb. ft. and a bullet having a maximum diameter of .50 inches.

Soldado – Spanish for soldier.

SWAT – acronym for a police Special Weapons And Tactics team.

Zodiac boat – a small, inflatable, motorized boat for transporting cargo and personnel.

###